Praise for *Bianca's Cure*

"A masterful storyteller. Berardi's narrative is both imaginative and persuasive—a tale relevant to women in science today, and with a plant that still attracts considerable scientific attention: *Artemisia annua*."

—Ruth Lydia Richter, botanist in the natural science section at the Goetheanum (CH)

"Navigating the Medici court in Renaissance Florence was not for the faint of heart. Neither was curing malaria. Determined to prevail in both despite threats and innumerable obstacles, Bianca in *Bianca's Cure* inspires those who dare!"

—Esther Erman, author of *Rebecca of Salerno*

"Gigi Berardi's voice-driven narrative skillfully describes the tortuous path a woman scientist takes to do her work and at the same time manage children, household, and realm. Readers of both historical fiction and science will enjoy this unforgettable tale."

—Ruth Sofield, professor at Western Washington University and coauthor of *Introduction to Environmental Toxicology*

Bianca's Cure

Bianca's Cure

A Novel

Gigi Berardi

SHE WRITES PRESS

Published in 2026 by
She Writes Press, an imprint of The Stable Book Group

32 Court Street, Suite 2109
Brooklyn, NY 11201
https://shewritespress.com
Library of Congress Control Number: 2025918831
ISBN: 979-8-89636-070-4
eISBN: 979-8-89636-071-1

Interior Designer: Kiran Spees

Printed in the United States

To my children, Ian and Emily,
wondrous artists and scientists.

1

Venice
A Death and a Beginning
1558

No one heard Bianca as she moved on her stockinged feet to the sickroom where her mother lay dying. She'd practiced walking through her aunts' palace like a cat, softly, silently. Cats had a good sense of smell, too, and could recognize chemical changes in the air, maybe even disease. The same way she could tell, from the woody fragrance of the root she'd been simmering for hours, what the broth she'd created could do.

Yesterday her aunts forced Bianca out of the room before she could give her mother a steeping cure. Tonight, she had made herself wait until the clock struck three, then four, before slipping down to the cellar where the women in her family had made alchemic recipes, using dried herbs, for generations. Once there, Bianca had removed her shoes, leaving the door ajar so it wouldn't click, placing the copper pot on the iron ring over the fire without making a sound. After adding some of her mother's wormwood extracts, she crept upstairs. Now, she slid around a corner into the dark hallway, finding her way by pressing a palm against the cold frescoed walls. Her other hand clutched the cup that held her herbal brew. Her aunts mustn't see the light of a tallow candle or smell its burning fat. If they caught her, they'd stop her. *A sickroom is no place for a girl of ten. You're underfoot, Bianca. A priest was poking his nose in here again. If he sees you and your "cures . . ."*

Bianca was closer to being able to cure malaria with her herbs than the aunties had ever been. Her mother had taught her to see the rhythms of plants growing and creating seeds, writing their biographies in the shape and curl of the leaves that opened and closed each day. This herb, artemisia in the deep fall and just at the start of flowering, was the most expressive of all. And it had gestured to her. The bitter plant was the medicine her mother needed. Mama had shown the aunties, too, but they didn't believe her, or they didn't care.

Mama practiced science, testing ideas and writing about new cures in her notes. Mama knew about how the plants interacted with each other, and how she could extract their healing substances, one by one, with her new alembic. But she'd gotten sick, and no one would help Mama with her ideas except Bianca. According to the aunties, distilling extracts was men's work, an insult to the remedies they'd been making for generations. The aunties followed recipes, but didn't understand the chemistry behind them. Mama did. They'd want to become scientists, too, once they saw what Bianca's cure could do.

Pausing outside her mother's door, Bianca cracked it open wide enough for a cat to slip through. The room smelled of acid vomit. Her mother lay in the bed, unmoving, her breathing ragged. Almost all the thick dark hair was gone from her head, and shadows made caves of her closed eyes. Bianca set the brew on a small table by the bed so she could raise her mother up on the pillows. Her skin was hot to the touch. When Bianca lifted the bitter broth to her swollen lips, her mother groaned. Was she trying to say her daughter's name? Bianca hardly breathed. Her mother's eyelids flickered.

The door behind Bianca slammed open.

No time to hide, let alone run. Bianca's aunt burst into the room. Just a few years older than Bianca's mother, she was tall and had the same dark hair. But never had her mother looked this furious.

Bianca's aunt reached her in two strides, swiping the cup out of her hand. Warm liquid splashed onto the bed and stone floor. Sniffing, her aunt looked around the room. "What are you doing, stupid girl?"

Bianca curled her hand into a fist around the root in her pocket, all that was left from her night's efforts. The woody plant bit into her skin. Good. Its strong oaky fragrance would help her focus. She tried to make her face hard. Her aunts' were like stone, from years of fighting with each other. Was her mother the only kind one? Maybe they wanted her to die?

Her aunt didn't wait for Bianca to answer. "So, we're playing with roots again? What damage have you done now?"

Bianca shook her head. "I wasn't hurting her." Which was more than the aunties could say. Their purges and sulfur poultices had made her mama bald and left her pale and shaking. But Bianca bit her tongue. "I just thought . . ." No, she knew. She knew what she was doing because her mama had shown her.

Mama was going to use artemisia to end the heat disease.

Your aunties are clever. Never doubt that, Mama had told her. *But they are only as clever as every woman who's come before them. Anything they see as new is a threat. That's why they won't use artemisia extracts the way I do. Someday I'll take you to Florence and we can learn more from the alchemists there how to distill the herbs, separating out their purest essence. For now, we do what we can, one day at a time.* Mama hadn't settled on a cure yet, but she had said she was close, and close was better than the aunties' treatments. If her aunties couldn't see that, they weren't clever at all.

"You thought?" Her aunt stiffened. "You're ten, Bianca. Too young to think anything." The slap hit her on the cheek and Bianca tumbled sideways, her forehead cracking against the wet flagstone floor. The cold stone numbed the pain. Whimpering, she sat up, pressing her hand to her head. But it was no more than she deserved. She'd gotten caught again, without any hope of getting the brew to her mother.

Dabbing the corner of her eye, Bianca blinked back a tear. Couldn't her aunt hear her mother gasping? Bianca got to her feet, swaying. Mama's breathing was too fast. She needed Bianca.

"This is not a game, girl." Her aunt's fingers gripped Bianca's elbow. "You challenge us?"

"My mother would, if she wasn't sick." Bianca tugged her sleeve out of her aunt's bony grasp. She shot a glance at the few sticky black hairs matted together along the side of her mother's head, and the many sores from the smelly, stinging poultices. "Mama was making a cure. A cure that saves lives. She gave it to the gardener's son, remember? And he got better."

Her aunt followed Bianca's gaze, moving her eyes from her niece to her sick sister. "That boy was barely ill. And what about the man last month? She treated him and he died." With one arm, she pulled Bianca toward her. "Listen, when your mother could still think, she welcomed our treatments. She begged us—not some child—to save her."

Bianca lifted her chin. "Auntie, no—"

Her aunt touched a cold finger to Bianca's face. "There, there—copper-gold hair, pearl-like skin, but such an empty look in your eyes. I can't see why she entrusted any cure to you, pretty girl." She brushed Bianca's cheek with her palm. "She spoiled you, too."

Jerking her head away from her aunt, Bianca fell back a step. "Mama loves me whether I'm pretty or not." What Mama had really said was that some people would hate Bianca for being pretty, and some people would love her for it, but that pretty was just like anything else, something she could use. All Bianca knew was that she couldn't use it to make friends with her cousins. They'd stopped wanting to be seen with her because they said she made them look ugly. "I don't care about pretty. Once I'm a scientist, I'm going to cut off all my hair and cover my face with clay."

"Hmm. So you think the clay can do something about your face?"

Her aunt shook her head. "And I assume that charmed artemisia spilled on the ground was supposed to reverse your mother's disease?"

Her mother's breaths were getting quicker. Bianca's own chest grew tight. "Yes. Artemisia will save her. I've simmered the roots as strong as I could, with Mama's extracts in it." She swallowed. Her mouth had gone dry. "Mama said it has to be pure."

"Pure?" Her aunt's eyes narrowed. "We Cortese blend ingredients that heal, recipes passed down from plants grown here over generations. Over centuries."

"There's a different way, Auntie. And some of our plants come from the ships in the port. Mama knows how to use alchemy to unlock the secrets of one plant at a time. Mixing so many brews the way you do weakens the medicine. Strong extracts with the wormwood helps the body to heal itself. And so—"

"A different way?" Her aunt leaned in, her voice a hiss. "Meaning *better*? Better than what we have created here since the Cortese name graced Venice's streets?" They stood inches apart, her aunt's moist breath warm on Bianca's face. "All this talk of 'purity.' That's a man's alchemy of metals. Men separate. Women blend." She stepped back, but spoke again before Bianca could draw a breath. "Listen to me: strong gets noticed. When we make a little noise, we're seen, then we're vulnerable. You may be young but you can't pretend you don't know what people call her." She tilted her head toward the woman in the bed. "I know you think Pellegrina had a cure for malaria, and you wanted to use it to save her. But Bianca, you know nothing. People are afraid of your mother and her ideas. If you use her spells to save her, they'll say the devil brought her back. We must heal her in the ways we've used for centuries. If this disease takes her now, after all our treatments, at least she doesn't burn at the stake. Have you thought of that? We don't need the alchemy of men, their costly equipment, their forges and distilleries. We have our methods. We work in our own ways."

Had her aunt's chin and cheekbones always jutted so sharply, or had meanness shaped her face? Bianca met her gaze just for a moment, those eyes gray like Mama's, but so much colder. "What you're doing isn't helping, Auntie."

"Your mother still lives, doesn't she?"

Barely, Bianca wanted to say.

"I suppose next you think you're going to discover some laboratory to work in—like your mother tried?" Her aunt snorted. "To share our recipes with outsiders? Give away our secrets? Study side by side with men?"

Surely that would be better than keeping silent, or keeping secrets that revealed nothing about cures. Her aunts' recipes were odd combinations of things, more superstition than anything else. Bianca dug her hand into her pocket, her fingers catching on the scratchy root.

"Why not just run away to Florence and be done with it?" Bianca's aunt folded her arms. "Whore yourself out to one of those Medici. Men of science, but what kind of genius needs fancy equipment to create a cure? They call themselves alchemists, with their laboratories and charts of the night stars, but none of them have cured anything, have they? Men build themselves big workspaces like in Florence so the world will think they're doing something, and your mother, she was always just like them, with that studio in the annex of your father's palace. Bored of the old ways that actually work. Afraid she'd fail if she followed in our own mother's footsteps. And she taught you the same. Well, let me save you some time and heartache, Bianca. You'll fail. We would have taught you here, but you insist on going your own way. Your mother is ours, and there is nothing for you to do. If I catch you in this room again, your father will hear of it. He'll lock you up in one of those big houses of his, Bianca, and we won't plead for your release—certainly your mother won't."

Bianca bit her lip. She tasted blood.

Her mother lay still, save for her heaving chest. The aunties couldn't save her. And the puddled mixture that might have helped her now stained the bedsheets. It would take Bianca days to make more. And even if she could . . . *Your father will hear of it.* She couldn't come back. But how could she leave?

"Go." Her aunt placed her hands on Bianca's shoulders, forcing her backward, step by step, until she stumbled out into the hall. The door slammed in Bianca's face.

"No, please." She beat on the heavy wood until her hands burned. "Open the door." What if her mother called out and Bianca wasn't there? And her aunt ignored it? She pressed her ear against the door. Silence.

There hadn't been silence in that sickroom for days, not since the fluid had entered her mother's lungs. Something was wrong.

Bianca ran to the stairwell and then up the stairs, up farther, into the stuffy attic, through the piles of stale-smelling books and musty canisters. Carefully she climbed out the window onto the rotted, narrow ledge, following it step by step. Soon she was peering down into her mother's room. A crack in the bleached boards covering a small window showed her aunt bent over her mother's bed. Bianca pounded on the boards, each blow becoming fainter as her hand began to throb. Her aunt's shoulders stiffened, but she never turned around. Instead she took a cotton flannel and covered her sister's face. The image before Bianca blurred. Her eyes stung. Grabbing the artemisia from her pocket, she shredded the failed root till the last earthy flake fell from her fingers.

She had nothing.

Bianca stood rigid in the last place she'd ever stand in a world where her mother had lived. Move, and Mama's death would be real. Bianca would leave here half an orphan, in a city where the sickness already had killed so many. How did this happen? Her mother knew things, her mother could have cured the heat disease, in time. But she hadn't been given time, not even another day. She'd been given Bianca, and Bianca hadn't saved her. No one had.

The reddening sky lit the glass in the window. Bianca remained still. The sun's reflection caught in one of the frames in the hazy morning. With the back of her hand, she wiped away a tear. It didn't matter what her aunts said about men's work or her mother's infusions. The aunties had let Mama die, but Bianca would finish what her mother had begun. Walking back along the ledge, she clenched her teeth till her jaw ached and shook her hand at the brightening sky. She'd find a cure. Her aunties couldn't stop her, nor her father. Nothing would.

2

The Sick House of Venice

1563

The stench from the Sick House still filled Bianca's nose, even here in the palace annex that had once been her mother's. It was the odor of illness, of fear and of hope, of some people getting better, and others not. It meant her bitter brews might help as healing remedies. It meant that Bianca was doing what her mother would have wanted.

Since her mother's death five years ago, she'd made recipes in the annex, and often in darkness. In the early morning, Bianca wouldn't light a candle. Better if no one noticed she was up. The aunties would have thought this bigger than any workspace they'd need. But then, what work did they actually do? People came to her aunties not only to be healed, but more often, to change the way they looked—from wan to fair, from freckled to glowing. Those were the arts her cousins were learning. Bianca had been banned from such lessons, but she didn't care. Her aunties brought no one from dying to living, but Mama's alchemy could. Making the infusions was a first step. The next: to find the dying.

It had taken a long time, but she'd found them in a Sick House. A hopeless place, yes, but her mother wouldn't have called it that. It held the possibility of, with the right cure, recovery. Bianca didn't have that cure, not yet, not one that could save all or even most of the feverish patients who wound up at the Sick House. But she had her mother's notes, and she'd filled almost a whole book with her own. Bianca grabbed that book now, stashing it in her basket. What else would she need? She'd made a tincture from artemisia leaves based on notes her mother had left behind, and brews from several other wormwoods. She gathered the carefully labeled bottles, adding a jar of the extract from the santolina leaf. Soaked in cotton, it made the insects in her wools disappear. If she found the right dose, in the right dilution with water, the santolina might repel disease as well. Bianca packed the jars into her basket, going over her latest infusions and extracts in her head.

Earlier in the year, she'd followed a rumor to the door of the Sick House. The nuns would take in anyone to wash bedclothes or change bandages or scrub vomit from the floors. At first, Bianca had volunteered for the worst tasks. While she bathed bodies that reeked of illness or of soaked blood from already-stained bedclothes, Bianca stole every moment she could to jot down what she noticed about the heat disease, and how the sick responded to the nuns' treatments. At home in the annex, Bianca had organized her recipes. Steeped herbs, with plenty of leaves and added tinctures, were the easiest. But the first time one of the younger nuns caught her giving a dose to a man who seemed near death, Bianca thought she'd be thrown from the Sick House. Only when the man, gasping, had told the nun he'd begged Bianca to help him did the nun pause to listen to Bianca's story. When Bianca described her mother's work and how she'd been following her mother's recipes, trying to strengthen the solutions that, when her mother died, were still too weak to cure, the nun slowly nodded. "Fair enough." And something lifted inside Bianca's chest.

The next day, Bianca had returned to find the man dead. But the nun, a hint of kindness in her stern face, had told Bianca that even though his fever had lessened, nothing short of God's angels could have saved him. From then on, that nun and a few of the others allowed Bianca to treat patients with her tinctures. Many, though, refused to let her near the men most ill, and so they'd sickened and died on the nuns' weak brews while Bianca watched.

If she'd told the nuns who she was—Bianca Capello, not some obscure merchant's daughter as they thought—would her father's name give her authority to override them? He was one of the richest men in the city. He could close down the Sick House with a word, or give it ten times the money the church had allotted to keep the place running. But if anyone in the Sick House told her father she was there, Bartolomeo would put an end to his daughter's visits. He'd force her home and probably put her to use by marrying her off the very next day to whomever he most wanted to impress.

So Bianca let the nuns believe she was simply some well-to-do man's daughter. But she couldn't help asking questions. Once, she'd overheard two of the sisters discussing the studies of the Medici duke in Florence. One nun laughed. "Planetary forces affecting metals that heal—heal humans? These men believe nothing is sacred."

"Hush," the other nun said. "Look who's listening."

They'd both turned. Bianca felt her face grow red, but she had to know. "What did you mean?" Bianca asked. "Planets and metals? How?"

But the nuns shook their heads. "Not here, Bianca." And she held her tongue. If she angered the nuns, it would cost them nothing to send her away. It would cost Bianca everything.

Today, the clanking of the glass jars in her basket beat like a drum, tapping louder than the clicks of her heels on the wet cobble as she left the palace annex. Wind whipped her linen jacket, and she slipped in more than one puddle in the predawn light. Counting her steps, she entered the side street where the grim forms of sick men and women hunched against the front wall of the Sick House. The storm the night before had soaked up some of their pungent smells. She slid past a man blocking the entrance.

The porter nun opened the door and beckoned her inside. In the first large room, moisture dripped from the ceiling. Bianca forced her lungs to draw in the thick, now-familiar air. Whimpers and sobs erupted from dark corners. Those sick with the most virulent form of the pox lay clustered in the middle. The beds along the walls held those sick with the heat disease, some delirious with fever, others gasping for breath, suffocating on their own foul air. A seizure pinned one man to the hollow of his bed as he rocked back and forth in between spasms. No women lay in the ward, confined as they were to the back of the Sick House where Bianca had rarely been. Forgotten, and without treatment, few of them survived.

A nun ministered to those in the center sickbeds, bending over one restless figure, a bowl balanced on her knee as she used water with vinegar to clean the open sores of the most recent admit. His shrieks echoed through the ward as the harsh, pungent liquid trickled into his wounds. Like all the critically ill, he lay on sopping bedclothes drenched in his own vomit and sweat.

Bianca set her basket on a small table among bloodletting tweezers and needles and the leather sacks for fermenting blood. She didn't need to search any further to know what treatments those with malaria had been given, though the ones who had been bled looked just as sick as the rest. A side table held urine bottles. Bianca's mother had taught her about checking for sweet in the urine. The nuns did some things right.

Laying out her ceramic cups and jars, filled with brews and tinctures of varying strengths, Bianca organized them according to type of plant. Here were the wormwoods, here the fragrant menthol, here the santolinas. Together they might cure, she knew they could, if she could only balance them correctly. Perhaps today would be the day when she got the proportions just right, or the steeping time or the size of the tiny leaf pieces for the brew, as her mother had tried to do for so long. Perhaps today she would heal at least one man. Then she'd earn something other than sidelong, skeptical looks from the nuns.

She approached the closest nun, an older woman who'd helped her before. Picking up a small crock, she waited to catch the nun's eye. "Would you heat this new infusion for me? I know you don't want me underfoot in the kitchen. But once it's warmed, I have tinctures to mix in that should cure—"

"Listen, mistress." The nun's jaw tightened. "Before you give us orders, know that we've noticed you're being rather selective in whom you're treating. Prefer to treat men with the heat sickness, do you?" She shook her head. "You're with us now to clean up after all of them, and to do what we say. If you want to ease their pain with some of your brews, we won't stop you." The nun waved to the cluttered table. "But don't come in here talking about cures. There are no cures for the dying. Nothing in your potions can save them." She spoke slowly, as if talking to a child. Bianca bit her lip. "You must leave the men in peace. God decides when to call them, and we are here to help them on that journey." With two fingers, she lifted Bianca's chin. "Stay far away from the dying. You cannot stop their final crossing."

Bianca glanced at a patient she'd been watching in the closest bed, doubled over, muttering something confused, when he wasn't completely unconscious. "The dying, like him?"

"Bianca, you're not listening to me. What do you think you're going to do? Give him another one of your brews too bitter to keep down? We've seen that over and over." She sighed. "You entice them to drink, Bianca, your skin so pale, your golden-rinsed hair. I don't know whose daughter you are, but you've never had to suffer, that's clear. This is all some pastime to you, a game you play. But it doesn't matter how striking you look. Ravishing has no place here among the sick. If anything, you're a distraction to these men who need to be following the saints' paths, resisting temptation as they prepare to give themselves to God. If you can help those who are going to live, fine. But don't think you can change the fate of the dying. Use your skills where you might actually do some good."

Bianca closed her eyes, trying to shut out the nun's harsh voice. Had Bianca moved too quickly into the sick wards, scrubbed too few floors, made herself too visible with her medicines? Whatever trust she'd begun to win was ebbing away. If these women only knew that the good Bianca was doing ran far deeper than any one man's life. She opened her eyes, forcing herself to hold the nun's gaze. "But what if we could learn to cure all . . ."

"There's no time for learning." The nun's face tightened.

"But I can cure them." Though she couldn't save them all, not yet. Maybe her mother could have, but if she'd found the perfect recipe before she'd died, she hadn't written it down. "I'm trying to help them," she said. "Please." Bianca picked up a bottle, its label penned in the neat script of a nun, and held it out. "How did you and the sisters learn what you know? Someone had to experiment, to try a cure in order to know that it helped. That's all I'm doing. Now, please . . ."

"Experiment?" The nun took the bottle and set it firmly on the table. "I think I know what you're trying to do. This illness that is sweeping the city—of course we want to stop it, but that is God's decision. Bianca, I warn you to be careful. When you first came, I wanted to let you stay. You seemed a bright girl, ready to learn our ways. But people are starting to talk, and I must say, I don't blame them. These men are ready to see God, and you mustn't stop them."

"Some of the men could have lived, if . . ." She couldn't stop her voice from shaking. "The conditions here . . ." She kicked a pile of soiled cloths on the floor. Couldn't the nuns see the filth? Her mother never would have used old cotton to clean wounds, or rusted knives for removing bandages.

"We use what we have. If you're worried about doing more harm, then what of your brews?" The nun seemed ready to say more, but at that moment the man in the bed Bianca had pointed to began to writhe, clutching his right side. As one, Bianca and the nun turned to him. The nun lifted the man's cotton smock. "See how he holds his stomach? He's dying, but we can ease his pain."

Bianca grabbed a stained cloth from the table, barely catching his vomit.

"Quick, Bianca, we need to give him some of the lime powder. As much as he can take until the stomach pain goes away and he can keep down his drink."

Bianca reached for the powder, then turned the man on his side. "Once the retching starts, if he chokes—"

"Don't argue, Bianca. You're working for us, to learn. That's why you're here, isn't it?" The nun handed Bianca a cup of water to hold while she tapped the pale powder into it, then swirled the liquid mix into a putty. "Give him this. Make sure he gets all of it." She thrust the chalky brew at Bianca and walked away.

Bianca stared down into the cup. Lime powder? What might ease the man's discomfort quicker? Ginger, or mint? But the nun was probably watching. She spooned the treatment into the man's mouth. Death was the known quantity in this room. The unknown, even if it promised something better, yielded nothing in the nuns' minds.

Somewhere else—Florence, maybe—Bianca could experiment until she had a cure to offer men like these. But that cure would be too late for the men here. Bianca shot a quick glance at the nun who, grim-faced, was turning to the next bed. Bianca didn't have a cure yet, but she had more to offer than these nuns did. Under their watchful eyes, though, the hours Bianca had spent teasing out the secrets of her plants would be of help to no one.

Bianca waited till all the nuns seemed busy, then walked to the darkest corner of the room. The men here required less of the nuns' care; they weren't as sick, which meant Bianca would learn less from treating them, but it also meant the nuns wouldn't care what she was doing. She gave each of several men a slightly different brew, some smelling of menthol, others, yellowish and grassy. A clock rang, a hollow tone, on the half hour. One man before her gasped, her cure churning its way out of his stomach and up in a spew of thick vomit. The nun was right, the herbs she used were too bitter, even after all these years that she'd been trying to perfect a recipe. Bianca inhaled sharply, her chest tight. Through the high windows in the sickroom's outer wall a thin ray of sun fell, the dim light of a waning afternoon.

She'd never stayed this late before. Her father's days were busy with brokers and traders, but he'd expect her at supper. He'd married again, but his wife had no interest in Bianca and was often away for weeks at a time. Pouring one last swallow of golden liquid down a gagging man's throat, she held his head as he swallowed. If he could keep it down long enough, the medicine might ease his symptoms. *Everybody receives healing differently. Some can't receive it at all,* Bianca's mother used to tell her. That was why Mama kept such careful notes on the different doses. *Write down what works and what doesn't and for whom.* For this man, the medicine seemed to be too harsh, irritating his stomach. Yet on at least a few others, it had broken their fevers. Any good healer would stay to watch the results, but Bianca had to go.

She pivoted, too quickly, bumping into the table behind her. Liquid sloshed over the rims of the ceramic cups of infusion she hadn't yet had time to use. Well, what did it matter? As soon as she left, the nuns would pour all her efforts down the infirmary drains.

Grabbing her basket, Bianca walked through the sickroom and pulled open the main door. One of her companions for the day had barely glanced up. Bianca could have treated fewer men and left with plenty of time to spare, but she'd made a choice, and now she had to run. Should she risk hailing a carriage to take her home? Surely no driver would recognize her. No one would expect Bartolomeo's daughter to reek like the worst corners of a sick house, with sour vomit smells to match the stains on her skirts. Gusty air caught in her throat, another thunderstorm looming. The lady of the House of Capello was no noblewoman now, just a healer who'd spent the day caring for men who could all die in spite of her treatments. Or because of her, the nuns might say. But the nuns knew nothing. Like her aunties, they feared anything new. No doubt they'd have hated Bianca's mother, too.

A carriage ground its way through the mucky streets. Bianca wavered. Hail the driver, or let it pass and hope to remain unnoticed? She closed her tired eyes. *Breathe.* When she opened them, she screamed. In the shadows, all that showed of her father's expression as he vaulted from the carriage was the fierce white flash of his grin.

"As I thought." Somehow he was already in front of her, his fingers digging into her shoulders. Sickroom odors no longer made Bianca gag, but now, with her father's hot breath in her face, her stomach lurched.

"I was working," Bianca said in a low voice.

"As I've been told." He curled his lip. "But you have no work."

He'd said the same to her mother. Bianca used to hear them at night, Bartolomeo raging at the hours Mama spent bent over her brews.

"I do," Bianca replied, just as her mother had. "I'm saving lives. I have—"

Her father yanked on her arm. Bianca stumbled, tasting copper as her teeth caught her tongue. "Come with me, girl," her father snapped. The tang of blood mixed with acid in her mouth. She pressed a hand to her stomach. She had no choice but to follow.

3

Cassola, near Bassano

Locked In

One day bled into another, then another as Bianca watched the quiet landscape of her father's country estate sleep and wake. For the third day in a row, Bianca opened her eyes to a spill of golden morning light and the knowledge that this room was now her world. She walked to the window and looked down on a courtyard marketplace, already busy even this early in the morning. A baker's boy went by, pushing a barrel of fresh bread. Fishermen, up since the previous night, were already bringing in their day's first catch from the river. Someone shouted and a stall owner slapped down a slippery fish. Women hurried about, hawking eggs and rolls. Low-pitched bells called out the morning service, sounds that must be so much louder to those below, some rushing toward the church. All moved through the yard as they wished. They were visible. None glimpsed Bianca locked in her room, hidden, with nothing to do but watch them from a single window.

Pacing didn't help. Her bare feet already knew each crack in every floor tile. Her days of imprisonment had already been three days too long.

What will you do when you get sick, and no one has created a cure to save you? That's what she would have asked her father when he found her leaving the Sick House, if his voice hadn't drowned out hers. "You're my daughter, a Capello," he'd shouted over the rumble of the carriage wheels. "Not some simple servant stinking of house waste." The yelling didn't stop once they'd arrived at the Capello palace. "Pack a bag," he'd said. "We're leaving Venice. Until you learn how to behave, you'll stay in the country, out of trouble." They reached the estate, nestled in a river valley, a full day later by carriage. As exhausted as Bianca had been, she'd still heard the click of the lock when her father left her to settle into her apartment.

That click, now that it sounded several times a day, hadn't gotten any softer. But it was nothing compared to what he might have done. If he'd really wanted to punish his wayward daughter, he could have destroyed the place she'd been escaping to. But even her father would have been afraid to do that. He might not like Bianca's actions, but he wouldn't put the city at risk just to punish her. Disease, Bartolomeo took seriously. It was only his daughter's skills he dismissed.

The sun barely inched across the sky. What would the nuns be doing? Morning was a time to offer prayers for whatever sick men had made it through the night, and for the souls of those who didn't. In the afternoon they worked quickly, despite the clamor and distractions, to prepare for the evening.

And as night fell? Bianca stood by her window and imagined the sounds of coughs rising, congestion setting in as fevers spiked and the sick moaned, tossing and turning. The longer she stayed in her father's country estate, the sicker the men would become. Bianca couldn't have saved them all, but at least she could have offered soothing hands, a cool cloth on infected skin, brews to ease symptoms and pain.

Night, though, was such a long way off. The sky still hadn't lost the rosiness of dawn. What would her mother have done if she'd been trapped like this? Bianca knew the answer as soon as she'd thought the question. Her mother would have worked, no matter what. She would have done what she could with whatever she had. Even if all she had was a room, endless hours, and . . . a maid.

By the time Maria, the girl her father had ordered assist Bianca, had tapped on the door and slid the key into the lock, Bianca had a plan. "Maria," she said as the maid laid out Bianca's breakfast and collected the supper tray from the night before. "I want you to do something for me. My father doesn't watch you closely, does he?"

"No. I don't think so." Maria was staring at herself in Bianca's mirror.

"Then you could bring me things. Books, for instance?"

"I don't think I'm allowed." Setting the tray on a table, Maria said, "Am I?"

A question better left unanswered. Instead, Bianca rose and crossed to her wardrobe. Something small—a silk scarf. "Take this." Bianca held it up, unfolding it to show a square of pale green with a deep garnet border.

Maria's eyes widened. "Really?" She took the scarf and twirled it in the air before arranging it around her neck. "How does it look? I mean—books, yes." She glanced at Bianca. "I'll bring you what I can."

Bianca felt a smile spread across her face. "Thank you, Maria . . . and check my mother's room first? Bring me anything that's hers." Maria could have scrounged more of her mother's books in Venice, but surely there would be enough here for Bianca to study.

The next day Maria received an earring in exchange for a book filled with Pellegrina's ideas in her own handwriting—not those of long-dead men unspooling across pages. Bartolomeo Capello might well have Maria jailed for wearing the earring if he spotted it, but Bianca had seen the longing with which the maid eyed her jewelry. Of course, the girl would be discreet. Bianca would have given much more than that if she could've pressed her own notebook into Maria's hands and told her to deliver it to . . . someone. Anyone who would recreate what Bianca had done and use it as Bianca herself couldn't do, locked in Bartolomeo's cage.

Every day that week, breakfast came with a few more books. Most were useful, but Bianca itched to scan a full bookshelf herself. On the sixth day, Maria handed her a volume with her mother's notes scrawled in the margins. But all the notes referenced another text, one Bianca didn't have. When Maria set the breakfast tray down, Bianca shook her head. "Take it away. Take everything."

"You don't want breakfast? Just some bread? You have to eat, mistress."

"No I don't. Maybe if his only daughter starves, my father will pay attention. He might care what the rest of Venice would think about it." Her aunties used to say Bianca was so desperate for knowledge, she'd whore herself to a Medici to get it. Well, for now, she'd whore to herself, using her body to make a point. If the family asset was a little more drawn and pale, at some point her father wouldn't be able to ignore her. A little hunger would be a small price to pay to be visible.

"If you don't want it, then . . ." Maria picked up an orange and dug a fingernail into its skin, starting to peel it. "If there's no meals to bring, though, when will I get to see you?"

"You'll still bring me food. I just won't eat it. Here, put that back." Flushing, Maria dropped the orange. Its sharp scent made Bianca's mouth water. "If my father is going to know I'm starving, we need the food as evidence."

"I suppose." Maria licked juice off her fingers.

"Oh, fine." Bianca picked up the orange, handing it back to Maria. "Finish the orange. One fruit won't matter. But nothing else. Tell my father, or have the cook tell him. I'm not eating. Tell everyone."

"Everyone?"

"He doesn't care about me, but he cares what others think of him. Wait . . ." Bianca took some paper and wrote, the scratchiness of the tip of her pen the only sound as Maria finished peeling the orange. *I am motherless, and now fatherless. You must give me what I ask for, or else . . .* Bianca handed the note to Maria.

Maria's eyes skimmed across the page. "If I show him this, you'll start eating again?"

"If he pays attention to what I need. We'll know soon enough."

Maria nodded, gathered the full tray, and left.

Hours passed as Bianca waited. The sun was sinking outside her window when heavy footsteps stopped at her door. Bianca got to her feet. She was standing in the middle of the room, poised, as the door burst open. She forced herself not to flinch as her father marched in, kicking the door shut behind him.

"You dare mention your mother to me." His voice was low, but she heard every word. "Your mother, killed by those witch sisters of hers, or else by some concoction she came up with herself. She'd be alive now if not for them. Or she'd have died a peaceful death. She'd have died by my side, not theirs."

Bianca gritted her teeth. Did her father truly think any death from malaria could be peaceful? He was right to blame her aunts; her mother's dying had been made even more painful by their attempts to cure her. But it was Bianca who'd helped her live as long as she had. "Mama knew more about healing than anyone else." Bianca spoke without looking at him. It was the only way she could keep her voice from cracking. "If she was a witch, I'm happy to be a witch too."

Out of the corner of her eye, she saw his hands ball into fists.

"Your mother was a perfect woman but for her sisters' corruptions. When she fought me it was always because her family's traditions had led her astray. I want to hear nothing more from you until you take a husband."

Bianca opened her mouth to speak. She didn't get the chance. Her father stomped out of the room.

She darted to the door. Locked again. She stood with her back against it. Enough. There had to be a place, somewhere, where a woman could create a future outside of her father's schemes. A place like the Sick House of Venice but less set in its ways, where they'd understand what it meant to use a new cure that a woman had created, rather than one that had been failing for centuries. Bianca sat down at her desk and began to write.

She woke early the next day, walking straight to her jewelry case. She lifted out a necklace. Its double strands of crystals glinted in the dawn light from the window. As it caught the light and bent it into rainbows, she could imagine the crystals ground into a fine powder or a single mineral. Was that what the alchemists studied in Florence?

At the sound of Maria's key in the lock and the door opening, Bianca pooled the crystal strands in her palm. Certainly she had no need for jewelry now.

"Maria," she said as the girl set down a tray. "I want you to do something else for me. I want you to deliver a message." She touched the girl's forearm. "See it's received. And bring back a reply."

Maria eyed the necklace. "Mistress?"

Bianca closed her hand around the jewels. From the side pocket of her skirt she pulled the letter she'd written the night before. "See that this reaches Padua."

"Padua?"

"The Sick House of the nuns there, yes. I have recipes they'll be interested in that I wish to share." The girl looked at the necklace peeking out from Bianca's hand. "In exchange, I've asked them to give me a space to make my cures. I know they'll want me. Bring me back their reply as quickly as you can." Bianca pushed the letter into Maria's hand, then let the necklace fall into the girl's open palm. "Crystal will look good on you."

"Padua is a long way, mistress." But Maria's fingers had already closed around the necklace. She gazed at the floor, shifting foot to foot. "What about your father?"

Bianca studied the girl. Could she trust her? "He's angry. I can't ask him for anything. But I won't have to, not if you pass on this letter." Bianca clasped her now-empty hands in front of her. "Listen to me, Maria, I have distant family in Padua. I'll write them as well. They'll ask my father to let me stay for a while."

"Will I get to come with you?"

"Maybe."

"I've never been to Padua. I wonder how the ladies dress?" Maria's eyes glowed. "I'll make sure it gets sent." She slipped from the room.

It wouldn't be the same as helping in the Sick House. They'd know her in Padua, and her father would keep tabs on her there. But even under watchful eyes, Bianca could visit the nuns, to learn and make progress on her cures again. Her aunties had no faith in her, and even the nuns of Venice wanted only her hands and strong stomach, not her mind. Padua, though, was a place of learning. It wasn't the Medici's Florence, but it was easier to reach. If the nuns invited Bianca to join them, her father would have to allow it, if only to avoid the shame of having it known how he'd kept her a prisoner.

That night, she slept well for the first time in days. As long as Bianca's imprisonment was between herself and her father alone, Bianca could do nothing. Once the nuns at Padua learned of the knowledge Bianca had to share, though, her father wouldn't be able to ignore the invitation they would extend to her. He wouldn't be able to marry her off, either, at least not right away, not before she'd had time to finish her mother's work. She could entertain suitors in Padua if it kept him happy, so long as she had time to study. Who knew, maybe one of the men she met there might respect her for the scientist she was becoming.

For the next several weeks, Bianca jumped every time she heard Maria's step outside. Maria learned to shout out "Nothing" as soon as she came in. Finally, at the end of the third week, Maria entered, her face empty. Holding a finger to her lips and nodding, she turned behind her, and a man, maybe ten years older than Bianca, followed her into the room. He was slight, but handsome enough. Bianca's eyes skimmed over him. Maria held a letter in her hand.

Wordless, Bianca took it and tore it open.

Mistress Capello: We regret to inform you there is no place for your work here. While we are always glad of additional hands to help us in our sickrooms, help is all we need, and you, it seems, seek much more. Our Sick House is not a place for experiments. We know nothing of this science—perhaps in Florence? Perhaps Sant'Elisabetta there? Here, we heal, and those we cannot heal rely on us to ease their passage. We pray that you find success in lessening further suffering. With respect . . .

Science. The aunties used that word, too, but always meaning something harmful. Science, trying out ideas for cures on real people, was exactly what she wanted to be doing. The signature was almost illegible. Mother Superior. Padua. Bianca's hands shook. However much she blinked, she couldn't clear the sting from her eyes.

"Mistress?" A deep voice, with an accent that wasn't from Venice. The man behind Maria cleared his throat. Had she seen him before? He might be one of her father's deputies, or maybe a clerk. If she'd ever known his name, she'd forgotten. He was barely a head taller than Bianca herself, and Bianca, unlike her mother and aunts, could look few men in the eye. He had the build of someone who labored indoors, his hair thick and dark, his smile wide. He seemed familiar enough with her, whether she knew him or not. The look he gave her was bold. "Your maid enlisted my help in this errand. I'm a clerk in Venice, but with some business in Padua—I took the letter there for you and brought back the reply. The nuns were . . . quite stern, almost forbidding."

"Forbidding? Meaning what?" Bianca failed to keep the sharpness from her voice. The clerk, though, didn't seem to mind.

"Whatever you wrote them didn't meet with favor," he began. "I wouldn't like to see their harsh faces again. Although," he added, grinning, "I'd do it for you."

Bianca tightened her lips, then looked at Maria. Who was this man? And why had Maria brought him here to witness Bianca's shame? This rejection wouldn't stop her; nothing would stop her. But he didn't know that. He'd see her as a silly girl whom no one valued.

Her eyes met those of the eager fellow. He held her gaze until she looked away. "Thank you for your help," Bianca said. Tossing the letter on a side table, she turned. "Maria?" The girl's eyes lit up as Bianca handed her a pair of crystal earrings she'd found to match the necklace. What to give the clerk? He'd have no use for jewelry. "What's your name?" Bianca asked him. "I'll put in a word for you, perhaps you'll be promoted." She shot a glance at Maria. "Without telling anyone how you served me, of course."

"My name is Piero." Hand on chest, he lowered his head.

"Piero." Bianca rolled the "r" the Florentine way, as he'd done. Was he blushing? She thought he was. "And where do you work?"

"I work for your father on the Salviati bank's behalf." He paused. "I'm returning to Florence in two months . . ."

Whatever else he said she didn't hear. Florence. She'd been right about his accent. Bianca's stomach fluttered. Could it be as easy as this?

"What would you like, then, in payment?" Bianca whispered, stepping closer. Piero's breathing sped up. Standing before him, Bianca brushed a strand of hair from his face, letting his eyes take her in. The light shift she wore clung to her curves.

Piero dropped to one knee. "Simply, to serve."

Bianca reached down to take his fingers in hers, placing her other hand on his cheek. Piero turned his head to kiss her palm.

Two months. Men had fallen in love in less time than that. Bianca, wife of a Florentine, could surely go where Bartolomeo's daughter couldn't: straight to the heart of the city where she would finally test her knowledge.

4
Escape to Florence

Bianca settled into the chair across from her father. Eight weeks in, these meals with him still felt strange. He'd summoned her for the first time just after she'd received her letter from Padua. His message had been no more welcome than the nuns' harsh response. *In order to prepare for your future as a wife, you'll join me nights for supper. Any time not spent at my side will be spent in your room.* When Maria had handed her the note, Bianca nearly choked. She'd just formed her own plan, one involving a certain clerk, in Venice. Had her father somehow guessed? But after the first few days, when her father mentioned nothing about any messages Bianca might have sent to Padua, or any clerks who suddenly seemed distracted, Bianca relaxed.

Tonight she filled her plate, her heart racing. But she couldn't let her father notice, couldn't let him guess that this Manor supper was to be their last one together. She fixed a smile on her face.

The note Maria had delivered that afternoon had made it clear. *Midnight. Be ready, tonight, my love.* By now, Piero's handwriting was almost as familiar to Bianca as her own. The smooth paper had an inky parchment smell mixed with the sweat she'd come to know. Piero's kisses weren't everything she'd ever dreamed a man's could be, but the way her name sounded in his Florentine tongue made up for that. What did she care if he had little interest in her science? He'd soon be taking her to Florence.

"You look well." Her father's voice cut through Bianca's thoughts, as did the smell from the fragrant spice stick grinding in his mouth. Licorice, or possibly it was star anise seeds. Did her father have access to all her stores in the palace, when she only had a few herbs she'd left in her room here the last time they'd spent a week away from Venice? Not that it mattered now. "Behaving like a lady agrees with you, I'd say." Her father lifted a fork, eyeing her. "Just what a husband wants."

A lady? Bianca looked down at the table, waiting for the heat in her cheeks to fade. Tonight, her father's power over her would end. And he had no idea. *Be ready tonight . . .* Bianca had slipped the note into her sleeve. She could pull it out right now and tell her father, "I'll soon have a husband." Instead, she lowered her eyes, tucking her chin into the trim on her collar.

"The year is almost ended." Her father gazed at her, still chewing. "It's time to have you married. Yes, Bianca?"

Bianca met her father's eyes. "If that's what you wish."

"Good. We'll return to Venice next week. I have a woman there who will prepare your trousseau."

At the word "trousseau," he raised his eyebrows and a small trail of drool dribbled down his chin. Chew enough of the sweet root and it could numb one's tongue. Chew more and one could choke on the pulpy mash. Bianca said nothing. Let him chew till his tongue became too thick to shape words. Wouldn't that be sweet, if, when she left that night, her father couldn't even forbid her from going.

"Something to look forward to, Father." Bianca sat back in her chair. Piero had asked her what jewels she'd bring, but certainly wouldn't expect a typical trousseau of embroidered linens or bedding with fine hand stitching. He was marrying the Capello name, and that was far more than he ever should have hoped for. As for herself, she was marrying Florence. "Of course, I'll do as you ask. I look forward to meeting some suitable men." Bianca glanced down at her lap. "And I'll follow your guidance . . . and instruction." With a weak smile, she looked up. "Next week."

Eyes fixed on his well-behaved daughter, Bartolomeo nodded. Bianca tapped a linen napkin to her mouth. He might as well return to Venice next week. By tomorrow, she'd be gone.

An hour later, with the door of her room shut behind her, Bianca sat on the edge of the bed and slipped a pair of boots into her trunk. She hadn't changed after supper. The silk dress she had worn to please her father, blue for the Capello crest, clung to her body. Every place the silk touched, every curve she thought of as hers, soon would belong just as much to Piero.

Bianca stood up and walked to the mirror, staring. There, and there, Piero had kissed her. Those were the thighs he felt when he slid his hands under her dress. This was the face he told her was beautiful. But what did his words mean, really? Bianca leaned in close to the glass. Did he even know what color her eyes were? Or did he only see the curves of her body? Bianca had asked Maria to make her a scalding hot bath after each of Piero's late night visits. Once married and with her own house, Bianca could bathe whenever she wanted, however much Maria laughed at her for it now. By then she would have gotten what she needed. By then she'd be free of her father.

Bianca looked in her closet, searching for a dress that didn't hug her figure quite as closely as this one did. There—a light lime shimmering brocade, something beautiful from home, but attractive to Piero, too. She'd learn the easiest ways to give him what he wanted. He, after all, was giving her Florence. And he could be kind, looking at her like a jewel, some expensive object he'd never thought could possibly be his. But she was his, wasn't she? She was a young man's possession, and soon, a *wife*. Leaning against the bed, she pressed her hands to her stomach. Was this how her mother had felt before her wedding day? *Wife. Wedding.* The bed she lay on might be the last she'd ever have to herself again.

Bianca could hear her own breathing, her heart pounding. The excitement she'd struggled so hard to contain while sitting with her father didn't feel like anticipation now. It felt like a heavy stone pestle lodged in her gut. Why wasn't her mother here to talk her through this? She had never even met the man Bianca would marry. Bianca shut her eyes, sinking into the bed, letting the familiar dips and creaks of it cradle her.

Behind her closed eyelids she could almost see her mother's hands separating dried flowers from their stems, her mother's lips as she kissed Bianca goodnight. She could hear the sound of her voice calling from a corner of the nearby woods. Leaving Venice, Bianca would be on her own, exploring paths and grounds on which she'd never walked with her mother. Would Bianca start to forget what her mother looked like? Everything she'd ever told her? About brews. About her garden. *Follow one thing, and follow it with your whole heart,* her mother used to say. She certainly hadn't meant a husband. But Bianca wasn't following a husband. She was following a cure. She was following knowledge.

Bianca opened her eyes and stood up. Whatever faults Piero had, he wasn't her father, he wasn't anything like him. Bianca was leaving with Piero, tonight, and if she didn't change and finish packing, she wouldn't be ready when Maria arrived.

Choosing what possessions to bring was easy. Bianca grabbed another pair of shoes. This dress would serve, this dress wouldn't, and none of it really mattered. She used the brocade dress to wrap the books Maria had brought her. Hesitating a moment, she took most of them, also packing the notebook she'd filled so carefully from her time in the Sick House. Ideas for cures were all this bride needed.

And several pieces of glassware wrapped in cotton wool, a wooden box for her magnifying glass, and some tweezers.

And herbs? Her father had forbidden her entry into the country gardens, but Bianca had taken with her some bundles of artemisia rootstocks stored under a loose board at the back of her closet in Venice. She packed them into her trunk. Weeds to some, yet surely in Florence people would recognize their value. Still she longed for her packets of seeds, and the stores of herbs she'd so carefully harvested and dried in the Venice annex. Had her father tried to destroy them before they'd left Venice? Maybe he'd given them to the aunties, so they could waste them while making the same useless treatments they'd brewed for centuries.

Bianca leaned over a small jewelry chest and took her mother's pearls and a handful of small gems. She'd wear the pearls, and her mother's ruby ring, and a few other pieces. The rest she folded into a small linen scarf, tucked inside the brocade dress, adding a jar of clay face powder to make her look the lady if she needed to. Then she slammed the trunk shut. Next time she lifted the lid, she'd have started her new life in the city of alchemists. Just four days of travel, maybe five, and she'd be one of them.

Someone knocked, two light taps on her door.

Bianca crossed the room. The maid pushed open the door, face flushed with excitement. "Bianca, let's go." Maria had wrapped her hair in a thick scarf. She passed Bianca the plain cloak she carried over one arm. "For you, mistress."

The cloak fit loosely over Bianca's gown. "Careful, Maria, the trunk is packed with books. We can each take an end." Together they lifted the trunk, pitching side to side as they walked. Bianca backed out the door, Maria following.

"This would be easier with Piero's help," Maria panted. "He could probably carry the whole trunk himself."

Bianca shook her head. "I do as much physical work as he does,

Maria. Or I did, before my father locked me up." She shifted her fingers, adjusting her grip. "But where is he? Why didn't he come with you?"

"He's waiting outside. He was afraid your father would see him." Maria put down her end of the trunk. Bianca stumbled, catching herself before the trunk tilted too far and knocked her off-balance. "He's strong, Bianca. And don't you think he's handsome?" Maria rubbed her cramping fingers. "And he's smart. He took cover in the stalls, readying your father's fastest carriage even before your supper."

"Why hide? My father's in his rooms. He'll be there until morning. But come on, that doesn't mean we've got time to rest."

"No, mistress, Piero said there were candles lit in your father's study."

Had her father chosen tonight of all nights to stay up? They'd have to get out without going past him. "Then we really have no time. Come on, Maria."

The girl sighed and hoisted her end of the trunk again, matching her steps to Bianca's as they made their way down several corridors and into another, past the closed doors of unused bedrooms. At what had been her mother's door, Bianca paused, lowering the trunk and reaching out to touch the handle.

Far behind her, someone called her name.

Her father? Distance made the voice hazy, but it had to be him. From the sound, he could be in her room, searching for her. Bianca's breath caught. Had Maria heard? No, the girl, busy stretching her fingers, was too distracted to notice.

Good. Maria would panic, and they couldn't afford delays. Bianca found a back staircase and stepped onto the first flight of stairs, slow and cautious. Once they inched down it, they could take the servants' door at the bottom and be outside.

The *thump* when Maria missed the last step and dropped her end of the trunk was only slightly louder than her cry of pain. "My foot!"

"Hush." Bianca scrambled to hold her end of the trunk as Maria bent over the banister for balance, cradling her foot, her face squeezed in pain. "Maria, quiet. If my father hears us . . ." She reached across to grab Maria's arm. Were those footsteps on the floor above them? "Listen. We have to run."

"I can't." Maria fell back onto a step.

"You said you'd help me. You have to." But Maria didn't move. Was her foot broken? The trunk was heavy enough. "Hide, then." Things would be much worse for both of them if Bianca was discovered with her. "The kitchen closets are just through that door. Please try not to be seen until morning. And Maria . . . thank you." Right now she wanted to shake the girl, but she had to make herself say it. "Thank you for helping me, I mean, us."

"I know. It was so romantic, watching you and Piero fall in love . . ."

Bianca shot a pointed glance toward the kitchen.

"I'll hide . . . when they find me, I won't say a word . . ."

Bianca took Maria's hand, then pulled her into an embrace before stepping back and nudging the girl gently away. Finally Maria hobbled to the kitchen door, flinging herself through it. Bianca eyed the trunk. She couldn't carry it on her own. Quickly, she yanked the lid open. Nestled on top was the bundle of books in the brocade dress. She grabbed it and the artemisia roots, and slid them under her cloak. Heavy footsteps drew closer. Bianca lunged for the door that led outside.

Rain lashed down, its roar loud enough to cover the sound of the door closing behind her. A faint light glowed in the stables across the yard. Gathering her baggy cloak around her waist, Bianca ran, mud splashing up her legs. "Piero!"

"Bianca, love." Piero sat in the seat of her father's carriage, the reins of Bartolomeo's only two carthorses in his hands. Transport sturdy enough to have held Bianca's trunk, if she'd been able to bring it. "Your bags . . . ?"

"No time. He's coming." Bianca hopped up beside Piero, tossing her bundle of books on the floor.

Piero frowned. "What about your jewelry? And your silks? I'll go back for your trunk. Wait here." Piero vaulted from the carriage before Bianca could grab his arm.

"Piero." The beating rain muffled her voice. "Don't be a fool," she said as he moved toward her. "I barely packed any jewelry. It's my mother's books I'm going to miss. At least I have her notes," she said underneath her breath. "But Piero, there's no time—he's going to catch us. Look—" Across the yard, light spilled from the opening door.

Piero jumped back into the carriage and smacked the reins against the horses' withers. "All right. You'll be safe now." His breath steamed hot in her ear, even as she shivered. His hand crept around her waist as he slapped the reins again. "You're safe. I've got you. Maybe later we can send for your things. Now I have you all to myself, Bianca Capello."

And he did. She imagined her father, framed in the doorway, most likely shouting. She couldn't ever come back, Piero had to know that. The horses cantered forward, the rain beating on the carriage roof. By the time Bartolomeo could mount a chase, they'd be gone. Her life here and in Venice would be gone. Bianca Capello, royal daughter, would be gone.

In her place: Bianca the scientist. Bianca Capello of Florence. Until they got there, Piero might think she was his, but soon he'd find out that he was hers and that this was Bianca's escape all along.

The horses kept up a steady clip southward. The rain began to ease, and the rich odors of damp soil wafted into the carriage. Piero rested his head on her shoulder. She turned away, flinching as his hand tightened around her waist. There was little enough she needed Piero to protect her from. She needed his connection to Florence, and then his job would be done.

They drove the rest of that night, stopping only now and then in the grass by the road, the faint moonlight letting the horses find their way. Bianca had thought she might sleep in the carriage, but each time she began to drift off, her head slumping on Piero's shoulder, she'd feel his thigh chafing against hers. By the time watery light poured over the pine woods around them, Bianca's head was pounding. Finally they reached a village nestled at the edge of a marsh, the air heavy with the sounds of insects. Bianca swatted one from her arm as Piero guided the horses to the gates of an inn. Hardly more than a way-stop, it was small, only two stories, and built of rough pine, so it almost blended in with the woods that fringed the town. Bianca had never stayed at an inn before. Those she passed in Venice were much larger than this. But those inns would have smelled of street muck and weary travelers. Here, the sweetness of pine bark filled the air.

"I don't know if we should stop," she said as Piero, closing his eyes, dropped his head over his chest. "Piero, are you listening?"

Jerking his head forward, he yawned. "We've come far enough. No one will be looking for us."

"You don't know my father." Bianca sighed. Too easily, though, she could imagine Piero falling asleep with the reins in his hands, even at daybreak. This place, with its narrow, quiet roads, did seem too far out of the way for her father to search. No one would expect to see Bartolomeo's daughter here. And Bianca wanted a bed.

Piero handed the reins to the inn's stable boy and led the way inside. When he asked for lodging for himself and his wife, Bianca blinked. *Wife*. But the innkeeper just nodded and took them to their room.

Once inside, Piero shut the door, smiling. "Take your dress off." He pulled her close, slipping his arm around her. "You're my wife now, or nearly so. Wait." He lifted her hand. "Where's your ring?"

He must mean the one he'd bought for her, a tiny garnet set in silver that he'd slid on her finger when they'd made their plans to run away. It always felt a bit too loose. Maybe Maria would find it.

One last trinket by which to remember her mistress. "It must have fallen off."

Piero shook his head. "I spent all I had on that ring." But he forgot his anger quickly as his hands found the buttons on the back of her dress. "We've never done this in daylight before. Bianca, let me see you."

"Can't we just sleep?" But there was no stopping his eager fingers. Bianca let her dress puddle on the floor. His hands tugged at her shift, and at her underskirt. "Wait, Piero. At least we can lock the door."

Her life as Piero's wife had begun.

5
Florence
Unhappy Wife

Bianca shook herself awake. Several weeks sharing this bed with Piero, and still she opened her eyes expecting the familiar silk sheets she'd grown up with. There, she woke to the sounds of birds warbling outside her window, not the snuffles of Piero's sleeping mother just on the other side of the thin wall. At least she had the bed to herself for the moment. Piero had risen an hour ago, content with stale rolls and whatever else his mother mustered before she fell back into bed. His clerk's job kept him from the house most of the day, leaving Bianca with Anna, her mother-in-law. The words still sounded strange, though she and Piero had married within a week of arriving—something the Medici court had arranged, although she had no idea why. Surely her father couldn't know she was here? Piero's mother hadn't smiled once during the service. Or since.

If she had, Bianca would have seen. Anna was always in the small house they shared, shaking her head, growling instructions as though Bianca didn't know how to sweep and wash after months of cleaning sickrooms. Bianca had been called useless as she attempted to knead bread, stretching and folding the dough until Piero's mother elbowed her aside and pummeled it into a tight loaf. The woman had a hoarse cough that shook the house at night and she tired easily, yet Bianca, it seemed, was the weak, incompetent one.

But what did Bianca care if her bread tasted salty, or if she wasn't quick enough sweeping the floors? The hearth in the room she shared with Piero was part of her studio now. She was making brews again, buying herbs from the Florentine markets, places even busier and more bustling than the ones back in Venice. She'd even treated Anna once when the rattle of liquid in the woman's lungs became too harsh to ignore. Anna had improved by the next day, but she'd refused to admit it had anything to do with Bianca.

Piero's small, stuffy house wasn't what she'd imagined Florence to be, but out in the market the city came alive. Anna had been happy enough to hand off the shopping duty. Bianca was buying everything for the household, not just her own herbs. Merchants sold sweet-smelling spices from roots or leaves or seeds of plants, but also raw fabrics and spun silks from faraway places. Florentines from wealthy houses swept by in finely carved, gilded carriages, kicking up dust. Once she even caught a glimpse of the Medici coat-of-arms, someone from the household out on royal business. Most afternoons she'd return to find Piero's mother back in bed, huddled down in the cold, short days of winter and the luxury of having the household's labor divided. It hadn't taken long for Bianca to realize she could stay out until early evening and not be missed.

She rarely lingered in the market. Really, there was only one place she wanted to be.

Every day once the shopping was done, she walked to the gates of the Sant'Elisabetta convent. She watched nuns enter and leave. These were the nuns she'd heard rumors of in Venice, the ones mentioned by the superior in Padua who'd read her letter and dismissed her. They'd built an apothecary her mother had dreamed of visiting. Their knowledge, her mother had told her, surpassed that of any women or men anywhere else. Within those walls, the nuns practiced healing at a level Bianca could only imagine—independently, and surely with their own laboratories and sickrooms, especially for women and children. They created cures and wrote about them, Bianca was sure of it. They had no shortage of patients. Women throughout the city, and men, too, came to the nuns. Did they leave healed? One day Bianca had watched a woman approach holding a swaddled bundle, only to depart an hour later, empty-handed. On another, a man came to the gates wracked with a cough, a cough she could have easily healed. A nun let him in. She watched until dusk, but didn't see him come out again.

One night last week she'd returned home as she always did to help prepare the light evening meal and to sit at the table with her husband while his mother peppered him with questions about his clients. The woman was hungry for gossip, especially when Piero's clients were wealthy like the Medici. But Piero reported nothing about their alchemy or their social lives. Bianca glanced out the window. The moon was full.

But . . . it couldn't be. Her monthly bleeding hadn't come for the second month.

Bianca didn't hear another word spoken at the table that night. She visited the chamber pot so many times in the next few hours, Anna asked whether the supper she'd prepared didn't agree with her "Venetian disposition." All through the night, no blood appeared on Bianca's nightdress. The longed-for pain she usually dreaded didn't come.

Now, as Bianca lay in bed, her stomach started to churn. In a moment she was hovering over the chamber pot again, retching into it as silently as she could until her stomach emptied. Finally, gasping, she sat back on her heels. Was this to be her life? Wife to Piero and mother to his baby, a baby who'd grow up watching his mama, a royal Capello, washing the floors on her knees? No. Her plan was to study, not to care for Piero's child and his troublesome mother, nor scrub tile floors to keep the cramped, dark rooms clean. But soon she would be out of time.

Once Piero knew she was pregnant, any freedom that she'd carved out for herself would be gone. No. She couldn't wait. She couldn't merely keep watching the nuns at Sant'Elisabetta, trying to diagnose their patients from afar. She needed their knowledge. She needed to convince them that they needed hers.

After barely sleeping through the night, Bianca rose, shifting her weight from one foot to the other as if to distract herself. Was the sickness past? Yes, but she'd seen enough of her cousins pregnant to know it would be back tomorrow morning, and the morning after that. Anna would notice if Piero didn't. What Anna might say about the mission Bianca undertook today, she didn't want to know. The work Bianca chased, work that drew on the practical arts of women and men, would surely get her punished in Venice, but here? Anna, who crossed herself regularly and prayed every day, might be the first to call Bianca a witch, or worse. Bianca hadn't come to Florence to please Piero's mother. Still, she needed to be cautious.

She dressed quickly, lingering over the pieces of jewelry she'd been wearing on her hurried journey with Piero. Sliding her mother's ruby ring onto her finger, she packed the pockets of her overcoat with some of the herbs she'd bought in the market. Then she left the bedroom, pausing only to stoke the fire. Start the bread? No, let the old woman fend for herself. Any woman could make bread. Only Bianca Capello, Pellegrina's daughter, could find a way to cure malaria, and she planned to do it, within Sant'Elisabetta's walls.

6

Sant'Elisabetta

1564

Outside, the streets were full of people scurrying about in thick coats, the sun's early rays making Bianca blink and shield her eyes. She drew her woolen overcoat tight, its heavy folds pressing in on the herbs she'd packed in its deep pockets so that scents of santolina and sage trailed after her in the morning air. She was going to the nuns prepared, a scientist ready to learn. She just needed their equipment, and a little of their knowledge, to help her create her herbal remedies and test them. She just needed someone in this city to see her for who she was.

Half an hour later, Bianca stopped in front of the door she'd spent so many hours watching. The facets of her mother's ruby ring flashed in the sun as she reached up and pulled the cord. As the bell inside tolled, Bianca twisted the ring on her finger. When Mama had passed the ring on to Bianca before becoming sick with malaria, she probably hadn't pictured her daughter using it as she planned to today. But Mama, of all people, wouldn't mind.

Bianca held one hand on the clasp of her coat, letting light play over the surface of the gem. Had no one heard the bell? She reached for the cord again. Her hand was still in the air when the door before her swung open.

The nun in the doorway stood at least a head taller than Bianca, her heavy habit hiding all but her face. Keen dark eyes assessed Bianca from beneath the folds of the nun's veil.

"How far along?" the nun asked. "Six weeks? Eight?"

"What?" Bianca took a step back. No one else had even guessed that she was pregnant. This nun, though, would be more than familiar with soon-to-be mothers. "Probably eight," Bianca said. "But I'm here about something else." Though what if she wasn't? Some women entered these walls as mothers and left free, unfettered.

"Something else, is it?" The nun's eyes flickered over Bianca's face, then to her hand, which still hovered over the clasp of her coat.

The sun caught the ring's gemstone as Bianca let her hand fall to the side. "Please, may I see the superior here?"

"You're not from Florence, are you?" The nun opened the door a little wider. "Very well. Come in."

What had given her away? Maybe her accent, or perhaps the nun knew by face every woman in Florence who could afford to wear such a ring. As the nun stepped aside, ushering Bianca in after her, Bianca tucked her hand into the folds of her inner cloak. Her mother's ring had been seen. It had gotten her in.

A candle flickered on a table just inside the door. Carrying it with her, the nun plodded down the long stone hallway toward a small door at the hall's far end. Just as in the foyers in the Sick House in Venice in the winter, the air was bone cold and dry. Any brew that needed to be served warm here would chill within minutes. The nun knocked several times and the door swung open, warm air rushing out. Bianca swayed in its draft. An old woman stood before them. She thanked Bianca's escort, the porter, who turned on her heel and left.

The edges of the wimple under the old nun's veil seemed to sharpen the lines of her face. Her skin hung crepe-like on her cheeks. Only the black eyes that flashed to meet Bianca's didn't look old. Those ageless eyes traveled up her, then down. With one bony hand the woman gestured toward a stiff-backed chair in the middle of the room. Bianca tiptoed in and closed the door as the nun sauntered to her desk.

The room offered little comfort. A small window with an ornate grille let in a glimmer of light, and embers glowed in a grated hearth, but the room itself was almost bare. Bianca sat and opened her coat, breathing in the warmth.

"You look tired, child." The nun stood before her, her forehead creased, hands folded beneath her robe. "I'm the Mother Superior." Bianca looked up to meet her gaze. "If you came wishing for us to take your baby, the Sister wouldn't have brought you to me. Yet I can't think of any other reason for you to be here."

If you came wishing for us to take your baby. The child within her was only an idea, wasn't it? Bianca's breath caught in her throat. Let someone take away this strange thing inside her that made her vomit more than any of her strongest brews? The tie to Piero she wouldn't be able to shed? Was there some way she could hand this woman her baby now, and walk out of here freed? No, of course not; the nun would think her mad. But then, didn't the porter think that was what she wanted to do? Birth the baby, leave it, and never think of it again.

No. She didn't have that luxury. She had a task to do, a task that would use up all the favors she could ask for here. How could she convince these nuns to see her as worth listening to if, in seven months, Bianca asked them for the same escape every woman who came to Sant'Elisabetta wanted? She'd handle motherhood when she had to, but not having a place to experiment would kill her science. That alone was reason to have come.

"I can't say I wish to be a mother," Bianca said. "But my wishes about that don't matter. I want to study. To work with, and to learn from, you. My mother taught me what she knew about herbs and healing. She nearly found a cure for malaria—"

"A cure?" The nun shook her head. "That's impossible."

"Mother, please. I can explain." Bianca leaned forward. "She was creating a cure when she herself got sick. I was ten, but she taught me everything. Ever since she died I've been trying to finish what she began. I couldn't do it in Venice. So I came to Florence. I want to work with you . . ." Bianca's voice trailed into silence.

"Work with us? Our work is to shelter children, teach the young." The nun's wrinkled face gave away nothing.

Bianca drew a breath and clasped her hands. Yes, there, the light from the hearth glinted faintly off the ring. Had the nun seen it? "Surely, you do more than that."

The nun shook her head. "Nothing that would interest you."

"I understand that apprenticeships require payment. I'm prepared to part with my mother's gift to me," Bianca said, tilting her head toward the ring, "if you'll allow me to study here."

"This is a place for labor, not for study." But the nun's eyes were on Bianca's hand.

Slowly Bianca slid the ring from her finger, the ring her mother's skin had once warmed. In the second it took to drop it into the nun's waiting palm, Bianca closed her eyes. It was done.

The nun's hand disappeared up her sleeve so quickly Bianca might have thought no exchange had just occurred, except for the empty place on her own finger. "If you wish to work, we do need skilled hands. Learn along the way, or don't. Your first duty will be to complete whatever task is in front of you. If this is acceptable to you, we'll expect you back tomorrow."

Had Bianca just bought her way in? She let out a breath she'd been holding for too long. The nun had made no mention of any trade of information. Bianca hadn't even shared her recipes yet, or shown the nun her herbs. That plan, though, seemed almost laughable now. These nuns had no need to let Bianca in as an equal. She was useful to them only as an extra pair of hands. Still, drudgery opened doors. Bianca tucked her hands into her coat pockets and buried her fingers in the dried herbs that were probably poor relatives of the collections of plants these nuns had at their disposal. It didn't matter. Nothing mattered. Only this: *We'll expect you back tomorrow.*

"I'll work hard," Bianca said, as the nun walked her to the door.

The nun nodded. "We shall see."

Walking back to Piero's house, Bianca stepped more lightly than she had since coming to Florence. The hours she used to pass watching Sant'Elisabetta, she'd now spend inside. Lying to Piero to explain her absences would be easy. She suffered from women's troubles, it ran in her family, she had gone to the nuns for treatment. They'd be able to help her, but she'd need to go to them every day. Anna would probably gloat, her worst fears about Bianca's suitability as a wife and mother confirmed. She'd be irate if she knew Bianca had just willingly agreed to work in a nunnery when Anna had tried for weeks to make Bianca her toiling servant.

That evening it all went to plan. Piero presided over supper, telling and retelling stories about bank clients he'd assisted. Someone in the Medici court had slighted him, an insult felt deeply by Piero and even more so by Anna, who spent the meal praising her son and complaining about every person in the city of Florence who had ever failed to appreciate him. When Bianca mentioned in passing that she would be receiving treatment from the nuns at Sant'Elisabetta, Anna responded as Bianca expected. "Good. See if you can learn from them how to be the wife my son deserves."

"Nothing would please me more," Bianca said under her breath. A man with Piero's wandering eye didn't deserve any kind of wife at all. He'd come home twice smelling of a perfume Bianca didn't recognize. Shouldn't Anna be paying attention to that? But if it meant he touched her less, Bianca didn't care.

The next day after morning chores, she walked to Sant'Elisabetta and tugged the bell pull. The same tall nun let her in, without a smile and with barely a word, but at least today the set of her jaw looked slightly softer than stone. Bianca, wide-eyed, followed her through the corridors that smelled of different herbs and along garden paths, between beds of mints and sages, a thicket of rue, and herbs even Bianca couldn't name. Her tasks that day, however, had nothing to do with gardens. She buffed pitted floors, swept away dust, and polished glassware from storerooms that, she imagined, must have been used in the making of countless cures. It was important work, she reminded herself each time the bell tolled and she had to stop and kneel for the hourly prayers upon which the nuns insisted. Someone had to do the chores, and if this was what it took to gain the nuns' trust, then Bianca would clean and polish better than any novice.

By the end of the day, though, Bianca's knees ached, and her back could barely straighten. Exhausted, she got home just in time to help Piero's mother prepare the evening repast. Between washing the dishes and joining Piero in bed, Bianca barely found time to write down the few observations she'd managed to make in her day at Sant'Elisabetta. *Two nuns smelling handfuls of earth in the mint garden. Then digging into the soil, possibly to determine its fineness? Try to find out why. Large glass funnel in storage outside apothecary—what is it for?* Mostly Bianca wrote down questions without answers. But the answers, she told herself, would come.

When Piero reached for her that first night, Bianca pulled away. "We can't. The nuns said I have to wait."

"I thought they were going to help you get pregnant. Don't you need me for that, too?"

"Soon, Piero. They told me we must wait until the treatment has time to take effect."

Piero sighed. Within minutes, his breathing slowed and he slept. Good. She needed sleep herself. The last thing she wanted was to waste a day with the nuns because she was tired.

Late one morning, several weeks since Bianca first passed through the gates of Sant'Elisabetta, the Mother Superior ushered Bianca into a large room of cabinets full of labeled herbs and liquids in smoky gray bottles. Far beyond the windowless stone room came the sound of nuns chanting. Tucking her hands under her long-sleeved cowl, the Superior gazed at Bianca.

Her heart pounding, Bianca looked down at the floor. But before she could ask if she'd done something wrong, if she'd displeased the Mother Superior in some way, the old woman spoke. "You meant it when you said you could work, didn't you? No need to look so frightened, girl. I'm giving you to Sister Angelica. Go through that door—yes, there. She's waiting for you." Without another word, the nun turned away. The tapping of her heels echoed down the corridor.

Bianca crossed over to the other side of the room and nudged open a door. At a corner table along a far wall in the next room stood a nun wearing an apron and gloves, and sorting a big pile of dried herbs into neat stacks of lady's mantle, pennyroyal, and comfrey. She was younger than any of the nuns Bianca had talked to so far, her long, narrow face framed by a white wimple, with just a lock of nutmeg-colored hair peeking through. Her smile, when she glanced up at Bianca, was quick and warm. A small gray cat rubbed against her legs.

"You must be Bianca," the nun began. "I'm Angelica. Please, take a look around."

Shelves lined the stone walls. One large table of heavily polished wood in the center held raw fiber and cuttings of chamomile and mugworts, baskets full of freshly harvested herbs, and a few books—all in the shadow of flickering wax candles. On the nearest shelf sat one small alembic with a rounded flask and a thick glass column to condense and collect steam, the boiling flask much like her mother's back in Venice. Besides this, there was nothing here that matched the rumors of nuns practicing men's alchemy. No salt niter to force minerals silver, nor bowls of mercury sulfide or copper pots of calcinated talc—the mark of metal transformations. Still, Bianca knew her face had to have shown her excitement as she fingered a familiar bundle of aromatic woody stems.

"That space is for you." Angelica pointed to a nearly empty table along a wall, a basket of coltsfoot claiming a corner of its surface. "Show me what you can do, my dear. The Mother Superior told me you have ideas."

Bianca winced. That might or might not be praise, coming from the inscrutable old nun. But she began scanning the tables around her, searching for herbs whose powers she understood. And there it was, the plant she knew the best. She pushed a clump of dried artemisia cuttings toward Angelica. "This herb is the best for the heat disease."

Picking up the bundled stems, Angelica smelled the wood. "You think this cures malaria? After all the simmering, the decoction from it is so bitter."

Bianca gave a tight nod. "I sweeten it. With anise and fennel seeds, or grain syrup."

The young nun lifted her eyebrows. "And that helps?"

"Yes, I think so." Would Angelica, like her aunties and like the nuns at Padua, scold Bianca for inventing such a medicine? Surely any healer would know bitter medicines could be sweetened. Bianca skimmed the nun's collection. What could this room tell her about their methods—outdated, inventive? They had an alembic, so why didn't she see any distillates?

"Are you looking for more alchemy, Bianca?" Her guide hadn't missed Bianca's wandering gaze. "The Mother Superior didn't tell me to show you. But, she also didn't tell me not to. Come with me." She turned on one foot, her veil still folded neatly over her shoulders, and motioned Bianca back out into the hall. "Down this way, there's another corridor." Bianca, scanning the doors that lay ahead, almost ran into Angelica, who'd paused. The young nun smiled. "Just a minute. This is the best view of our gardens."

Bianca gazed through an opening to the enclosed grounds beyond. The manicured yard was a picture of vibrant growth. Neat hedges surrounded gardens that even in winter shone verdant green. Some of the hellebore plants were in flower, faded pink or dusky rose or with wine-colored blooms. Branches of mulberry spread across stone walls. In spring, the foliage would burst, food for silkworms. Would she still be here to see the death, the sacrifice that happened next? Each caterpillar feeding on the mulberry would spin a cocoon. Boiled, it would never emerge, its life the price of the fine silk the nuns would weave from it.

"Beautiful, isn't it?" Angelica's soft voice was barely audible over the birdsong outside. "I love this place. How could anyone ever leave?" Bowing her head, she started down the hall again, her habit brushing the doorframe as she passed into a large workroom. Inside, a half dozen or more liquids chortled, boiling in thick glass receptacles around the room. Bianca, heart racing, inhaled. An acrid steam stung the inside of her nose.

This was where she belonged. Studying the room, Bianca saw some things familiar, but many new. Bitter herbs, tucked in the corner on the far table. On the one directly in front of her, a ring of sweet-smelling distillates in flasks. This was the science Bianca sought—a practical chemistry, distilling herbs into substances so pure they could heal disease. Would they be better than her mere infusions and simmered decoctions, her tinctures? Her fingers itched for her notebook. She jumped when a hand brushed against her arm. Angelica.

"Bianca, I need you to pay attention," Sister Angelica cautioned. "It's dangerous until you know your way around. You have to let me teach you if we're to work together."

"Work together?" She was to do more than clean this room, then? Bianca leaned over the closest boil, then flinched.

"Do you know what that is, Bianca?"

"Something fruity."

"It smells sweet. I can see why you'd think that. But it's not." The nun patted Bianca's arm. "It's opium poppy . . . and bitter. Milky latex found in the unripe seed. Look, we have others. Smell the sweet apple on the table, and here, a smoky boil."

Bianca leaned over, then straightened, wrinkling her nose.

"Wood tars." The nun raised a finger to the pungent steam. "Insect repellent."

"For moths? I've used wormwoods with bay laurel to do the same." But Bianca had to admit this distillate smelled like it could be a good chemical.

The nun's smile broadened. "A wise woman of Venice would have much to offer us if she cared to share."

"What would you like?" Bianca asked softly. "An infusion against indigestion or colic, a cream for healing a wound?" She looked down at the nun's hands. Sister Angelica, following her gaze, twisted them to hide faint purple lines. Even these holy ones were vain. "Something to keep female hands beautiful?"

"Are those the secrets you think we want?" The nun moved to another table, picking up a glass bottle. "We're creating strong extracts—"

"With your tars?"

The nun nodded.

"And cures?"

"Only God cures," the nun said with a slight bow of her head.

"Doesn't God give you your skill as a healer, urging you to discover what your extracts and tinctures can heal?"

"We're cautious in gleaning such knowledge." The nun folded her hands. "Knowledge can be put to many uses. Those who value their souls think hard before they reach for what only God knows."

Bianca's mother had warned her about insisting too strongly on her own knowledge, all that she was fighting for now, her kind of alchemy. At some point Bianca would have to stand her ground. But was Angelica the woman to have this fight with? Not until Bianca knew for certain she'd keep quiet. Angelica might understand, but she might not.

"I know, Bianca," Sister Angelica said. "You want to make medicines and perhaps dispense them in the apothecary."

Had the nun peered inside Bianca's soul?

"You should have gone to Santa Catarina. Few of our distillations are medicines . . ."

"But Sister Angelica, their medicines are salves and infusions, powders maybe, no distillations, no testing, no . . ."

"Testing? There are no experiments here." The nun's voice was gentle but firm. "Knowledge is a gift, Bianca. You think it's created, and that yours is powerful." Sister Angelica reached for a potted aloe, then took a large pinch of soil. Meeting Bianca's eyes, she said, "Knowledge takes time, fermenting like this soil does, until it's ready to go elsewhere. And we decide when."

Watching the specks of soil tumble from the nun's hand, Bianca forced herself to nod. All this knowledge, sealed in a nunnery.

"You must want this very much."

"Yes." Bianca rubbed the finger that had once worn her mother's ring.

Sister Angelica turned to face her. "I assume you gave them something to get in here?" At the look on Bianca's face, she laughed. "Oh, don't look so surprised. I know how the Mother Superior operates. How do you think we can afford this workroom?" She set down the aloe and took Bianca's hand in her own worn fingers. Pressing her fingertip into Bianca's palm, the nun traced the shape of a cross. Their eyes met. "Shall we make it worth it?" The nun lifted her chin. "Bianca, work with me? We both have lessons to learn from each other."

7
The Blunder That Couldn't Be Buried

Growing up, Bianca used to imagine having a medicinal distillery at her fingertips, but she'd never thought about who might keep her company there. Even when she had first entered Sant'Elisabetta and begun searching for its secrets, she'd looked for a room full of distillations staffed by pious old women. What she hadn't expected was a partner. No matter that the nun's day was evenly divided into work and prayer. What Angelica began in the early morning, Bianca finished in the afternoon. The nun's chemistry, distilling dyes to their purest state to color silks, was practical, as were the distillations to keep moths at bay. Her alchemy was cautious, as any incident Angelica caused would have her back weeding and bagging herbs with her sisters. She was eager for Bianca's stories of her mother's experiments with artemisia. The idea that reducing a substance to its purest form could not only increase the potency of dyes but also cure disease made Angelica's eyes light up, as Bianca's must have when her mother first started sharing with her daughter the secrets of alchemy.

Had Pellegrina, surrounded by sisters who were skeptical of anything new, longed for a companion like Angelica with whom she could share her ideas? Surely she had, Bianca thought one day as she cleaned a large workroom alone, Angelica having been called away for evening prayers. Earlier, Angelica had been showing Bianca how to use the larger alembics, a skill Bianca was eager to practice and Angelica was willing to share. Now, Bianca soaked up the condensation from within the wider glass tubes. When she finished, she surveyed the room, now clean, and sat on a stool with her notebook. She hadn't told Angelica what she intended to do with the practice distillation she'd made that day. She had shown the young nun the notes, though, in which her mother had laid out the recipe that, based on Pellegrina's reading and experiments, would make an effective cure. *It will have an impact on the heat disease,* her mother had written. *What remains to be seen is how the body will respond. Giving it to a patient would tell us much about how to manufacture something that heals more than it hurts.* Bianca had read the recipe over and over till she was convinced her mother was right: the artemisia distillate would be effective, but only if the ingredients that helped cure and even make it drinkable didn't harm the patient. Only if there were no impurities. Of course, at the moment there was no patient. There was only Bianca.

Brimming with finished distillates, the glass container she and Angelica had filled sat on the table before her. Bianca lifted it to her lips and downed the bitter contents in one swallow. So, it was done. Bianca stood up. She didn't feel any different so far. She cleaned out the beaker and quietly left.

The workrooms, the narrow stone halls, and the dormant gardens shaded with muted light felt more like home than did Piero's apartment, but his was the house she still had to return to at the end of the day. Her husband and his mother continued to tolerate her absence, secure in their belief that Bianca was in treatment for what they took as her barrenness. Soon she'd have to tell them that Sant'Elisabetta's "cure" had succeeded. But even then, she could insist that her pregnancy was so fragile, she'd lose the baby if she didn't keep seeing the nuns.

The baby. Bianca placed a hand on her stomach as she left Sant'Elisabetta and began walking. The baby had just taken an experimental cure, too. Well, this baby's mother was an alchemist and a scientist, like its grandmother, and always would be. Someone like Angelica should be carrying this child. More than once as Bianca knelt, pulling weeds along the thyme-lined walkways, she'd heard a burble of laughter, followed by the sight of Angelica running up the path with a small boy or girl on her hip. Angelica, though, had promised herself to her god. Bianca had promised herself to alchemy, but the price of that vow had been a husband, and so, a child. All too soon, it would be Bianca responsible for a living, breathing, crying being.

When Bianca went to sleep that night, rolling so her back was to Piero in bed, it was with a feeling of cautious optimism: pregnant or not, she'd created a cure, a strong dose, and with no ill effects.

The next morning, Bianca's eyes flew open. She was certain she'd just spent the night dreaming more vividly than she ever had before, though already the images were fading. What refused to fade was the rash that confronted her when she faced herself in the mirror. All across her neck and arms, Bianca was red. Was it the mugworts harvested for the extract she'd made days before? Or the comfrey? Bianca sighed. Her cure wasn't ready.

That morning she completed her kitchen duties as quickly as she could, slipping from the house as soon as she heard Anna stirring. She stepped into the piazza, then across another, into Sant'Elisabetta. She could avoid her mother-in-law's questions. Dodging Angelica's would be much harder. She needed to mix up a salve quickly before Angelica saw her. Maybe some calendula . . .

"Bianca!" Angelica cried, the moment Bianca entered the workroom. "What on earth did you do to your neck? Whatever's wrong?"

"Nothing." She'd thought she might have a few hours to herself, as she'd left Piero's early. But Angelica, it seemed, was there early today, too.

Angelica shook her head. "I'm familiar with herbs, Bianca. Do you really think I'd look at your skin and not know that you had taken something? What was it? Is it the distillates we mixed together?"

"Just to experiment. Now that we have so much distillate, why not?"

"Hmm," Angelica continued, as if she hadn't heard her. "Did you drink something else, too, maybe with wood nettle? It doesn't always do that, but in certain combinations . . . and, as a distillate . . ." Angelica began digging through baskets of dried herbs, searching for a treatment to lessen the rash.

Bianca stood in front of the nun until Angelica turned to look at her. "Besides the medicine? Not wood nettle, Sister, but several days ago, comfrey, maybe mugwort."

"Comfrey? Harvesting that without gloves?" Shaking her head, Angelica reached into the basket again. "You can try this. I'll get it steeping for you. And if it was mugwort, I'm guessing you had wild dreams, too."

"I . . ." Bianca hesitated. She could lie, but wasn't Angelica her partner? "I was checking something on myself. A cure. I wanted to know how a healthy body would react to purified herbs, combined. It's what my mother planned to do, but she didn't have any such distillery to purify the substances. One body, of course, doesn't give me much information. But still . . ."

"Bianca the scientist. I should have known." Angelica shook her head, but her eyes showed a gleam of interest. "Well, what do you think? Have you learned anything?"

"I think so." Bianca took out her notebook, opening it and quickly jotting down her symptoms. "So if we take out the nettle, and add instead . . ." She caught herself. *We?* "This is what I'll try next," she said. "Another distillate of artemisia, no stinging plants . . ." Beside her, Angelica nodded.

"I almost wish I'd get malaria." Bianca set her notebook on a table. "Otherwise, how would I know if my cures do anything?"

"One healthy body tells you very little," Angelica agreed. She crossed to the hearth, stirring the embers for the day's work. "If you like," she said in an even voice, her back to Bianca, "I'll be a second body. You can try out the cures on me. And I'll help you with the herbs."

Bianca had wondered what it would be like to have a partner she could trust. Now she knew.

Each day, with Angelica's help, Bianca felt she was twice as close to finding a cure. When one brew made Bianca's heart race, or another made her break out in welts, she knew it was the fault of the treatment if Angelica reacted the same. Bianca could barely remember how she'd thought to learn anything alone. And the other nuns asked fewer questions when Bianca only had to secure half a recipe's required herbs in the woody gardens. Angelica collected the rest during her shifts. After drinking the distillate, they'd compare their findings.

Bianca had a recipe for rose extracts, oil that softened diseased skin, one her mother had circled in a book, but without explanation. Puzzled that her mother was interested in such recipes, Bianca began to scrutinize the variety of tinctures and oils she'd written about. Other procedures were for distillates of wormwoods, with some unusual artemisias. After Angelica read the notes, she, too, began trying out a formula or two Bianca's mother had written down but, as far as Bianca knew, had rarely tested. Another called for willow, its smooth, slippery inner bark simmering to a brown liquid that yielded pain relief. Angelica tested this one on herself one morning when she woke with a headache. That day, Bianca watched as Angelica's grimace turned to a smile within the hour. After that, any doubts Angelica might still have had were gone.

Unbeknownst to her sisters, Angelica, when called to a sickbed, began giving Bianca's poultices to ailing nuns. She'd describe the nuns' symptoms and Bianca, or sometimes Bianca and Angelica together, would sift through Bianca's mother's notebooks and the growing number of volumes Bianca herself had filled. The cures they created didn't always have an effect, but enough did that Bianca began adding more and more of her own twists to her mother's recipes. Angelica had fewer new ideas, but she executed Bianca's perfectly. Bianca could not have imagined a better partnership. And while the tasks that earned her a place here left her hands red, causing Piero to grumble about their roughness, she didn't mind. Even cleaning the workrooms was a sort of meditation. Rarely was she disturbed.

"The nuns like you, Bianca, or they're starting to. I know I do," Angelica told Bianca one day. "We're learning a lot about your cures. The laboratory is yours as much as mine; it's God's will."

Bianca smiled. With Angelica's trust and her willingness to try risky treatments, Bianca was confident she'd find the cure that had been so elusive in Venice.

Early the next day, everything changed.

Quick footsteps in the hall were her first warning that the will of Angelica's god might no longer be on their side. Bianca had been given the task of cleaning one of the distillation rooms alone, since Angelica was on duty caring for the children. But as Bianca sponged stains from a table, trying not to think about how tight her dress was growing, the door burst open. Angelica was flushed and out of breath, an empty basket swinging from her hand. Sweat-soaked tendrils of hair clung to her forehead. "Bianca, come quickly. It's one of the girls. She's . . ." Angelica swept an armload of bottles off a shelf, piling the extracts into her basket. "The heat sickness—a flare-up. She has infusions, some with extracts, but . . ."

"Not those." Heart racing, Bianca grabbed her own basket and began throwing in the things she'd need, stronger treatments, including a large flask of new distillate. By the time she had it all assembled, Angelica's breath had evened out, the wild look in her eyes fading.

"I thank God you came to us when you did," Angelica said as they left the room together. "If anyone can save her, it's you."

Save her? Bianca's breath caught. She hadn't saved her mother, or the penniless men in Venice who dragged themselves to the sick ward, dying, only to drink Bianca's medicine and still not live to see morning. She and Angelica might have learned a great deal, but a cure? Was she ready? Angelica believed she was.

"I'll try." But Bianca couldn't meet Angelica's eyes.

They found the sickroom occupied by only one nun attending, standing by the bed with a cool compress in her hands. "I'll take another turn now," Angelica told her. She took the nun's compress and handed it to Bianca. It was nothing but a clean cloth dipped in water. Bianca shook her head as the nun left. She and Angelica might have a cure or they might not, but at least they had more to offer than cool water and prayers.

She joined Angelica by the bedside of the restless girl. Soaked in sweat, she smelled nothing like the earthy scent of the children playing outside, like freshly sprouted seeds. Instead, pustules bulged on her neck and down her arms. As Bianca watched, the delirious girl cried out, her eyelids flickering, her body shaking until she screamed. Then she stilled.

A fire already burned in the grate. Bianca stirred its embers to burn hotter, then put a pot on to simmer.

"What are you warming?" Angelica's voice shook.

"Some powdered root in water. That's for later, to settle her stomach. For now, she'll have the artemisia distillate." Bianca squeezed Angelica's hand. "It'll be a strong dose. But anything less won't help her. Should we proceed?" Blinking away tears, Angelica nodded.

Bianca removed the stopper in the flask she'd brought, then knelt by the bed. The child gave a weak cough, her breathing erratic. Bianca coughed too, but at least she could draw air deeply into her lungs, however much the air reeked of sickness.

Her first attempt to administer a dose ended with drips down the barely conscious child's chin. Bianca tilted the girl's head back, coaxing the liquid until it slid into her throat. A feeble hand pushed Bianca's away.

Behind her, Angelica spoke. "It may be too harsh . . . the distillate, I don't know."

"We've waited too long already." Bianca stood. Would Angelica see the fear on her face? She tried to keep her voice steady as she spoke. "Angelica, listen to me. If we'd gotten to her sooner we could have gone more slowly. But warmed brews aren't enough now. We have to try more distillate."

"I believe you." But the flask in Angelica's hand shook. "Only—"

"Only what? We've studied my mother's notes. We know what we're doing." She looked into Angelica's eyes. "The infusions alone help only sometimes. It's the alembics, Angelica, that give us the medicines." Bianca pointed to the hearth. "Not the kettles."

The slight angle of Angelica's head, the way her fingers gripped the flask, told Bianca the young nun doubted her.

"It has to be this strong. Otherwise we can't save her." Bianca poured more distillate into the cup. Angelica didn't answer. But she didn't try to stay Bianca's hand.

At first, the child resisted. Her tongue pushed weakly at the cup and a thin stream of liquid trickled from her mouth. Behind Bianca, Angelica let out a faint whimper.

"Swallow, child. It's going to burn, it's bitter, but is death any better? Drink it, live, prove it works." The thought of the girl sickening more made Bianca's chest tighten, but . . . what if this was her moment? What if, after today, she'd be the woman with the cure? Gently, Bianca pinched the girl's nostrils. Almost at once, the weak throat opened and swallowed. Angelica breathed in sharply. The girl's chest rose, her heart thudding under Bianca's hand. "She's taken it." Bianca drew away. "It's in her, she's breathing—"

"Angelica." Both jumped as the rough voice of an older nun cut through the sickroom's heaviness. The child moaned, drops of liquid still glistening on her lips. As Angelica went to greet the nun at the door, Bianca tucked her cure out of sight beneath the bed, moving so her skirts hid the flask and other bottles. Nothing, however, could hide the scent in the room.

The nun entered, eyeing Bianca. "I didn't expect to find you here." She tapped on Angelica's sleeve. "Sister, there's another child sick. Less severe, but we need you."

Angelica shot a quick glance at Bianca. *Go,* Bianca mouthed. Angelica had to know they'd done all they could, and they'd been right to do it. The child was quiet now. Her raspy breathing no longer filled the room.

"Let's go," Angelica said, pulling on the nun's arm. "Take me to the child."

The nun sniffed. Bianca held her breath. Then the woman turned and Angelica followed after casting one quick glance back at Bianca.

Bianca returned to the bedside. The girl lay peaceful, as though no illness had ever touched her small frame. No need to give her any more brew. Bianca retrieved her basket from beneath the bed and began gathering the rest of the cups and bottles. She'd leave the kettle; it was still too hot to carry. The rest she'd cover with a cloth until a nun came to relieve her of her nursing duties. And by then the child's recovery might be clear and Bianca would have nothing to hide.

But something was wrong.

The room was too hushed. The girl's breath hadn't just quieted. It had stopped. More than sweat soaked the bed; there was bile in the loose, bloody liquids. Nothing else new, no redness, no oozing pus, emanated from the motionless body.

Had time frozen? Any second, wouldn't the girl's chest rise again? If Bianca herself didn't breathe . . . if the whole world held still . . .

Bianca squeezed her eyes shut. When she opened them, shadows jumped into view and candlelight made prisms at the edges of her vision. But the girl remained silent. Frozen.

Bianca had failed.

Every note she'd made, everything she'd read, said that this cure should have saved, not killed, the child. But here she lay, dead, a blunder that couldn't be buried. Liquids soaked the mattress. Under it all lingered a ripe smell that every nun would recognize as something that didn't belong in this child. Bianca looked at the girl lying before her, so different from the shuddering, coughing one she'd dosed less than an hour ago. Quiet filled the room. The girl's knotted face was now peaceful, all lines erased. Bianca bowed her head. She pressed her palm against the girl's chest, and then to her own. When, at last, she reached over the body to cover the girl with a dry sheet, her hands shook. What had gone wrong? The distillate had ruined the child's gut, maybe even her liver, but how?

Picking up a bunch of herbs in her basket, inhaling the weak fragrance, she looked around the room. What answer could she find? Mugwort eased gut swelling. Had she not added enough mugwort to the boil? She fingered the woody stems and leaves in the bottom of the basket. Perhaps she should have soaked the herbs first. Or had the boil been too strong?

She'd been careful, but working with distillates was still so new. She'd need years, not months, of careful work before she could expect to trust this treatment. Bianca shook her head. Look at how long her mother had worked to find a cure—longer than Bianca had been alive. These things took time. But she hadn't had time, and wasn't it better to have tried than to let the girl die?

Bianca shook her head. Later she'd look at all her notes again and try to pin down what had gone wrong. But right now she had to concentrate on the next thing to do.

Another nun would be here soon. They'd blame Bianca for this death. And Angelica? Bianca's throat clenched. She had to leave, and she could never return. The years, maybe decades, it would take to find a reliable cure, all the things she still had to learn, distillations she hadn't yet tried . . . That would have to happen somewhere else, if it happened at all. But even if she could stay, would she? Would she risk another death like this? Bianca leaned into the bed frame, then pulled away. Candlelight behind her, the shadow of the child's form and Bianca's was starkly planted on the wall. If anyone caught her now they'd drive her from the city, or maybe worse. And Bianca couldn't blame them. She'd never bring the child back. The best she could do was to continue working, so that this girl wouldn't have died in vain. But not here. Bianca could never come back to this place again.

Bianca shivered. Was this to be her future—death after death? First her mother. Then countless others at the Venice Sick House before she came to Sant'Elisabetta. Florence had drawn her because of the Medici, and Sant'Elisabetta, but its doors would be closed to her now forever. She'd been so sure of her knowledge, of her cure, and because of that she'd lost her place here. Yet she couldn't stop trying. That much, at least, she owed the dead.

Bianca brushed the wet filth from her skirts. The only place she could run to was back to Piero's. At least he'd never know what had happened. All she'd have to do was assure him the nuns' treatment had succeeded, and let him lay his hand over her gradually swelling belly, and he wouldn't ask her any more questions. She'd go back to being his wife. Soon she'd play the role of mother, too. Somewhere in the back of her mind, Bianca knew, she'd always hung onto a hope that the nuns could have taken on the burden of this child. They could have cared for it while she worked, or perhaps someday she'd have found a new name and guise for herself, secured the baby with the nuns, and left Piero and his mother behind. Now that door was closed. But somehow, someday another chance would come. It had to.

With the back of her hand, Bianca brushed the child's cheek, then her own. Both were cool, but blood from the child's was pooling quickly. She pulled the sheet over the child's face and turned to the door. She'd be smarter from now on. This time, she had leapt at a chance to cure when she should have waited. Now she would experiment by herself, and if there were mistakes, the price would be hers alone to pay.

8
Florence Streets

Leaving the dead girl behind, Bianca pulled the door shut with a thud, the sound merging with the midday bell's call to prayers. She stood for a moment, trying to breathe deeply. If she slipped out now the nuns wouldn't see her, or smell her stink. For these few minutes, they'd be turning their thoughts toward their god. By the time they looked earthward again, she'd be gone through the nearest iron gate, onto a side road that would take her from Sant'Elisabetta into the rest of the city.

Into the hallway and down a corridor she stepped. *Quiet as a cat*—that was what she used to tell herself, creeping past the aunties to get to her sick mother. Could it be that, so long ago, her aunties had been right about the risks of Bianca's cure? Bianca paused when she reached the door outside, then softly turned the handle. The gardens beyond were empty.

As she shut the door behind her, a breeze caught her skirt, making it billow like a banner announcing . . . what? Her arrival as a soulless woman, with no future. A child lay dead. There'd be no forgiveness. Bianca's task was to make that child's death matter. She followed a path to the gate in the outer wall. It creaked as Bianca pushed it open. Would the nuns hear it over the chant of their prayers? No nuns came running, and a moment later she was through.

A noisy street stretched before her, occupied by Florence vendors nestled in their stalls to escape the bright noon sun, none suspecting or even wondering what the girl with her back pressed against Sant'Elisabetta's iron gate had just done. Bianca gulped air, her heart pounding so loudly that surely the nuns must have heard it. They *should* hear it. Bianca had just killed a girl. She needed to run but . . . wasn't anyone going to stop her? Was she going to be allowed to just go, back to a husband who wanted her, her own child quick in her womb? Someone should punish her. Unless there was some reason for her to be spared?

"Bianca." A voice called out.

A voice so familiar, but the tone was cold, lifeless. Bianca peered back through the grated iron door. In the gardens she'd just left stood Angelica, haloed by the sunlit strands of hair escaping from beneath her veil. Her face drawn tight, tears welled in her eyes. But when she spoke her voice was flat, toneless. "Go home. You can't come back."

Go. The word hit like a stone. Bianca searched Angelica's face for something else. Hatred, disgust, fear . . . a plea for Bianca to stay and face her punishment? Could it end like this between them? With silence. With nothing.

"There's no time to talk, Bianca." Angelica's voice was bleak. "You don't want any of the sisters to see you."

A woman's reedy voice called Angelica's name. Angelica glanced over her shoulder and nodded. If Bianca had ever known the face to put with the voice, she couldn't think of it now, but Angelica knew the woman. Angelica belonged here, as surely as Bianca didn't and never had. Bianca turned away.

"Bianca." Angelica's voice shook.

Bianca paused. She waited for the words: *Stay, Bianca. Stay.*

"The Medici are alchemists, and chemists, too. Go to them." Angelica blinked, swiping a hand across her eyes. "Go," Angelica said. "Just go."

Then the young nun turned toward the convent, and was gone.

The walk home passed in a blur. Could it have been only this morning that Bianca last came this way, anticipating nothing more than a day by Angelica's side? Now the route seemed endless. The calls of merchants and hawkers made her head spin. Then all at once Piero's house loomed before her. Her future: those dim rooms, Piero's ailing mother who was probably lying in bed now, waiting for Bianca to come home so as to listen to her day's complaints. Bianca paused, the busy piazza all that separated her from a future under Piero's roof. Maybe she shouldn't go in. Maybe she should just keep walking.

Her feet started moving again. If she went home now, in the middle of the day, there would be questions. She'd go back in the evening as she usually did. Until then, she'd try to clear her head. Angelica had spared her for a reason. Bianca had to figure out what that reason was.

The Medici . . . Go to them.

She'd walked past it many times: the Medici's Church of San Marco, beyond which the plants in Duke Cosimo's gardens stretched in orderly, too-neat rows. Nothing useful grew there, so Bianca had rarely paid it much notice. Yet it took only minutes for her to arrive at its outside walls. Bianca leaned into the gate, looking at the gardens. The Medici were meant to be scientists. Why did they waste their time raising lilies and roses, when all this rich soil could have grown medicinal herbs? Bianca crossed the street, circling around the church to sit down on a bench with a view of what looked like a walled patch of woods. From what she knew of the Medici, some of their science lay in directions different from hers. The duke followed astrology, as did the oldest son. Bianca smiled grimly to herself. Perhaps if she, too, knew the secrets of the stars, they could tell her where to go from here.

She closed her eyes. So far, she'd always forged her own path. She had chosen Piero and followed him out of Venice. She had talked her way into Sant'Elisabetta, with the help of her mother's ring. She had studied her mother's science and added to it by trying out remedies on herself. Even her partnership with Angelica was something Bianca had worked to build, winning Angelica's trust, however badly Bianca had ultimately betrayed her. If she were to follow Angelica's advice, she'd have to do it soon. Her clothes were tight, her pregnancy becoming harder to ignore. Tugging on her bodice in front of the mirror this morning, Bianca had seen a woman who looked older than fifteen. The winter coat she'd brought from Venice fit well, but in a few months? And after the baby was born, what small freedoms she had now would be gone.

Just this morning, she'd had the whole world open to her—the Sant'Elisabetta gardens, the nuns' distillation rooms. Now she was starting over, something her mother hadn't known. If her mother was like an olive tree with firm branches spreading in clear directions, what was Bianca? Impulsive. If she was going to make inroads with the Medici, she'd need to do it soon. Bianca didn't need the cosmos to guide her. She guided herself, and her steps had taken her to Florence, and now, a bench near the San Marco church. Perhaps the Medici could not or would not help her. But she wouldn't be her mother's daughter if she didn't find out.

Bianca didn't know how long she sat there, the sun warming her closed eyelids. The moment ended with the rattle of carriage wheels. She opened her eyes.

Wisps of wind in the street carried along shards of broken pottery, rattling even louder than the clatter from the carriages. The wheels of one stopped just steps away from her. The lightweight carriage's side bore a coat-of-arms everyone in Florence would recognize. She'd seen it before, living as close as she did to the building down the road whose door bore the same shield. But the man in the carriage certainly wasn't the duke. He could only have been in his mid-twenties, and he drove his own carriage, his face reddened with the exertion of guiding his horse. As he stepped down, Bianca smiled. She liked his dark eyes, and the way he stood, leaning forward slightly as if eager for wherever his path might take him next. Judging by his clothes, he had to be quite well off in the Medici household. The Medici themselves, of course, would never travel the city alone, without bodyguards . . . And yet she'd seen the same features in portraits of the royal family. Angelica had told her to go to the Medici. Could it be that already she had?

The man paused at his horse's head, tying its lead rope to a nearby mounting block. Leaving the carriage, he called out to her. "Mistress, are you lost?"

Bianca pulled herself up from the bench, running her fingers through her hair, then brushing the dust from her coat. The man had a small, neat beard, a gentle smile, but what serious eyes. He loosened his collar as he approached, and his furrowed brow eased. His hands looked strong, though calloused and scarred as if he used them more than most men of his rank. And what kind of lord would drive his carriage alone?

"Perhaps you're not lost," the man said. A slight smile played on his lips. "You look like a woman who always knows where she is. But do you know who owns the garden before you?"

"Someone who grows weeds." Bianca waved toward the wall. "And scrubby woods. What a waste of good ground inside."

"That's Venice in your voice, isn't it? And so, what brings you to our city of beauty, so far from home?" He leaned in closer. "Surely, it's not gardening."

"No, I live just a few steps from here." Bianca pointed to the peak of Piero's roof, barely visible down the road.

"Ah." The man's gaze followed her finger. "One of the Salviati bank clerks lives there." He turned back to Bianca. "How can it be that a beautiful Venetian with a poor opinion of my woods lives there too?"

Bianca stood, bowing her head and dropping into a curtsy.

His woods? That made him one of the duke's son's. This had to be Francesco. A younger brother, Ferdinando, was a cardinal. She had followed a whim and Angelica's advice to find herself a Medici—but the heir himself? Francesco, the alchemist? This man could open more doors for her than anyone else but his father. From him she could learn the parts of the Medici alchemy that she needed. If he took her into the palace . . . if he shared his science . . . Looking up, she met his eyes.

They were warm eyes. Brown, the color of one of her mother's rich brews. Once she met his gaze, Bianca couldn't seem to look away. Why did her face feel so warm? Why did she feel like his eyes actually saw her—her, not just her body or her name? What a fool she was being. She might well use both to get what she wanted from him. Angelica had told her to find a Medici for a reason; she hadn't said how.

"I have nothing against weedy woods," she said. "Other things simply interest me more." She watched his face. "And you, as well, or so I've heard. If you are who I believe, though how a duke's son would come to be driving his own carriage, I don't know . . ."

"What interests me is how a clerk came to have such a beautiful wife, and what she might be doing walking the streets alone." She wasn't ready for the feel of his fingertips as he reached for her hand. Old burns roughened his fingers. He laced them in hers. Bianca concentrated on the texture of his skin. These were chemists' scars. "If I'm not mistaken, my father knows your father. I'll admit, I was aware the clerk had taken a wife. You're Bianca, yes? Bianca Capello?"

Bianca nodded. If she was so well known, why hadn't Bartolomeo come after her, then? As quick as she thought the question, she realized the answer. Bianca was no longer of value to him; her reputation had been ruined as soon as she'd left with Piero, and her father had no reason to come find her. Instead, the Medici heir had.

Francesco gave her a wry half-smile. "Your father's rather quick to anger, isn't he?" Bianca raised her eyebrows and shrugged. He'd hear no argument from her about her father's temper. Francesco continued. "I thought it was curious, that a nobleman's daughter would marry a clerk. Especially one like Piero. He doesn't seem particularly remarkable."

"Ah," Bianca said, tilting her head. "But he lives in Florence. The city of knowledge—of science."

Francesco laughed. Bianca smiled to herself at the sudden gleam of interest in his gaze. His honest laugh matched his eyes. "Science, is it? I'm biased, but that seems like a good reason to me." Francesco tightened his clasp of her hand. "Though it's a pity he, not I, was the first Florentine you found. Tell me, though, how does a beautiful Venetian lady come to have an interest in science?"

"My mother was a scientist." Would Pellegrina have described herself that way? Possibly not, but that was how Bianca viewed her mother's work. It wasn't a lie, and the word might open doors. "Since the day she died I've continued her work. She told me of Florence. She dreamed of coming here."

"And you as well?" He smiled. "Perhaps now you'll fulfill mine. Come. Will you walk with me, in this charmed city of ours? I am Francesco, by the way. A duke's son does indeed drive his own carriage when he tires of his father's men reporting back his every move. I loathe my father's bodyguards. They'd advise me to continue about my business. But please, Bianca, distract me. Allow me to show you Florence."

He offered her his arm.

Bianca took it, surprised at how comfortably their strides matched as she and Francesco began walking. She'd been in the city for months, but no one had ever given her a tour. Francesco gestured to several buildings near them. Some looked deserted, with boarded-up windows and peeling paint. Broken bricks and warped metal spilled from an open door. "My offices, my studio. Well . . ." He laughed again. "It's not much now. But it's going to be my casino."

Bianca almost laughed. What work of any importance could he possibly do here?

He wasn't laughing, though. "You said you came to Florence for its science. If that's so . . . well, then, you're like no woman I've ever met. But if you care for science, this is where it's practiced." He lowered his voice. "Alchemy."

"Ah, as in transforming metals?"

"I do change things, one from the other, but I'm most interested in porcelain." He turned toward the building. "This is my studio. Right now, as my father says, it's a wreck. But I need a space, hidden. Perhaps you understand, if you practice science yourself. It takes time. It's a secret art, not for public view. But neither my father nor his artists can tolerate my furnace in the palace, so my porcelain making needs to happen somewhere else . . . in the casino here."

She'd been right to present herself as a serious scientist. Was that how Francesco saw her? The Medici's science was something of an open secret, widely acknowledged but not widely understood. The fact that he would speak of it directly to her was promising. Then again, perhaps his openness didn't mean he'd share his science; perhaps he had no real science to hide. The buildings before them didn't look very practical. "Have the Medici no laboratories, then?"

He shrugged. "We have some. My father has his workrooms. Do you know much about alchemy?"

Bianca laughed. "Yes, I might."

"Look," Francesco said, squeezing her fingers. "The wall behind you? The woods, the weeds hide a garden. A very young Michelangelo trained there."

"Beneath that messy canopy of trees?" Bianca squinted. "I see nothing." The rumors she'd heard of the Medici—did it all come down to this? The ruined garden of an aging artist and a duke's son who intended to study alchemy, but didn't yet have a laboratory? She should feel disappointed. But at the moment, she couldn't. However small his laboratory, she couldn't shake the feeling that this red-faced man with the scarred hands offered some kind of a new beginning.

"The ruin of the garden, Bianca, that's nothing. And the way my casino looks from the outside . . . well, it is a mess. But don't be fooled like my father into thinking the outside speaks to what's within. I already have a group of men working even as the building is being repaired. I myself am creating a porcelain. The vessel is as important as what's in it, you know. My porcelain will reveal the purity of its contents. Make the ceramics delicate enough, yet strong, and add a touch of arsenic in the glaze—and you might have a glass that shatters at the hint of poison. That would be useful, no?"

Useful for the Medici, perhaps. If rumors were true, more than one of Francesco's kin had died of poison. Those who didn't wield the influence or draw the envy that the Medici did might have less occasion to benefit from Francesco's project, but he clearly was a scientist, though he may not use the words; she could tell his interest by how his face lit up when he talked. But there was a warm flush to his cheeks.

Bianca had seen the signs often enough. Francesco, at one point, had had malaria. And those who caught it once often sickened again and again. Francesco's porcelain could be useful, but even he, a Medici, was more likely to die of malaria than of poison. What he needed far more was the alchemy Bianca had to offer, herbs that could cure.

Francesco turned and walked back toward Piero's house. Bianca would have kept going. But he knew where she lived now, and their shadows were growing long in front of them. "I suppose I should leave you." Francesco stopped outside the door. Bianca looked up at the drab building before them. No alchemy could be found within those walls. No team of scientists waited within. "I should,"

Francesco continued, "but I don't want to. I intend, Bianca, to see you again. I'm holding a ball soon. It's Candlemas season now, the beginning of spring. If you do not attend, I'll be devastated, and shall have to swallow arsenic to end my sorrow." He held both her hands. "So, you'll come to my ball. Do I need to invite your husband, too?"

In spite of herself, Bianca smiled. Candlemas season—spring? There was a bit of the mysterious in these Medici. This one wasn't, perhaps, the alchemist in command of the fully functional laboratory that she'd imagined, but he had plans, and he had a team of men. And being in the palace certainly would get her closer to the Medici science. As for the way his touch sent warm shivers up her spine, well, she wouldn't let that get in the way. She could do what it took to get a laboratory, and enjoy herself, too.

"Don't bother with the arsenic," Bianca told him. "But yes, you'd better invite Piero. It'll save me having to answer tiresome questions."

"Having met you," Francesco said, stroking her hand, "that might be an attachment I don't want to encourage. But, if I must . . ." With a flourish, he produced a sealed envelope from within his cloak. "I was on my way to deliver this last invitation to a good friend of my father's, but let my father do that himself. You are invited, Bianca. And your husband. Here . . ." With a stub of graphite pencil, he wrote their names on the outside and signed it. Then he pressed the parchment into her hand. "Until then." Francesco made a short bow. "It won't be long."

Francesco got into his carriage and hurried away. Once he left her view, would this whole day turn out to have been nothing but a dream? The girl's sickness and death, the sadness and betrayal on Angelica's face, Bianca's walk back into the city, and now this. In the span of a day she had gone from apprentice to the nuns to friend of the Medici. If "friend" was the right word. She'd explore that further when she next saw Francesco. Which, it seemed, would be in the ducal palace.

As the duke's son passed out of sight, Bianca looked down at her hands. She still held the parchment, the invitation sealed with the Medici crest. It was real, then, all of it. She'd found herself a Medici, an inroad into the family that held Florence's greatest scientific secrets. And getting what she wanted from him promised to be more pleasurable than her affair with Piero had been. She turned to go inside. She didn't have to worry what to tell Piero about Sant'Elisabetta. The invitation would drive all questions from his mind. Francesco de' Medici had just asked both of them to a ball that no other clerk in Florence could ever dream of attending, and if the only man Bianca could picture accepting a dance from in those halls was a prince with hands scarred by science? Well, that was something Piero didn't need to know.

9
A Ball

Twenty minutes seemed an hour, Piero peppering her with questions the whole ride to the Medici palace. In the several weeks since handing the invitation over to the man who now sat beside her, Bianca had been able to think of little else except this night. Piero, it seemed, hadn't either, but for very different reasons.

"Didn't you ask him, Bianca? I wish I'd been there. I should have been there. Tell me again exactly what he said to you. You may not have understood what he meant, but tell me, Bianca. It'll make sense to me." Piero couldn't be silent for even one moment, not when a promotion was pending. He'd talked of nothing else in the days since she'd met Francesco, insisting it was the sole reason the two of them would have been invited to a ball. Bianca had listened and nodded, speaking when she had to. Yes, Francesco had known who Piero was. No, he hadn't mentioned a promotion. Yes, that did seem the only possible explanation for the invitation. Yes, Piero would surely end this night a richer man.

Bianca twisted a fold of her skirt between her fingers. She'd rather walk than sit here next to Piero, but he'd insisted they arrive in the closest thing to high state they could muster. The carriage he'd borrowed from a fellow clerk, though, was a long way from blending in with the carriages they saw along the way, with silver fittings and intricate carvings, carrying the crests of wealthy families of merchants and politicians. With all this traffic, they must be close. And yes, there ahead of them the ducal palace glimmered, tiers of lights rising up over the city, each window its own star looking down on Florence. Music echoed out into the streets.

"Look, Piero. The palace."

Piero gripped the reins of their carthorse, his mouth open in awe. Bianca didn't blame him. Her father's palace had been elaborate, but nothing like this, a massive building set evenly with large blocks of textured sandstone. Ornate statues lined the drive through the piazza up to the doorway. She'd seen it before, but never this close, and never lit up the way it was tonight. Never before had its open gates ushered her in.

A guard, dressed in the Medici red and gold, stepped out to greet them. "Dismount here, please," he told them. "I'll take your horse. And welcome, sir and lady, to the Medici ball."

Clutching her skirts as they left their carriage, Bianca stepped over a puddle. Piero guided her past the worst of the mud in the cracks of the cobble, his hand on her elbow. Pausing in the foyer near the stone steps that led up from the wide-open palazzo doors, Piero nudged Bianca, hissing in her ear as another guard approached. "Show him our invitation. Make sure he can read my name."

Bianca laid her hand on Piero's arm. The Medici would no sooner have invited a clerk to their ball than a beggar off the street, but if Piero insisted on believing the invitation was for him, let him. The guard looked only at the Medici insignia on the gilt-edged parchment she handed him, then ushered them through.

Moving a few paces ahead of Piero, Bianca let her skirts touch each step as they climbed toward the great hall, the sound of guards talking below giving way to loud strains of music from the landing above. Bianca turned to Piero. "At the ballroom door, we stand apart."

"What? Aren't you proud to be my wife? Wife of the soon-to-be—"

"It's just how it's done at balls, trust me." Sometimes she was sure Piero forgot that the woman he'd married had grown up wealthy. No doubt Piero had as little understanding as she did about the Florentine rules for ballroom etiquette, but she didn't want Francesco to see her first on another man's arm.

The top of the stairs opened up to the massive Hall of the Five Hundred. Five men standing upon each other's shoulders couldn't have touched the flat paneled ceiling, and its length might have filled half the Piazza San Marco. The vast hall could fit ten of her father's ballrooms, or better, a hundred sickrooms for patients. The frescoes looked moist, as though the artists had just set down their palettes. Scenes of towns and countryside filled the panels, the landscapes strategically placed to fold in on themselves at one central location: the hills outside Florence. A whole world stretched before her in those paintings. The small life she'd been leading with Piero was about to get bigger.

Beneath the sparkling arrays of candles, each reflected in the myriad crystals of the chandeliers, the hall pulsed with voices and laughter. In the center of the floor, couples danced in lines or whirled in tight circles. From the back of the hall drifted the honeyed and spiced aromas of meats and drink. A man strode past, his thick hair and flashing dark eyes fitting with his assertive aura, the furred hem of his cloak brushing Bianca's skirt. His face, and the camphor smell of the fur, were still uppermost in Bianca's thoughts when she glanced up and saw his twin in a golden-framed portrait.

Piero had seen him too. "That's Cosimo, the duke."

Bianca turned to the paintings along the wall. Yes, there was the man, again and again. Bianca studied each portrait's face, the eyes, the nose. Word of the Medici fascination for art collecting had reached even Venice, but she'd never imagined such large paintings, framed in gold, the most prominent lit by their own sconces of candles. In her ear, Piero chattered on about the Medici duke, but Bianca's attention had been caught by a portrait of a young man with dark, serious eyes and a slightly flushed face. His father's eyes. Francesco. The portrait was small, but so rich in color and detail it seemed constrained by its frame. Why wasn't Francesco's portrait a full-wall fresco?

And she'd held his hand. Bianca's heart skipped. High stakes for her ambitions, being in the house of a prince. At least she'd dressed well, judging from the stares of the men and women in the ballroom. She hadn't worn this gown, hastily packed on the night she'd left home, since the day she'd become Piero's wife. She'd hurriedly taken out a few seams this morning. It still fit her tightly, but didn't look any worse for that. Its lime brocade glimmered with newly stitched gold threads that she'd also used to plait her hair, their gleam almost lost in her honey-thick braids. Around her neck, she wore her mother's pearls.

Bianca let her eyes wander from the painting of Francesco. Piero was gone. He'd sniffed out an opportunity halfway across the hall and now stood deep in conversation with a cluster of men at the front of the room. A few business ventures could emerge for Piero from this night.

Her eyes darted next to a small, chattering entourage of men and women moving toward her. The man at their center might have been his own portrait come to life. Bianca smiled, taking a few steps forward. She'd worked her way into this palace. Now she was ready to find out what it would take to stay.

A glance from Francesco quickly turned into a gaze fixed on Bianca. He waved with open arms, as if making a proclamation, *This is for you*. Imagine if, indeed, it was all for her. The long-tapered candles, the bright white, sweet-smelling roses, the romantic madrigals. The crowd would turn toward her, following Francesco's lead. Chairs would knock against each other as guests rose, the festive sounds of glasses clanking would welcome her: Bianca. Bianca. Bianca the wise healer, the woman scientist.

But no. The crowd had no idea yet who she would be to them. The only person looking at her was the handsome son of the duke, pushing through the crowd until he stood in front of her. He offered a small bow. "Signora Capello? Or do you go by your husband's name, Bonaventuri?"

She acknowledged him with a slight curtsy. "Call me Bianca. My own name."

Lightly touching the back of her arm, he moved her along to a quiet corner. "I've been waiting for you, Bianca. Sit? If we stand, we're interrupted."

"Have we so much to say, that we can't allow interruptions?" Bianca found a chair and sat, arranging her skirts so the curve of one leg showed from beneath her silk shift. "I wish you'd sit as well, Francesco. There, that chair isn't taken."

Francesco pulled over the chair, close enough that, if he wished, he might reach out and touch her. The look in his eyes suggested he wanted to. "I remembered a stronger accent. Your Italian hardly gives you away as a woman from Venice. I think I must have been looking for it that first time we talked, not believing that a woman so beautiful could have been born and raised here without our having met."

"I do have a Florentine husband, as you know. And I have other reasons for wanting to make myself understood in Florence. I came to study. Not," Bianca added, "to be a clerk's wife."

How much to tell him? She'd never explained to the nuns at Sant'Elisabetta exactly who she was, but the Mother Superior, at least, might have guessed, especially if it was well known among some families here that Bartolomeo's daughter was in Florence. If Francesco was going to be part of her future as a scientist, he'd find out sooner or later how she practiced, and how it sometimes ended. That would threaten her work more than would her relationship with Piero, but was the threat greater if she revealed all tonight? She'd tell him what he needed to know for now, Bianca decided. If he discovered more himself later, hopefully he'd see her as a scientist, not a killer. "I imagine I lost most of my accent studying herbal preparations with the nuns at Sant'Elisabetta," she said. "The day I met you, in fact, I had just left them. I won't be going back there. My methods for practicing science don't agree with theirs." She lifted her chin. "But I learned a great deal from them, before I had to leave."

"Hmm, I know Sant'Elisabetta, but you studied with them? A married woman?" Francesco leaned forward. "Were I your husband, I'd hesitate to let you out of my sight, even with the nuns. In fact, I'm surprised not to see him by your side. Is he here?"

"Piero's somewhere." Bianca shrugged. "He's going to spend all night chasing after important people, trying to discover why he was invited. He's convinced it means a promotion for him." Bianca glanced around the room. "He'll spend hours talking money in the corner"—she tilted her head toward the front of the hall, where she'd last seen him—"to anyone who'll listen."

"And pay you no mind, if you should, for example, wander off for a tour of the ducal palace?" Francesco stood, his limbs loose and easy, as if he'd next twirl her around the room. He reached for her hand. She let his hang there a moment, then grasped his fingers, allowing him to pull her up. "I'd love to show you what else we Medici have to offer besides all this sparkle. I'm glad you're willing. If you hadn't been, I'd have had to coerce you."

If he only knew who was coercing whom. She had come here determined not to leave until she'd uncovered some Medici secrets. Bianca clasped her hand around Francesco's. "Oh, it's force for me now? Not with Medici poison?" She'd forgotten the shivers his touch sent up her arm.

"No, not force," Francesco agreed. "Something without poison. I admit my family has an unfortunate history with it." He nodded in the direction of a side door. "This way." Leading her along the edge of the great hall, Francesco's step was sure as he moved them past knots of conversing guests. Arriving at a corner door, he motioned for her to follow him through into an adjoining room. Conversations waning behind them, they slipped under a low doorway and up a staircase. The highest step soon opened onto a landing, bringing the ballroom below into an expansive view. Francesco wove his warm, firm fingers through hers, pulling her into the corridor beyond, the sound of the music fading. They found themselves in a small chamber. The only light came through the open door behind them.

"My mother's apartment."

She liked how soft his voice was when he talked about his mother. Her eyes widened as she scanned the room. "Francesco, the designs on the wall? So elaborate. I see parrots and other birds. Look," Bianca tilted her head back, "even on the ceiling. There's birds, hunting animals, citrus fruit . . ."

Francesco slid his arm around her waist. "Hmm, like the fragrance I smell on you." Bianca leaned away but he took her hand and pointed to an alcove. "She had a little office here, a study."

"To study what?" Bianca let go of his hand. A small desk anchored the space, with one shelf of books along a short wall. The spines were worn, the titles unreadable in the dim light. A sooty ring on the desk's surface showed where a lantern had been.

Francesco shrugged. "What every woman studies?"

Bianca raised an eyebrow. "Oh? And what would that be?"

Francesco looked startled. "Organization of the house? The children? Or, well . . ."

"Did you ever ask her?"

"Clearly I should have." Francesco reddened. "I was young, and perhaps I hadn't yet met a woman forthright enough to correct my ignorance."

Not the answer she'd expected, a man confessing his ignorance. And was he blushing?

"If this study had been yours," Francesco asked, "what would you have done with it?"

"I'd study herbs. That's why I came to Florence."

Francesco braced his hands on the surface of the desk. "For what purpose?"

"Cures, Francesco. I'm going to cure malaria."

"Malaria." He looked down. "My mother died of it. Two of my brothers, too. Giovanni, Garzia, and our mother, one after another."

"I know." News of the duchess' death a little over a year ago had traveled to Venice. "Malaria." She reached for his hand. "My mother died as well from it."

"And you . . . ?" He searched her face.

"I've never been ill."

"How have you escaped it?"

Bianca shook her head. "If I could tell you, I would. My mother hadn't had it before, either, until it took her life. Perhaps we have a certain smell, warding off the bad air." She laughed.

Francesco reached for her other hand, clasping them both together. "Seriously, Bianca, my entire family has been ill."

"I'd like to think some divine entity has been sparing me till I can figure out the cure. But I don't believe that. God didn't save my mother and he won't spare me. It's only my cure that will stop it. I'm sorry . . . I'm not very religious," Bianca added. Would he pull away? No, he still held her hands. "I know your brother Ferdinando is in the church."

Francesco laughed, a sound without joy. If anything, his grip felt tighter. "Consecrated when he was younger than you are now, and never lets anyone forget it. No, I agree, God spares no one. You must be familiar with herbs, then?"

"Quite. I can't cure others if I first succumb myself. And yes, I have experience, and so far I've been spared." She lifted her chin so he could see the clear pallor of her skin. "See for yourself."

"I do see. Your face is, well, almost white." Finally he dropped her hand, but only so he could brush her cheek with his fingers. "You look as though you've never been sick."

"I haven't. But don't let my face convince you that Venice has fared any better than Florence. It happens in different ways. Some escape, but in the end it's always the same—streets littered with carts of dead bodies, and the filth from decay. One can't pass through the city without full cover for mouth and nose."

Francesco nodded. When he looked at himself, could he see as clearly as she could the sickly tint that lingered in his skin? His reddened face?

Francesco's finger trailed along her collarbone. He touched his own hollow cheeks, his eyes never leaving hers. "When it had me in its grip, I wanted to die."

"I'm well aware of what the disease does. I know what it has done to you." She held his hands tightly. "I can see its traces, the redness behind your eyes?" She touched his lightly sweating brow. "Tell me what you're working on to help yourself, and I'll tell you how to do it better. I promise you, I'm closer to finding a cure than anyone."

Francesco raised an eyebrow. "You'll do it better, will you? Have you experimented with arsenic, then?"

"You meant it about poisons." Bianca wasn't sure whether to laugh. "Has arsenic cured your illness?"

"Not yet. But it might. Or you might." Francesco moved closer to her, his ripe, salty smell, tinged with an undertone of metal, filling the air.

Bianca looked into his eyes. "Are you going to give me the chance to try?"

"I think I'd be a fool not to. What can I give you, Bianca, that will allow you to help me?"

"Knowledge," Bianca said. "The Medici are scientists. Share your knowledge with me."

"And in return?"

"A cure. A life without disease surely is enough?"

"That depends," Francesco said. "Is it a life with you in it? Or are you going to cure me, then leave me to languish without you?"

Would he see in her smile permission to do what she needed him to do tonight, and her willingness to answer his need in turn? That was, she was almost certain, what she saw in his.

Bianca folded her arms. "How about this? I'll answer that question at the end of the night, *after* you've convinced me that the Medici deserve their fame as the greatest collectors alive of pieces of art—and science."

Francesco laughed. "Stubborn, aren't you? All right, then. I can show you some of my family's secrets. My own . . . well, some of it's here, but my real alchemy I do in my casino. There's plenty to see in the palace, though." He kissed her cheek. "Follow me."

Bianca gave him her hand again and Francesco led her through three rooms, maybe four. He gestured to the paintings, talking in a rush of words, but her thoughts were on the warm current Francesco's hand sent through hers, and she lost track of the number of shadowy doorways. Finally, squinting in the dim light, she followed him into a large room, its walls partly bare. A floor clock dominated the space, its heavy ticks filling the silence. She crossed the room, leaning in to see the detail on a star chart that seemed to be the room's only point of interest. It was skillfully drawn, but worthy of a whole room?

All at once she felt Francesco's hand on the small of her back. "Look up."

She did. The ceiling was a half-painted fresco, the night sky stretching out above them more vividly than if they had been outdoors. Constellations Bianca knew, and many she didn't, floated above them. Hours, days, years of work must have gone into their depiction. Francesco left her side, lighting the candles that stood on side tables along the walls, each set of stars growing a little brighter after he passed. When he'd finished, he returned to her side.

"This is my father's astronomy room. He claims it's the center of the palace. The stars and planets, he says, hold the answers to all questions, if we only read them true. Were my father not the duke, he'd spend his every waking hour here. The work was done by his very best artists, and he oversaw almost every brushstroke."

"It's beautiful. And precise." Not what she sought, but if the son's training was as meticulous as his father's knowledge of the heavens, perhaps his alchemy would have much to offer after all.

Francesco took a step closer, his shoulder brushing hers. "There's another room, a little studio, where I do some of my real thinking. Actually it was my mother's. It's nearby." He hesitated. "I don't take anyone there."

Bianca touched Francesco's chest, laying her palm flat over his pounding heart. How long had he been looking for a cure? "If you get malaria again—when you get it—I may be able to cure you, Francesco. At the same time, I can learn from you." In the meantime, his poisons wouldn't save him, and she wouldn't save anyone either, as long as she was stuck in Piero's house. If she was to work, and if he was to live, he needed to trust her. She took a step closer, making no effort to fix her dress as it slid a little further down her shoulder. "How often do you laugh?"

"Other than with you?" Francesco's eyes traveled down the curve of her neck.

Taking a pin from her hair, she said, "Give me your hand." Bianca drew it along his palm, watching Francesco's face soften. She set the pin down, then let her thumb trace a small circle at the base of his wrist. His pulse fluttered under her fingers. In the full gleam of the candles he'd kindled, she saw Francesco's face, gaunt, stippled, the heat disease a too-recent memory written across his skin. Bianca's stomach tightened.

Francesco took her hand and she gave it readily, easily slipping it into his. Strange: instead of making a cure to save hundreds, she was thinking now about making a cure to save this one man. Of course, it amounted to the same thing. But how much time would she have? "These stars . . ." Looking around the room, she shook her head, running her fingers along the polished groove of a side table flecked with little nibs of lustrous shell. "Francesco, I see a room of stars and planets, constellations, heavenly details on display. It would make a good place to study. But this is not science."

"You must be patient." He spoke softly, leaning in, his breath tickling her ear. "I see only a strand of pearls on your neck, no alchemy, but we know there's more there."

"Do we?" Bianca glanced down, then peered into his eyes, searching his face. "Francesco, it's late, I've seen little. The studio you mentioned—"

"Shhh." He nodded, his reluctance apparently forgotten. "You're practically there." In one move, Francesco reached for a candle and opened a paneled cabinet, revealing a hidden façade to an entryway with a partially open door and a chilly hallway beyond. "After you."

Leaving behind the tick of the clock in the astronomy room, Bianca took a step into the corridor. Even the door, once Francesco closed it behind them, didn't completely muffle the clock's sound. Or no—what she heard now was water, countless drips leaking from the hallway's dank walls and ceiling. She lifted her skirts, following Francesco down the wet hallway on tiptoe. All the smells were wrong for a laboratory. Mildew, must. Fetid, like a cesspool. Any parchment or herbs stored here would rot in hours. And what about the damp filling her lungs?

Just then, the dark and shadowy corridor gave way to pungent air. Bianca drew in a deep breath as Francesco walked ahead, barely glancing to the sides, his candle fluttering. The small light almost went out when, at the far end of the walkway, Francesco swung open another door, its draft pulling at the candle flame and making it flicker. Bianca followed him through. Bookshelves lined the walls. A staircase inside led to a small window. Though the room was empty, the faint sound of strings filled the air.

"Francesco, music?"

"It's the ballroom. We're so high up, no one below ever notices the little window." He turned to her and smiled. "You're curious. Take my hand."

Bianca climbed with him up to a small landing. The window above it looked out on all the guests below. The hundreds of candles burning in the chandeliers made everything glitter, as though each jewel worn by each woman emitted its own light. Wherever Piero was, he meant nothing to her from up here.

"A much better place from which to enjoy your ball." Bianca sighed. "Still, it's not alchemy."

"You don't stop, do you, Bianca Capello. Come." Francesco waited as she stepped down from the window's top step, then slid his arm around her waist, moving toward a table in the middle of the room. Beneath the scents rising from the ballroom, another odor rose: must.

All the table held, however, were a few rocks. Their surfaces shone, reflective and dark. "They're wet. Where's the water coming from?" Bianca looked up. Damp stained the ceiling, a leak clearly responsible for the earthy fragrance, water on rock. And he considered this room a studio? "Who's worked here?"

"My mother, Eleonora, claimed it once, through a secret door from her chapel." Francesco gestured to a door's faint outline on the other side of the room. "But she preferred the little nook in her apartment that I showed you."

"Your mother hasn't been in this room for a long time. The leak?"

"That's from winter of last year. I keep meaning to have it fixed."

"And the rocks?"

"My collections. I come here to take notes sometimes, to think."

"I expected a workshop, with tools. Thinking isn't practical science." She stepped closer to the table, picking up a small rock, then setting it down again. Its surface sparkled with mica, but what had mica ever cured? Bianca shuddered. Without Francesco's arm around her waist, the room felt cold. "This is what you wanted to show me? Stones?"

"There's more." Francesco pulled a sooty book from the shelves. "From the Medici, dozens of years ago. My father's side of the family." He looked up at Bianca. "Written by a woman, my father's grandmother—"

She put her hand over the book. "Is this all you have to show me? I thought the Medici palace would be full of chemicals, etched glassware, gilded porcelain containing unusual herbs harvested in secret by Medici hands." Bianca shook her head. "I've seen old books before. I want to find something new." She handed the book back to Francesco, letting his fingers brush hers as he took it from her. "I want to see your laboratory. This may be your thinking room, but it isn't where you do science, is it?"

Francesco set the book on the table. "Bianca, you have many questions tonight. But truly, is nothing all you've found?" He took her hands. "Perhaps you've found more than you even realize. Do you recognize a man's heart when you see it? Isn't desire a discovery, too? Surely love has its own alchemy—we just need to find it. Or create it. I'm sure you understand." He moved closer, his cheek touching hers. "Or practice it." His breath in her ear made Bianca shiver. She opened her mouth but said nothing.

"I told you, Bianca, I have a laboratory—near your residence." Francesco held her wrists, circling his thumbs along the inside of her palms. "I know you've seen its outside, but to others it's hidden, like a lot of what we do. There, I have equipment. I have a team of men who work with me—but never in the palace here, and never directly under my father's eye. I'm very careful about whom I take there. This, you must understand."

Bianca closed her fingers over his. "What might convince you to let someone in?" His hands were warm.

Francesco smiled. "You're obsessed with laboratories."

"I'm obsessed with not having one."

"While I," Francesco said, drawing her toward him, pressing against her chest, their hands still entwined, "might quickly become obsessed with not having you."

"Is it a consort you want?" Bianca could hear her own heartbeat. How easy this was turning out to be. But she couldn't get carried away. She had a goal, however much she enjoyed its pursuit. "I am serious, Francesco, and I come with a price." She tried to keep her voice steady. "I won't be a decoration."

Francesco kissed her cheek, freeing one hand from her grip so he could twist the ties on the front of her dress. "A few Medici secrets for the chance to laugh? I'll pay the price."

Bianca didn't move to stop him. "I want a man whose mind matches mine."

"You and Piero don't talk about your work together?"

"Piero barely knows what alchemy is. But he is my husband, and—"

"And?" Francesco raised an eyebrow.

Bianca's heart beat faster. But there was no point trying to hide it. "And I'm pregnant with his child."

"And?" Francesco whispered.

"And nothing." It was her turn to laugh, a burst of relief. Her ties to another man wouldn't cost her a Medici. The casino might still be hers. Francesco couldn't match her in wits, not really, whatever he thought of his own pursuits. But he could help her, and was willing to, wedding ring or no. "I suppose I have another four months, maybe more. Once the baby's born Piero and his mother will barely know I exist." Piero's mother would have eyes only for her grandchild, that was already clear—and this could only work to Bianca's advantage. "Four months, and you'll show me your laboratory. Yes?" She waited until Francesco nodded. "Till then . . ."

"Till then we'll be very careful." Francesco loosened another tie on her dress. "This may be our last meeting for a while, yes? I shall have to leave you in peace." He laughed softly. "Do you even know what peace is?"

"I'll have to find out, won't I?" Bianca tried to say the words lightly. *Peace* wasn't the word she'd use to describe the months she'd have to spend confined to Piero's house as she waited to give birth. Yet she would do it, and how much easier those months would be now, knowing what waited for her on the other side.

Breathless, Francesco asked her, "You're not looking for peace tonight, are you?"

"Why, no." Peace wouldn't ensure he'd remember her four months from now.

"Then . . ."

His touch made her shudder in a way Piero's never had. She untied his belt and his sash fell away. Francesco moved his hands along the back of her brocade dress, loosening the ties along her spine until her skirts fell to the floor, then up the seams of her silk slip, edging his fingertips into her bodice, loosening ribbons with almost painful slowness. Her back arched as he cradled the soft swell of her breast.

She'd gotten what she'd come for. She had her Medici, and an invitation to his laboratory, at last.

10
Virginia

The months before Bianca's water broke were as peaceful, and as long, as Bianca had feared. And yet, the moment came too soon.

Wet sheets. Half-awake, Bianca balled the damp fabric in her hand. She'd been dreaming . . . what? A leaking ceiling, in Francesco's secret apartment. But no, this fluid was sweet, sticky, and it had come from her. Bianca shot up in bed. She wasn't ready. She needed more time. Another day? The contractions, the pain, she wasn't ready for any of it, and after . . . Afterward there'd be a baby.

Bianca slid her feet to the floor. Where was Piero? Either he'd left already for his latest clerking job or he hadn't been home last night. Bianca barely kept track of whether he came home or not. What if she, too, could vanish, without a word to anyone? As she peeled off her soaked nightdress, a contraction ripped through her. Crouching, teeth clenched, Bianca stiffened, waiting until it ended. She shouldn't be here alone. Soft voices grew louder—maybe Angelica was here? She'd know what to do. Bianca had often heard the screams of women in labor at Sant'Elisabetta, with Angelica assisting. Angelica could hold her hand now, could tell her how long each rippling contraction might take, could help her face the pain.

Another contraction gripped her. Bianca screamed.

Angelica? What had Bianca been thinking? There was no one. She was alone. The world swung into focus. She was on the floor, but then someone pulled her back onto the bed. Not Angelica. Then who?

"Bianca." Her mother-in-law stood before her, joy on her face. "Soon."

Anna's voice, then more pain.

Was she falling? Windmilling over the stairs into a bottomless chute, arms flailing, breaking the fall with her head on the cement floor? No, not cement, a pillow. Agony rushed up to greet her, blood, that coppery smell. Crushing pain, the baby forcing its way out into the world, but it was killing Bianca. A tide rushing in to drown her, then a jagged pain splitting her in two.

And then the world blurred into Anna's rough hands. What was she saying; how could Anna sound so calm? Liquid oozing, someone running, shouting. The world, continuing as if nothing else were happening, unaware of the pain spiking in Bianca's body, devouring anything in its way.

Finally the baby slipped free.

Was it a baby? It looked like a slimy marine creature she might have known in Venice. If she tried, couldn't she, too, slither from her torn body, find a foothold, and climb one ragged rock after another to smell the salt air?

That cry, though. That was an infant's voice. It must be a baby in Anna's bloody hands. Piero's mother holding a baby. Bianca turned on her side, kicking away the covers from the weight of summer heat, smelling the blood that painted her body.

Anna's mouth shaped a word: *daughter.*

"Hold her," Anna said.

Bianca wanted to sleep, but instead she opened her arms.

Such a little weight. Such a red, scrunched-up face. How much pain this little girl had demanded, just to be born into the world. A daughter, from a line of Venice women, strong, no-nonsense, hard-working. And this baby would know none of them.

Until her death, Mama and the aunties had all been mothers to Bianca. But this baby—this baby, whose mother needed to put science before everything—would barely have one.

"Such a beautiful baby girl," Anna fussed. "What will you name her?"

A name? Was the baby's cry asking for a name? But what?

"You name her." Bianca barely recognized her own exhausted voice. But Anna heard her. Never, since arriving in Florence, had Bianca seen such a wide smile on her mother-in-law's face.

"Virginia," Anna breathed. "Let's call her Virginia, shall we? Our pure, innocent little girl."

Bianca closed her eyes.

"Unless you wanted to call her Francesca," Anna taunted, a sharp edge in her voice. "I think you cried that name out, in your pain."

Bianca's eyes flew open. She'd called out for Francesco? What a fool. "No," she said quickly. "Virginia is perfect. Name her that."

Anna nodded. The baby wailed. It was done.

The first weeks after her daughter's birth passed in a blur. Bianca wanted sleep but never got it. The baby's hungry mouth tore at her breasts until Anna took her and handed her to the wet nurse. Then Bianca's too-full breasts would ache. Virginia cried every night as soon as Bianca laid her head on a pillow. If Piero was home, he complained about the noise. The one time Bianca, tired of rolling out of bed to tend the baby, suggested that Piero go soothe his restless daughter himself, he called her a crazy witch and left the house. Finally Anna suggested they move the baby's cradle to her room, where the wet nurse could spend nights sleeping on a pallet.

That was how, three weeks after giving birth, Bianca finally slept the night through into the following morning. When she woke it was to find Anna rocking the baby, beaming.

"Sleep well?" Anna said.

"Yes," Bianca told her, and went back to bed.

The next day Bianca woke at dawn. Neither Anna nor Virginia was stirring. Outside, early birdsong and the calls of market-goers filled the air. Bianca dressed and stepped out onto the street. A boy in messenger's livery was passing. She only hesitated a moment before calling out. "Would you deliver a message to the palace?"

The letter she wrote was brief. *Baby delivered. Mother ready for alchemy.* "For the duke's son, Francesco de' Medici," she told the boy. As his eyes widened taking in her plain dress, Bianca smiled. Let him wonder. But her smile was short-lived. What if the boy was right? What if she, Bianca Capello, had no claim whatsoever on Francesco's time?

All that morning, as the sun climbed and she helped Anna start the day's bread, and later into the midday meal, Bianca couldn't stop glancing out the window. Every messenger that passed made her heart skip. Of course, it could be days till he answered if he answered at all. Of course, he could have forgotten all about her. Of course . . .

At a sharp knock on the door, Bianca dropped the bowl she'd been washing and ran to answer it, ignoring the angry glance Anna cast her way.

It was the same boy. "Message for you."

Bianca took the scroll and ripped it open.

We'll meet outside the palace tomorrow at noon, Francesco had written in the same scribble she'd seen before. *I'll come for you there.*

11
The Medici Mistress

Less than a day after receiving Francesco's message, Bianca stood, once again, in front of the palace. This time no music echoed from within, no guards waited outside to greet her. It was daylight, and the windows shone no more brightly than the streets outside. Bianca's heart, though, pounded as it had the night of the ball. She'd left her house quickly, barely checking herself in the mirror before pressing the baby into her mother-in-law's arms. Anna, happy to have her granddaughter to herself, hadn't even asked Bianca where she was going.

Glancing at the noonday sun, Bianca heard hooves clopping a triple meter on warm pavement, as if repeating the syllables of her name. But it was only a merchant's wagon. A voice made her heart skip. Francesco.

He'd appeared from a smaller entrance around the corner of the building, dressed as a duke's son in his ruffled white shirt and black velvet. A gold pendant hung around his neck. Bianca looked down at her own clothes. They paled in comparison, just a smock and a few layers of cotton fabric. The only linen she wore was a skirt, nothing showy, no puffs or slashes in her sleeves, no cuffs. Her bodice still felt more snug than it had before her pregnancy, her breasts tender, her body not the same one she'd used to entice first Piero and then Francesco. She looked up and met his eyes.

She'd forgotten how dark they were. And she'd forgotten how warm Francesco's gaze could be.

Francesco bowed, then took her hand, holding it to his chest. "You're more beautiful than ever." From the way his voice caught on the words, she could tell he meant them. Heat spread through her, and with it, relief. He still wanted her. "I insist on escorting you," he told her. "To our secret room, but through the palace, as befits a duke's lady."

"I'm not a duke's lady," Bianca pointed out. "You're going to get us caught, Francesco." But she couldn't help laughing as he hooked his arm in hers.

The door that opened onto the Hall of the Five Hundred was staffed by only one guard this time. The man bowed to Francesco. Bianca felt his eyes following her as they passed by him. "Francesco, is this the only way—"

"Of course not." He raised his eyebrows. "There's a shorter way, Bianca, just not today." Beaming, he kissed her cheek. Francesco led her along the edge of the great echoing hall, empty now and seeming even larger than it had on the night of the ball. By the time he finally guided her up the stairs and through the palace apartments, Bianca's head spun from glimpses of gilt-framed portraits in full daylight, rooms draped in velvets and gold brocade, and the occasional courtiers they passed, all of whom stepped aside for Francesco and watched Bianca until they were out of sight. If Francesco noticed he gave no sign, chattering on instead about which bust had been carved by which artist in each opulent room. He only fell silent when he reached the map room corridor and opened the small entry to the secret apartment.

"Welcome home," he told her with a quick bow. "At least, home for now."

The room had changed. It no longer smelled of must. Instead, thick tapestries lined the walls. Francesco's rock collection had been relegated to one small cabinet with glass doors, leaving room for a luxurious bed with a trundle underneath and silks hanging from its frame, an empty bookshelf, and a small table set with wine and sweets. Francesco circled the room, arms wide. "All ours, Bianca. What do you think? Tell me what books you want, and I'll bring them. Tell me your favorite wine and it'll be yours."

"Volumes on chemistry." Bianca drew her finger along a freshly polished shelf, then turned to Francesco, smiling. "And maybe the texts you use in your alchemy, too." She could see it already, a library of her own making.

Francesco laughed. "Of course. I should have known."

Already this small apartment seemed comfortable—and practical. She could keep some of her herbs here, and Anna couldn't take them to cook with. The books she'd longed for when she'd been trapped in her bedroom in Venice would be all hers now. At least, they'd be hers while she was here.

Francesco looked at her expectantly, his face like a little boy's. "I'll get you anything you want, so you never have to leave."

"I wonder if you've forgotten I'm married," Bianca said. "And I'm a mother now, too. I can't exactly move in—"

"Maybe not officially," Francesco said cheerfully. "But you'll spend as much time here as you like. Don't worry, my father will give your Piero work. All you have to do is come along with him—and then, go off for a stroll in the gardens. Only really you'll be with me."

Could she? Anna would gladly watch the baby, and they both trusted the wet nurse. Piero, whose mood had darkened since the ball had failed to yield much new employment, would be thrilled. And Bianca would have a place of her own with time to study. Study—and do other things.

"I suppose so." Bianca reached for his hand. He was a persuasive, if not practical, man. But a dreamer, too—and with a big imagination. Bianca stroked his palm, barely grazing his skin. Even looking down, she could feel his warm breath on her cheek. Then Francesco leaned in, planting his lips squarely on Bianca's.

His grip as he guided her to the bed was gentle. Bianca barely knew who pulled off whose clothes first, just that now all she wore was her sheer shift, all he wore was a thin shirt, and his hands were sliding down her bare back, pillows toppled around them. Her body, still tender, stiffened. She hadn't let Piero touch her since the birth. But Piero wouldn't ever be as gentle as Francesco.

He noticed her slight flinch. "Bianca . . . too soon?" He drew away, sitting back against the headboard.

She reached for his hand. "Would I be here if I didn't want you?"

And want things from him. Francesco laughed, and Bianca felt herself relax. If they could laugh, they could talk. Both were key to getting what she needed. And right now, all she cared about was Francesco lifting her shift and finding that comfortable fit of their bodies she remembered so well from the night of the ball.

Bianca woke to see Francesco staring at her. The yearning in his eyes made Bianca forget all the changes the last months had wrought on her. She was still beautiful, and he still saw it. More important, though, this body had a brain. And that, she reminded herself, mattered more than anything.

Settling into the soft mattress, Francesco ran his hands across Bianca's stomach. Faint silver lines marked where, for nine months, a child had been. The tenderness of Bianca's breasts served as another reminder. "You may have a plan," Bianca admitted. "Get Piero employment, and Anna will let me leave the baby with her if she thinks I'm going with him to his work. She'd love to see me that devoted to her son. But it's going to be difficult."

"It won't be difficult at all." Francesco rolled over, reaching for a scrap of parchment on a table by the bed. "Here, I'll write the order right now and give it to my father today. I think your Piero already has had some tasks in the offices here—more work won't be a problem. He'll hire your Piero. You have work you can do here."

Was this work, what she was doing now? It didn't feel like it, and certainly that wasn't what Francesco meant. Piero's mother might have a word for it, but if Bianca was using Francesco . . . well, this work gave her much more pleasure than seducing Piero had. "Yes." Bianca smiled. "I do have work. And Anna's perfectly capable of mothering my child."

"Hmm, the woman I love, mother to the daughter of a man I've only seen from a distance. Or, have I met your Piero and forgotten?" He drummed his fingers on her arm. "From everything you've told me, and from what my father's said, he's not an impressive man. You said as much the day we first met."

"He isn't."

"Say the word and your Piero will suffer an accident." He grinned. "And you'll be free to become . . ."

"Become what? Your wife?" Bianca shifted on the pillows. "Your father would never let you marry me, a runaway from Venice."

"And so . . . ?" Francesco ran a finger down her arm.

"Listen to me, Francesco." Bianca rested her hand on Francesco's, stilling his finger. "Your father will select a wife for you."

"You may think I need a wife." He withdrew his hand so he could lean back on one elbow. "But I know for certain you don't need a husband."

"Do you?" Bianca sat up. "Piero's too careful to have an accident. Besides, I need his mother. With the wet nurse, Anna's more than happy to look after Virginia."

"Drop her on the nuns' doorstep. They can take her."

Had Francesco heard something about her work in the convent? She took a breath. "Which nuns?"

"The Medici nuns, Sant'Elisabetta, the ones under our patronage."

The Medici nuns? All at once Bianca couldn't trust her voice. She shook her head. A Medici connection there all along.

Francesco pulled her toward him, nuzzling his face in her hair.

"All right, maybe not. But when she's old enough, your daughter will be welcome in my court. It happens all the time, rich men, or men who wish to be rich, sending their daughters to serve as maids-in-waiting until they can snare a lord for a husband. Have your mother-in-law watch her till she's older, and then she'll come to the palace to live among the best young women in Florence, and you'll never have to worry about her again."

It was so easy for Francesco. He wanted Bianca, so he'd make his father hire Piero. He wanted privacy, so he created a secret apartment for the two of them, in a room he'd barely been using. Still, wasn't that why she'd sought out the Medici in the first place, so she could unlock a little of that power for herself? It would do no harm, letting him make her daughter a courtier in the palace. No mother could offer their child a better life than one lived in comfort, educated among the wealthy of Florence. And Bianca needed freedom. She had a cure to build.

Bianca eased back against the pillows, studying Francesco's face. Dark circles smudged his eyes and the color in his cheeks seemed too bright. He needed her body, or thought he did, but his real dependence on her seemed too far from his thoughts.

She brushed his cheek with her fingers. "Francesco, have you been sick again?"

Francesco gave her a thin smile. "No, of course not. But I am curious about your malaria treatment. I suppose you haven't been able to make progress, these months with your husband."

"Not much." In the last week she'd read and reread all her notes, written down a few ideas she wanted to try, but she couldn't accomplish anything in Piero's house. Bianca withdrew her fingers, resting her palm against Francesco's bare chest. Whatever he said, he'd need her cure soon. She didn't have time to waste. Here in this secret room she could study, she could plan, she could read about artemisia. Knowledge wasn't enough, though. She'd have to apply what she learned. "You want me to be free to practice my science?" Bianca waited for Francesco's nod, then continued. "Then take me to your casino."

Francesco looked away, shaking his head. "Truthfully, Bianca, the casino is in ruins. With all the construction, it's half useful at best."

"But you've been going there these past months. Or do you wish me to believe you've just been sitting in the palace?" If he had been, he wasn't the scientist she thought he was.

"Well, no. I've been there. But the casino is not a place for . . ."

"Women?" she said, before giving him a gentle shove. "Because of the foundries, the caustic chemicals? Then it should be too dangerous for men as well." Shaking her head, she sat up. "Francesco, what are you worried about? The grime, the smells . . . lime, sulfur, urine? Which of those in your casino will offend me?"

"Bianca, listen. You don't understand our alchemy."

He had to tilt his chin back to look up at her. Bianca touched a finger to his lips. "So teach me. And I'll teach you mine. I've read of how alchemists here think of energy, combining and subtracting elements. You divide metals, I create medicines. It's just that I don't dip mine in allegory. And I'll use mine to save lives, including yours."

Francesco rolled over, shifting so he could sit up too. He didn't meet her eyes.

"Francesco, look at me; your mother and brothers died of the heat disease. You're sick with it." Was he even listening? "I see things. I make herbal infusions, tinctures. Distillates too, when I have the workspace. The bitter apple growing wild, artemisia in the woods, all of it has power for those who study it."

He looked at her. "It sounds like you want a garden. Not a casino like mine."

"I want both. My herbs can help you, Francesco. Even more as distillates. The extracts, too, have power—surely as an alchemist you understand." She looked around the room. What could she say that he'd want to hear? "I'm curious about what powdered stone can do, too. My mother used lapis." Not to any great result, but if he insisted on minerals as therapy . . .

Sure enough, a glimmer of interest showed on Francesco's face. "And arsenic, Bianca? It has remarkable powers."

"Francesco, do you really want to die playing with ground-up poison rock?" Bianca tried not to grit her teeth. "When has such a cure ever helped you? When you're sick, you get bled, then there's a tincture to calm your nerves. Then your physicians give you laudanum, and more, to make you sleep. But no infusions." She raised an imaginary cup to her lips. "No, not even one. Too womanly, am I right?"

Francesco looked at her, shaking his head slowly.

"You think you know my alchemy, but you don't." She laid her hand on his. "Take me to your casino and I'll show you what I can do."

Neither spoke for a moment. Then Francesco sighed. "You truly think you'll learn something there?"

"It's a place for chemistry, yes? Chemistry's what I practice. Plants produce chemical substances that combine with each other as surely as your metals do."

Even before Francesco nodded, Bianca knew she'd won. His crooked smile said it. "I truly can't take you there now. It's pure debris. But soon, Bianca. I promise."

"How long does the mistress of the duke's son need to wait?"

"You don't give up." Francesco held Bianca's face to kiss her, then swung his feet out of bed. "And I? I can't say no to you. We'll go in a week."

Bianca felt for her cotton stockings under the covers, hiding her face so he wouldn't see the pure delight she knew her smile must show. She had done it. Francesco stood to collect his clothes and Bianca emerged from the bed, her face composed now. Half-dressed, Francesco paused to slide Bianca's chemise onto her shoulders, easing it over her still tender breasts. She reached for her cotton garments and seamless linen skirt, such simple clothes. "I don't give up," Bianca said, pulling on her smock, her back against a wardrobe. "And you won't regret showing me your casino, where you'll play with arsenic." She smiled, taking his hands. "And where I shall save your life."

12
The Casino

The first time Francesco had pointed out his casino to her, Bianca barely knew the man. She'd never heard him laugh, not really, and he hadn't known about her herbs and her kind of alchemy. It was late summer now, not winter, but little enough about the building had changed. As she took his hand to dismount from the Medici carriage, Bianca still couldn't convince herself that the casino building belonged to a wealthy family. Less construction wreckage cluttered the outside, but sunlight had further faded the yellow paint on the door. Small weeds grew from cracks in the faded walls and between the rough flagstone steps of the entrance. The air was heavy with the rotten stench of sulfur.

She'd spent months alone, waiting to give birth and waiting for this moment, too. Perhaps she'd let her hopes get too high. But Francesco was watching her eagerly. "A little neglected still," Bianca said.

"Nevertheless, a great artist has touched this place." He kissed her on the cheek. "The gardens were good enough for Michelangelo."

"Decades ago, Francesco."

"Hmm. All the more reason to return the building to something valuable, even if it takes years."

Bianca swatted at a mosquito. Another buzzed in her ear. The gutters were rife with them. At least she could slap them away; not so the buzz of gossip. From the people passing, Bianca drew the same kinds of glances as in the palace. Everyone knew Francesco by sight, but many stared at the thick-haired woman with him, dressed in linens instead of the thin silks and finely woven satins that would befit a companion of the duke's son. Yet what did Bianca care if people wondered, or if a sultry gust of summer air blew her hair loose? The miles she'd traveled, the things she'd given up, and now here she was, companion to a Medici prince, minutes from setting foot in his studio of science, even if it was in an old building with a peeling yellow door.

Francesco's fingers tightened around hers as he led her up to it. "Bianca, love, I can see you're not impressed." He turned to her. "If I spent time making the place look attractive, I'd have less time to do science inside. Besides, do you know how much money fresh paint and new roof tiles would cost? My father could pay for it, of course, but he says the casino is my madness and refuses to waste any more Medici money. Stocks of chemicals and glass are expensive. And my men like to get paid. But here, you have to see what's inside before you decide anything." He opened the door. "Welcome to my alchemy, Bianca."

The air outside had been rank, but inside was ten times worse. A sharp, acid smell assailed Bianca's nose even as she buried a cough in her sleeve. When she looked up, she had to squint in the small, dim entryway. She took another step into the foyer. Torches cast shadows on the broken bricks, twisted lumps of metal, and shattered glass piled along the walls. A cat brushed the hem of her skirt. This shadowy place must be full of rats. So different from Sant'Elisabetta, where the only cats Bianca ever saw were those content to sleep in the sun.

"I did tell you," Francesco said. "It's in progress. But that's what science is, isn't it—always building on what's come before." He shrugged. “I know what I’d like to do with it, but my architect has his own ideas. The man thinks he knows more than I do.”

Bianca laughed. “About building? Are you so sure he doesn’t?” But Francesco didn’t laugh with her. She’d have to be careful; Francesco was serious about his casino. Still, she wished the architect were here now to explain to her how this structure was even standing. If this was what Francesco practiced science in, Florence would wait a long time before he created anything useful. The cure for malaria depended on her, not him, but if Bianca was to accomplish anything, she needed a building that wouldn’t fall down around her ears.

“May I?” Francesco took Bianca’s cloak, hanging it with his on one of the large carved pegs by the door. It was the action of someone ushering a guest into a beloved space, but the drafty room was no warmer than the street had been, and she shivered without a mantle. At least she’d worn boots with heels high enough to keep her dress off the floor. In the corridor leading out from the entrance, shadows flickered, cast by the light-play of candles. She touched a handkerchief to her face. Next time she’d infuse it with oils, and maybe her clothes, too.

Hiking up her skirts, Bianca tripped over an uneven ceramic tile as Francesco called out. “Bianca, make way . . . Careful with that,” he added, speaking to someone ahead of her. Bianca peered into the dusty air. Two men with rough faces and untidy beards barreled toward them, their muscled arms straining under the weight of the chest they both carried. One man grunted as they passed Bianca and Francesco. The other barely glanced their way. “Pay them no mind; there’s a lot of equipment to transfer from one room to the next. You’ll meet my men in a moment. Look.” Francesco tilted his head toward a door. “Our storerooms are to the right.”

Bianca looked through the door as they passed. There it was, treasure buried in chaos. The shelves were well stocked with glassware, large alembics, a small portable oven, and what looked like bundles of dried herbs. So it was true: the effort Francesco failed to muster for the outside of the building all bore fruit in here. Her fingers itched to pull open the doors and drawers of the storeroom's locked cabinets. Francesco, though, was already ushering her on.

Whatever he might have been saying, Bianca couldn't hear it. The roar of a foundry grew louder as they walked down the corridor. Its smoke made Bianca cough, but something about this stink drew her in. It smelled of science. And it smelled of Francesco. Still, as they passed the foundry room, Bianca covered her ears and couldn't help ducking as a shower of sparks lit the air. Francesco shouted something to one of the men transferring the molten metals to molds, and to another, a dark shape busy in the act of grinding metal who raised his hand in some kind of answer. Even after it faded behind them, Bianca thought she might never stop hearing the foundry's banging in her head, nor smelling the fumes that could poison them.

"Is there always this much smoke, Francesco?"

"And ash. That's why my father wouldn't let me work in the palace. The soot could destroy his paintings and tapestries."

Bianca took another deep breath through her handkerchief. "It certainly could." She'd want the gigantic foundry out of her residence, too. But did Cosimo know what it was like here for the men, this tiny casino under repair, and all inside breathing in the foundry grime, not to mention the fumes of acids and fine metal dust?

The passage they followed grew wider. Bianca lifted the handkerchief from her nose and fanned it in front of her face before returning it to her pocket. Maybe it would be splendid. Now it smelled like sewage.

Francesco leaned in. "It's all a mess, isn't it?" He said the word *mess* as though it were a good thing, and his smile was one she hadn't seen before, proud, almost a little shy, the smile of a man showing off his greatest accomplishment. "It's a mess—but magnificent, too?"

On some men, the satisfaction on his face might have seemed

arrogant. On Francesco, it only looked boyish. If she were a true partner to him she'd find a way, carefully, tactfully, without crushing that childlike certainty, to show him how wrong this place was, and to help him make it what it should be before it all came crashing down. But first, she'd need to get to know his casino. And that was making her head throb. "Well," she said. "It . . . might be magnificent someday." As his face fell, Bianca added, "I want to see where you make your porcelain. The one that's so sensitive to what it holds."

Francesco brightened. "Down the hall, then." Slipping his arm around her, he gestured ahead of them.

Bianca placed her hand over his where it rested on her hip. "Truly, Francesco, it's incredible. All my life I've wanted stores like you had in that one room. There might be just a few things you could change." Starting with the chaos. Accidents happened in messes like these. Surely Francesco's alchemy required exactness. She'd have to go slowly, helping him improve the place without crushing that persuasive confidence. But not too slowly. She had important work to do.

"It'll get better, I promise." Francesco brushed his lips across her forehead. "But come, you haven't seen the best part yet. In one of the rooms behind us is where the rough manufacturing and finishing happens. Down here," he said, waving his arm to the hallway ahead as they walked, "is where my porcelain is born. Among other things. Wait." He whispered as she moved to step through the open doorway that marked the middle of the corridor. "Close your eyes?"

Close her eyes? And risk losing her head to some flying piece of metal? Still she shut them, her body tensing as he led her a few steps forward.

"Well?"

"Francesco, I hear a rumbling furnace, bellows beating . . . the clanking of glass . . . heavy thumps on tables. The air is humid; there must be simmering liquids?"

"And the smells?"

Bianca lifted her chin, taking in a deep breath. "Sulfur, mostly sulfur. And soot particles in the air, carried in fumes." And no fresh air.

Francesco's hand pressed against her closed lids as he led her a few more steps. "All right. We're here. You can look."

Bianca blinked as he lifted his hand. Her eyes widened. A large U-shaped room stretched before them. In the middle and at the end were wooden tables, and beyond that a furnace. All throughout the room, workstations fed one into another, men carrying metals to be forged or some bringing pottery to a kiln. Francesco's men were like shadows, large dim shapes moving in and out of the light cast by flickering candles and the fires of the forge. The smell of hot metal hit the back of her throat, with something putrid underneath, something dead, a rank animal odor like the air of Venice's grassy marshes. The rotting scent of death. Were they fermenting carcasses? Yes, experiments were happening here, but from the smell it seemed more a morbid science than one of healing and life. Was there room for what Bianca did? There had to be. Somehow she'd make room.

"Show me, Francesco." She turned to him. "Show me everything."

He led her to the forge first. A man bent over one table, welding something amid a flurry of sparks. He nodded to Francesco, then ran his eyes over Bianca. She held her head high.

They walked past cluttered tables she dared not touch for fear of getting a splinter or burning her hand on a hot liquid. Several workstations lay beyond the forge, some with small cauldrons of molten ingredients. "Here we purify metals," Francesco shouted in her ear. "Changing their color and weight."

"Alchemy," Bianca murmured.

Francesco pointed to deep shelves of boxes. Their labels bore the names of different types of clay. Some held plaster molds. "And here, my ceramics." He put a hand on her arm, halting in front of a potter's wheel. Behind it a small furnace sat warm, waiting to be stoked. "The thinnest possible vessels, so delicate they sense poison and refuse to hold it. In fact, I've been adding minute amounts of arsenic to the glaze. It makes the porcelain even more sensitive. When the vessel itself is toxic, it recognizes any other toxin it touches. And it shatters, or it will once I've perfected it, rather than hold a substance that could kill."

"Francesco, that's madness." She bit her tongue, but the words were out. "I just mean—you drink from these cups that are made of arsenic, poisoning yourself just so you'll know no one else has? How can you risk yourself like that?" And *why* would he, to no purpose she could see? But she didn't ask him that.

"The arsenic in the glaze isn't enough to kill, not even close." Francesco drew a box from behind the potter's wheel and lifted out a thin white cup. "Look, you can almost see my fingers through it. It's taken me months to get the porcelain this fine." He took her hand, wrapping her fingers round the cup's handle. "It feels as though you're holding air, no?"

The cup did have a delicate beauty, its soft pearl-like sheen unlike anything else in the casino. "May I, Francesco?" Bianca took the cup in both hands and held it up to the nearest candle, the brightness giving it a luster. Curiously fragile and light. Still, it wasn't sentient. How could he think there was some chemical carrier in the cup that might sense a poison, and then shatter? Gently, Bianca handed the vessel back to him. "I can't say I share your ideas about science," she said. "But the cup is beautiful."

"Come along, I'll show you soon where we smelt the ores, to get the purest form for the glaze, but first, where we distill the sulfur." Francesco nestled the cup back in its box and took Bianca's hand. At the next station, a man hunched over the largest alembic Bianca had ever seen, watching it boil. If she had this equipment, she could progress twice, even three times as quickly as she'd been able to at Sant'Elisabetta.

Francesco spoke to the man operating the distiller. "This is the Lady Bianca, she's asked to see our alchemy. You'll show her, cousin?"

The man shrugged and raised a beaker from the table before him. He was heavyset, and Bianca couldn't picture his lips ever smiling. The man shot a hard look at Bianca. "Don't touch it. A spill will sear your dress, and if you drink it you'll get a nasty stomachache. One you won't recover from." He snorted, swirling the dark liquid as he held it to Bianca's face. "Smell that? Nice perfume, isn't it? We do more than play at pretty potions."

Taking a step back, Bianca kept her voice even. "I'm not interested in pretty potions." The man's dull gaze traveled up and down her body. "Francesco told me what you do here. He has yet to convince me that arsenic is as useful a substance as he claims it is. But as I'm a scientist, I wish to learn as much as I can. Only then will I be able to judge whether there's a place for poison in my own work."

"Your 'work?'" His eyes opened wide.

"I'm finding a cure for malaria," Bianca said. "Francesco, let's go. I'd like to see where I'll be doing my experiments." She could feel the eyes of Francesco's cousin following her as he led her away, though when she glanced back the cousin appeared busy with the sulfur solution in front of him.

Francesco faced Bianca. "My cousin there . . . the men are good workers, good scientists, but they're rough, Bianca. Perhaps you see why I waited to bring you? If you don't want to work here—"

Bianca cut him off. "Oh, I do." If she'd been questioning her decision before, the scorn of the man with the sulfur had erased the possibility of giving up. "My science is worth as much as anything else that's being done here." Or more. "A man like your cousin isn't going to scare me away. He can look at me however he wants to. You'll be with me, yes? He'll know he can't do anything to me. He's the one who'll be in danger, or his pride will, when he sees what I can do."

Francesco rubbed his forehead and nodded. She couldn't tell if he was worried or relieved. "We have an empty workspace over here. This way."

The cramped space he led her to was half what each of the men seemed to have. But she could move a table, shift a crate of broken glass, bring instruments from the central tables, and she could store books and notes. She'd keep her own area tidy, and if she did perhaps the men would do the same, and the whole casino would be a little more orderly. If she brought an oil lamp, for example, and the men saw how its even light allowed for more careful fabrication and precision, wouldn't it be only a matter of days before they all did the same, abandoning the gloomy haze of the flickering candles? And she doubted any of these men took notes, but perhaps they would when they saw her doing it. She'd have to be careful, of course. Any ground she gained she'd attribute first to Francesco, the man who'd brought her here. That way the men would accept the changes she introduced. If she did it right, Francesco himself would never know how big a role she'd played in taking this casino from a mess of a place to one of calm, of safety. Francesco needed her here, whether he knew it or not.

"I'll take it," Bianca said, laying her hand on the scarred wooden surface of the table. "I couldn't imagine a better place to work." The lie was worth it for the grin that spread across Francesco's face. Her task now—as though she needed another—would be to make the lie come true. "Show me the storerooms I can use? And please, if you have a spare apron that would fit me?"

"You want to start working now?"

Bianca laughed at the bemused look on his face. "Of course, even months ago. Let's start working and I'll show you what I can do."

13
Francesco's Men
1565

How quickly the months passed, Bianca reflected one day, laying out tools and herbs on her worktable. They'd been busy, to be sure. Most of her hours here she spent organizing her work surfaces and stocks, meticulously preparing recipes with incremental changes, writing down everything she did. From her workbench she could almost see Francesco's. He was there now, setting up as she was, both of them readying themselves for the work of the day, although soon he'd be circulating among the men. Over the past months she'd watched from this distance as he'd helped pour glass into molds and test the thickness of porcelain. Often she'd look up to the shattering of ceramics as his latest experiment proved too delicate. He'd catch her eye, give her a rueful grin, and keep working. When he asked her what she thought of his work, Bianca tried to give ambiguous answers. He had to know what she thought, had to know how trivial porcelain seemed to a scientist working to cure the heat disease, but Bianca had decided long ago it wasn't worth fighting over. Let him practice science however he saw fit. He'd given her the space to practice hers.

And she was, but slowly. So much slower than she'd hoped. Bianca braced both hands on her table, scanning yesterday's notes once again. She was getting results, yes. But most days she still longed for her mother's practical knowledge of plants. She missed the herbs she'd had access to at Sant'Elisabetta. Without the nuns' ample stocks of dried leaves and roots, she had to wait whole seasons to find what she wanted in the marketplace. That alone had set her back months. And while she'd been here most days, she'd had to miss weeks when Virginia was teething, and Piero's mother, ill, couldn't watch the baby alone. After each absence, she returned to find Francesco happily enjoying the porcelain manufacture, having accomplished little, if anything, new. He was content, though. And Bianca was too. If she'd gotten less done in a year than she'd hoped, well, she had many more years ahead of her. That was the gift Francesco had given her: her own workspace and time.

She reached for her apron, tying it on as she glanced over again at Francesco. He wasn't working yet; a young man, barely more than a boy, wearing the Medici colors, was talking to him earnestly. The boy held a rolled parchment in his hand. Francesco's face was still—too still. Bianca caught her breath. Then Francesco turned from the boy, his eyes finding hers across the crowded casino. He looked away quickly, but not before Bianca knew something was wrong.

By the time she reached them, the boy had left. Francesco held the parchment, staring down at it without seeming to read. He looked up when Bianca stopped in front of him.

"What's happened?"

"It's a message from my father." He shook the parchment closed before she could read its contents. "I don't want to talk about it in here. Can we go outside?"

Without waiting for an answer, Francesco turned and began making his way through the casino. Feeling suddenly cold, Bianca followed, past the thumping foundries, past showers of sparks and the glances of Francesco's men—men who, after all this time, still barely spoke to her. She was used to that, as she'd grown used to the stale metallic air and the clouds of smoke, but she still drew a deep grateful breath every time she stepped from the casino to the street outside. Despite the filth and rubbish in the streets, today the air was fresh, with a hint of the coming fall's crispness, but even breathing it in, her lungs felt tight. She turned to face Francesco, but the sun was behind him. Hours seemed to have passed since Bianca first caught sight of the messenger boy, yet it was still early morning.

"Francesco," she said. "Tell me what's happened."

Finally he moved so she could see his face, drawn and worried. He'd twisted the parchment in his hands till it shredded into tatters.

"Bianca, do you remember what you said right after you had your baby? About me needing a wife?" Bianca nodded. "My father has decided that he wants an alliance with the Habsburgs—now. It seems it's my responsibility to seal the alliance. He's been talking about it more these past months. I've been trying to put him off. My days working here with you, our nights together when we can get them . . . This is what I live for. But my happiness doesn't concern my father. The message he sent today informed me I'm going to leave tomorrow. All this—you—what we had . . . it's done."

Bianca sighed. She'd never seen him look so defeated. And she felt . . . what? An image of the workspace she'd just left flitted through her mind. Surely *everything* wasn't over. "Francesco. This is unfortunate, but—it's not forever."

"Of course it's forever. I'm leaving soon. How many months I'll be away, I don't know. There's other diplomatic business too. And when I come back, I'll have a Habsburg princess for a bride." He moved closer, touching a finger to her cheek, then tracing the curve of her collarbone, saying, "Understand, Bianca, please. I don't want any woman in my bed but you."

So that was what he was worried about? "I know that, Francesco. But this was bound to happen sooner or later. Nothing between us has to change."

Francesco let out a sharp breath. "Doesn't it? That's what I hoped, but . . . you'll still love me? Even if I'm married?" The tension in Francesco's face eased. "My wife will never know about our secret room. We might not go there quite as often, but . . ."

"You'll slip away from your wife just as I slip away from my husband." Was this all his sad face had been about? "I never wanted to be your wife, you know that. What we have has nothing to do with anyone else. Being apart will be hard," Bianca added. Though she'd get more done. This past year, Francesco had often wanted to spend time together in their secret room—time Bianca enjoyed, but, precious as her moments away from Piero were, it always felt like time she could have spent working. "Go do your duty. Keep your father happy so he won't close down your casino. When you get back, our secret room will be waiting. And who knows, I might have found a cure by then."

"A cure?" Francesco's brow, smoothed by her words, furrowed again. "Bianca, surely you don't mean you'll keep working. When I get back of course, but while I'm gone, the casino . . ."

"Is my casino too now, is it not?" Bianca's pulse quickened.

"My men . . ."

"Are *your* men—just flesh and bone, Francesco." Like cogs in a wheel, laboring in a room full of sulfur and other sharp smells—nothing more. "They barely know I exist." She wouldn't be a woman among men, just one scientist among others. "Tell them you trust me. I'll get as much done as I can while you're gone. Then, when you return . . ." She brushed her lips across his. "We've waited for each other before. We can do it again."

Francesco leaned into her kiss. She let him, his body pressing against hers. When at last she pulled back, Francesco's face looked peaceful. "You're right. I'll let them know they're to help you in whatever you need, and leave you to your work otherwise. And when I come back . . ." Finally he smiled, squeezing her hand. "I'll miss you, Bianca Capello."

Bringing his hand to her face, she whispered, "And I, you." She'd won—but won what, exactly? Was she being a fool, assuming she could keep working alongside these crude men while Francesco was far away? No; she'd be a fool to let fear keep her from pursuing her work. The men had never hurt her, only looked at her.

"You probably have to pack," Bianca said. "Go back to the palace. I'll meet you in our room at dusk, before I go back to Piero. Yes," she said before Francesco could interrupt, "I'm going to continue working today, and every day while you're gone." Some women might have wondered if, by then, he'd still want Bianca in his bed, but the way he slid his arm around her waist was answer enough.

"Very well. I'll see you tonight." Head bowed, he turned and started back toward the palace. Bianca watched till he was out of sight, took one last breath of clean air, and returned to the casino, alone. She, Bianca Capello, who'd stood up to her aunties, fought her father, married a foreigner, found refuge with nuns, wouldn't stop now. She was Bianca, Francesco's love, unshakable.

For the first few days Bianca was sure that Francesco's men, though they might not admit it, accepted her presence even with Francesco gone. Following Francesco's departure, she arrived in the casino early each day before most of the men, so that when they descended with their loud laughter and rude jokes, she already had her head down over her experiments. But even wrapped in a leather apron, her hair coiled under a scarf, she felt their eyes on her. She wasn't an extension of Francesco now; she was a woman in her own right. Much as she wished to deny it, something had changed. They looked at her straight-on now, instead of ignoring her as they'd done in Francesco's presence. Bianca told herself that of course they'd be uncomfortable. They were used to women sitting at home washing household laundry with lye soaps, or sweating over pots simmering with scraps from the previous night's repast. They were probably just curious about a woman who, while they were experimenting with improbable things like porcelain designed to shatter, was doing real alchemy, finding a cure for the heat disease. If she felt threatened, she told herself, that threat was all in her head.

Her first morning alone she had felt the men watching her, but when she swept her eyes around the room no one's gaze met hers. One man busied himself at the forge. Others bent over glass beakers, maybe invoking a bit of Medici astrology in the words they whispered to each other. Or in the comments they were making on the dress Bianca wore or the clip holding back her hair, but their words and glances couldn't do any real damage. What mattered was the small alembic she'd claimed from the storeroom when Francesco was still here, the glass containers and clay vessels, the endless supply of parchment on which she noted everything she did. Bianca tried to cram months' worth of plans into those first few weeks, preparing for all the experiments she'd read or thought about during the past year.

But again and again, the results she expected didn't come.

The day she learned why started as every day had, since Francesco left. Bianca left the dawn-lit streets of Florence behind her and entered the dark casino. At her workspace she tied her leather apron's frayed strings in a double bow at the small of her back, then smoothed the front of it, breathing in the thick leather smell. She set about organizing her table as she had every morning the past few weeks, glassware in the middle, herbal extracts across from her, burners at the far end. She'd perfected the placement of her tools and herbs, bringing in what she needed from Francesco's storerooms or searching the market for herbs. Even now, after working in the casino with Francesco for almost a year, she caught herself wanting to ask someone questions like, *If I use oil of anise from the market instead of distilling it myself, do I save time, or do I weaken my remedy? Which beaker dissipates heat better, the sturdier one, or the one made of more delicate, sensitive glass?* When she'd last had a space to experiment, Angelica had worked beside her. Now what Bianca wanted to ask her was why, despite all Bianca's careful measurements, despite the recipes she checked again and again, almost nothing she'd created since Francesco left had come out the way she'd predicted. Herbs she'd had little trouble with before somehow had lost their potency. Solutions simmered when they should have boiled, and unexpected particles surfaced in her brews. Angelica might say . . . Bianca shook her head. Imagining what Angelica might say couldn't aid her. Certainly Francesco wouldn't have been any help. Even if he was here, tinkering with his porcelain, she wouldn't have bothered to ask him a question about herbs whose names he probably didn't even know. Hadn't she gotten used to working alone after her mother died, and now, in the casino?

Hours later, after setting up her equipment and going over her notes from the day before, her world was reduced to hot water and steam. Bianca watched the boil writhing in the cauldron, the tang of cooked herbs shutting out everything else. She wasn't torturing the water; she was coaxing out its elements. A slow churning boil, bubbles building in perfect circles on the bottom, increasing quickly in width, breaking explosively at the surface. The earthy bite of artemisia drifted up, as it should, but other scents overpowered it. Was that . . . tar?

Bianca staggered back from the cauldron, gasping. Where was the gentle aroma that would soothe a patient's inflamed lungs? She took another step away. This heated mixture would choke a sick man before it could save him.

She raised her head and looked around the room. The brew in her cauldron was not the one she'd prepared. Only then did she notice how silent the workroom had grown. Only then did she feel the weight of every man's eyes on her.

"What," Bianca cleared her throat, stepping out of the steam. "What's happening?" Several men looked away. Others met Bianca's gaze, their eyes revealing nothing. "Did someone meddle with my formula?" she asked. "Sulfur, and pine bark, and . . ." Cautiously, Bianca inhaled, lightly tasting the steam on her tongue. Certainty set in as she continued. "Antimony. Antimony with some resin. There's poison in this pot." Her words rang into the silence. Had Francesco's casino ever been so still? "This amount, with the artemisia, could kill." And it would have. Bianca shivered. Before giving this mix to some poor sick Florentine, she'd planned to test it on herself.

A man spoke, his voice a grindstone rasp. "Then you'd better stop, hadn't you, before you burn your pretty face dropping something in your pot? Witches who play with plants wind up killing people, we all know that. When that happens, don't think any of us will stand up for you. We all told Francesco before he left. We won't take the blame."

"Will you take the blame when your own work kills?" With effort, Bianca kept her voice steady. "Or will you blame me because you can? If you'd let me do my work, all the blame I'd ever have to shoulder would be from those who complain when my cures start saving lives. I imagine all of you would be among that small group, willing to find whatever fault you can any time a woman accomplishes something you haven't managed. Until you or someone you love suffers from the heat disease. Then I suppose you'll try to take credit for the same cure you sabotaged. And when Francesco comes back? What are you going to tell him?"

"We'll tell him you gave up and left," the man who'd made himself spokesman said. "Any normal woman would have already gone, and you're about to."

"Witch," someone muttered from behind her.

"If he finds out otherwise, we'll know it came from you," another man said. A large block of half-carved wood sat on the table in front of him. "You think he's watching over you? Francesco doesn't use spies, just like he won't have a man drive his carriage. He doesn't trust anyone not to tell his father all his secrets. So he may be a Medici, but he's as blind as any man. If he hears, we'll know it was you. And if you tell him anything, then . . . this." And he held up his blade.

Bianca's stomach clenched. Surrounding her were several big, bear-like men whom Francesco had chosen for their intelligence, surely, but also for the strength of their bodies, able to shape metal and wield tools in ways Francesco never could. He needed them, and they knew it; they were proud. Of course they wanted her to fail. And if she didn't—if, as they might already have sensed, she was closer to success than any of them were—they'd see to it that her miracle cures killed, that all her recipes went awry. The moment they had a Florentine's death to put on her shoulders, their problems would be over. The woman—the witch, the trespasser—would be gone.

She could stay. Didn't she need to stay, to prove to these men they hadn't won? But she'd never be able to trust anything she made, not now that she knew Francesco's men would tamper with her science. She'd have to sleep here, guard the work with her life to make sure it stayed clean, uncontaminated. Her cure would be at risk unless she let go of her pride—and left. But for where?

She took a deep breath. "I now have to fix someone else's errors. We'll call them errors, shall we? After that . . ." Bianca swallowed. "After that, I'm finished. Your stores, your equipment, everything that is still by rights mine, I'll keep, but I'll do my work elsewhere." Where, she had no idea. It would still be weeks, maybe months, before Francesco returned. She could do nothing here, though. Bianca turned away from the men's satisfied grins. The one who'd first spoken met her eyes, spat, then returned to his forge.

Bianca turned to her table and the simmering cauldron. She reached for the ladle, but her fingers fumbled the well-worn handle. Her hand was weak. She'd been twisting the bracelets on her wrist, leaving her skin pale and bloodless. She needed fresh air, away from the smoke and all the odors it absorbed. She began gathering her notes, taking everything she could. Let the men clean whatever mess she left behind. Without glancing back, she headed out of the room.

Bianca wasn't done with the casino. Francesco had opened his laboratory to her. If she had to wait until he came back to resume her studies, well, she'd waited before. But surely somewhere there had to be an unused corner, close enough to give her entry into the Medici stores, but private, hidden. Let the men wonder where she'd gone. What if she could find a place right under their noses, and continue in secret until Francesco returned?

Bianca paused in the corridor. So many parts of this rambling building she'd never set foot in. Instead of turning left toward the yellow door, she turned right, around the corner and down another hallway, then up a flight of stairs. She paused at a balustrade. The window above it looked out onto a matted mess of weeds and woods. Bianca leaned against the rail, gazing through the window at the tangle of woody plants below.

All at once she was on the Florence streets again, walking for the first time on Francesco's arm. He had pointed out his casino, and beside it: "Michelangelo's garden," Bianca breathed.

She hurried down the same steps, back through the corridor, turning just before the hallway to the foundry rooms. She stumbled, a small ripping sound signaled that, yet again, her dress had caught on a doorway. This, too, had been happening almost daily since Francesco left. Clumsy craftsmanship, she'd assumed, but she hadn't remembered tripping this much before. Who knew, maybe someone had pounded nails into the door frame just to catch the skirts of the only woman who had ever passed this way. She bent over to release the snared material, then tiptoed past one room after another into a dark hall. Unless she'd completely lost her sense of direction, she had to be close to an outside door.

And there, ahead, an exit. At the broken door jamb, she took one long breath, peering through a murky window. Surely the garden of an artist would have some sort of outbuilding, one she could quietly claim. Bianca reached for the door handle. Before she could turn it, though, the bells of San Marco rang out, so close that the sound shivered through the metal under her fingers. Bianca stepped back. The men soon would be gathering their supplies, heading home for the day. The last thing she needed was for them to find her here.

Quickly she turned, making her way back through the corridors, through the faded yellow door, and out onto the evening streets. Tomorrow she'd dress for crawling through the weeds and brush. As long as they didn't see her enter what had once been Michelangelo's haven, she'd be safe. The men she was fleeing would never imagine the possibilities in a garden of brambles, a place of unwanted plants. Tomorrow Bianca would begin again to chase her cure. In earnest. And this time, without men.

14
A Garden of Cures

The next day Bianca rose before the sun. She wound a kerchief around her hair, filling her coat's deep pouches with rusted kitchen utensils, a sharp pair of shears, and a small spade she'd found discarded at the edge of a nearby garden. Piero barely stirred. The baby, tucked in a cot in Anna's room, slept too, accustomed to waking to a bottle of goat's milk and the arms of a grandmother who, reveling in taking care of her beloved granddaughter, seemed to have chosen not to question Bianca's long absences during the day. Within minutes Bianca slipped out into the streets, heading toward the casino and its yellow door.

But this time, once she passed through it, she didn't turn toward the foundry and a day spent among men who resented her. Instead she kept going, slipping down the corridor she'd discovered the day before. Since Michelangelo and other artists had left, had anyone even walked this way? Here, again, was the door to the outside. Bianca brushed a spider from its lintel as she reached for the handle. Soon this garden would carry a different, more heroic history. It would be the place where malaria was cured.

Most wouldn't think twice about the tattered door, hinges rusted, in a musty casino corridor. Bianca pressed her face against the smoky glass of its square window panes. She coughed, and the pane released a few layers of dust, still revealing nothing. Catching her hand on the rim of some rough wood, Bianca pulled away too quickly, a splinter ripping through the skin, blood beading in its wake. Bianca put her finger, with its copper taste of blood, to her mouth as she scrutinized the door. Thin veins of moss had rotted the planks, but the handle was still intact. Just a small pull, and the old, loose boards released their woody perfume. Bianca stepped through into air that smelled alive with plants setting their fruits, engulfing their seeds with sweetness.

The door closed behind her without a sound. Just one step and she was covered in burs. Bianca blinked in the dim light that filtered through thick patches of stinging nettle, rosemary, and thistle sage. She slipped her hands into the fleece-lined pockets of her coat, then felt around hidden pouches for something that would help her clear a way forward through the dense, woody growth. If Francesco were here, would he have forged her a path? Probably not. He smelled of ink and metals, but never of sap. Bianca's thoughts went next to Angelica. The young nun's knowledge of herbs, her readiness to take on any task, her laughter perhaps most of all, would be a boon here. But that door was closed, and Bianca was alone. Only a songbird's melody broke the silence.

Bianca reached into her deepest inside pocket and pulled out the shears. The first briar she cut snapped back, scratching her face. She hissed through her teeth. She'd take thorns over hours spent in that foul-smelling foundry among men who wished to see her fail. Bianca opened the shears again and hacked at another stem, stomping down small shoots with her feet. Steadily, she moved forward. Slowly, a path began to form.

A vine caught her ankle. She fell to her knees, bracing for pain. But the velvet touch of the mossy stones on her face was soft, cool, moist. Her cheek met earth, a woody taste filling her mouth. She spat out the dirt, then pushed up to standing. What rich loam. Between her fingers, she crumbled the dark soil. Fertile ground.

Reaching into a barbed briar of trailing roses, she touched a thorn. Her finger left it red. She'd christened the garden, or it had christened her. Straightening, Bianca froze. Half a face, cracked and blank-eyed, stared from behind a tree. Then Bianca laughed. Wading through vines, she cut through the bramble, pulling back a thick canopy that revealed . . . broken plaster. Figures of half-finished goats and toppled pedestals lay in fragments, and here and there a hand or a horn reached out from the weeds. Her first guess, it seemed, may have been right. The place hadn't been touched since the famous sculptor, and any young artists with him, had left it. Surely only shards remained.

Pushing through the briar, Bianca leaned over to pick up fragments of marble, smooth and rounded, shaped into pieces of muscle, something part of a larger piece. How had these bits of stone and clay survived here so long? Whatever spirit the artist had imbued them with might have faded, but the pieces themselves endured. Would anyone ever say the same of Bianca? A cure for malaria was so much less tangible. But a life . . . *I am alive because of what Bianca Capello did.* Would people claim that, generations from now? Because of what Bianca Capello was about to do in this garden. Working in a sculptor's shadow.

Bianca returned the chunks of marble to the tangle of weeds beneath her feet. Ahead, a beam of light streamed through the trees, touching onto an old trail that was still partially cleared. It must have been well-used, to have lasted this long. Moving more quickly once she reached it, she forged a path through the weedy groundcover until she stood before a building otherwise hidden from view. It smelled dank, of rotting wood, with water pooling all around it. Stepping closer, she peered through a cracked window into a small room, the first of two. Shapes loomed inside, some broken, but not all, the occasional bust or marble arm beckoning to her from the gloom. In the recesses of the shed, wooden boxes lay, cracked and stained by mildew.

Bianca tested the handle of the door. It gave, and the door groaned open. A sliver of light brightened the shed. Squinting, she pushed through what seemed to be bags of stones and plaster, and pedestals with toppled statues.

Inside, she ran her fingers along a central table in the larger room, avoiding any rough spots. Low shelves lined the walls, heavy with ceramic bowls. Other tables displayed tools, brushes, chisels, and bags of powder or sand. A small satchel, now half mildewed, held more tools—although what must have been engraved initials, or even a bit of text or poetry, had been worn away. She waved away the cobwebs, thick tangled gossamer threads knotted with dead insects. Two large slabs leaned against the wall, one of which had been etched. She traced the fine incisions. What would the old artist have said if he knew a woman had been here? The mistress of a Medici, a woman alchemist, whose medium was plants, whose work was extraction. Not too different, perhaps, from the sculptor who cuts shapes from raw stone.

To accomplish anything, she'd need to clean up. She'd also need glass of all sorts, bowls, and drawers for her herbs. These she could collect from Francesco's stores. Alembics and distillation columns would be more difficult. She'd have to take them away in parts from the casino, then reassemble all. But she'd do it.

If she could work anywhere, it would be in an isolated place such as this. No interruptions, no questions or interrogations. No one would blame her for her failures or fear her successes. It was her garden of useless brambles—disordered, shabby things. And in the shed? With more light filtering through the windows' overgrowth, she could see the interior differently, tidy and organized, clean after being buried underneath years of layers of dust.

All hers, and no one needed to know about it. Certainly not the men in the casino, nor even Francesco—the secret was safe with her, only her. She could tell him when he got back, show him this garden so full of possibility, much more than the small corner of the casino that had briefly been hers. Already she doubted whether she'd want to go back there, even under his protection. She'd never be comfortable. If she told him what the men had done, they'd never forgive her. She didn't think Francesco would blame her, though he might. Worse would be if he blamed the men. If she closed her eyes she could still see the dull light of the forge gleaming off that one man's blade. So far she'd done nothing to them, and still they hated her. If she set their duke's son against them, she'd never be safe walking alone in Florence again. No, she'd do whatever she needed to do to protect her secret from her enemies and Francesco both. She'd keep quiet. What she'd found was too valuable to lose.

Here she could be a scientist in pursuit of a cure, without having to be first a mother or wife. People didn't remember Michelangelo as simply a man; to the world, he was an artist. Bianca Capello they would call . . . what? Not merely "wife" or "mother." Not "woman," but "scientist." Not "mistress," but "healer." The one to end the heat disease, when no one else could.

15
Distractions

A growing season, Bianca reflected, was a lifetime in a garden. Just in the past few months, thanks to an unusually warm fall, so much had changed. Herb seeds had germinated, with leaves emerging in shades of green. Slender stems had grown into sturdy stalks, reaching out in all directions, for she made sure they had had room to do it. Now, in autumn, the plants died back, releasing their seeds for another chance at immortality. Woody plants chose another path for survival, dropping their leaves, the stalks and branches remaining, bracing themselves for the winter cold.

Only when the fading light made her notes impossible to read did Bianca step away from her table, bracing her hands against her back to relieve the stiffness of another day in her makeshift laboratory. What she'd needed from the casino she'd taken in the early morning hours before Francesco's men arrived.

Over time, she had put each nook and cranny of her small space to use. The biggest change, though, showed in the garden outside. Although the outer wild tangle of brambles she'd waded through her first day was still there, the inside gardens were lush, with a logic Bianca had imposed through hours of weeding and pruning. She'd found several herb beds with parsleys and thymes, leggy and wild, which she'd pruned back and cultivated. Now she could harvest fresh leaves daily. She'd sown seeds into prepared beds of loamy clay, letting them grow a little before their next burst of growth in the spring. She'd no longer have to haggle in the market for wilted specimens with which to brew her treatments. Instead Bianca could take part in each plant's life from seed to harvest. She now studied the forms of their leaves as they grew, reading in each unfurling frond or leaf what that plant would become over the next weeks.

Today, like every other since she'd claimed this sanctuary as her own, had passed too quickly. As the last light faded, ever earlier with winter's approach, Bianca bundled up into a wool coat. She reached above the front lintel for the rusted old key to lock the shed, leaving another day's work behind her. Winding through the gardens, she stopped to check a batch of seedlings she'd planted several weeks before. Was their soil too dry? No, when she got down on her knees and dug her fingers into the earth, it was moist. Bianca got to her feet again, then made her way to the door, hesitating before she entered the roadway that her haven shared with Francesco's casino. Hearing no voices, she slipped through the gate. The city was usually quiet at this time of evening, the familiar walk back to Piero's house the perfect time for Bianca to think over her day's progress. She'd made a good start on extracts from dried yarrow and could finish them tomorrow. After that . . .

A sound made her pause, her foot catching on a loose cobble just outside the casino as she stumbled to a halt. Voices, coming from the casino doorway up the road. Francesco's men. What were they doing here this late? She always timed her exits far enough into the evening that she wouldn't meet anyone. It didn't matter when she got home. Piero would be out of the house until sometime after midnight, when he'd return smelling of wine and another woman's scent. And his mother was happy enough caring for the baby.

Bianca had every right to be here, but why risk an unpleasant encounter? The men she'd been avoiding might not see it that way, and she had no desire to draw their notice. Her supply runs to Francesco's storerooms, first thing in the morning when just a few men were beginning to fire up the furnace, were timed with the intention of meeting no one. The one morning a metalsmith had caught her taking a few glass cylinders, she'd dropped them and run before he could ask her anything, his guffaws as she fled louder than the sound of shattering glass. He hadn't chased her, but she'd spent that whole day in the garden listening for footsteps. And that was in broad daylight, with plenty of people out in the street. She'd gone to great lengths never to be a woman alone at dusk with those men. If they saw her . . .

Someone called out from inside the casino and a deep voice answered, a familiar voice. She'd made that voice laugh, and listened while he spoke to her of alchemy.

Francesco?

No. He couldn't be back yet. She had too much to do.

But that was his voice. And she should be thanking some deity that Francesco was *here*, that she wasn't about to be alone with his men. Francesco was her champion, wasn't he? True, the last thing she wanted was someone to distract her, to shatter the peace she'd built in the garden. But if he saw anything at all in her face to make him doubt she was glad to see him, he might decide his Habsburg bride was more interesting than the Venetian alchemist after all. Bianca the scientist stood to lose everything if Bianca the lover failed now.

The casino door burst open as she was in the middle of inspecting her muddied skirts, the dirt under her fingernails, her disheveled mess of hair. Bianca stepped back into the shadows. The workers spilled out first, a sulfurous reek following them as they pushed in one mass past her and down into the piazza below. Only a few men glanced her way. Let them think she was just some serving woman. She could almost wish she was. But no, she was mistress to the insignificant-looking man who walked behind them, buried in his faded ochre-colored traveling cloak, heavy with metal clasps and thick ties. Though he was smiling, his eyes kept wandering from the men laughing around him. She thought for a moment that he'd walk right past her. Could he? Did she want him to?

She kicked a pebble into his path. Their eyes met.

"Bianca." A smile lit Francesco's face as he stepped toward her, taking her into his arms. She clasped her hands behind his neck. He'd been gone for months, yet in his embrace, wrapped in the familiar musky smell of him, Bianca could believe that no time had passed at all.

In her ear he breathed, "I've been looking everywhere for you."

"Now you've found me." His touch was gentler than she remembered, but his embrace was the same familiar squeeze, his grip firm. "Francesco, you feel the same." She stroked his face.

"And you," he said, kissing her cheek. "I'm sorry I had to leave you alone."

Alone? Bianca almost laughed. She'd been the freest she'd ever been, occupied only with her work, barely playing the roles of wife or mother—or mistress—until she went home at night. All those weeks she'd spent locked in her father's house, all the months pregnant under Anna's gaze, waiting for the first glimpse of Francesco's casino, this life she had now was what she'd dreamed of. Since she'd claimed Michelangelo's garden, she hadn't once felt the lack of companionship. The Medici stores of glassware, soft beeswax candles, vials of solvents, mineral powders, tins of oil. All this she had made use of without Francesco by her side, his name ready enough on her tongue to justify the use of his equipment, but his face growing a little distant. From Francesco, she could be separated. From her work, no.

Still, he was her sweet, deluded man, and if he wished to think himself indispensable, let him. "I missed you," she told him, because in these past months his smile had crossed her mind, sparking a little bit of loneliness. "Don't worry, though. I've gotten a great deal done, Francesco, projects, cataloging my herbs . . ."

Francesco drew her toward him, nestling her under his chin, then took a step back to look at her. "You're as beautiful as when I left, Bianca."

Would Francesco demand her time now, pulling her into the present with no eye to the future other than one they could share? She touched his face. He'd grown paler since she last saw him. Dark circles ringed his eyes. Those shouldn't be there. Soon, though, he'd be resting easy in her arms, his head on her chest, she stroking his face. She'd won her freedom through Francesco. She had to remember that.

"I thought I'd find you inside with the men?" His voice sounded husky.

Bianca opened her mouth to explain. Words stuck in her throat. It would be so easy to tell him, but would he believe her? And if he did, could she really trust that he'd be able to stop his men from coming after her?

A secret kept could be held a little longer. A secret told could never be taken back. "I was collecting plants for my studies," she said cautiously. "Here, smell." She turned her palms up, holding them out to him. He crinkled his nose at the earthy scent of artemisia, an odor Bianca herself barely noticed anymore. Then Francesco took her hands in his. When he let her go, his face was drawn.

How much did he know? What had the men told him?

"My cousin says you haven't been working," Francesco said. "Yet you've just told me you have been."

"I . . . it was difficult." Bianca stuttered to a halt. "I'm grateful for the casino, the equipment. I use it when some of them aren't there, or . . ." Or they'd taint the distillations. Make cures into poison, and accuse Bianca of witchcraft while they were at it. She thought of those angry men standing around her on the day she'd discovered their plot. Were these the kind of men her aunties had in mind when they'd warned her what ignorant people who identified Bianca as a "witch" would do to get rid of her? Maybe someday she'd share her garden with Francesco, but not now. Not until the men had forgotten her. Besides, she didn't mind keeping that peace, that solitude, for herself alone.

Bianca drew breath to tell him another lie, something that would let her keep her secret. For now, though, Francesco didn't seem to need answers. Stepping aside as a horse cart rattled past, Francesco took her hand, his grip almost too tight. "Bianca, listen . . . please. I'm going to be married." He glanced down. "Next month, December."

Bianca's stomach unknotted. "That isn't news, Francesco." Bianca took his chin in her palm. "I know you've been playing the diplomat for your father, courting the Habsburg princess. You need a bride and we both knew it wasn't going to be me."

"I've been running after this woman and her family for months." He brushed his cheek against hers, then took both of her hands. "When the only woman I wanted was you."

"I'm *married*. Or had you forgotten?" Bianca tugged on her apron. "I'm no more or less yours than I ever was."

"But . . ." Francesco let out a long breath. "It's as you said it would be then, before I left? Nothing's changed? I know you said this wouldn't have to come between us, but I worried."

Such relief in his voice. Had she really doubted he'd still want her? But his face looked drawn. "You're not happy. But why? Do you want me jealous of a woman with no freedom, whose life will be lived entirely in the eyes of the court? I'm grateful to her, this Habsburg who's meant to bear your children, sit beside you at those endless court affairs, give some of her blue blood to your line. I can't do those things and I never wanted to. I have a cure to create."

The lines in Francesco's face eased. "You said as much before I left. But I wasn't sure. You don't mind?"

"If I'm wrong tell me now, but last I checked our apartment is still waiting for us in the palace. Your new wife will be just one more person who's not in on the secret. I feel no differently with a real wife there."

Slowly, a smile spread across Francesco's face.

"Her name is Joanna," he told her. "And she is nowhere as beautiful as you."

"I'm more beautiful than Joanna? Is that all?"

"And more clever." Francesco nodded toward the road. "You're right, to our apartment."

"And this Joanna?" Bianca asked. "The poor woman needs to live somewhere."

He took Bianca's arm, guiding her down the road to his carriage. "She's not in the city yet." Francesco shook his head. "Until the wedding, she'll stay in a villa outside Florence. My father will see to it."

"Then tonight, enjoy your freedom." No one knew better than Bianca how precious a thing that was. "When she comes, though, remember, Joanna isn't the enemy. She'll make your court life easier, and you know I never wanted the Medici name. Medici science at my fingertips and a Medici prince in my bed—that's enough for me."

16
Red Robes

In the days running up to Francesco's wedding to Joanna, Bianca's routine was even more tiring. But she didn't mind being tired if that was what it took to have everything. Rushing to the palace apartment in the early evening to head straight for Francesco's arms, as she was doing now, was hardly a price to pay for days spent in the garden. She'd be home to Piero's house often close to midnight, where she'd slide into bed, trying not to stir her husband from his snoring. Sometimes, she stayed the night with Francesco.

Strange, Bianca thought. Once she'd hated Piero's mother and wished the woman would disappear. Now Anna counted Bianca useless, to be sure, and probably cursed the day Piero married her, but she was happy to care for Virginia, and Bianca couldn't imagine life without her. A time would come when her mother-in-law would become too frail to chase after Bianca's growing daughter, and then . . . well, better not to think about that. Almost dusk; Francesco would be waiting for her in the ducal palace.

Bianca walked through the palace doors, ignoring the artwork in the entranceway depicting Francesco's bride's homeland. Yawning, she paused before reaching the stairs that would take her to the grand hall and through to the Bronzino chapel with its secret door. Francesco would be waiting on the other side in their apartment.

She'd gotten in a full day's work, distilling an autumn harvest of artemisia, and now she'd have her prince. That was enough. Stepping inside, she turned the corner and collided with a wall of red.

Francesco had told her his younger brother, the cardinal, was in Florence to nose around the palace and gossip about his brother's soon-to-be bride. Francesco had been complaining about him, his meddling, his criticisms, his scorn for Francesco's alchemy, but Bianca had yet to lay eyes on him. The man standing before her, though, was unmistakable. The red robes, of course, but he also had Francesco's face, though twisted into an unpleasant sneer. And he, clearly, had no doubt who she was.

"Bianca. I've been wanting to meet you." His voice was deep and smooth. "Such an interesting woman, from all accounts. Oh, don't look so surprised. Francesco's never been subtle. There's talk of you all over the palace." He tilted his head. "The only thing more talked of is the wedding in December. Of course you've been told? You must have heard the hammering for the new ceiling in the great hall each time you slip through the rooms here to find my brother."

It was true, the hammering was hard to miss. Once or twice Bianca had passed what must have been emissaries for the Habsburg bride, and the architects designing the projects for the nuptial preparations were everywhere. Some were overseeing renovations of the Pitti Palace on the south side of the Arno River, soon under repair for the princess. Joanna would have a palace of her own. And a title. But her husband, she'd be sharing.

"I hear it." Bianca's eyes met his gaze. "All of Florence knows Francesco's to be married. I don't know why you feel you'd need to tell me that, Cardinal." She shook her head. "Do you want something?"

"I'd like my brother back." The cardinal dropped a hand on her arm. The gesture might have looked innocent, but his fingers dug into her flesh.

"You have him. All of Florence has him, and the Lady Joanna as well." She tugged her arm free. "When I come this way, this route you think I know so well, do you know what I see?"

Their eyes met. Younger than Bianca, perhaps Francesco's little brother had never been afraid of anything. Bianca was used to stares in the palace. Porters stole glimpses of her. Ladies in waiting hid their faces but glanced from behind veils or fans. Perhaps it was the cardinal's red robes that gave him the courage to look the open secret, Bianca, in the face.

"Tell me, Mistress." His mouth twisted around the word. "What do you see?"

"I see the foyer busier each month." Her eyes narrowed. "Look at the frescoes, Your Eminence, of Habsburg cities. All to make the Austrian princess feel at home. And I'll be the first to welcome her. No one could be happier than me that Francesco is to be married." She gave him a cold smile, and before the cardinal could reply, she slid past him and strutted up the stairs.

"Your brother disapproves of me." Bianca closed the door of the apartment and slumped on the bed, curling up beside Francesco. "I met him outside." She laid a hand on Francesco's chest, his heart's rhythm just a little faster now that the specter of his brother was in the room. Bianca, too, could feel her pulse racing. "He thinks it immoral that you have a mistress. I spoke with him, but I doubt he's done. This is a line we're going to have to walk for years, Francesco. You'll always be Joanna's husband, and I'll always be in your bed."

"My brother can worry about morals, Bianca." Francesco pulled her toward him. "I've been thinking, I'd like you to have a palace of your own—in Via Maggio. It'll have everything Joanna's has. My architect will design the interior. But the Pitti Palace will be for the woman I'm forced to marry, and the other will be for the woman I love." Bianca shook her head. Her own palace so close to Pitti? The idea was ridiculous, but it was pure Francesco. His eyes glowed with that boyish enthusiasm for a project anyone else would have seen as unpractical. Still, how could she object to a palace of her own? "It'll be a place we can be together without sitting under Joanna's cold nose," Francesco continued. "Or my brother's." His voice hardened on the last word. "What happens outside the royal palace doesn't have to concern him. He'll know, but if I make it convenient enough for him to look the other way, he'll go along with it." He touched her lips with his finger, making Bianca smile. "A married man I may soon be, but you and I will have our secrets."

And Bianca had hers. Francesco knew she spent her days searching for her cure, but he'd been so busy preparing for the wedding he hadn't had time to notice that none of her work happened in his casino. He'd barely been there himself. If Bianca dreaded the wedding, it wasn't because Francesco would be legally bound to another woman, but rather because once he no longer had to plan the biggest event Florence had seen in years, he might have time to wonder how Bianca spent her days—and where. "I see nothing wrong with secrets." Bianca wrapped her arms around his waist. "But you do know," she added, "that you and I aren't one of them?"

"Are you listening to the chatter of the Florentines? They'd gossip about an angel. Since when do their opinions matter?"

"They don't to me. They do to your brother." Bianca was about to say more. Something in Francesco's face, though, made her stop. Sweat beaded on his skin. "Let's not talk about it," Bianca said. "We'll worry about him later." *No sense fretting yourself into a fever,* she almost added, but he wouldn't want to hear it. Francesco's sickness, the heat disease that stayed deep within him, was another thing they'd worry about later, when they had to.

17
The Heat Disease
1572

In the years following Francesco's wedding, Bianca never heard much from him about the ceremony. Rain delayed it for days. He did tell her Joanna had hated the herald trumpets blasting, and the crowds of Florentines in their red velvet hose carrying huge flags and shouting. Palace gossip, the little that Bianca had gleaned, told her that Joanna didn't care for the sound of Italian, nor understand it. As for her royal home, the palace hanging over the Pitti piazza like a blot on an otherwise sunny square, Francesco had said that after the wedding she'd wandered around as though dazed. The only pieces of art she'd wanted for decoration had been dour paintings from her native Austria. Seven years later, the palace still looked like nothing so much as a pale imitation of a cold, unfriendly land.

Francesco reported that Joanna's mood seemed to lift, though, when she became pregnant within months of the wedding. Once or twice during that first year Bianca caught sight of Joanna, her head held high and a proud look on her face, one hand resting on her growing belly. The woman believed she had accomplished what she'd been brought here to do. Even when the first child, and then the second, the third, and the fourth were born—all girls, one living only a month and another a year—Joanna's smug smile of satisfaction didn't waver. At least, that was Bianca's impression. As the years passed, Bianca didn't find it difficult to stay out of Joanna's way. Why would she? Francesco was building her a palace.

Bianca had worried at first that once the wedding was over, Francesco would expect a greater share of his mistress's time—time she needed to work on her cure, however much she enjoyed Francesco's company. Those fears proved unfounded as his court duties as Cosimo's regent only increased. Francesco complained about not having time in his casino, moaning over his own missed days of work rather than asking after hers. Once Bianca would have found this lack of interest frustrating. Now she was simply glad she could continue her studies in secret. She'd told Francesco she'd found a place apart from his men to experiment, but not where, and not why. Thankfully, that seemed to be enough for him. If her work had been more visible—if, for instance, she had found a medicine that cured—even Francesco, busy as he was, would have had to wonder where she'd done it. To Bianca's frustration, though, seven years had yielded few results. She wasn't surprised: plants, unlike Francesco's metals, were temperamental. She couldn't rush her harvests, and she still couldn't shake her fear of moving too quickly as she'd done with the girl at Sant'Elisabetta. Still, she'd hoped to make faster progress. A garden shed too cold and damp to use in the winter, a leaking roof that dripped on her stores, plants with spring root rot or a few harvests lost to powdery mildew, and her own caution had ensured that she hadn't. She knew so much more than she did when she started. Less stems and roots and more leaves, early morning cuts when the leaves were still turgid and moist with dew, different solvents for extraction, and changes in steeping time. Bianca knew she would get there, but her patience was running low.

Today, as Bianca walked again through the humid Florence streets at dusk toward the ducal palace, something else worried her. In the nearly nine years Bianca had been in Florence, Piero had become uninterested in their marriage bed, and Bianca certainly hadn't minded. She didn't know or care with whom he spent most nights, and the woman's perfume had become familiar to her. Did Anna know her son had a mistress? If so, she looked the other way. And Piero ensured that she could, always making it home at some point before dawn so he could eat the breakfast Anna made him and head off to whatever task the royal court had for him that day. Anna would smile proudly and tell quiet, wide-eyed little Virginia how important her father was at court. And Bianca didn't say a word.

For two days, though, Piero hadn't come home. Anna was frantic. Bianca had almost skipped going to the garden today, but she'd left off at a critical point in a procedure, and if she'd let it sit over one more night, a week's work would have been ruined. She could have bypassed going to see Francesco. That would please Anna, though the woman would still find something to complain about as soon as Bianca walked in the door. But she needed to talk to Francesco.

That night Francesco, who'd just returned after a week's absence from the city, was waiting for her in their apartment. He'd lit only one candle, his face in shadows, the bed a nest of blankets. Bianca didn't have time for its temptations, though. She sat on its edge, next to Francesco. "Piero's gone," she told him. "I think—"

"I know." He reached for her hand. "Bianca, they found his body. He's dead."

Bianca shot him a quick look, but it was too dark to read anything in his face. "You know? Francesco, how?"

"I didn't kill him if that's what you're wondering. Though I can't say it never crossed my mind." Francesco sighed. "But no. It was the family of his mistress. Someone saw a nephew stab him and throw his body into a street near a bridge."

Bianca looked away, shaking her head.

"I don't know why they waited this long, but . . . Bianca?" Francesco clasped her hand. "Are you all right? Surely you're not sad."

Was she? For the hopeful young man who'd rescued her from

Venice, maybe. But he'd hardly rescued her; she'd rescued herself, as much from the life he'd brought her to as from the life she'd had before. "I never wanted him," she said. "I just wanted him to bring me to Florence. To you, if I'd only known it at the time."

"Now you're free to marry me." Francesco's voice was heavy. "But I'm not free to marry you."

"I don't want to marry you." Nothing had changed for her. "I'll have to keep living with Anna, at least for now. I need her to watch Virginia. She's only eight and she's shy and, well, I barely know the girl, but Anna's devoted to her. She'll keep her safe. I might be able to spend more nights with you. But I'll have to make Anna happy too. And you have Joanna. And . . ." Bianca leaned in, pressing her cheek to his. Then she stiffened. Pulling away, she could still feel Francesco's heat on her skin. "Why didn't you say something, Francesco? You're sick."

"I'm not." But then he began coughing.

Bianca lit two more candles from the one he'd kept burning. Yes, the flush was there, and the glazed look in his eyes. "How long has it been since you were ill? A year?" Since his marriage, Francesco's malaria had flared up several times. So far the bouts had always been brief. Now, though, heat radiated from his skin even as he began to shiver, his fever higher than it had ever been before. Bianca began a mental inventory of her garden shed. What distillates did she have? She'd had plenty of space and time to work, but no real cases to study. The shed was more full of notes and new distillates than actual cures.

"We need to get you to a sickroom here in the ducal palace," Bianca said. "Joanna will want you in Pitti, but I want you here, where I can keep an eye on you. Can you stand? We'll call a servant and have them set up a bed and prepare a wash basin and linens. And another one to tell Anna I've been delayed. I'm not going home again while you're like this."

She could lose her husband. But her royal lover? She was going to make sure Francesco lived.

The worst of his illness lasted several days. As she bent over his bed, thoughts of the girl at Sant'Elisabetta wouldn't leave her mind. Still, he responded well to what she gave him. Bianca didn't go home to her daughter and mother-in-law. Instead she slept in an apartment near the sickroom, making it known to the servants she was there as a healer. No one was fooled; they'd already seen her slipping through the halls at all hours to meet Francesco. But Bianca didn't care. She needed everyone to know where to find her if Francesco worsened.

After three days, Francesco was well enough that Bianca felt she could leave his side. She sat at the dresser in her borrowed apartment, staring into the mirror, using a brush to tame strands of the coarse, thick tresses she'd barely had time to touch since Francesco sickened. Soon she'd bring him his morning treatment, a simple infusion with additional extracts—but he was already cured. It sat on her nightstand, sweetened with peppermint and a drop of honey to ease the bitterness.

"Signora?" came an earnest voice from the other side of her door.

"Yes?" Bianca set the brush down and turned.

The woman at the door's face was drawn, her hands clasped and pressed to her waist. "I'm sorry, I—"

Bianca stood. "What is it?"

"Ma'am, the duke regent has a visitor. The door's closed."

No rest for Francesco. Could just anyone find their way in?

"It's . . . it's the cardinal," the maid said.

Bianca slapped one hand on a table. Not just anyone. Francesco's little brother. "How long?"

"He was here when I—"

Long enough. The maid's voice faded behind Bianca as she hurried down the hall. If she had to pummel Francesco's door open, she would. The last thing a sick man needed was a visit from the brother most likely to cause him pain. The cardinal thought nothing of belittling Francesco, mocking his alchemy, berating him for being so much less of a leader than their father. Every visit from him left Francesco defeated, even when his health was strong.

She pushed the door open as soon as she reached it. The cardinal stood over the bed, droning in Latin, his fingers massaging oil on his brother's forehead as it ran down the side of Francesco's face, into his ears, and down his neck. Were holy oils his idea of treatment? Adding to the smell of sickness was some spicy scent.

The cardinal looked up and, without breaking from his prayer, met Bianca's gaze, eyebrow raised, the pleated brocade of his red robes rustling.

Francesco didn't stir, and hopefully wouldn't till she'd gotten rid of his brother. "I'm his healer," she told the cardinal, over the sound of his muttered Latin. "I'm taking care of him."

The cardinal finished whatever phrase he'd been reciting, then crossed himself. Only then did he turn to face Bianca in the doorway. "I know what you are. All of Florence knows. We've met before, Bianca, or have you forgotten?"

"I thought you might have forgotten, Cardinal. It's been years." She hadn't spoken to the man since their miserable encounter before Francesco's wedding.

"It has, hasn't it? And you're still here. My brother and his foolishness." The cardinal reached for a jar of liquid and started to spoon it into Francesco's mouth. "It's only thanks to God's grace he's not in an even worse state. Brother, take some of this."

Whatever the cardinal gave him was as likely to be poison as anything else. Bianca stepped across the room close to the cardinal, knocking the spoon from his hand. Clear liquid spattered across Francesco's sheets. He stirred, eyelids fluttering. "Bianca?"

"Francesco, please." She leaned over him. "What has he given you?

What's he doing here?" But Francesco didn't answer. He'd fallen asleep again.

Bianca straightened. The cardinal eyed her as he would some wild animal. Maybe she looked it, her loose hair more like a thick golden hood concealing her face than a delicate coiffure for a noblewoman.

"The Lady Bianca Capello." The cardinal walked around the bed, opposite Bianca. "You think you can do better than us Medici with our medicine, our pharmacies, our hospitals? Added to whatever charms you already possessed, now you cure malaria and—"

"Yes." Bianca cut him off.

"And tell me, Mistress. What do you know about this disease?"

"I know that it kills your family. It can kill Francesco—and you."

"Not me." Pursing his lips, he touched the cross that hung round his neck.

"I wouldn't be so sure, Cardinal."

The cardinal leaned over the bed and clamped his hand on her arm.

Bianca didn't think. She'd noticed the open jar of fragrant oil on the bedside table as soon as she'd walked in; it was good quality, something she'd like for her workroom. Now she grabbed it and flung it in his face. As he stumbled back, she picked up a salve from the same table. Digging into it with all her fingers, she balled up a greasy wad and threw it at his robes. "Don't touch me. And if you give your toxic cures to Francesco again—"

"You witch." The cardinal scrubbed at the stains on his robes. The dark oily blot only grew bigger.

"Bianca?" Francesco rolled his head on his pillow, opening his eyes. "What's happening?"

"You have a visitor. Your dear brother." Bianca bent over the bed, making sure to keep the cardinal in sight. His hands were fists, but he didn't move to touch her. "He was just about to leave, weren't you,

Cardinal? Or would you like to tell Francesco what you just called me?"

It was a risky ploy. For all she knew, the cardinal didn't care if Francesco learned his mistress had just been called a witch. Francesco, though, was regent for their ailing father, and the cardinal wasn't. The look Ferdinando cast Bianca was full of fire, but the man turned to go. Muttering something, he slammed the door behind him.

"What did he call you?"

"Never mind." Bianca wrapped her arms around Francesco. "It's all right, love."

"He's gone?" Francesco leaned back on his elbows, and Bianca helped him sit up.

"I don't know why he even came. Did you summon him?"

"Of course not. Maybe the servants?" Francesco drew a raspy breath. "He hates you. I'd never ask him here. He'll have heard I was sick. He's a vulture."

Bianca shivered. That was the cardinal, a big red scavenger, circling. Always watching, with a vulture's keen eye, but this time she'd sent him running. "He does hate me," Bianca agreed. "Now sleep, don't try to talk. When you're better, we'll get you out to Poggio; you can rest in the countryside." The cardinal wouldn't show up at Francesco's hunting villa, beyond the civilized walls of Florence. If he did, Bianca couldn't answer to what she'd do.

18
Desperate Women
1574

The day Cosimo died began like any other. Bianca slipped unnoticed through the back halls of the casino just after dawn, picking up a flask and some bottles, then opening the garden door. Within, her private sanctuary was bursting with springtime flowers. It had to be the most peaceful place in the city, she thought, and not for the first time. It wasn't until she was crossing her garden, dewy sprouts brushing their tender leaves against her skirts, that the bells began to toll, Santa Maria del Fiore and San Lorenzo first, then the other churches across the city. Bianca froze. Calls to prayer never rang out this early. This was something else. The bells' doleful rhythm could only mean one thing: death.

Beyond the garden wall, voices began filling the streets. Bianca closed her eyes, letting out a deep breath. It couldn't be Francesco; she'd seen him last night. He'd been healthy, though tired, his last bout with malaria several years behind him. Cosimo? He'd been growing weaker, unable to breathe easily at night, leaving Francesco with more of his father's duties. Mourning bells would toll for a grand duke . . . or for a royal wife. Joanna was ill again, her weak spine twisted in what must be unbearable pain. Every time Bianca saw her she wondered how much longer the woman's body could keep going. Either way, father or wife, Francesco would need Bianca, and the cures she'd been trying out again on herself for the past month would have to wait. She retraced her steps, turning her back on the garden's hopeful buds.

By the time she emerged onto the street again, a crowd had begun to funnel toward San Marco, the church's doors now open wide, and also the Duomo. Bianca pushed against the flow of people until she reached a side entrance to the ducal palace. She waited for Francesco in their apartment. He could be there soon, or it could take him hours to arrive.

She'd barely had time to select a book and settle on the bed to stare, unseeing, at its pages before the door burst open.

"Bianca." At the sight of her, relief rushed over Francesco's face. He hurried to her side. "I was hoping you'd heard the bells. It's my father. My God, Cosimo is dead."

One tear rolled down Francesco's face. Was he mourning the loss of his father, or was he grieving for himself and the future that awaited him? Bianca pulled him down onto the bed beside her, both of them sitting with their backs resting against the pillows. His body, pressed to hers, quivered with tension. Francesco, now a duke. The grand duke of Tuscany, inheriting the title won by his father's efforts. And Bianca, the grand duke's mistress.

"I can't stay." Francesco reached for her hand. "I have to go. My duties . . ."

From the dazed look on his face, she doubted he knew what those duties even were. But being held by his mistress right now certainly wasn't one of them.

"Francesco, your father . . ." What could she say? Florence had looked up to a devoted Cosimo, but she knew Francesco wasn't the only person who thought of the grand duke as cold. Should she say, "Your father was proud of you"? The ambitious man had commanded armies, but also countless artists, styling Florence as a city of political strategy and of paintings and sculpture. Francesco might add "science" to those accolades. But was Cosimo proud of his son? Probably not. More likely he'd feared what would happen to Florence in the hands of his regent. Francesco was far from being the governor of state his father had been. Then again, at least Francesco, not Ferdinando, was the heir. Bianca shivered to think of the cardinal with more power in his hands.

"I'll wait for you tonight." Gently Bianca disentangled her fingers from his, cupping the back of his neck to pull him to her, inhaling before letting go. "Until then, be careful. Your brother soon will be in Florence."

"He's not welcome. I have no time for him." Francesco shook his head. "Bianca, a dozen people are waiting for me in the palace chambers, waiting to make me a grand duke, after my father. My father's embalming—I don't care much for it—but I have no choice. But tomorrow, I'll still be the same Francesco married to the same Habsburg who has yet to birth an heir."

Bianca nudged his shoulder with hers. "Go, Francesco. But meet me later in Via Maggio. You'll still have the same mistress, waiting for you in the palace you designed for her." She kissed his cheek. "For us."

"And that's where they'll have to look for me when they want their grand duke."

"Or in the casino, busy with his alchemy." Bianca nudged him again. Francesco tried to smile, and Bianca did too. If the past months were anything to judge by, being duke would leave little time for science. But she hoped, for his sake, that's where he'd be found.

During the last weeks of spring, a full day's work behind her, Bianca pushed back from her table, stretching her arms and rolling her shoulders to loosen the tension from hours spent over her notebooks. Cosimo had died just over a month ago. Since then Bianca had hardly seen Francesco, he busy in court—sometimes with Joanna by his side—and she spending hours bent over a chamber pot or soaking in a bath, weathering the effects of whatever cure she was testing that day. She was proceeding much more carefully than she had the first time with Angelica. She'd thought about trying the same treatment again on herself and tracking how her body reacted. Instead she started over again, in the comfort of her garden shed, trying infusions from flowers as well as leaves, harvested at different times, steeped in different solvents. But she'd need to keep experimenting, with tinctures and extracts, too, to develop an artemisia medicine that a body could keep down, without the crippling nausea. With artemisia, that'd be half of building a cure. This part she certainly could test on herself. As for the other, testing her herbs' ability to fight off malaria, she still needed people with the heat disease to take the treatments. She was ready, or almost ready. But who would be her patients?

Deep in thought, Bianca shut the garden gate behind her. Crossing a street, she hesitated, stepping aside for a group of women coming from the market, some of them burdened not only with baskets of fruits, cheeses, and meats, but with children in slings or perched on their hips. Bianca didn't envy them, these tired women who faced their own mortality each day, pregnant or with infants, scrounging for wood and water, bartering for food, fighting illness. They knew what sickness meant, for themselves and their children. They'd do whatever they must to not orphan their babies.

Bianca paused. In the Sick House in Venice, she had almost always treated men. But if she wanted subjects who'd be willing to take her cures, willing to risk the unknown in order to stay alive . . . motherhood or even just the practice of surviving, Bianca reflected, gave some women the courage to try anything.

The young mothers passed out of sight. Only one woman remained, standing alone against the monastery wall. Older than Bianca, but probably pretty once. Sharp cheekbones, her eyes set deep inside their sockets, with a narrow face, but alert. Her dress, fine still, a shimmering red silk, was better suited to a palace social event than here. Many a wealthy man who'd just come from such a gathering would notice this woman right away. Hip cocked, face half hidden in a tattered shawl, she scanned the street. For a second her gaze met Bianca's, her shawl slipping so the evening light caught pox scars marring her face. The heat disease probably ran rampant, too, hidden and untreated, among women like her. She stepped toward Bianca, then pivoted. Walking up the street, she slipped into an alley. Women knew the price of life and the price of death, and none were more desperate than the city's prostitutes. Desperate enough to do anything to stay alive.

Crossing the square, Bianca darted down the same alley and soon had the woman in sight again. Bianca followed her to a stone building, two stories high, with only a small sign outside, *Welcome*, with painted-on stripes—a signal to customers that whores for hire lived there. The woman opened the door and stepped inside. A muffled cry, then a silence that stretched for minutes before the door closed.

Bianca marked the cross streets, then retraced her steps, already mentally cataloguing what treatments she might use in a place like that. When she returned tomorrow, she wouldn't want to come unprepared.

The next day she stood outside the door. The basket in her hands held bottles of tinctures and distillates, the ingredients for poultices, a few powdered herbs, and pages of notes—years of work, packed with care. She waited a moment, listening. No laughter or music rang from within. Distant but clear, someone wailed. She knocked.

The woman who cracked open the door was the same one she'd seen on the street yesterday. She still wore the same red dress. This close, the disfiguring welts of some sickness on her face looked fresh.

"I'm sorry, we're closed." The woman stared at Bianca. "And you are?"

"Here to help." Bianca tapped on her basket. "And you can help me."

The woman's eyes traveled over Bianca, her clothes, her body. "I doubt we can." But she didn't close the door. "You should go to Madame Sclera on the far side of the city if you want employment. Her house is clean, no sickness. Here, no man has passed through our doors in weeks. Anyone who enters leaves in a coffin."

"I understand," Bianca said. "Yourself excepted, it seems. You had the heat disease, I can tell. But you've recovered?"

"You say so." The woman stifled a cough in her sleeve. "I'm well enough to mind the others. I go out and buy what food we can afford." A scream echoed from within the house. The woman paled. "You'd best leave, mistress, whoever you are."

"My name is Bianca. I'm a healer. I have cures."

"No one can cure what we have." But the woman eased her grip on the door.

"I think I can." Bianca took out a flask from her basket, holding it to the light so the woman could see, then tucking it in again. "I've been working on a cure, using it on myself." She'd woken feeling dizzy from the distillate she'd taken last night. Despair had swept over her then, less from the lightheadedness than from the fear that her cure wasn't ready. But all the strongest treatments had some side effects, especially those with wormwood. Dizziness was far better than vomiting or stomach cramps. Besides, she'd woken this morning with no other symptoms, not even a headache. She would go slowly, carefully. But she had to move forward. "I think I have a treatment that can save your friends' lives."

"Why trust you?" Harsh though the woman's voice was, hope glimmered in her eyes. "You're not like us. You've never been desperate or starving, have you? You're a lady. We're the last ones someone like you wants to save."

Bianca held out her hand. "I'm a woman, too, and a healer. I want to stop the heat disease, whoever has it. My mother wanted the same thing. But before she could cure it, she died of it."

"Sounds as though she might have been a witch," the woman said. "Sounds as though you might be too."

"I'm not, and neither was she. But if a witch could save your life, would you choose death instead?"

The woman hesitated, then shrugged. "Come inside. But we can't pay you." She pulled the door wide, allowing Bianca a good look at her. Bone thin, the flush of sickness colored her face and neck.

"I don't want payment, I just ask that you trust me. I want to treat you." Bianca opened her hands. "I'll save as many lives as I can, and I'll learn to make better cures. I wish I had a perfect cure to offer you now. But I won't know what to change until I've tried what I have on those who need it."

"Meaning us." The woman pointed to herself. "You'll try it on us? No, I imagine your rich lord and lady friends wouldn't stand for sampling your cures." The smile she offered Bianca was dry and grim. "You need someone desperate, and that's who you've found."

The woman clearly grasped Bianca's plan. This time, Bianca wouldn't take risks on anyone who hadn't asked for it, but she was nonetheless experimenting. "I can promise nothing," Bianca said. "But I think you know the alternative to treatment for this disease."

The woman held Bianca's gaze, then turning, motioned. "Follow me."

Bianca entered the front room. Like the woman's dress, it had once been fine, but now only peeling wall designs and stained couches remained. A square cut-crystal mirror on the wall showed countless reflections of Bianca's pale face and the woman's flushed cheeks. The woman led her quickly into a corridor, then into the first of the sickrooms, large and reeking of urine and vomit. The beds crammed inside held several women each. In the nearest bed, a woman barely more than a girl called out, while beside her lay another, her face a mass of red swelling. Across the room one woman sat with her back braced against the wall, head down as she coughed into a basin.

Next to her, swathed in blankets and softly moaning underneath her breath, a form lay motionless.

What to do first? A poultice for the woman with the swollen face, steeped thyme for the one coughing. For the one under the blanket, something stronger still from her garden, a new distillate. Bianca set her basket on the floor and knelt between the beds.

Would the woman who'd let her in notice that her hands were shaking? But it was the contents of the basket that had caught her interest. "You brought all your potions. To help us?"

Nodding, Bianca poured a citrus-smelling liquid into a cup. She turned to the motionless form and drew the blankets away from the bed and the sheet back from her face. A girl, barely the age Bianca had been when she first came to Florence. Pressing her hand to the girl's chest, she counted breaths, watching the sheet over the body stir a little. The panting girl probably had fluid in her lungs. Gently she raised the cup to the girl's lips. The first drops slid down her chin. Then her tongue moved, and she swallowed.

"If she lives, we'll thank you. If she dies . . ." The woman in the red dress sighed. "Certainly none of us can offer her any other fate. If that's me in the bed in a few days, it'll be you who cures me, or no one."

Bianca looked around the room. Who next? The dark eyes of the woman in the red dress met hers. Bianca dug in her basket and held up a bottle. "Here, this is another tincture I've prepared. Drink it, please. It will bring your fever down. And then, can you bring me water and clean cloths? And—"

"We have nothing, can't you see that?" The woman took the bottle, unstopping it. Eyeing the liquid within, she wrinkled her nose at the sharp scent. "Strong." But she swallowed the contents in one gulp, coughing some of it back up. "I'll get you water, yes, but there's not much else here."

Hopefully it'd be enough. Bianca would pack a larger basket

tomorrow. It would be up to her to bring these women back to life. If she failed, they were dead anyway. The next chapter in her fight against the heat disease had begun.

19
House of Sin
1575

Rain slapped against the stone walls, rattling the wooden shutters of the brothel windows. Thunder broke, cracking through the sticky heat that held all the women in its grip. Bianca swiped her hair, brushing it back with one hand and clamping it in place. Even that small action was more than many of these women, fevered and weak, could do to help themselves.

The room she stepped into now teemed with restless cries. Someone cried out for water. The air reeked, malaria forcing the infected to empty their stomach and bowels anywhere they could. Even with the clammy heat, some shivered as though their veins flowed with ice. Who to fear for the most: the ones who burned, or the ones who didn't?

In the year that had passed since the woman with the red dress first led Bianca into the sickrooms, time had started to lose its meaning. Weeks or maybe months after that first day, the last of the malaria cases seemed to be over, some cured, most ending in death. The woman in the red dress who, though gaunt and scarred, had made it through, told Bianca where to go next. When Bianca knocked at the door of the infected house two streets over, hammering loudly to be heard over the moans coming from within, the whole cycle started again. As soon as one woman recovered, another fell ill and took her place, sometimes to recover in turn, sometimes to die. Bianca was now treating women in a third brothel. Or could it be her fourth? And how many more would she need to treat until she could save all the women—or even half? So often they died before she could track the effects of her treatments. She needed to follow the progression of the illness from its beginning to the edge of death, but there were too many sick that needed cures now. Their cases all urgent, Bianca's remedies often came too late. When she'd gained the first woman's trust at the original brothel, Bianca had expected to learn quickly, to save so many lives. She'd saved a few, and had learned a great deal more about what death looked like. And she'd learned, again, what her mother had also known: finding a cure could take a lifetime.

Today, like so many days, Bianca leaned over to wipe phlegm from one woman's face with the corner of her apron, the sour smell of acids and half-digested foods making her gag. Swallowing and closing her eyes, she breathed in through her nose until a wave of nausea left her.

She had had successes. A woman's fever breaking, another eating for the first time in days. All were recorded in Bianca's notebooks. She'd learned more this past year than in all the years before. Still, she hadn't found a logic to her findings, she hadn't found the artemisia cure that would work in every case. Strong doses as in extracts, those that should have done the most good, often caused the women to vomit before their healing properties could take effect. Bianca had a whole notebook devoted to infusions she could give to reduce the nausea caused by the cures. The back pages, though, were full of jotted questions. Did this woman vomit because of the cure or because of her sickness? What if the women's bodies were right to reject the distillates? What if, by making the teas palatable, Bianca had convinced a woman to take a dose that was so strong it could harm her? Or could that woman have been healed if Bianca had been able to treat her earliest symptoms? Bianca knew little about the first hours of the illness. She saw patients only when they were already in its hold. Without being able to dose them as the illness progressed, she could only guess at the body's ability to strengthen, much less recover, if given the medicine early on. Most women were either too close to death to survive, or not sufficiently strong to take the medicines. In the end, most died.

Of the three women in this room, one, Bianca knew, wouldn't make it. She had hope for the other two. The patient next to her, sitting up in bed to sip a cup of brew, had taken Bianca's latest cure. It was a weaker dose. Still, Bianca hadn't been sure her patient could stomach it. If the woman could keep it down, she'd get stronger. But the look on her face told Bianca everything she'd just swallowed was trying to come back up again.

Brisk steps rang outside the door, someone with heels. Bianca turned. This woman had recovered a month ago and, like others before her, had stayed to help. "Another of the sickest is refusing to take the infusion," she told Bianca. "Please, hurry."

Bianca sighed. And then there were those who, rather than taking the cures only to vomit them up again, refused to swallow the liquid altogether. She made her way around piles of soiled cloths, to the back of the building with its smallest rooms. Shards of several broken cups littered the floor.

"Mistress." A woman strained to raise herself to her elbows, coughing blood onto dirtied sheets. "It's just bitter brew. I want medicine." She clutched Bianca's arm as Bianca knelt by the bed. "It's not making me better. Women are dying here."

Bianca eased her arm free. "Listen, please, you must be patient."

"You're not a doctor, are you?"

If this woman didn't trust Bianca, it was because she'd been raised to place her trust only in men's hands. "Please, let me show you what I have." Taking a cloth bag of herbs from her pocket, she cradled the fragrant fabric, holding the sack close to the woman's nose. "Smell, it's mostly artemisia."

“Artemisia. My mother used to grow that.” The woman studied Bianca’s face. “Is this the medicine?”

“It’s a kind of medicine. Not everyone receives the same—there’s different strengths.” She stood, crossing to the small hearth where someone had set water to simmer that morning. “You see,” Bianca turned to the sick woman. “I pour hot water over the dry leaves, and to this I add a little distillate.”

“Distillate? What’s that? I want the best.”

“This is the best. I’m giving you some steeping herbs in the mixture, the way most people take it. Look, I’ll try it myself.” Bianca crumbled the dried leaves into a bowl, carefully pouring the hot water over them. Squinting into the pungent steam, she added several drops of the distillate she carried in a vial in her pocket. “We wait a minute for it to mix together,” she said. The woman nodded. Bianca breathed in the steam. She had tested this mixture on herself already. She knew it wouldn’t cause a healthy woman harm. As for this woman . . . Bianca poured the blend into a cup. She sipped, then lowered the cup, wiping her face. “None of what I have will kill you.” Bianca sat on the edge of the woman’s bed. “Will you try it?”

The woman drank it in one gulp, choking it back.

“Shall I sit with you while you take it every morning?”

With another small nod, the woman lay back against a pillow.

At the end of the day, Bianca wrote down her notes. The woman whose mother had grown artemisia was sleeping peacefully. A woman in the front room had died.

Fifteen minutes after closing the dead woman’s eyes, Bianca reeled toward the brothel’s exit, pausing at the closed door just to lean against the solid wood. Not that anything besides a bed could offer her the repose she needed. She told herself that the woman who’d died today wouldn’t have lived this long if not for Bianca’s care. Still, she’d start making mistakes if she didn’t get rest.

Bracing herself for the onslaught of heavy rain, she opened the door. Water ran in the street and hid the buildings on the other side, now lost in a heavy gray mist. Fog engulfed the road, distorting voices, so that at first when she heard her name, Bianca turned to look behind her, toward the rooms she'd just left. But no, this was a man's voice, coming from the street, not the brothel. A form loomed in the haze, a colorless shadow that darkened to red as it approached. She flinched, but sharp fingers grabbed her arm. She felt her knees caving.

In those robes, anyone in Florence would recognize him. And Bianca, though she hadn't spoken to the man in years, only needed to see his half-familiar features, Francesco's nose and eyes transposed over sharper cheekbones, to know who gripped her arm even as she sank to her knees in the street. The sneer on his lips, though, was one she'd never seen on the face of his older brother. What was the cardinal doing here? Was he visiting the San Lorenzo basilica, his father's grave? Surely he couldn't have been following her. But the smile he wore was the smile of a man who'd won a prize.

"Cardinal? You're here . . . the Medici tombs?" Bianca staggered away, trying to stand only to slip to her knees again in a slush of mud. The cardinal's fingers loosened for a heartbeat, then tightened again as Bianca tried to hang onto her basket, lifting it clear of the river that had once been a street. One hand on the basket, the other arm trapped by his fingers, she couldn't get back up out of the muck, or even wipe the mud and tangled hair from her face. It was the cardinal who finally wrenched her to her feet.

"I wouldn't worry about my family's crypt, Bianca. You'll never see it. Let's talk about you, here, shall we? A brothel, Bianca?" he hissed. "Not only did my brother find himself a mistress, he dragged one straight from the gutter. What am I supposed to think you were doing in there?" He tugged at the basket with the hand that wasn't clasping her arm. "Hmm, sweet-smelling santolina, were you making balms?"

"You'll blame me for tending to the sick, then?"

He spat on the ground. "In a whore house?"

She lifted her chin. "I'm a healer."

His nails dug into her wrist. "I am, too, but I don't need to go into a brothel to find my flock."

"And what of those in need? Are they free to find you?" The woman who hadn't wanted to take Bianca's brew had blamed Bianca for not being a man. But a healer like the cardinal would have done that woman no good. Bianca's jaw clenched. "You practice your skills in Rome or Florence and no one questions you, a man in red robes. Yet many who need saving have never seen your face. Let me go and I'll tell you what I'm doing."

If the cardinal heard, he gave no sign. "I'm going to ask again, Bianca, a brothel? In an alley in Florence? Look around," he said, waving toward the street. "How many women from the court do you see here?"

Clearly it didn't matter what she said. "Just take me to Francesco. That's what you're going to do anyway, isn't it? So you can tell him where you found me."

"And he'll put you aside, as he should have done years ago."

Would he? Bianca would show him the cardinal's red handprint marked in bruises on her arm, she knew that much. If the man held her any tighter her fingers would go numb. Francesco might not be happy about what his brother had to tell him, but she'd never once seen him take the cardinal's side on anything. "I suppose we're about to find out which one of us knows your brother better."

The cardinal's only answer was to start walking, pulling her after him.

Water splashed over her ankles as she walked behind him, the shape of his carriage rising from the gloom. The waiting horses shivered in the rain, heads low, barely stirring as the cardinal tugged at the door and pushed Bianca in, climbing up after her.

Carriage secured, he finally let go of her arm. Bianca set her basket between her feet so she could rub her hand over the marks his fingers had left on her skin. Her wet skirts clung to her legs, capturing every draft as the carriage lurched forward. The rest of the way they rode in silence.

In the palace, gusts of moist wind blasted through the halls, brushing against the worn wall tapestries, cooling the clay floors. Bianca's skirts left trails of filth on the ceramic tiles. The cardinal kept a few distasteful paces between them, nostrils flaring as he tried to protect his perfect red robes from Bianca's sickroom stink. *That*, Bianca thought, *was probably the only reason he'd let go of her arm.*

If the cardinal thought he was marching her toward certain doom, he was wrong. Francesco would know she was no whore. What he'd think of the treatments she'd tried in the brothel, though, she wasn't sure. And how would she explain the cures she'd been testing when, as far as Francesco knew, she still had no place to work other than a corner of his casino?

Flinging open the door to Francesco's private chamber, the cardinal pushed Bianca inside. The smell of disease followed her into the room. Bianca stared straight ahead, her heart pounding. The windows hung ajar, their shutters partially open to the blowing rain. Francesco stood looking out at the whirling stormwaters. Only when his brother spoke did Francesco turn.

"I found her in a brothel." The cardinal's voice boomed as if filling a packed theater.

Bianca spoke up. "I have a name."

"A name, Ferdinando." Francesco's voice echoed in the spacious room. He looked tired. If he wasn't careful, stress would make him sick again. "Bianca was born a year before you were, little brother. Treat her with respect, please. And she's under my protection." He pushed past the cardinal to Bianca's side. "Are you hurt?" He held her hands, taking them to his face, his nose wrinkling. "*What* have you been doing?"

She stepped back but he still held her hands, his grip as gentle as his brother's was harsh. "I was visiting—"

"A brothel. In an alley near the Medici tombs." The cardinal stood tall. "How did you not know of this, brother? Our father knew every single thing that went on in Florence, and who was doing it. Or am I to believe you knew, and did nothing?"

"Unlike our father, I don't set spies on those I love, though I have no doubt you would, if you were in my place. Not all Medici are cut from the same cloth, brother."

The cardinal drew breath to speak. Bianca cut in before he could. "Francesco, please listen to me. The women there are sick with the heat disease. They need treatment. Men like your brother refuse to see that, but I do."

"Yes. You would." Francesco's face was still, a mask Bianca couldn't read. He moved his eyes to the cardinal. "And so, brother?"

"I snatched her away from the whores, to save her from herself."

Bianca wrapped her fingers round Francesco's. "Francesco." She lowered her voice to a whisper. "Tell him to leave, I can explain."

"Explain what?" the cardinal cut in. "Your cult-like alchemy? Or," he turned to Francesco, "science, you call it?" The cardinal spit out his words. "Francesco, our father is barely in his grave for a year, and you'd let her disgrace your name like this? I put up with her when you were regent. Don't think I will now that you're grand duke. Punish her as you should, or don't, but I'll be watching. The next violation this woman commits will be her last."

Bianca closed her eyes, letting the voices wash over her. She didn't need to see the cardinal's furious face as he stomped out of the room.

In the silence afterward, neither spoke. Then Francesco sighed, finally letting go of her hands. "Well, Bianca?"

She met his eyes. "The women at the brothel, their sickness is real.

They're the first patients I've had in years to treat. I've come a long way with my cures. Perhaps," Bianca whispered, "further than you realize. But I need to know if what I'm doing is enough."

Francesco's mouth formed a thin line. "Isn't that what hospitals are for, love? And besides, you've cured me. What more proof do you need?"

"Hospitals don't experiment." Bianca clasped her hands in front of her. "Listen, Francesco. You haven't been sick enough, and that's just it—I can't learn on someone who'd likely recover anyway. Even with your last illness, yes, your fever was high, but it only lasted a few days." She shook her head. "My aunties thought that cures used for hundreds of years would save the sick today, and yet people died. New is what we need when the old fails, but only the desperate will allow me to try things that haven't been tried before. The brothel whores are desperate."

"I see." She wanted him to touch her. Instead he crossed the room, turning his back to the storm so he faced her, the window behind him. "Bianca, I had no idea you were working like this." His face looked drawn. "My men say you're never at the casino, that you'd given up your science. And you never talk about it anymore. How can you expect me to understand you've found a way to cure these women if I thought you hadn't been working?"

This had been her fear—not that he would cast her aside but that, in trusting her, he would finally require that she in turn trust him, telling him everything. Francesco's science was much more chaotic than Bianca's, but he'd know she couldn't have made any progress unless she had a space to experiment. He was right; she never talked to him anymore about her search for a cure. If she had, she'd have had to explain about the garden, and why she'd needed to leave the casino. Whether he'd blame his men or Bianca herself for that early sabotage, Bianca didn't know. Her science was safest if she practiced it alone. And as long as her garden workroom remained a secret, nobody could take it from her.

But then she pictured her shed, her stores of herbs and chemicals taxed to their limits since she'd started bringing cures to the brothel. How much more could she do if she had a sturdier roof, one that wouldn't leak on her valuable herbs? She'd tried so hard for so long to keep Francesco unaware of what she'd built for herself, yet she couldn't explain her need for the brothel without also explaining the garden and its laboratory . . . and her time there. Bianca counted off the years in her head. A little over ten years she'd spent in the shadow of the casino, yet working outside its reach. Even though each season was different, her progress had been slow and careful. Twice she'd lost entire crops to pests and disease. One summer, mold had gotten into her stores. Plus she could barely work in the winter, bundled up in thick wools and blankets, with only bundles of straw to keep out the draft. Some years she'd barely been able to learn anything. Francesco couldn't even begin to comprehend the dedication required when working with plants, or the burden of fear that grew heavier each time she took a cure herself or gave it to another, untested. Bianca was dealing in life and death. He wouldn't understand unless he saw it for himself, just as, so long ago, she'd needed to see his casino before she could truly see him. Perhaps once he knew all she'd accomplished, she could even enlist his help. First, though, she'd have to share her secret.

Bianca breathed deeply. "Francesco, I don't care about being seen in a brothel." He had to understand that first. "These women are on their deathbeds. And yes, I'm helping them." She joined him at the window, taking his hand. Would he resist? No; he wrapped his fingers in hers. "That's been my sole work for years. All this time to develop the cure that will save you."

"Has it been that long?" A shadow crossed his face. "It's ten years since I married Joanna. Imagine if I'd married you instead." He pulled her closer. "Maybe I'd have known about this mysterious science of yours—and helped. You wouldn't have needed a brothel then."

Bianca raised an eyebrow. Typical Francesco, to assume any project he was involved in would succeed. If indeed she'd been his wife for ten years, she'd probably have accomplished nothing. All she said, though, was, "Let me show you."

"So where would it be, these cures of yours? A secret workroom? Some palace closet?" He kissed her cheek. "I thought I knew all the secret places."

"Nowhere in the palace." Bianca held his gaze. The time had come. "Do you remember when you pointed out Michelangelo's garden? The day we first met."

Francesco's smile broadened. Then her words sank in. "Wait, what are you saying?"

"The door to the grounds of the casino wasn't locked. There's a little shed. And now a garden."

A look crossed his face, part surprise, part . . . what? Perhaps he wished he'd discovered the artist's studio himself. Outside, thunder rumbled.

"And I have his tools."

"But what has this to do with the brothel? Unless . . ."

"I've made it mine. Michelangelo's garden is my laboratory now."

"And that," Francesco said, shaking his head, "is where you've developed this cure? When I thought you'd lost interest. I've wondered, but I didn't want to ask, in case you felt . . . I don't know . . ."

What was he thinking? For all he knew, what she'd given him each time he'd gotten sick could have been made in any kitchen. He might have asked, but at least now she knew he'd thought about it. Bianca softened her tone. "I'm never losing interest, Francesco. Malaria will be cured, and I'll be the one to do it. The brothel's part of it, a necessary part, unless you want to give me others with malaria to try my cures on." Bianca paused, then swallowed. "I've devoted more than half my life to this already. Do you remember how young I was when you left to court Joanna, and I had to make my way alone? I was barely a girl then. I'm wiser now. The brothel's been an important step. You'll see I haven't given up my science; I just have another place in which to do it. If you want to understand it all, Francesco, I can take you there tomorrow. I can show you where the remedy for your heat disease will be born."

20

A Secret Shared

Early the next morning, the calls of magpies and larks greeted Bianca and Francesco, a dawn ruckus as short-lived as the rain that still clung to the leaves of her herbs. Within an hour, the birds would be gone, settled in nearby woods to avoid the new day's heavy after-storm heat. The mice and snakes that scuttled along the overgrown path at Bianca's step would soon be hidden. To Francesco or anyone else who didn't know the place, this part of the garden would seem abandoned, the only sign of human life the bits of fabric stuck in the brambles leading to the shed.

Bianca guided Francesco down the path, not faltering even when a thorn caught her skirt and pulled another loose thread free. She'd told him to meet her outside the casino at dawn and he'd been waiting there at first light, though she'd half expected, and half hoped, that some duty would have called him away. Inside the garden, she led him through the even rows of her perennial artemisias, and past the patches of annuals she was training to release their seeds for next year's crop. He followed, silent but wide-eyed. She kicked aside some shards of glass, remnants from her first attempt to carry a box of cylinders and stirring rods while avoiding resident hawks. She knew where their nest was now, and how to sidestep it, as she'd learned the garden's other secrets, like the hidden holes of loose grit and slippery moss-covered rocks. Now, the two stood in the middle of her refuge.

"Bianca, how . . ."

"Listen, Francesco, this has been difficult for me." How could she make him appreciate what she'd achieved here? "Your whole life in the palace you had what you needed, what you wanted, so you could study your alchemy." She took his hand. "I've had very little, only the hope that someday I might have a cure."

"I still don't understand," Francesco said. "You seemed happy that year you spent in the casino with me. When I left for the Habsburgs, you insisted you'd keep working, but I never saw you there again. All the time I've put in there, all the scientists I've gathered together, and you'd rather do your work among weeds?" He leaned over, dropping her hand so he could pick a single chamomile flower. He tucked it behind Bianca's ear. "A nice place, Bianca, but this is where you do your science?"

"I'll show you." Bianca turned down the path. The trail took them past some woody stalks, the morning light slanting through the leaves. Crossing under a tall arch of jasmine, they walked to a fragrant part of the garden, full of rosemary, sages, and thymes—the plants' shallow roots signaling quick growth after their leaves were cut. Francesco reached over to pick whorls of purple-blue flowers, handing them to Bianca. "What's this?"

"Clary sage. Its scent is almost as strong as sweet freesia in the early spring." Bianca smiled, pointing to a clump of tall stems with green-yellow leaves. "Even extracts of lemon verbena yield a fragrance."

"There's no end to your secrets, Bianca. Show me the rest?"

Just a few steps ahead, chamomile grew with calendula, feverfew, santolina—and the artemisia, its harvest ready at the start of flowering.

They stumbled through thick vines toward the mound of morning glory from which, between trellises, one window of her laboratory glinted. The eastward-facing shed rose in front of them, their shadows cast toward it. The worn boards and peeling paint looked dull in the early morning light. The vines and woody brush choking the shed added to the gloom, even as a lark's joyful call rose up from the weeds.

Francesco twisted the handle on the building's weathered door.

"I keep it locked." Bianca stepped forward, inserting the rusted key that always rode in a pocket at her hip. For a moment she stood there, the metal growing warm in her fingers, the scent of mint rising from the patch she'd planted just outside the door. This was the last moment in which the place would be hers alone. But she couldn't keep it to herself any longer, not if she wanted to be able to explain her cure and how important it was to test it. She unlocked the door and pushed it open.

Walking into the room, Francesco kicked away a pile of discarded stems. The dusty shadows gave way to thin slivers of light from a window. He coughed, clearing his throat as the room's musty smell hit him, turning to skim what must have looked to him like nothing more than shades of darkness. But the shadows delineated different worlds, each with a separate language. Almost ten years ago Bianca, too, had entered this room for the first time. How had it looked to her then? Now all she could see was her familiar space, her haven. Only Bianca knew the history and purpose, say, of the small table positioned next to the door, strewn with mounds of fresh herbs and clods of soil—long, scraggly, woody stems, but also tender shoots with delicate leaves. The wormwood piles released the strongest odors, sage-like but not as sweet, pungent and musty, Bianca reminded herself, to those who didn't associate its odor with healing. But all smelled like hope to her.

Tucked in the corner on the far side of the room, emetic herbs occupied a low shelf, their surface-dust undisturbed. The shed's middle table offered a different language of healing in the strong acid odors of its stacks of pale green stems, soft with fine hairs and feather-like silver leaves. Small heaps of yellowish disk-like artemisia flowers, the first of the season, littered the surface, a contrast to the tidy table across the room, an artist's workbench with its thick veneer that Bianca polished at the end of every day, keeping it spotless, wiping away any dust or dirt. Darkness preserved the aromatic herbs, but windows at the shed's far end cast light on her distillation chamber, an alembic with its glass column clamped to a metal stand. It marked the space as a scientist's. And so, the geometry of the room, the progression of healing herbs to potent medicines, precisely mirrored the journey of the woman with the malaria cure.

Francesco's gaze settled first on the teeming shelves, then the old cloths that hung from the walls. He pulled open the drawers packed with papers, quills, and inkpots. One overflowed with her notes. "You really have been working here." He took in the glassware on a nearby stand that had no other home. "I didn't even know there was a shed in this garden. How did you find it?"

"I cleared some of the brush. The shed was buried underneath." She shrugged, smiling.

"From the outside, it looks like it still is."

"That's the idea."

"Why?" Francesco turned to face her. "You still haven't said, Bianca. Why not let this place be found? Why keep everything you do a secret? Why shame yourself sneaking off to a brothel instead of just telling me what you needed?"

"Would you have believed me?" Bianca raised her hand as he tried to speak. "No, listen, Francesco. If I'd told you that your men were sabotaging everything I did, poisoning my cures, then threatening me when I caught them, that I felt unsafe every time I walked in that casino door, would you have listened?" Even now, almost a decade later, saying aloud what had happened made her heart speed up. "Or would you have said I was overreacting, a woman causing trouble? You wouldn't have—couldn't have—dismissed all your scientists in order to keep me."

"My men? Sabotage?" Francesco reddened. "They wouldn't have hurt you. I told them to protect you. When they told me you'd left, none of them mentioned—"

"Of course they didn't. They were probably terrified that I'd tell you, but if I had, I'd have had to watch my back every day for all these years in case one of them took his revenge. I didn't know how long you'd be with the Habsburgs, and I couldn't afford to waste time making cures that others were tampering with, trying to undermine my every step. If I hadn't discovered what they'd done, and had taken one of the cures with their poisons in it—"

"Bianca, no—" Francesco took her hand.

"I had to find my own space. Then you came back. You were so busy with the wedding, and I'd built myself what I needed here. Why should I have told you anything?" Shaking her head, Bianca pulled away. "Nothing had to change. If your brother hadn't interfered at the brothel, I'd be treating those women right now, learning what I need to know in order to someday cure you. If even one man had stood up for me, all those years ago in the casino, maybe I'd have made progress there, but one didn't. So I made my own way. And that's the way I've worked—alone."

"I don't know what to say." Francesco braced both hands against the surface of her worktable, a helpless look on his face. "I had no idea any of this was going on. But I suppose that's what you're saying, isn't it? I didn't know what my own men had done, and I should have. I didn't know you were still working, and I should have. What do you want me to do now, Bianca? Do you want me to punish them?"

Some men wouldn't have had to ask that question. Bianca's father, for instance, could be harsh, but if anyone had even so much as threatened her mother, that man would have been lucky to merely wind up in chains. Such treatment wouldn't help this situation, though. And Francesco, thankfully, wasn't her father. "I want to continue as I've started," Bianca said. "That includes caring for the women in the brothel I'm treating until the malaria has run its course."

"If you're seen there . . ."

"I won't be. No one's seen me till now. Maybe your brother followed me, I don't know. I'll be careful. Once the illness runs its course, I won't return." Listening to her own voice, she realized she spoke as if she had a cure after all. "Surely, Francesco, you wouldn't have me leave these women to die, just to make your brother happy."

Francesco's jaw tightened. "Cure them, then. After that, though . . . I don't know. I have to think about what people say, now that I'm grand duke."

"If you don't want me in a brothel, then give me what I need to do my work here." She'd still require patients, and she had every intention of going out and finding them, somewhere, but she'd have to be more careful, treating fewer cases and so learning far less. If Francesco was going to make her pursuit of a cure harder this way, the least he could do would be to help her build a larger workroom. "Keep looking around. See what I've done, and what I don't have that any scientist in your Florence should. And then you can make up for your men's bullying by helping me get it."

Francesco nodded. He walked farther inside, peering and sniffing, as Bianca lit candles ahead of him. The worried look on his face gradually gave way to wonder. He stopped in front of one of the half-formed busts Bianca had pushed into a corner out of her way. "This might be a relation of mine, on old Cosimo's side of the family," he muttered under his breath. Turning to Bianca, he said, "And what of the old artist? He's been dead ten years now. Have you found any of his designs?"

She paused. "No, nothing like that." A few half-drawn sketches, unsigned, but those felt like a gift the artist had left for Bianca alone.

Her own discoveries were hers to share, but the ghost of the artist she sometimes felt here could choose to reveal himself to Francesco or not.

"A pity," Francesco said.

Bianca sighed. Couldn't he regard her lifesaving alchemy with just a little of the awe he lavished on the artist?

Now he turned to her library, but even there, he ran his fingers over the spines of the texts written by others, not her own notebooks. "These books, then, you brought all of them here? You've read them?"

"Many times." Was that so astonishing? "Francesco, it's what I've used those books *for* that I brought you here to see."

Francesco lifted a cloth, revealing squares of marble, but also a few of Bianca's drawings. He picked up one. "Artemisia," he whispered to himself, "rosemary, thyme." He fingered a sachet hanging from the edge of a shelf. "The sweet scent of artemisia. That's the smell that clings to you some nights, isn't it? And other herbs, too." He glanced over the rows of tightly bound bundles, hanging from the one strong rafter. "Is that lungwort? And catmint—what do you do with that? Still, more artemisia than anything. These distillations smell of it." He turned to her, taking in a deep breath, then letting it out slowly. "You did all this?"

Did he see any assistants, ready to spring out from behind a dusty table? "I've had ten years, Francesco." Bianca tried to keep the sharpness out of her voice. "Keep looking. There's more."

Francesco crossed to the cabinets and pinched some herbs on a shelf, the aroma wafting upward. He tugged at a drawer stuffed with lenses and parts of dried cuttings that spilled into his hand. He clasped the leaves and roots with a familiarity that told her maybe he'd studied some of these same plants. Did he recognize now how much she'd done here?

She moved to stand beside him, trying to see the rooms as he saw them. Yes, he should have cared more about her science, he should have questioned his men when they told him she'd stopped coming to the casino. But had she done so much better, understanding his? She knew of his ampoules of anti-poison oils and his flasks of lime water and medicine syrups. And his porcelain cups that he'd showed her in the casino, so pearly-fragile, his face bright with pride. Yet she'd never bothered to ask what his alchemy of stars and metals and porcelain could tell her about her own, or how much he in fact already knew about the things she was studying. Perhaps she could have learned more from him if she'd trusted him sooner with her own work.

And maybe, now that she had, he was finally starting to see her. Gazing again at her books, the reams of knowledge lined up neatly with their spines facing out, Francesco said, "Not everything here was written by others, I see." The narrow shelves were stacked with her notebooks, her scribble transformed into science. "These are yours?"

"Yes, those are my notes. But the information won't make sense unless you see how I got it."

Still, he took down one of the notebooks and began thumbing through it. "You write down everything. The time of distillation, the temperature, the solvents, even . . . what's this? 'Climbing vines splayed on different sides of the shed?' You mark where you grew the plant? Does that make a difference?"

Bianca nodded. "Francesco, that's one reason the work has taken so long. Every growing season I can only do so much. How much sun a plant gets, what's in the soil, it all makes a difference. A plant grown in a droughty soil behaves differently from the one grown in full rain—or shade. Everything has an impact on the plant's potency, and I have to know all of it. I can't leave that to chance; I have to test everything. Imagine if your arsenic came in many varieties and you matched each with different porcelain clays. How long would it take you experimenting to make a single perfect cup? Do you see why I've needed all this time? I started testing in the brothels a year ago. Before then, I didn't have a single recipe I could trust. Now I do, but I still don't know nearly enough about how to use it. That's how it was with my extracts, but I'm making distillates, now, carefully, systematically. Your brother wants me to stop practicing my science. That would mean years' worth of work wasted. And then years of experiments just to rebuild what I've done."

"But why not just make as strong a dose as possible?" He touched the alembic. "This could give you a very high concentration. Why not distill to its full potency and be done?"

"Because I want to save you, not poison you. Francesco, this is about using the least amount of substance to yield the greatest amount of good. Too potent and the medicine becomes hopelessly bitter. Long boiling times means that sensitive, maybe protective, chemicals in the medicine are destroyed. High doses can kill."

Francesco swallowed. "Kill?"

"I don't know, but think of it like your arsenic. You put the tiniest amount in your porcelain, your glazes, yes?" Francesco nodded. "If you used more, one drink from your cups would kill." They might do so anyway, but that was her opinion, not his. "The wormwoods are poisons if used too freely. I'm looking for a balance and part of that is making a distillate that the sick can keep down. Kill the sickness, not the body. It's an art."

Bianca opened a worn leather satchel, then took Francesco's hand, pressing his fingertips to the grooves that once held gold leaf in the form of initials. "Subtlety, Francesco, sensitivity, look." Taking a small metal rod from the bag, she slid it toward him. "The young men here were artists, and maybe scientists, too, understanding how to do more with less. Like with this tiny tooth chisel. Small and fine for precise work, but yielding great beauty."

He sucked in his breath. "Michelangelo's?"

"I imagine so. The man used instruments like anyone else, and I found this among the shards on the floor. Delicacy is what such art requires, and science as well." Surely, if it had been the artist's, he wouldn't mind her using this one piece of metal he'd once held in his hand. Bianca rotated the chisel as Francesco stroked its edges. How to explain so Francesco would understand? "Listen." Bianca put down the chisel and looked him in the eyes. "Here, I'm making cures, cures in this tiny room. And right now the brothel is the only place I have to really see which brews and extracts, my distillates, best fight this sickness."

His eyes flicked from the chisel to her face. "You think you're close?"

How she wished she could say she was. "It will be years still before I have a cure I can trust. Years if I am lucky, and if I can keep working." She pulled out the chair she sat in to take notes, motioning for Francesco to sit. He did, flicking open the notebook she'd left there yesterday and flipping through its pages. "I haven't been able to follow the entire course of the sickness yet. Let alone test my cures at each stage. I'll need many more patients, and much more time. But . . . if I had those things?" Was Francesco ready to think bigger than he ever had? She let her gaze follow his to the page she'd filled with details of sick women. Better to look there than at his face. She could pretend, for one more second, that the answer was *yes*. That he understood her science.

She wasn't here to pretend, though. She turned to face him. "I was in that brothel because I have something real to offer those women, something I've created over years. Whatever the cardinal tries to tell you, what I'm doing is right and good, and if I'm allowed to keep on, I'll save lives. Otherwise, more women will die there. The brothel will become another tomb, so close to the Medici's own San Lorenzo. Now do you see what I meant when I told you I've come much further with my cure than you realize? Do you see why I can't let your brother stand in my way?"

"I can see you must continue your work," Francesco said slowly.

"And, yes. You've done a great deal with very little, and I can help you do more." Francesco looked around the room. "Solid walls with more clay and straw to fill in gaps, better yet, stone, some new plaster and a new roof, bigger alembics, you'd like that, yes? And maybe assistants. You've probably been pushing yourself too hard." He took Bianca's hand, then looked into her eyes. "My brother, though. If he knows you're still going out to places like that, he'll do everything he can to turn the Church against me. He already challenges me for being less than faithful to Joanna."

"Avoid him for a month, and then you can tell him I've quit the brothel. I can't abandon the women now, but the heat disease has almost run its course there; those I haven't managed to cure in a month's time will be those who are beyond saving. And then, yes, help me make this laboratory all that it should be." Meanwhile, Bianca would keep an old cloak in her workroom and a dirty kerchief to cover her hair for her trips to treat the city's forgotten women. Her healing in the future would have to be more furtive, slowing down her progress. But for a better space, this was a price she could pay.

"Fine." Francesco bit his lip, closing her notebook and looking up at her. "I can avoid a conversation with him for three or four weeks. But I'll need to tell him soon that you're finished. He's going to make things difficult for us, Bianca." A half smile spread over his face. "Sometimes I think you living in the Via Maggio palace isn't enough. I should have hidden you away, outside of Florence altogether." Francesco stood so he could slide his arms around Bianca's waist, keeping his eyes on her. "And it's time your daughter joined the other young ladies in court."

Bianca was silent for a moment. "As you like, Francesco." Would Virginia greet this news gladly? Bianca didn't even know. But he was right about the cardinal. "I'll keep on with my work here, and we'll both stay out of your brother's way." Her secret might be out, but her science would continue for now, uninterrupted.

21
Sickness at the Via Maggio Palace
1576

The Arno River divided the Via Maggio palace from the rest of Florence, the mercurial air holding its heat greedily during the day, winding its way around the solid stone palace building and walls at night. When Francesco had first shown Bianca the elaborate design for the inside of the palace, she thought it would never be finished. But he'd been serious about getting her out from under his family's scrutiny, and Via Maggio had been her private residence now for over a year. She watched from one of its windows as heavy rains pummeled the pavement below, stirring up sediment and debris. If Francesco hadn't restored the Via Maggio palace, if they hadn't had this refuge to share together, she might be sleeping in some closet in Pitti Palace while dodging Joanna and the cardinal's ever-present spies. Francesco was sick again, but under Bianca's own roof this time.

The disease had struck quietly, a redness in Francesco's eyes he'd blamed on late hours spent writing another angry letter to his brother. Then it reached his lungs, a hacking, dry cough that woke both of them when he'd stayed a night with her several days ago. She'd asked him if he wanted to return to the Pitti Palace and have her treat him there, but both of them knew he'd be better off at Via Maggio. Though the message he'd had her send to Pitti explaining his whereabouts had been vague, Joanna would know exactly where he was. Would

Virginia, now part of the Medici court, know too? She was one of the palace children now, but what went on in the prim, quiet little girl's head was as mysterious as ever. She'd become Joanna's shadow. Did Virginia know her own mother was Joanna's rival? If "rival" was even the right word. However long malaria kept Francesco here in Via Maggio, Joanna, Bianca suspected, wouldn't miss him.

Bianca turned from the window, the sound of driving rain following her as she walked to the corner of the bedroom where she'd set up a basin of water and handfuls of herbs for infusions. A thunderstorm this early in the day, not even noon? Francesco would have taken it as an omen. Wringing out a thin cotton sack, she filled it with a poultice. Later she'd add warm oil.

Although not as sick as others she'd treated, this was certainly the sickest she'd ever seen Francesco. Fortunately, she'd had enough of her cures ready in the solid-framed building that he'd built to replace her old shed. Damp couldn't ruin her stores of herbs in the new structure, and she was sure their potency from growing in rich soil was that much greater now. All this was due to improvements in the sections of the garden Francesco's men had made, tilling and mulching. The soil was so deep, she could push her arm into it and show Francesco her muddied sleeve—a mark of the fertility that enriched her plants. She would have been there today, despite the rain, if she didn't have to tend to a sick grand duke.

Though perhaps if she'd pulled herself away more often she'd have seen much sooner that Francesco was sick. Had the illness come so quickly, or had she just missed the signs? Since that first cough, gnawing heat and splitting pain had devoured him, malaria twisting Francesco's body into a shivering heap. The poultice she'd just prepared, now with warm oil, should make him more comfortable, hopefully cool his fever, but her duke was still a long way from well. If she lost him . . . Bianca shook her head. She wouldn't lose him. But saving him would take time.

Bianca set the wet poultice and bowl on the bedside table, smoothing his bedclothes, then sponging the cool water onto his forehead. He blinked up at her, unseeing. She'd always loved his eyes: large, chestnut brown. When Virginia was born, Bianca had hoped the baby's hazel-colored eyes would warm and darken, but no, they'd stayed as cool and bright as Bianca's own. Bianca touched a hand to her stomach. Her flesh was soft still, the change she'd first sensed months ago still little more than a thought. A thought she'd avoided as long as she could, a thought she could dismiss when working. But the baby was real. And, surely, this baby would have his father's brown eyes.

Those eyes were glassy now, and Francesco's breaths labored. She touched his forehead, but nothing would wick away the burning heat. Half-conscious, he pawed the side of his head, fingers smearing the beads of sweat on his face. She picked up his shaking hand, holding it tight. He'd teased Bianca about her alchemy, her herbs. "Your medicines are like pouring hot water over dirty laundry." Those infusions could help him, more than the little vials of sulfur vitriol that his courtiers would have him swallow.

Francesco thrashed around in the bed, a shudder traveling down his leg, before he called out, "Water." Suddenly he sat up, eyes wild and wide. "Bianca," he rasped. "My stomach . . ." Bianca dove for a bucket, positioning it just in time to catch the stream of bile from Francesco's mouth, both of them breathing in his foul air. More brew she'd have to get down him to offset what he'd lost. What else did she have in her cabinets here? Something to settle his stomach? Bianca reached for her mint. Or should she use the fennel she'd taken herself that morning? Her hand still hovered between the two when a growling sound from the bed made her breath catch.

Rolling his head back, Francesco groaned, his intestines spasming as brown liquid drained his bowels, leaving sticky solids in his linens. Tears rolled down the side of his face, pooling in his ear. Propping him up with more covers to sop up the sticky mess around him, she knelt by his bed, bowing her face and pressing her cheek against the cool wood of the frame. Who did she trust to hold her prayers? She looked up at Francesco. She had no one besides herself.

Opening a cabinet, Bianca reached for the distillate. She added it to the infusion she'd left on the side table, her hand shaking. Treating a lover or treating another patient—strange how much it mattered. Francesco lifted his chin as Bianca trickled each drop into his mouth. Gently she laid the warm oil poultice on his stomach, then brushed her hands across the backs of his. Hands that had stroked her back, that had wrapped around her, drawn plans to create her new garden workspace, reached for her after he'd been away. Bianca ran her fingers through his matted hair, but when he turned his head restlessly and tried to reach for her, he barely had the strength to lift his finger. Bianca pressed one palm into his, her other anchored over his heart, his chest gasping with erratic breaths. He burrowed deeper into the sweat-drenched bedclothes, writhing. Then, quiet. He lay, calm, as if death suited him.

But he couldn't die. She wouldn't let him. She said his name once, then more loudly. "Francesco."

His eyes, flickering open, were the clearest she'd seen them today. But his voice was weak. "Bianca? I'm so tired."

"I know." She sat beside him on the bed, holding his hand and ignoring the foul liquid she'd have to wash from her skirts later. "You've been fighting hard. But you can hear me?"

He shifted his head on the pillow. "I don't want . . . any more."

"You can't give up." She'd seen it before in patients, even ones who hadn't had to wage this war as many times as Francesco. After days of struggle, rest and an end to pain became the only things they wanted, and the promise of a cure couldn't change their choice. They chose to die.

Francesco might recover this time, but malaria lurked in his future.

He knew it and Bianca knew it too. From where he lay, weak in his own filth, would clinging to life seem worthwhile? Bianca thought back to this morning, the fennel tisane she'd swallowed upon waking, the way her dress had seemed just a little tighter when she pulled it on. Softly, she stroked Francesco's face. She waited till he looked at her. Those eyes. "You have to live," she told him. "I'm going to have a baby. Ours."

At first she thought he hadn't understood. His face was completely still, his shuddering breaths his only movement. Then slowly his lips curled up, his cheeks losing some of their gaunt shadows, his eyes lighting with so much warmth that Bianca felt herself redden. He tried to take her hand again, but she took his instead. Gently, she placed it on her belly.

"A son," Francesco said. "With you."

When she pictured a baby born with those brown eyes, it was a little boy's face she saw in her mind. A son, born of a strong Capello woman. Joanna still hadn't had a son, though she kept trying, each pregnancy wearing even more heavily on her frail body, her twisted spine. Even if the Habsburg princess did produce a boy, would he be strong enough to live? Bianca had never meant to carry the Medici heir. But she couldn't mistake the hope in Francesco's eyes.

"A son," he said again.

"So you see, Francesco, you have to live."

"Live." Could the red in his cheeks be, already, just a little fainter? "Of course I'm going to live," he told her. "You're curing me, aren't you? You, the mother of my heir. Joanna never lets me hold my babies, but you will, I know you will. I can't wait to see him." He finished, still a little out of breath. "I hope—I'm sure—he'll have your eyes."

22
A New Garden
1577

Bianca dressed quietly so as not to wake Francesco, still asleep in the bed she'd just left, the bed he'd commissioned for them—along with everything else at Via Maggio. She peeked into the crib in the next room, smiling at Antonio's creamy face and thick hair. A Medici face, and, when he was awake and exploring the world, deep brown Medici eyes. For once, as she slipped through her bedroom door, both Francesco and Antonio slept without stirring.

What a relief it was to move freely, without carrying the weight of a baby, without the swollen feet and aching back that had made her work in the garden so much harder. More than a year after her son's birth, she still didn't take for granted this feeling that her body was her own again. But Francesco had loved her pregnant, running his fingers along her taut curves. By the time Antonio was born, the shadows had faded from under Francesco's eyes and he'd become well again, ready for his son. Even though just months ago Joanna had given birth to a boy, it was still Bianca's Antonio whom Francesco laughingly, happily, lifted with his calloused hands.

For Francesco, becoming a father again had been easy. Bianca envied him. For her, the first several weeks after Antonio's birth late last summer had passed in a daze worse than that of her pregnancy. She'd labored most of the day and night to bring him into the world, and hadn't slept for weeks after. Born small and, at first, refusing to nurse, Antonio couldn't find comfort anywhere until he'd gotten used to sucking goat milk from a glass flask. Francesco liked to feed the baby, but he also slept right through Antonio's cries, and Bianca never knew which nights he'd be able to spend at her palace. Many times during those first weeks she'd thought of the nameless women who'd left their babies at Sant'Elisabetta's gates, babies who nuns like Angelica had raised as their own. Had Bianca been any other man's mistress, she almost could have done the same. But then, she'd look at little Antonio and see herself in him, so much of that curiosity and imagination she'd searched for in her daughter, Virginia, who'd become a mannered young girl in the Medici court. Never did Virginia run outside with her hair unbraided and soil under her fingernails, as Bianca used to do. Antonio, though, at nearly a year old, seldom seemed to want to take his fingers out of her potted plants on the terrace. Could she truly wish he hadn't been born? Soon Francesco had hired nursemaids for her and her routine each day had grown easier. On mornings like these, when she was able to retreat to her garden sanctuary leaving Antonio safely sleeping, his birth was no longer something to regret. She had her family, and she had her freedom.

Tightening her cloak, Bianca slipped down the hallway and stepped out into her carriage. Soon, Antonio would want to know where she was all day. "Working," she'd have to say. When he was older, would she bring him with her? The only garden he'd ever know would be the one Francesco had helped her build, with its solid-framed building instead of her old shed, its plots of soil Francesco's hired laborers had cleared of bramble. Antonio would see beds of moist, rich soils, with extra loam and silt added for her greedy herbs, so different from the wild jumble of woody plants Bianca had first tamed.

Half an hour later she arrived at the casino, protected now by a solid windbreak of cypress trees Francesco had installed. Passing through the strong, carved gate that had replaced the creaking original, Bianca fixed her eyes on the newly roofed building, its heavy door unlocked by light, shiny keys. Whatever she'd wanted, Francesco had provided. And so what had taken almost ten years for her to half finish, Francesco's workers had completed in nearly two. If Bianca touched her tongue to the soil in her beds and tasted that phosphorus was missing, Francesco's men would haul in chicken muck. Or, sliding slick clay between her fingers to form a ribbon, she'd know that cow manure was what was needed to transform it into soft, stable clods. It had taken several years of cool muddy springs and humid, stagnant summers to build up the rich soils, but Francesco's landscapers and engineers had done what she'd asked, giving her drainage ditches as masterful as anywhere in Florence.

Opening the door of the once-shabby garden shed, Bianca surveyed the laboratory Francesco had helped her create. A different man might have given Bianca more, but Francesco had given her enough. The shed a distant memory, what she had now was palatial by comparison. Brushing her hand along a table, she could gather only seeds, no splinters. Tinted lacquers added a warm glow to the tables, as well as an impermeable barrier for any chemicals that might spill. The two workrooms were now three. Real vents, and plenty of them, exchanged the air around the countertops set with alembic distillers and bulbous glassware. Gone were the smells of experiments without good aeration, the rotten egg reek of sulfur, the sourness of nitric acids, the tang of acetic chemicals. Instead, fresh garden air flowed through new windows, with handcrafted shutters that sealed tightly when closed. Details like these made Bianca's heart lift, though Francesco hadn't been able to stop there. Cabinets with inlaid stone? She'd laughed when she'd seen them. "Spend your money on building me more plain work surfaces," she'd said. "Though I'll happily spill my mixtures on anything you give me." Everything, Francesco had said, must be lovely for her.

Now she set down the bag she'd brought from her palace and hung her cloak on a peg. Even that was more ornate than she needed, a bone hook carved by one of Francesco's artists. Though it made her smile, it was also a reminder that the space was no longer just hers. Francesco could follow her here, curious and questioning, ready with advice as to how to prune perennials whose names he didn't even know, pushing his alchemy ideas when the only evidence supporting any of them lay in the mysterious constellations of his astrology charts and in cryptic texts. There were days when she had to remind herself how close she'd come to losing him in his last sickness, or she wouldn't be able to keep the harshness from her voice when she stopped him from ranting about some new thing. She'd promised herself to stay gentle. And mostly, she did.

Today she got in several hours' work before Francesco appeared. She was weeding a flowerbed outside when she felt his shadow. She sat back on her heels.

"I come out here expecting to find you brewing the cure that will help me live forever, and instead you're in the dirt pulling weeds." Francesco frowned. "Can't one of the assistants I hired for you do that?"

"I like pulling weeds." The assistants had been Francesco's idea. The two young men, serious boys from well-to-do families, were sometimes useful, but Bianca still preferred to do most things herself. "Caring for a garden is how you get to know its secrets. The plants in this bed, Francesco, do you see? So close to the ground, with leaves that sit perfectly into the woody stems, the roots swelling with starchy sugars. And I ask how is it that it survives the winter, the sweet brush feel of its plump leaf evident even now."

"Why do you need to know how it survives?" Francesco waved his arm, encompassing with one gesture her entire garden. "It does, and you harvest it."

"That's what makes me who I am," Bianca said. "I ask questions."

"Me, as well. But grander ones."

Taking his hand, Bianca pulled him down to kneel beside her. "The answers to yours are in rocks and stars; mine are right here. In the garden, but also in the rising steam of my alembics. The twirling air cools into clear distillates and I find new medicines, but to do that I have to understand the parts of the plants I use and how they affect the herb's potency. Every plant's powers peak differently, in every season. It takes time."

"Stars." A grin on his face, Francesco gestured to the sky.

Bianca raised an eyebrow. "Maybe."

"I still think you should experiment with my metals, too." Francesco pointed toward the casino. "Just a touch of gold dust in your soils. The arsenic I use in my porcelain—"

"The arsenic is going to kill you, after I've gone to so much effort to keep you alive. Have you forgotten the apprentice you brought me who'd managed to get just a bit of it in his mouth? I've seen firsthand what it can do, and that boy was fortunate I had some clay to give him." Even so, Bianca had doubted whether she could save him. "I suspect you're still not writing down your experiments, either, or keeping track of your powders so that doesn't happen again. Test and record your results and you avoid errors. The best alchemists are scientists, too."

"So you say." Francesco shrugged. "What about the men you use to test your medicines on, though? What protects them from error?"

"You mean the three you brought me in the past year who died before taking any of my cures?"

"Bianca, love, listen." Francesco stood, brushing dirt off his knees. "I bring you what patients I can. By the time I hear of one, though, the illness is already serious. The malaria progresses so quickly."

Francesco still didn't understand her insistence on testing everything, and carefully, even when she reminded him how her medicines had saved his life. His reluctance to let her have patients meant that she'd mostly had to settle for learning as much as she could from the plants themselves.

"If you went out looking—or if I did—malaria cases would be all too easy to find." In fact she had gone out looking, and had treated a few more since she'd revealed her garden to Francesco. Not enough, though, and the men he'd brought her were poor substitutes for her brothel residents. What could she learn from patients who died before she poured her first treatment through their lips? Nothing—and Bianca didn't have time to waste on *nothing*. Francesco may have flung himself full-tilt back into his casino again, but every time Bianca looked at him she pictured her lover lying weak and helpless in a bed, sweat-drenched, depending on her.

Glancing up at the sun, Bianca braced one hand on a knee and stood. More time had passed than she'd realized. "I know you wanted to fire a batch of porcelain today, didn't you? And I'm planting root-stocks today."

Smiling, Francesco leaned in to kiss her cheek. "I'll see you tonight."

Before he could leave, though, one of Bianca's assistants came rushing toward them. "Madam Bianca, Sir." He bowed his head. "A messenger just found me as I was passing by the garden gate. He asked me to give this to you." He glanced at Bianca, then Francesco. "It's about your wife."

"I'll be inside," Bianca told Francesco.

Grim-faced, Francesco nodded.

Bianca was sorting a harvest of red nettle when Francesco called to her from the garden, his voice heavy. As he trudged in and sat down across from her, Bianca searched his face. He looked gaunt, years older than he had in her garden just a few minutes earlier. One person alone could make him look so dour. "Is Joanna sick again?"

"Of course. Is she ever not?" Francesco bowed his head, folding his hands. There was bitterness in his voice, the bitterness Bianca heard only when he spoke of his wife. "They don't think she's dying—this time. Each sickness leaves her weaker, though. But it's not just her, Bianca."

"The baby?"

"Yes. Filippo too."

Bianca reached across the table, taking his hand. After Antonio's birth, Joanna had finally had a son. But the boy was ill more often than he was well. "I could help Joanna, help both of them. Do you want me to go to her?"

"Go to her, and she'll write to my brother, and he'll cut you from my life as neatly as you snip wilting blooms from your herbs. And I can't lose you. You're all I have."

Cut the cardinal off instead, Bianca almost said. All these years later, she still remembered the man's sharp grip on her arm, his eagerness as he hauled her in from the brothel to the ducal palace. She couldn't say those words, though. She'd said enough against the cardinal. Even now, mentioning him had drawn a curtain over Francesco's face.

Bianca touched his chin, making him meet her eyes. "You have an heir, Francesco."

"Antonio." He sighed. "If Filippo dies I still have a son, is that what you're saying? And you're right, and Antonio is strong and bright, while Filippo . . . Filippo is his mother's."

Bianca knew what he meant. All of Joanna's children shared something, a certain docility, a bland acceptance of their own fragile constitutions and their simple lives at court that Bianca feared Virginia, too, had adopted. Bianca needed Joanna, needed her to mother those children. But only Antonio possessed the curiosity that the heir to a dukedom like Florence, much less Tuscany, should have.

Francesco stood, coming around the table to take her into his arms. "Antonio's so . . . he's so *alive*, Bianca. Is it wrong for me to say that, while little Filippo might be dying?"

"Filippo is Joanna's." She pressed a finger to his chest. "Antonio is yours."

"Ours."

"Ours. And you have him, you have an heir, whatever happens. You married Joanna as you were required to do. And you have a son. Two sons." Poor little Filippo. "Go to your wife now," Bianca said. "I'll prepare what I can and have it sent to her. If the cardinal asks where it came from, I don't know, say a friend of yours in Venice." She would pore through her notes, creating a strong treatment for Joanna. The woman needed strength more than ever—comfrey extracts to ease the swelling in her spine, infusions of willow bark for the pain in her crippled legs, gently distilled licorice for her gut. And Bianca needed Joanna, whether Francesco fully realized it or not. Joanna, mother to all the royal children and Francesco's partner at court, fulfilled the duties Bianca had no interest in. She bought Bianca time to do her work, and time, above all else, was crucial to her science. Even if, as Francesco believed, Joanna would get well from this current bout of sickness, time might be running out for his wife. And that meant for his mistress as well.

23
Joanna Laid to Rest
1578

Bianca jumped, dripping ink onto the page before her as carriage wheels rattled on the cobbled street outside, a sound too bright for a funeral. Setting down her pen, she walked to the window that opened onto the cortège below. Francesco, dressed in the thick mantle he'd told her scratched like a hair shirt, sat atop a black mare. He rode behind an open gilt-edged carriage. Gone were the usual cushions, their lush velvet deemed unsuitable for a time of mourning. Besides Joanna's ornate coffin, the carriage carried another shaped like a miniature cradle for her dead infant, what would have been her second son—the child that had broken her, almost a year after the sickness that, it turned out, had heralded the end.

The rest of the procession shuffled around the corner onto Via Maggio, pipes and horns droning, Medici flags flying, on the road right beneath her window. On a muggy day in April, Bianca couldn't be faulted for standing there. With the streets swept clean of any sewage and debris, perfume from the urns of lilies below drifted into Bianca's rooms. She hadn't seen Francesco since Joanna's death, but surely he was the one who'd insisted his wife's cortège pass along this route. There he sat, ramrod straight, his jaw tense, riding gallantly behind Joanna's casket like the staunch companion he'd never been for her in life. Long before he could possibly make out Bianca's dim shape in a window, his face was angled directly toward where she stood. A true companion would have kept his eyes on the coffin. Bianca leaned farther out over the sill. Francesco could have chosen to keep his gaze on the people lining the streets, or on the casket ahead of him. Instead, he let his eyes find hers.

Bianca waved. And Francesco? Yes, there, he'd lifted his hand, dipping his chin in the slightest bow. Bianca kept her face still. Surely many in the crowd knew she'd be here, but Florence wouldn't see her smiling. What was there to smile about? Gossip might have painted Joanna as her rival, but Bianca had done the little she was allowed to do in order to keep the hard-faced woman alive.

The entourage moved on even as the din faded, the intensity of the church bells reminding Bianca of the woman's painful passing as they commended Joanna's spirit to somewhere other than here. Birthing the boy had been only the latest of Joanna's trials. Despite her spinal deformities, she'd managed eight pregnancies, each more difficult than the one before. Still, Bianca had heard whispers. Joanna might have survived this last birth had she not fallen and gone into early labor. More quietly and to the point, maids and gardeners wondered how Joanna had wound up crumpled and broken at the bottom of the palace stairs.

When she'd first heard two servants whispering to each other that Francesco had pushed his wife, Bianca aimed such a glare their way that both had scuttled from the palace hallway without another word. As more rumors circulated, though, and as Francesco failed to appear with an explanation, Bianca had begun to feel uneasy. More likely he'd pushed her into bed, not down the stairs, but the end result of Joanna's death had been the same. He'd fathered the now-dead child, and was responsible for her crippling pregnancy, if not directly her dying. The man could be selfish, thinking about heirs more than about Joanna's well-being. But then who was she? How many times early on had Bianca unlocked the large gate beneath her rooms in Via Maggio into the damp underground passage to the Pitti Palace, squinting in the yawning darkness to light a candle, sneaking along it to meet Francesco while his pitiful wife was confined in the last months of another difficult pregnancy, or busy raising children, including Bianca's own daughter?

But Bianca never would have hastened her death. Francesco must know that Bianca had tried in the last year to aid his wife, if only by befriending a kitchen cook to give her some extracts. He couldn't have thought that this funeral was what Bianca wanted.

The city, certainly, grieved for its grand duchess, filling the streets to witness the procession. Francesco's slight nod to her told her he saw the same truth she did: the city mourned an angry, bitter woman. What else could his face tell her, though? She wanted answers she hadn't yet received. Busy though he'd been with court duties, couldn't Francesco have made time to seek out Bianca, if only to tell her that all the rumors she'd heard were lies? He would come to her tonight though, surely. And when he did, he'd lay to rest any feelings of doubt she might have.

Of course, it was also possible he'd have a question, too. One that came with a ring.

Bianca opened a palace window wide enough to catch the last rays of sun. Today it would set for the first time over Joanna's tomb. How long would Francesco wait before asking Bianca to be his bride? She'd had time enough these past few days to decide on what she wanted. If Francesco needed her publicly bound to him, then she'd ask for more power for herself—the ability to test her cures, and the freedom to manufacture them. Marriage was a high price to pay but, she suspected, a necessary one. Francesco's last sickness should have convinced him she needed more freedom to find a cure. But whenever she had broached the subject over these many years, he would mention his brother and tell her the risk of the Church's censure was still too great. Logic wouldn't win him over, not in the face of his fear of the cardinal and his own pride. She had to find out if a fair exchange—a wedding for space to test her cures—would.

Bianca turned away from the window. She wanted to return to her notes, but she couldn't get the questions out of her head. What if she hadn't cured him in her palace at Via Maggio? If Francesco had died, would Joanna not have fallen—or been pushed—and be alive today?

It was past midnight before Francesco's heavy steps echoed on the stairs. He appeared at the bedroom door, face drawn, shoulders slumped with the weight of mourning, though he mourned, Bianca suspected, what his marriage should have been more than what it was. Sitting on the bed with a sigh, he kicked off his heeled boots, ten hours shuffling around in public having erased all their sheen. It took him a full minute to realize that Bianca was still sitting at her dressing table.

"Bianca? What's wrong?"

"I need to know." Crossing the room, she sat next to Francesco, looking into his eyes. What she wanted was to touch him, to smooth the worry from his tired face, but she couldn't, not yet. "They're saying you pushed her, Francesco. That you'd been fighting, that she flew out of your bedroom, that you followed her to the top of the stairs, and then . . . I know you hated her. I did, too, at times. But you didn't . . . ?"

"I've heard what people are saying. But I swear to you, I followed her and she fell." Francesco sat forward, reaching for Bianca's hand. Did he feel it stiffen as he wrapped his fingers around hers? "True, I didn't love her as I should have. I gave her what she needed, though, didn't I? It's not my fault she wouldn't let me touch her, wouldn't let me talk to her. We were in her bedroom and I was asking her what she wanted, and she just left, running. I tried to stop her. I took her arm, she pulled away. I hung on and the stairs . . ." Francesco shook his head. "She broke free of me, sort of flinging herself, and the stairs were right there."

Bianca could see it; she could see it so well. Francesco never understood when people resisted him, when they didn't like him, when his offers for some absurd project were rejected. Had he no idea what his keeping a mistress must have meant to the woman he married? Of course, Bianca was as guilty as he was, or guiltier. She did know, and she let Francesco into her bed anyway. Francesco the impetuous, quick to anger and quick to apologize. But not quick enough this time, when it was too late for forgiveness.

She shook her head. "Joanna never should have fallen down those stairs. If you'd thought for a second or paid attention to where you were going, she'd still be alive."

"Maybe. But I didn't kill her, not on purpose. You thought I could do such a thing?"

Had she? Looking at his face, hearing his voice, Bianca realized how misguided her doubts had been. He'd been so busy at court, and she in her garden. How long had it been since she'd really looked into his face? Had she forgotten who he was, this man she'd pursued so long ago, and won? "I'm sorry. I know you're upset." She slid closer to Francesco. "I knew you couldn't. But I had to ask you."

Neither spoke. Francesco brushed her cheek with his fingers. "I had something very different to ask you tonight. Now, after this . . . I thought I knew what you'd say. If you believed that of me, though, maybe I was wrong."

Bianca's chest tightened. Francesco had done his share of harm over the years, but when had he ever meant any of it? Now his eyes, searching her face, looked lost in a way she'd never seen before. She'd always known he wanted her; she'd used that desire plenty of times. But she'd never seen the other side of that; she'd never seen she could wound him. She knew what he'd been planning to ask her, of course she did, and she'd already decided on her answer. She had her conditions, but she'd try to make them without hurting him.

"Ask." Bianca lifted her face toward him. "I'm ready."

Francesco took her hand. "Are you, Bianca? Are you ready for my proposal for you to become my grand duchess?"

Grand duchess. The words would have delighted any woman. But Bianca wasn't any woman. "A proposal is never just a proposal. I know that, and I know what you want." All at once, the room felt stifling. She had known this was coming, but . . . Bianca stood, her hand still in his. "I'm not Joanna. This marriage would be different." She tilted her head toward the balcony. She needed to breathe. "Let's find some fresh air?"

Francesco followed her outside, sidestepping her potted plants. "I don't want you to be Joanna."

The faintest scent of lilies lingered in the air. She turned to face him, her back to the small table where, earlier, she'd sat reading over notes with a glass of wine, free from responsibility to the city or court or anything but her cure. "We've been together for a long time," she told Francesco. "You've given me so much."

"And?"

"And I want you alive." Leaning into his chest, she wrapped her arms around his neck. "I'm not marrying a dead man."

"Well, that shouldn't be a problem. You keep curing me." Francesco laughed, but the sound fell flat.

Bianca pulled away. "I can't cure you forever. You know that as well as I do. I have cures, yes. But when death truly comes for you, how can I fight back if I've never fought that fight before and won with any certainty? If I'm going to be your wife, you're going to have to accept that to save you, I need to test my cures. All you allow me are the dying."

Francesco watched her, his head still but his eyes following her as she paced. He put out a hand to stop her, taking her in his arms. "Just give me your brews. You don't need to check. Just use your common sense. I trust you."

She didn't relax into his grip. She couldn't, not yet. "Just give you my brews? That approach killed my mother, and probably yours." And, untested, the girl at Sant'Elisabetta. "You want the treatments people have been using for years, but for years people have been dying. And more will die today." Bianca stepped back, freeing herself from his embrace. "I've learned almost nothing about how the cures I have actually work since the cardinal found me at the brothel. I've been studying, I have ideas, I understand how to grow plants and use their medicinal properties better than I ever have . . . But I haven't witnessed any of it working. And you want me to use common sense? That's not enough, but even if it was, common sense alone isn't an option for me."

"Why not?"

"Because your common sense is valued more than mine. You play with ideas, build foundries, make porcelain with clay mixes and metal glazes." Bianca raised her hand, then let it fall on the rail of the balcony. Francesco twitched. "Men can guess; women have to prove themselves at every step. And I don't want to guess. I want to know."

"You don't have to prove anything to me." Francesco joined her at the rail, putting his hand on top of hers. "Just be my wife."

"Listen, Francesco. I know what I'm saying and what I need." Bianca slid her hand from beneath his to lift the abandoned wine glass from the table. She touched one finger to her lips, wetting it, so when she ran it around the rim, the glass rang.

"Venice glass, Bianca." Francesco would know; he'd bought it for her. "Beautiful, like you."

"Not like me." She tapped the glass. "It's delicate. It could shatter in an instant." Bianca held Francesco's eyes with hers. Did he know so little about her, even after all these years? "I don't shatter, Francesco. Understand the woman you want to marry."

"I do understand you, Bianca. I'm trying to. Only, I don't know what to say. What more do you want? I want you to be my wife. What can I do to make you want the same thing?"

"A cure is what I want—"

"And I, as well."

"Then it's being your grand duchess, not your wife, that I worry about. Our marriage could easily prevent my work. But it doesn't have to, if you're willing to listen." Bianca waited till he nodded. "That new villa north of here." Where he'd been spending the time he probably should have devoted to his pregnant wife. "It has space, yes? For outbuildings?"

"Pratolino?" Francesco frowned. "The buildings have been finished, yes, with fountains and galleries, but the park, no. It's going to be a wonder; I've hired the best engineers and architects, but . . . why now? You haven't been interested before."

"Francesco, I have, just not in your art, though I'm sure it's lovely." She could only imagine its scale, but that was just Francesco. "If I came along with you as your wife, though, I could use the grounds for my own purposes. I could set up workrooms, and a sickroom, a place where the diseased could come to me. And something else, the air is clear—a good place to heal."

"That's what these are for, isn't it?" Francesco patted the small clove sticks in his belt.

Bianca set the delicate wineglass back on the table and touched his hand. "Francesco, I know you think these sweet-smelling twigs help ward off malaria. But perfuming city air won't keep you safe. Look how sick you've been. In Pratolino's fresh air, if people are sick—and you know they are—it's clearly something else."

"But Bianca, love, even you have your fragrances. Your lemon, your . . ."

"Lavender?" Bianca shook her head. "Not to ward off disease."

"Very well. Cloves won't save me, then; I'll trust you. But others? When they see you bringing people there, they'll think you a witch."

She folded her arms. "I'm no more of a witch than you are."

"I know you're not." He tugged at her elbow. She kept her arms crossed. "But Pratolino is for play."

What would it take to make him hear her? "Play is for those who aren't trying to cure malaria, Francesco."

"Can't you do both? There's a water park, we can float in the deep swimming caves?" Bianca gave him a long look. Francesco flushed. Finally he nodded. "I want Pratolino to make you happy. If that means a sickroom, bringing people to you, then—"

"It does." She wouldn't mind hearing the warbling birdsong and hooting tawny owls and chirping crickets she'd find at Pratolino, but the only escape she needed from the city was a practical one. If the villa could be that for her . . .

"Then it's settled. We'll be married, and if you want to build your workrooms and sickroom there, well, I'll do my best to make sure my brother never knows." He reached for her and this time she let him, leaning into his embrace. Let him think he'd gotten the better part of the proposal, a prize after many long years' wait, a marriage, a grand duchess in a new villa. Let him believe her sickroom would be invisible. It wouldn't be, not at the scale Bianca intended it. A woman with a curing brew, one tested, and soon a Medici herself, could make the Medici name mean healing again.

24
Till Death Do Them Part
1579

As a girl, Bianca hadn't thought much of weddings. Her cousins would chat about the dresses they'd wear and the bridesmaids they'd have, but Bianca only remembered being bored by the talk. Her wedding to Piero had been, if anything, efficient. Bianca hadn't needed a veil or a church decked in roses in order to secure her ticket out of Venice, and Piero hadn't needed to dress his bride in white silk in order to bring a Capello to his bed. A grand duke's wedding, Bianca discovered, required much, much more than even white silk and flowers.

"We're already married," she reminded Francesco as they lay in bed together in her palace, a week before they would join hands and, in front of all of Florence, become husband and wife.

"Barely."

"Barely? We said our vows. Our wedding right after Joanna's funeral. Just us and that priest you found who was willing to keep his mouth shut. That was beautiful." Bianca drew a fingertip down Francesco's bare chest. "Plenty for me." That ceremony, in a private chapel and with a single priest, put a seal on what both of them had desired. Francesco would keep his promise to build her a laboratory at the new villa, and he had what he wanted too, the possibility of legitimacy for Antonio, his chosen heir even though sickly Filippo still lived. Their only nod to the weight of the occasion had been the massive ruby Francesco slipped onto her finger. Afterward, Francesco had waited months to announce their pending public wedding, but even that, Bianca suspected, had not been long enough. Francesco's brother, for one, seemed unsurprised but still outraged when he learned of his brother's coming public nuptials. "So the whore becomes a wife after all," had been the cardinal's response.

"You need a real wedding," Francesco insisted now. "*I* do. I've married the most beautiful woman in the world. She deserves to be recognized by adoring subjects." He placed his hand over hers, pressing her palm to his chest. "Can't I show her off to the world?"

"The only subjects I want to see are sick ones." She sat up just enough that she could reach for a cup of an herbal brew she'd left on a side table. She handed it to Francesco. Closing his eyes, he took a sip. "And just how adoring is this public of yours?" Bianca tapped his shoulder playfully, but the question was more serious than perhaps he knew. She didn't want a ceremony, and, despite what Francesco seemed to think, Florence didn't either. A lavish wedding—and more taxes to pay for it—would stir only wariness in those Francesco was meant to govern. Was he so oblivious?

Francesco laughed. "They'll be adoring if I tell them to be."

"Perhaps." Or perhaps not. But maybe she could earn their love. "Soon enough I'll be their hero. They'll take my cures, and they'll be glad you married a witch."

"Of course they will." Francesco blew into her ear until she laughed despite herself. Too many people wanted to give her that label. For as long as the women in her family could remember, healers with it in Venice had risked exile or worse. That was part of what had drawn her to Florence, and to Francesco. The Medici name would protect her. Wouldn't it?

Francesco sat up. "My witch. Have you settled on a dress? Show me."

"Your seamstresses have." Bianca slid free from the bedclothes and walked to the wardrobe, withdrawing a sprawling skirt. "Look." The thousands of pearls on her train made her eyes ache, but at least she'd talked them out of crystal beads and brocade bows.

Francesco stood up from the bed and circled Bianca. "You deserve this spectacle. The whole city will stop and bow before you. Dressed in pearls, in a chariot pulled by golden lions, carrying my beautiful and fierce bride."

"You'll make a fool of yourself as you want to." Bianca turned to thread the skirt's ribbons back onto the hooks. "But they won't like me any better if I'm dressed in gold or in nothing at all." Francesco began to speak. She touched a finger to his lips. "Listen, I know you're right to have a big ceremony. The more public we make this marriage, the harder it'll be for anyone to discredit it. Your brother, I know, would much rather we continue to skulk around in shame. But we'll say our vows and be done with it. It's taking up enough time as it is. And on the subject of your brother, have you spoken to him since you gave him the news?"

"He's spoken to me. Written, at least." Francesco's voice became heavy. "I meant to show you." He drew a folded letter from the pocket of the cloak he'd pitched onto the floor, handing it to her. "Not that he says anything we haven't heard before."

Bianca took the letter and read.

Brother, your choices are self-serving, small-minded, disastrous. Shocking in their disregard of our civic responsibilities, much less public sentiment. Your foolish projects bring shame on our family, and the ruin of Florence, literally. Putting the Medici name on mere porcelain, playing with arsenic, taxes, more taxes? Your court is a farce of pettiness and bullying, your patronage extends only to the corrupt court artists you favor. Ruinous for Florence. Cosimo picked Joanna not for you, but for us, and now both are gone. You chose the whore, and there'll be consequences. The Habsburgs will destroy you. And the papal authority? The Holy Office can take your titles, just as easily as it gave them. As for me, I'll bless neither you nor your union.

Hadn't he seen this coming? So much hate in this family. Francesco never spoke of it, but Bianca knew that one of his sisters had been murdered, and maybe a second, and there was a younger brother who had strangled his own wife. Bianca had seen the glare in Francesco's eyes when the cardinal, on her entrance, would leave a room. Their marriage could only make things worse. Bianca laid the letter down on the bed. "Well, it's nothing we didn't already know."

Francesco took it and tossed it onto the floor. "My brother will come around." His words were more certain than his voice. "For now, we don't need him. The same priest who married us once has agreed to bless us again, in public this time. No one will dare question the legitimacy of our union."

Confident words over the ceremony soon to be staged in Florence. But plenty of people would question the rightfulness, whatever Francesco believed—those who, like the cardinal, objected to Bianca herself, as well as those who simply felt it was too soon after Joanna's death to replace their grand duchess with anyone. The people of Florence seethed with anger. They weren't ready for a wedding. But Francesco, their grand duke, was.

It rained the day of the wedding, a soft, tapping drizzle, making Bianca's veil stick to her face as she walked out of Santa Maria del Fiore. It beaded Francesco's eyelashes so that, when he leaned in to kiss her with the city gathered as witness, Bianca couldn't hide a smile as the falling drops of water tickled her skin. He reached to take her hand, turning so that they both faced the Florentines who had braved the wet, and Bianca held her breath. She should feel something, shouldn't she? Curiosity? Expectation? But she already knew Francesco, knew his fiery outbursts, his impulsiveness, his complicated alchemy of metals and porcelain when hers seemed so simple.

A keen bystander to all that she wanted to do, Francesco knew about her science, her commitment to her cure. Somehow, each accepted the other.

His extravagant wedding made public what she and Francesco had vowed a year ago, but even those vows had merely formalized what each already knew. Francesco was hers, as she was his, their fates linked by more than the cure that would save him. He had protected her, her work, giving her Florence and its science. The marrying of their lives had begun years ago.

Still. "Did you have to bring lions, Francesco?" she murmured as they looked out to the city. "Arriving in Florence behind those beasts was the worst carriage ride of my life." She could only imagine how the lions had been mistreated in captivity, if not tortured, to train them for the ridiculous spectacle today.

"Come, what lady hasn't always wanted to ride to her wedding behind a team of lions?"

"The one you married," Bianca told him. The glee on Francesco's face had almost made the spectacle worth it, but she wasn't about to encourage him by telling him so.

They fell silent. She stood by Francesco's side, in a gown so expensive it could have bought for her the purest alcohols, and glass vessels and tubing to last a year. Francesco's jacket of woven gold silk glinted even in the damp. Before her, Florentines squinted up at them on the steps, their hooded forms indistinguishable as they eyed their new grand duchess in the rain. Whatever they felt, she couldn't read it in their faces. Whatever she herself felt . . . well. She was married. In public now as well as in secret, to the man of her choice rather than the first man she'd clung to as a girl wanting nothing more than a way out of Venice. Piero was dead; Joanna was dead; Francesco was hers.

Francesco pulled her close to him for one more kiss.

And then it was done. They made their way down the steps, the priest behind them. Bianca suspected she'd never see him again, as whoever Francesco had found to officiate would earn the cardinal's wrath. Francesco must have paid him well, one more cost to add to that of the whole show.

Her husband needed processions, spectacles, fireworks. As his mistress, she'd always been able to slip away when he'd insisted on having his fun. Now his fun—his everything—was meant to be hers, too. Bianca glanced up, inhaling the earthy air after the rain showers. The smell would have been even stronger with plant oils had she been in her garden. Already the crowd was dispersing. She waved her hand toward the city gate. A faint light shone through the clouds. "Blue skies, Francesco." She smiled.

"It's time for our wedding reception in Pratolino's grand pavilion." Wrapping one arm around her, he pressed his lips to her forehead. "The grounds—"

"—will have a sickroom built any day, or so you've been telling me for a year."

"You'll help me finish it—for our happy future together," Francesco reassured her. "Wait and see."

Bianca pushed away the faintest feeling of unease. Her sickrooms were still waiting to be built there. If being married to Francesco was anything like being his mistress, "Wait and see" would be a common refrain. If she'd learned anything in her casino garden, what she needed most was time—she couldn't allow herself to waste another day.

25
Mama Bianca

At the end of that rainy October wedding day, Bianca discovered that Pratolino could produce a ten-course meal, with dozens of dishes in each course, served on bright, embroidered linens, its tables decorated with sugar sculptures of the wood creatures Francesco claimed lived there. It could host firework displays and games in a landscape dotted with automated fountains. The villa itself was grand. But the park, though large and full of possibility, was unfinished.

As Bianca dismounted from their carriage, pulled, thankfully, only by horses, and set foot on the Pratolino grounds, she had to lean back just to take in the temporary pavilion for the reception that seemed to fill the sky. Beyond there was space for gardens, but most of that space was currently mud, caught in the changing whims of Francesco's designs and those of his gardeners. Yes, there were plenty of beds to seed, and the loamy earth received a good amount of sun. But if she wanted quiet in which to work, and finished grounds, she'd be waiting a long time.

Francesco must have seen the disappointment on her face. "Progress will speed up now that the wedding's over. The garden will be better if you help design it anyway, no? Here, let's join our guests—but first, a look at the villa."

Bianca followed him to the building. "These walls were finished months ago," Francesco explained. "But the scenes weren't quite right. And then the first artist we found . . ." Bianca half-listened as he described whatever fault had caused him to fire one artist and hire another. Patches of colored plaster still alternated with bare surfaces. Plinths held delicate sculptures in front of half-painted walls. "Let's eat," Francesco said finally, over the sound of musicians tuning their strings. "The banquet's ready, and so is the entertainment. Our first feast as husband and wife."

Settling beside Francesco at the head of the long table, Bianca couldn't help but think of her garden workrooms in Florence, well-stocked, arranged just so. Pratolino was different in almost every way. Still, she'd be able to build her sickroom. It would all be worth it. It had to be.

At least the bedroom Francesco had settled on for them was ready, with a high curtained bed and heavy drapes on the walls. After the end of the seemingly endless banquet, he led her to bed. But as Bianca curled up next to her husband that night, she could hear someone tripping over bins of limestone as she'd done herself, and when they woke in the morning, it was to the sounds of plasterers already preparing their surfaces and slapping down lime slurries.

"Francesco, you'd said that the building was done? It seems like you've been replastering once-finished walls?"

"I keep changing my mind." Francesco said with a sheepish smile. "We'll be back at Pitti tomorrow, yes?"

Bianca nodded. That place still felt like Joanna's, but as a state residence, she'd have to get used to it. They were publicly married and now, as grand duchess, she'd certainly need to spend more time there.

The next day found Bianca unpacking her bags in Pitti and settling into what was now her apartment in the dim, ghostly palace. In the casino garden, she loved the long shadows in her herb beds, and the smoky dawn ushering in a day spent in brewing and distillation, with the promise of one day pulling people from death's specter back into the light. In the lifeless Pitti, shadows just seemed gloomy. Joanna had died there, and so had half the children she'd birthed. And Bianca, the hated mistress, had never had the chance to find out whether her infusions helped any of the young Medici whose deaths Joanna had mourned until she followed them.

More than half a year after the wedding, Francesco burst into their room as Bianca was dressing to go outside. The fury on his face made her drop the cloak she'd been about to put on. "The nerve of him," Francesco said, pounding his fist into his hand. He threw himself down onto the bed. "He's going to wish he'd never set foot in Florence."

"Who?" Bianca tried to keep the exasperation from her voice. Another rage, Francesco's ruffled feathers to settle when all Bianca wanted was a quiet evening walk out in the palace grounds. "Tell me who, and what he said, and what you did that made him say something to offend you, because you know that's what happens." Bianca shook her head. "Francesco, you irritate people. Relax around your courtiers." She picked up her cloak and shook it, hanging it back in the closet. No peaceful walk tonight. "Talk with them, ask them about their families, and they'd trust you more. You stiffen up as soon as they approach you. They don't know you're shy; they just think you hate them."

"Well, I do hate them. This fool, anyway. He congratulated me on my marriage and I was going to thank him, Bianca, really I was, but then he said he wished me luck because I'd need it, since all of Florence opposed our wedding, and then he called you—"

"A witch or a whore?" Bianca sat next to him on the bed. "Francesco, you have to get used to it. This is our life until people have had time to see that I'm a healer with cures." She touched her finger to his flushed cheek. "I have to prove I'm the grand duchess they want. You have to learn to be their wise, diligent duke."

"You're right." Francesco leaned his head on her shoulder. "See how clever I was to marry you? But what you've said, it makes me think of something I wanted to ask you."

"Is it about being wise or diligent?"

"Bianca, neither. Now that it's springtime, we should spend a day with the children in the Pitti gardens, outdoors, under the sun. The children will love it, and you've barely seen Joanna's daughters since the wedding. This would be the perfect time for you to get to know them."

"Me?" She could picture Francesco happily romping with his children. But while he played, she'd want to be in her garden laboratory. "I know you love the children, Francesco, and I think a day with them is exactly what you need. But I—"

"—you need to show Florence you are their grand duchess. And you need to relax, Bianca. Come be my wife for a whole day, an afternoon. The gardens are my mother's, not Joanna's. I doubt she stepped into them once. Besides, all this science is draining you."

"What science? I planted late in the season last year. Now my harvest will be late too, by at least a month. I had to delay everything because of your extravagant wedding." But hadn't she just told him that both of them had to step into their roles? Francesco could be a better duke once Florence acknowledged her as a worthy wife for him, and mothering the royal children could only count in her favor. There was nothing she wanted more than to protest, but what could she say? That she didn't want to be a mother, when Joanna had devoted her life to the role? She had to let him see her try.

So, smiling, Bianca took his hand.

Francesco's delight almost made her glad she had. "We'll have cakes and games. The children will love you." He leapt to his feet and kissed her, as buoyant as he had been angry minutes before. "Tomorrow, yes? I'll tell the nursemaids to start making plans."

The next afternoon found Bianca not in her garden among afternoon bees seeking the first few days of spring warmth, but outdoors on the

Pitti terrace. Antonio, almost four years old, sat in her lap, a warm, unaccustomed weight. Across the garden, Joanna's two older girls each held a hand of the youngest child, leading him ceremoniously toward the table. They shot unsure glances toward Bianca, but mostly whispered among themselves. Bianca closed her eyes. What would Joanna be doing now? Presiding over them all, pouring watered wine into tiny cups of delicate china, part of a decorated set for the beautifully behaved children whose glances, with Joanna there, wouldn't have carried the hints of discomfort Bianca sensed even when Antonio looked her way.

Her vision of Joanna—a perfect mother, if a less than perfect match for Francesco—was broken by high-pitched banter, the younger children's feet stamping on the veranda tiles, their voices bursting into roars and giggles, with nurses following behind and Francesco in the rear. All afternoon he'd been wearing a cap with long tresses, roaring like the lions he'd insisted lead their wedding chariot, stirring the children up into a frenzy. "Lion!" he shouted now, curling his fingers like claws.

Small children screamed and ran, their snarls and growls settling into a steady hum as the older girls approached Bianca, each holding a corner of a lace mantilla that must have been Joanna's. Giggling, they placed it over her head. It sat heavy, as if weighted with stones, resting like a crown. "Come play," one shouted. Bianca winced at first as another scurried up, hugging Bianca's skirts, cooing "Mama Bianca." Smiling, Bianca reached out to pet the girl's hair. But she'd already darted away.

Would the moment have been sweeter if one of these girls had been hers? But Virginia was married now. Some count from Bologna had come to Francesco months ago, proposing that Virginia wed his son. At first Bianca was horrified. Her daughter, barely fifteen: at that age, or any age, Bianca would have hated anyone who forced her to marry. But Virginia had wanted it, and Bianca had been little older when she'd chosen Piero. "I've never asked you for anything,"

Virginia had said, standing before Bianca, hands folded in front of her. Bianca now wondered how much sadness Virginia had felt at the fact that Joanna, the mother she had chosen and had buried, had not been at her side on her wedding day.

Bianca shook her head. No point thinking about it. Not all girls had close bonds with their mothers. As for boys . . . Bianca brushed her lips over the crown of Antonio's head. He was almost asleep. He'd been quiet since the wedding. But he often seemed quiet when Bianca saw him, a bit older now and happy enough growing up in the palace with Francesco's other children. If he looked up at her with wide eyes, unsure what to think of the woman who cuddled him as though she had every right to, was that anyone's fault but her own?

Even Francesco seemed to have a better idea of what to do with the children than Bianca did. There he was, lion's guise tossed away, pushing a child's stick toy while his youngest daughter rode on his shoulders. But didn't Francesco's ease with the unruly children make sense? At court he bowed to every distraction, digressing into discussions of alchemy or art as though he was there to enjoy himself, not to rule. No wonder he plunged deep into the children's world of play. He was too much the child himself to listen to others' concerns and ideas, especially when they contradicted his own.

Bianca pushed the fringe of the mantilla the girls had crowned her with out of her eyes. Francesco played, but he wasn't responsible for the children, and no one expected him to be. Being the grand duke was enough. So shouldn't her true work—developing a cure for a disease that had taken Francesco's mother and brothers, and could take their lives as well—be enough?

A child planted a wet kiss on her cheek. Bianca pulled away before she could stop herself, then, glancing up, met Francesco's grin. But his smile faded when he saw the look on Bianca's face. Even the child, with Joanna's fair hair and sharp cheekbones, took a step back, eyes growing wide.

Bianca shifted her sleeping son to one hip and stood. She was no mother. Who was she trying to fool? "Let's drink," she said, moving toward the table in the middle of the terrace, handing Antonio to a nursemaid. Bianca sat down in front of a half-full wine glass, abandoned among a cluster of small items that were gifts for Francesco from the children. Shiny stones. Bits of ragged velvet. Jagged rocks. But also a pair of simple wire earrings, a paper fan. Were these for her? Bianca picked up one, then another. Let her appear busy, at least. Otherwise she'd have to help the nurses dole out fruit tarts and wipe children's hands.

They were all squealing now, from the smallest boy to the oldest girl, chatting and laughing as the sweet fruit met their tongues. Apparently they'd all inherited their father's sweet tooth. The tarts were apple, Francesco's favorite. Well, they were Francesco's children. What was she even doing here? Bianca lifted a half-decayed leaf, its skeleton showing, and set it back down on the table. As she withdrew her hand from its stem, another hand, small and pudgy, covered hers.

"I found that one."

Antonio had run to join the others. But now he climbed back into her lap, looking up with wide eyes, asking for—what? Approval? Praise? It was a pretty leaf. And so delicate. Not a thing she'd expect a child to notice. "Well done," she told him.

Antonio smiled. But it was a quick smile, gone in an instant. His eyes blinked as though he wanted more. What else was she supposed to say? Would a real mother know? In a minute he'd be crying. Bianca sat straight in her chair, but shifting her weight didn't make him hop off. Finally, she pointed to the table where the others had gathered. "Don't you want a tart?"

Antonio touched the leaf again, then, without a word, jumped off to find the sweets. He took the leaf with him.

Free. She was free of him. Bianca stood from the table with its gifts, letting the mantilla the girls had crowned her with fall to the ground. "Francesco?" As she met his eyes across the terrace, something wet splashed onto her skirt. In her haste, she'd hit the table with her hip, knocking over the wine glass. Clinking against the edge of the table, it shattered on the terrace tiles. One of the children's nurses saw, too. Gasping, she fell onto Bianca, followed by the others, a flutter of hands and cleaning cloths dabbing unsuccessfully at the red stain spreading over the tablecloth and Bianca's dress. The children stared at the splinters of glass, then at Bianca, tears running down the youngest's face. Bianca's jaw tightened. All this for a glass? "Please don't fuss." But the sound of her raised voice made the child cry harder. And now here was Francesco, looking just as anxious as the children.

"Bianca, what's wrong?" He took her hand, scanning her face as though searching for the secret to some tragedy much greater than a glass breaking.

"I can't be here." Bianca pulled away and started to walk toward the center fountain on the grounds.

Francesco followed her. "What do you mean?"

Bianca paused. "Let the nurses take care of the children."

"Is it so difficult?"

"Let's go somewhere else. Please."

To her surprise he nodded, walking with her instead of trying to stop her. "We can leave." He took her hand and began leading her away from the broken glass, the spilled gifts, the chaos. One of the nursemaids glanced up, whispering something to her companion. The children, mostly silent, watched them go.

Then one girl called out. "Mama Bianca?"

And other voices: "Papa! Come back!"

She'd seen his face, warm and relaxed, when he was around them. Low enough so that no one else could hear her, she told him, "You can go back. Keep playing with them if you want."

Francesco held her gaze. "What I want is for you to be happy."

Bianca kept walking and Francesco kept pace with her. "Then don't ask me to be here," she said. She chose her next words carefully. "Joanna was a mother. If that's what you wanted, you should have found another Habsburg." He shook his head, but she couldn't let him speak, not yet. "Please, Francesco." She took his hand. "This party was a mistake. You promised me space and quiet at Pratolino after the wedding. I'll stay at Pitti until you finish the grounds—however long it takes, and of course my work garden is here."

Francesco drew a breath and let it out, a long sigh. "This was what you meant when I asked you to marry me, wasn't it? You told me then you wouldn't take Joanna's place." He nodded. "I never should have made you come to the picnic. It seemed right. I think I was trying to give you everything my mother had. But that's not what you want, is it? You tried to tell me last night, and I didn't listen." Blushing, he took her other hand, holding hers in both of his. "I should be ashamed. I am ashamed. This was my fault. You want to work." Francesco looked deep into her eyes. "And that is what you'll have." He tilted his head in the direction opposite to the children they'd left, toward the Pratolino countryside.

"I could have said no last night, Francesco, and I didn't." No reason to berate him, really; he looked chastened enough. He had seen her today, he had heard her. Warmth surged through Bianca. Yes, he'd caused this mess, but how many men would have understood her need to flee that scene? "The children are happier with their nurses than with me."

As she left Pitti's gardens, her steps grew light. Even the distant shrieks of the children couldn't dampen her spirits. Let the nurses mother them. The children could call her Mama Bianca if they wished, and she'd drape a mantilla on her head now and then, but they'd have nothing to do with her future. Not unless they needed a cure someday, or would join her in her quest to create one. She pictured Antonio with his leaf and smiled. At least she'd rediscovered something of value. Give Antonio a year or two, and it might be time to show him her garden.

26
Like Mother, Like Son
1580

Bianca liked to be up before dawn in the early fall, waking earlier than the birds that nested outside the windows of her and Francesco's Pitti Palace apartments. Almost a year had passed since she'd publicly married Francesco. After the failed garden party that spring, she'd thrown herself back into her work, her relief tempered only slightly by nagging memories of Antonio's warm weight in her lap, of that leaf he'd been so proud to show her. Bianca had barely spoken with any of Joanna's children in the months since. Antonio she saw at night, when she peeked into his room before bed, but usually his nurses would have already put him to sleep. And Bianca, late as it always was, didn't want to wake him. Maybe soon she'd be doing all this in the new rooms at Pratolino, but today she'd make her infusions again in the casino garden.

Now, soft light filtered through the loose drapes on the window as she sat up against her pillows. Suddenly she froze, every nerve in her body thrumming. Someone was watching her. But it was too early for the maids, and Francesco was away, hunting near the Poggio villa. What if it was the cardinal, plotting another move against her while Francesco was gone? Bianca eased herself back down in the bed. Perhaps, with just one eye open in the darkness, she might still seem to be sleeping. The door had been pushed open, but no one was there.

Then a small voice. "Mama Bianca?"

Bianca sat up again. She'd looked right past him, he was so small. Antonio, standing in the doorway, his face turned up toward her like a flower's, his eyes wide.

"What's wrong?" Bianca slid out of bed. "Did you have a bad dream?" She peeked into the hallway. No nurses? His shoulder felt round underneath his thin nightshirt. What to do with him?

"No dreams," Antonio said. "I just woke up. Sometimes I do that." He took her hand. "When I wake up you're gone and Nurse says you've left, but I caught you today." He grinned.

"I have work I must do, Antonio. I make medicine, so people don't get sicker." Maybe a four-year-old could understand what so many adults didn't.

"Well, I want to do that too." Antonio pulled on her skirt. "Can I come help make medicine with you?"

Bianca laughed. As though a child could help her with anything. But what age had she been when she'd begun shadowing her own mother in a workroom? She was just six years older than Antonio when she'd made the cure that she'd hoped would save her mother. Bianca might have been five, or four, like her son, when she'd dried her first harvest of herbs. And that leaf at the party . . . even then, it had crossed her mind Antonio was as much her heir as Francesco's, and might someday follow in her footsteps. Someday. But, today? She'd have to make him promise not to trample her plants or chatter endlessly while she tried to think. As though a four-year-old could promise that. She'd be insane to bring him. Only . . . he'd have to start learning sometime.

"Please?" Antonio said.

If she said no, would he lose interest, maybe choosing the casino instead, the laboratory she'd rejected? What a twist that would be, and surely it'd fit with Francesco's plans. Francesco had plenty of wealthy men's sons to choose from, though, for assistants. What if she needed an apprentice some day?

"You can come," Bianca said. "But only for today. If you don't listen to me, if you break anything or stop me from getting my work done, then you won't be able to come back. Do you understand?"

Antonio nodded, frowning. His face so serious—was this what fear looked like on such a young child? He was the one who had come to her, though. It certainly hadn't been Bianca's idea. "Let me get dressed," she told him. "Go ask your nurse to get you ready. Wake her up if you have to; she can relax for the rest of the day." Bianca laid a hand on his shoulder. "Remember, your mama has important work."

"I'm going to do important work, too."

And he was gone.

Half an hour later, the two of them left the palace, both dressed in clothes they could move in freely. Clothes, it turned out, Antonio had worn to Francesco's casino. When she asked him more about it, he shrugged. "He took me there one time." He held up a single finger. "Working in the casino, that's what dukes do."

"That's what Papa said? What dukes do?" Then again, Francesco considered hunting to be a duty, too, and collecting curios, and chatting with a new favorite painter. Knowing him, he'd probably brought Antonio to the casino, then forgotten to explain any of the things the little boy saw there, pursuing his own interests and leaving Antonio bored. Bored, when there was so much to question in the world. No son of hers should have his questions go unanswered. At four, Bianca would have loved to have explored a garden like hers, full of medicines and secrets. Did Antonio even understand how important that was?

"Do you remember when you got sick?" Bianca asked him, taking his hand as they crossed a still-quiet street on the way to the garden. His first mild bout of malaria had struck only months ago. "Your nurse gave you all those medicines and you took them like a good boy and got better. Remember?"

"They tasted bad."

"But they made you well. And you still take them, right?" Her remedies were used more and more in the ducal household. For Antonio, she'd combined her infusions with mild distillates. He had pulled through quickly. For several months after, she'd still prepared a low dose for him in a mint infusion, which he was under strict instructions to take once a week. Could he understand how his mother's mysterious work, calling her away every day, might be making him as strong as he was?

"The whole time you were in bed then," she told him, "I was making your medicines in my workroom. The same workroom we're going to see today."

"Did you know my kitten has a workroom?" Antonio asked.

Bianca blinked. What was she supposed to say to that? The day stretching before her, she'd now given it over to her playful son. She half-listened as he told her more about his kitten, then about some silly game he'd played in the nursery, or maybe several silly games; she couldn't keep her mind on what he was saying. When he finally stopped talking, she glanced at him in relief, but he was looking at her as though to say, *your turn*. Bianca wracked her brain for ideas. What could she say to such a child? "Isn't it fun in the palace?" she asked.

"Not really. Filippo's too little. I'd rather be with you."

I'd rather be with you. Virginia had never once said those words. But Antonio wanted Bianca. He was like his mother, more than she'd even realized. Still, waste a day of work on a child? Her mother must have made the same choice so long ago. She could have given Bianca to others in the palace to care for. But she hadn't, and the aunties had tolerated Pellegrina bringing Bianca along to watch her mother weigh out herbs, steeping them in boiling water and in alcohols. Bianca could at least try to do the same for her son.

Reaching the garden gate, Antonio leaned against it, pushing it open. Running ahead of Bianca into the middle of the garden, he shouted, "What's this place? You said you'd show me your laboratory."

"Yes, this garden is part of it."

"This isn't a garden. Gardens have lots of flowers. And fountains. And paths. This is all tangly and ugly. And it smells." Leaning down, he touched his finger to the thorn of a purple thistle bush. "Is this poison?"

"Careful, no, it's just sharp. But there are poisons here."

"Can I see them?" His eyes opened wide. "Will they kill me if I eat one?" He grabbed his throat, running from her. "I think that bush is poison. I'm dying! I'm dying!" Laughing, she ran after him. Antonio turned and pushed her. She tumbled down, faking a fall. Lying on the ground for a moment, winded, she let Antonio crawl on top of her. She'd seen Francesco act like this with his children. But he'd grown up with it, his sisters and brothers all sitting around the same dining table as their parents. Then off to stories and play. Cosimo must have been a softer man when his wife was still alive. Still, how could the old duke and duchess have afforded the time, tolerated the child talk, clung so to those children?

They must have wanted to. And, today, she could almost see why. The little boy in front of her made her laugh. He was funny. Her son wasn't just a little baby anymore. He was a person, a clever mix of Medici and Capello, with his own personality, his own jokes, his own curious alchemy. Last week, the nurse had told Bianca he'd grabbed a handful of flour from the table and started dusting his and the other children's cakes with it. "The white powder's medicine," he'd said. "I'm 'sperimenting." Where had he even learned that word?

"Why didn't you ever bring me here?" Antonio asked, climbing to his feet. "I like poison."

Bianca stood up with him. Imagine if anyone saw a working Medici woman, a woman of cures, rolling in the weeds with a boy of four. "Well, this isn't a place for children. It's a laboratory, with chemicals and fires. This is where I made your medicine when you had the heat disease."

Antonio dropped to the earth again and grabbed his chest. "I still have it. I'm burning up."

She laughed again, pulling him to his feet. She hadn't thought of a little boy as being charming, but he was. And intuitive. "I'm serious. Malaria is serious. But you seem to be healthy."

"Yup. I'm all better. So why are we in this garden?" Antonio grabbed a handful of magenta-orange flowers and covered his nose. "It smells like that stinky drink. And these too. I don't like the yellow flowers."

He'd broken some of the lantana shrub, but the yellow was trailing licorice. "Stinky?" The perfect garden she'd carved out of prickly brush? Those neat rows of artemisia, bitter herbs that cured, at the cost of so many scrapes in taming the garden to begin with? "You don't like the smell of the brew I sent you?"

"Nope." He looked down, kicking a stone. "I hate it. It tastes like cat poo. I'm four now. I don't have to take it." He scowled.

"And that's good. But if you get sick, you might have to take that medicine again." Bianca pointed toward the artemisia in bloom.

"Oh, no." Shaking his head, Antonio grabbed her fingers, then looked toward her new workrooms, now in shadow.

"Antonio, do you want to play in the house there?"

The little boy nodded. He let go of her hand, bending down to pull up a plant—fortunately a weed.

"Let's go inside the big building near the bushes." But he'd stopped listening. He dropped to the ground, hunting for something. Bianca had to call his name to drag his attention from whatever he'd found.

Finally, knees muddy, he got up and clutched her hand. "All right."

Her heart beating harder than it should have, she squeezed back. His hand was so little; had she ever noticed? No doubt Francesco had, Francesco, who'd managed to be a guide of sorts to Antonio as well as a parent, while Bianca had offered nothing, no kissing after scrapes, no soft words at bedtime. But she'd never thought of herself as someone who could find the right words, or who could listen to children babble their selfish demands.

Was it so hard, though, to know what to say? He liked to play games and ask questions, and he wanted his mother to do the same. "I bet you can run inside faster than I can," she told him.

Antonio dashed forward, Bianca in pursuit, both of them kicking up leaves and grit. Bianca got to the door first, pushing against it, rattling the handle as though she couldn't get through. Antonio giggled, shoving to get past her till she unlocked the door and stood aside, pointing him into the building. Peering inside, he squinted in the dim light.

"There's no rocks or forges. Is this a real laboratory?"

So he had been to the casino. "It's a laboratory of plants, Antonio, to cure bad diseases." She lit a candle. How to explain her tender, healing science built on the meticulous testing of herbal chemistry, rather than caustic chemicals or giant boilers fired up and deployed on an alchemist's whim? Would Antonio even be interested, having already seen Francesco's workshop? Her work wasn't loud and showy; it didn't generate sparks or great eruptions of ash. Would anything she had here hold Antonio's attention?

Bianca opened the top cabinet drawers and took out small sacks of ground angelica and white peony root, and one of kaolin clay that she'd taken from Francesco's stores. A mineral, it was a good medicinal. And it was a white powder, like the "medicine" with which Antonio had treated himself and his brother and sisters.

"Come sit with me; then you can see better." Antonio climbed up on a stool and Bianca poured the contents of the bags onto the table, both of them sneezing and laughing as the fine, tumbling clay dusted the surface. "Like this, Antonio, protect yourself with the cloth here." Bianca pulled a cloth from her pocket and held it to his mouth.

He giggled, pushing it away. "You, Mama."

"All right, Antonio, can you look? These are made from plants, and this one's a clay, but see how they're all white? You might have seen that clay at the casino."

He dipped into the clay, wiggling his fingers. Like he'd done when he was a baby, grabbing for anything he could get hold of. Back then, when he'd just been born, how quick she'd been to enlist a nursemaid to hold his perfumed hand.

"This is like what I put on our cakes." He pushed some clay toward her.

"Oh, is it?" She took a pinch and smelled it. "Hmm."

"And leaves, too. They tasted bad, but it was medicine. It fixed us." He lowered his head, narrowing his eyes. "I mean it."

"That sounds smart." Bianca had wanted the same attention from her aunties when she said "I'll fix it" so many years ago, thinking that her mother would get better with her brew. "Very smart," Bianca told her son. Something they'd never said to her.

Antonio's face lit into a bright smile.

The flour did nothing to those cakes, but what mattered was that Antonio believed it had, and that he had ideas to improve on what others before him had done. One day when she wasn't looking, it seemed Antonio had turned into a scientist, though a reckless one. His nurse had better keep him away from Bianca's medicinal stores of distillates and powdered roots in the palace.

She leaned toward him. "Now, shall we do an experiment?"

"Like this?" Crumbling some dried herbs on the table, he spread them over the mound of clay, and pounded them down with one hand.

She grabbed his wrist. This was what she'd been afraid of, bringing a child here, but really, he wasn't doing any harm. "Are you done?"

"No." He tried to wiggle free, but Bianca held tight. Even a four-year-old had to learn rules.

"No more thumping, all right?" Bianca scraped the clay toward her. "What were you making, Antonio?"

"A 'speriment." Antonio clapped his hands.

"Well, let's try another one. You bring the alcohol while I get the glass containers." Antonio slid off the stool. "Sniff the jars over there on the bottom." Bianca pointed to the lowest shelves in an open cabinet. "And bring me what you think is the right one, the one with a light, sweet smell."

Kneeling on the floor in front of the shelves, he picked up a glass bottle, lifting the heavy stopper and sniffing. "Like this, Mama? I think it's this one."

Bianca nodded, smiling. "These are our secrets," she said, taking the bottle from Antonio and sitting him close to the table. "Don't tell anyone how we mix the potions. You understand, yes?"

"Potions?" He nodded. "Like poison?"

"No, we're making good medicine." She'd have to be careful what stories of her work she gave him to tell, especially to his troublesome uncle. Though hopefully the cardinal would never get close enough to ask. Did Antonio ever see him? Bianca didn't even know.

"Has your Uncle Ferdinando, the cardinal, ever told you what I do when I work?" she asked.

Antonio fidgeted on the stool. His knee hit the table and the bottle of alcohol he'd just brought her went flying. Bianca surged to her feet. "I don't like him." Antonio's voice shook. "He hurt me."

"Stay where you are." As long as he remained in his seat, his legs were far too short to reach the ground. Bianca grabbed a broom and swept up the shattered glass before he could step on it. As soon as she finished, she asked, "What did he do to you? Was your papa there?" And if Francesco was there, why hadn't he told Bianca what his brother had done?

"I didn't do anything wrong." Antonio squirmed in his seat.

"Oh, no, love, not you. Your uncle."

Glancing down, he curved his hands to make a small hollow. "There was water in a bowl, in the church." He looked up at Bianca. "I didn't want to put my face in, and he said I was bad, and he burned me." Antonio held out his hand. There, on his palm, a silver scar. "He said the candles were for God, and he would give me one, but then he hurt me."

Going behind her back to bring her son into the Church just because he thought Francesco hadn't? Bianca would hurt the cruel, careless cardinal if she ever got the chance. Fighting to keep her voice even, she rested both hands on the table. "You mean when he baptized you. Is that what he was doing?"

Antonio shrugged, playing with a thread on his jacket.

"He shouldn't have tried to get you to go in the water without me or your papa there. You weren't bad, Antonio. He's a bad man, and you should never trust him. Has he ever tried to hurt you again?"

Antonio shook his head.

"Don't let him. He's your uncle, so people might tell you to do what he says. But even if something happens to me and to your papa, you don't go with him. All right?" Given how the cardinal hated Bianca, she could only imagine what he thought of Antonio, the whore's son marked to be grand duke, unbaptized. Would he try to lure poor Antonio into some chapel with candles again? And then?

Bianca waited until Antonio nodded, then took his hand. "Let me show you something else. I think you'll like it." Bianca grabbed some artemisia flowers. "Come over here." They settled into two tall chairs at the middle table with its glass balls and sturdy glass cylinders, burners, and a new bottle of alcohol. "Antonio, be careful now, this is special equipment."

Antonio touched the bottle. "I like helping you, Mama."

She hadn't had a partner since Angelica. She hadn't thought she ever would again. An assistant from Francesco hardly counted. But Antonio so clearly belonged here, with her, working at her side.

"Don't sit too close to the glass." Bianca pushed his chair back. She kept her eyes on him as he leaned over to touch a tall column. "Look."

Bianca crumbled the artemisia and tossed it into a glass bowl. "Now, you pour." She held the bowl as he lifted the bottle and poured the liquid, back and forth, over the herbs. "Then after we light a little fire, we boil it." She'd have let the herbs steep for a week or two and used a water bath, but still, she could show some of her chemistry now, making the little boy smile.

How many children had the chance to practice chemistry with their mothers—lighting boilers, turning steam into something else? Bianca held her hand on top of Antonio's.

"Steady, all right?" She put the flint between his fingers and guided his hand to strike it on the stone. "Now watch the simmering herbs. With this liquid, we get steam very fast. You'll see it soon."

"Look, Mama, it's all smoky. In the glass tube, it's like a ghost."

"In the column, the steam will cool and become liquid again. Here." Bianca pointed to a mark on the glass. "There, it's too cool for the steam, so it just disappears. Like you when it's time for bed, I imagine."

Antonio squinted. "There it is."

"Ah, you see what happens with the water droplets that form?" She tapped softly on the column. "One by one, they drip into the glass tap in the middle."

"There?" Smiling, he pointed to the juncture in the column where she had inserted a siphon.

"Yes, and what we collect is medicine. For you." Bianca reached for him, but he wiggled away.

"I'm not sick."

"But you were." She wrapped her fingers round his hand.

"And Papa?"

"Yes, I've treated your papa too. We all need it."

Antonio's eyes were fixed on the glass column as he looked for the drops of vapor condensing into the clear, healing liquid. The malaria medicine. "I want to come here again to play. You're never around, not like Papa."

Bianca's chest tightened. Francesco often was away, yet it was she, Bianca, whose absence their son felt. "But isn't it nice to play with your sisters and your little brother?"

"Filippo's sick a lot. And they're not my real sisters."

"They're your half-sisters," Bianca said.

"Yes, but I like being with you."

"I think you can come back. You'll be good while I do a little more work here?"

Antonio nodded, clasping his hands as if praying. Where had he learned that? "May I have a hug, Antonio?" The boy leaned over to wrap his arms around Bianca. "And maybe you can help me again after today." How many more visits and how much more artemisia would it take to ensure Antonio would be the Medici who'd survive the disease, to be a grand duke like his father, and a scientist like his mother? And would he also inherit her battle with the cardinal?

No. Not if Bianca had anything to say about it. By the time Antonio was ready to follow in her footsteps, the whole world would know her work. It might take her years still to get there, but someday not even the cardinal would be able to deny what she had done.

27
Pratolino
1587

Bianca shut the workroom door quietly, as she always did. But how tempting it was to slam it, the way Francesco would any time something didn't go right. Not that slamming a door would bring back the Pratolino woman she'd lost today. Bianca finally had a place to treat the sick, and in the almost eight years since she'd first set foot on Pratolino's grounds, the people in the villages surrounding the country villa had learned to come to her when they had the heat disease. But many waited too long, as this woman had, her two grown sons carrying her withered form to Bianca's doorstep only after she'd fallen into the coma that Bianca's sickest patients never recovered from. Bianca would have dosed her with fluids and mild distillates, but death had the woman too firmly in its grip. Her fever had dropped, but her heart pumped blood with a pulse so much slower than Bianca's. She could learn no more from this woman than she had from the desperate women in the brothels. Catching the end of the illness wasn't enough, yet how would she ever track its course start to finish? No one would ever choose to get sicker so Bianca could watch the disease unfold. But because she didn't know enough, an hour ago the woman had died.

Bianca walked down the corridor into her laboratory, quiet now at the end of the early fall day. With its ornate window frames inlaid with precious stones and gleaming ceramic tabletops able to repel any spill, it was as much a gallery of fine art as an everyday laboratory. She'd imagined it as a space she would someday share, a beacon for others like herself. It had everything a scientist needed, from the fully stocked shelves of glassware to the tall chairs she'd designed for the different workstations, offering a perfect respite from standing all day.

Now, light from the large windows shone on the ceramic crucibles and the porcelain wash basins, gilding each surface as the late afternoon sun dimmed over the grounds outside. But what good were the vented stalls, the hand-carved cabinets, the books full of notes with cases to reference, if Bianca's patients continued to die? She had the laboratory of her dreams, but those coming to her were so ill she could neither learn from them nor cure them. And with each patient she failed to save, the villagers' trust in her lessened, making it that much less likely the next one to fall ill would come to her in time. Bianca paused to straighten a stack of notes, then adjusted the vent by the alembic and water baths to be ready for tomorrow. She loved these rooms Francesco had built for her, her shrine to her own kind of alchemy. But as she locked the laboratory and stepped out into the evening, she wondered if she'd ever be worthy of the space she now had.

"Bianca, why the long face?"

She jumped. Here came Francesco, sauntering around the side of the villa toward her. She forced a smile. "I thought you were in Florence still. The Duomo, did you . . . ?"

"The church is in ruins, according to my brother and everyone else in Florence. They say that every time I knock something down. And, yes, I'll grant you, it's a mess. Tearing down the whole façade might have been a lot."

Bianca shook her head. A lot? Francesco had fallen into a frenzy of activity with yet another disastrous experiment. He was doomed to topple every good thing he'd done; the wreckage lay in piles opposite the Duomo. It would take men hauling the broken stone all day, six days a week, to clear the church's steps. And still, dust and grime rising up in a thick cloud covered the piazza and anyone who traveled in it.

Yet all Francesco saw was progress. "When it's almost done, no one will even remember the rubble that's there now, let alone how it used to look, that gothic monstrosity. Buildings need updating. Florence needs a new face. And yours looks as sad as that of our Apennine Colossus. Walk there with me?" He took her hand.

Bianca let Francesco lead her to the colossus' crouched figure, partially lit by the setting sun. Surrounded by a burnished iron railing, the statue towered over them—just one of Francesco's many amusements at Pratolino, along with lifelike automatons spitting water, hedges with hidden sprays, and, tucked away in the belly of this very statue, caves of deep, quiet waters. Had this sorrowful giant, weeping its tears of stone, stooping from the weight of its dripping sandstone, also failed to save someone under its protection? The hunched, bearded figure, as tall as six or seven men, seemed to melt into the earth. One day, Bianca imagined, she'd walk past this place and find it empty, the anguished titan crushed into a mound of clay dust, filling the pond that now bathed its feet.

Francesco tilted his head back, taking in the figure's full height. "What do you think, Bianca? I want to bring the children here. Let them explore the caves under the statue."

"Hmm. Will Antonio try to climb to the top?" Her lips knit together as her gaze followed the weary statue all the way up to his drooping face.

"Don't look so worried." Francesco turned Bianca toward him and stroked her cheek. "Though you're right, our boy is an adventurer, isn't he? What he doesn't know, he has to find out."

Our boy. Filippo had finally surrendered to the weakness he'd been born with, and lay with his mother at rest. Antonio was Francesco's only son now, as he was Bianca's. "Pratolino is too far for the children," Bianca said, though she often wished she had Antonio here in her new laboratory. Any time she was back in Florence she took him to the casino garden and taught him a little more about herbs for her medicines and how to distill them. He was better off staying in Florence with his nurses and tutors than following her out here, though. Besides, how would she explain to him a day like today in her sickroom? If he was to be a healer, he'd have to encounter death. He knew a lot for an eleven-year-old. But not that. Not yet.

"You're right, of course. It's too far. Besides, he's so attached to his tutor, that bright young mathematician, he probably wouldn't want to leave. As for me, I can't go back there, not for a while." Cheery as he'd been discussing his project in Florence and the statue, Francesco abruptly sounded anxious. "Malaria is everywhere in the city, Bianca. I've told the nurses to keep the children close; they're getting lots of fresh air and sun. I feel I should be with them, but—"

"But you can't risk it." Bianca brushed her hand along the railing. "And the reason you can't? It's because your wife still hasn't found a cure for the dying. I lost another woman today."

"Oh, Bianca." Francesco wrapped his arm around her waist and guided her away from the statue. This time they followed the path toward Bianca's gardens, plots of herbs and flowers that, together with her casino garden, should have had Bianca producing cure after cure. The heat disease, after all, wasn't the only illness stalking Florence. It was just the first she needed to conquer—and even that, she was failing to do.

Ahead of them, square beds of deep soil grew kitchen herbs, rosemary, sage, thyme, and oregano, their flowers attracting honeybees and colorful butterflies. Much as she loved Michelangelo's garden, Bianca marveled at how much more quickly herbs grew here, either spreading upward or trailing along the ground in the Tuscan sunlight and the moist summer heat.

"Sage." Francesco picked several bright blooms. "You need a break from all this," he said, brushing the soft flowers across her cheek. "You work too hard, Bianca, you always have. What about a swim in the caves underneath our Colossus, no? A sulfur treatment."

Bianca closed her eyes. It was tempting. Deep and quiet, the sulfur water always invited escape from the day's worries. The steamy surface air would fill her pores, chasing away any concerns. She and Francesco could rest against the rocky barrel-like seats carved into the cave's rock, floating their arms on the surface, wicking away heat from the steamy hot water. More often than not, it was Bianca who'd hold Francesco afloat, her fingertips barely touching his back. There, she could pretend she really did have the power to protect him.

"An even better treatment," Bianca said, "would be the cure I could create if people, or even one person, would willingly allow me to observe them get sicker before they got better." Had she just said that, or only thought it, as she had for so many years? Touching the sage bloom in Francesco's hand, she moved closer to him. It was outrageous, this idea of hers, that anyone who came to her for a cure would then willingly wait for it so she could study the disease. But if Francesco was to understand the desperation she felt now, she needed him to understand this, too. Would he listen?

Francesco's brow creased. "Tell me more."

"Francesco, the patients who come to me are either close enough to recovering that they don't need a dose, or so near death that nothing can save them. And maybe it's not just one dose that the very sick need, but several smaller doses? And perhaps some sick patients die simply of dehydration or fluid in their lungs? I need to test my distillates and extracts in order to know if I have a cure, but by the time a patient is sick enough to warrant that, I don't know what other factors might be about to kill them, especially when I've only met them a few hours before. Don't you see that I can't understand the end of the illness until I've watched a patient from the early symptoms?

Once I've seen the progression, and not just in one patient, but several, I can start experimenting with the strength and the timing of doses. But who's going to come to me and say, 'I'm sick, I may die, but let me get a little sicker so you can learn if you can heal me or not?' All my testing says I have a cure. I can't promise, though, and until I can . . ." Until she could, and until she'd tested the doses on the right patient, she'd keep seeing the dead child at Sant'Elisabetta. Perhaps she would have died anyway, but that girl hadn't agreed to try Bianca's medicine. And Bianca hadn't been ready then to cure her. Now she was ready, she was almost certain. Almost . . . but almost wasn't enough.

She stole a glance at Francesco. He was silent, his face still. Wasn't he going to offer her reassuring words? Usually his quick dismissals of her problems frustrated her. He didn't know her work well enough to judge it. Now, though, Bianca would have grasped at any encouragement. Instead, Francesco simply frowned.

Finally, he spoke. "All right. You have him."

"What?"

"I can't give you a laboratory full of patients, but I can give you one. If I have malaria again . . ."

Bianca raised her eyebrows.

"When I do . . ."

"Francesco." Bianca held up a hand.

"You'll know from the first symptoms because you'll see them for yourself, I'll make sure of that. And then you'll get me to death's doorstep. Smaller doses, strong doses, distillates, extracts, Bianca, you decide." He took both her hands, bringing them to his cheek. "You chronicle the sickness—all of it. You learn what you need to know, and you treat me. You can give me Bianca's cure."

Why was her heart beating so fast? There was no way she could agree. No way she would have mentioned it if she'd thought he might volunteer himself. Withhold treatment? "No. You can't take that risk."

She had to say the words quickly, otherwise she might start to think about what his offer could mean for her. Certainly saving the grand duke would give her work legitimacy—as surely as killing him would bring condemnation from which she couldn't escape. At that thought, Bianca breathed a sigh of relief. She couldn't say yes to this. As soon as she had the thought, though, she caught herself. Wasn't this what she'd been wanting? If she didn't want it now, did that only mean *she* had been too afraid to take this next step? Francesco's other bouts had been relatively mild, even his illness at Via Maggio, but the next round? Hadn't she had enough of carting away the dead?

She had, but this was Francesco. She let her hands fall, balling them into fists. "If you get sick, I'm treating you right away—"

"Bianca, I thought the point was to gauge the dose?"

"To fine-tune it, yes, so that I can learn how to increase it to something effective." She wrapped her arms around Francesco. "But I can't sit by and watch you get sicker just so I can take notes. I might get closer to a real cure, yes, but that's too high a price."

Francesco gently pushed her away. "But it's not if it's a stranger?"

What price had the girl at Sant'Elisabetta paid? She bit her lip. Bianca couldn't have saved her, not as sick as she'd been. She hadn't purposefully withheld anything that could have helped her. Yet still she caught herself wondering at times how old the girl would be now, and whether she'd be a nun, a healer, a mother. How much more would Francesco's ghost haunt her if she watched him sicken but mistimed the treatment, giving him the infusion that could have cured him just after, instead of just before, he'd reached a brink from which he couldn't return? But Francesco was right. The fact that the patient she'd imagined was someone she didn't love—and that the one in front of her was someone she did—shouldn't change a single thing.

"As long as no sure cure exists for malaria, I'm going to die," Francesco said. "We both know it. If you look at it that way, I have nothing to lose. Either you do your experiment, develop your cure, your doses, and save me in the process, or I die the death that's been waiting for me for years. However my next illness ends, you'll learn, and you'll put that learning toward the cure. And I'll be famous as the grand duke that sacrificed himself for science."

"Oh, that's what it's about, is it? Your fame?" Bianca tried to laugh, one to match Francesco's muffled one. "Is it a better way to be remembered than as the grand duke who demolished the Duomo facade?"

"It is, truly." Francesco cast her an insistent look. "You'd mourn me, but Florence wouldn't. Unfortunately for Florence, though, I have no intention of dying. I know what I'm saying, what I'm offering. I don't have any doubts. Only you doubt yourself, Bianca. As for me, I trust you."

The words hung in the air between them. Was it the setting sun or the passion in his voice that made his face flush so? His eyes met hers, those eyes she'd known for so many years. She had to tell him no, had to say it now before this went any further. But what if Francesco's next illness was his last, and not only his last, but almost the last in Florence? What if, as he so believed, she really could save him?

The silence stretched, and Bianca didn't fill it with words. Instead she pulled him to her, wrapping him in her arms and resting her head on his shoulder as she'd so often done before. She whispered, "We'll do it."

"Good. Enough misery, Bianca."

"But I won't let you die, Francesco. I'm going to study my notes, writing down everything I know. I want to show my work to others, too—healers, scholars, anyone who might be able to review what I've done so far, to better prepare me. If—when—you fall ill again, I'm going to be as ready as I can be."

"Write a hundred pages or none. You're ready, Bianca." Francesco's words rumbled in her ear. He'd never understood her need to write, to document, to learn from mistakes instead of just forgetting them as he always seemed to do. The truth was, he'd never understood her work at all. It was Bianca herself, more than her painstaking science, that he was putting his trust in now. She could trust her kind of alchemy enough for both of them—couldn't she? "As for appraisal," Francesco continued, "the theorists and linguists of the Crusca Academy are the best for that. Don't think, though, that you can easily present your ideas to them. They're so incisive that even the Church dare not cross them, and they want everyone to know it. The philosophers will eat you alive."

If Bianca had had a notebook with her she'd have jotted it down then, *theorists at Crusca*. Instead she lodged the plan in her mind. She'd write until everything she knew about curing malaria was down on paper. Then, she'd present it at Crusca to Florence's greatest minds. After that, she'd take away whatever she learned and she'd be ready. Ready for Francesco's next illness, for which she'd never before felt anything but dread.

Bianca stepped back, a wisp of wind catching her hair. "Francesco, tell me this. If you believe in my science this strongly, why did it take you so long to give me what I needed? If I'd had this Pratolino laboratory ten years ago, the heat disease might already be cured."

"Did I know you needed it? Did you tell me?" Francesco looked genuinely surprised. And now Bianca laughed. Francesco frowned at her, looking so irritated that Bianca only laughed harder. "What? Bianca, what did I say?"

"Francesco, you clueless man, I told you a thousand times. Didn't I say the day we met that I came to Florence to do science?" How long she'd waited, first to even get inside the casino, then for a workspace of her own, one Francesco didn't even notice until he had to. But today none of that mattered. "Never mind, love. I have what I need now, and I'll use it. Your job is to not get sick quite yet." Bianca took his hand. "Don't go back to Florence. Stay here with me."

"As the grand duchess commands." Francesco brushed his cheek against hers. "It's getting late. And I'm quite tired. Fair scientist, would you follow your handsome alchemist to his bedroom?"

"I would," Bianca said.

She'd join him in bed now, but dawn would need to find her already awake. And the next day, and the next. How many pages, she wondered, could she write before sunrise?

When she woke the next morning, a faint golden light had begun to seep through the closed shutters of their room at Pratolino, soon to be filled with the bustle of servants, the beginning of a day. *What a reversal*, Bianca thought as she dressed quietly in the villa bedroom they shared. Years ago she'd have been sneaking into Francesco's bed, not out of it, stealing a secret night with another woman's man. Now Francesco had been Bianca's husband for almost ten years, and though his fingertips could still send chills down her spine, their intimacy was less urgent than the other kind of trust he'd placed in her, that promise he'd made only yesterday.

In one of her workrooms Bianca lit a candle and arranged her notebooks on a desk, the most recent on top. Its last page, describing the village woman's death, she'd only just filled. As she opened a new one, the flame's shadow danced across its linen pages, playing, too, against a roll of vellum that lay on a far corner, waiting for words. She uncorked a bottle of ink, rich and black, made from oak galls. Odd that a wasp building its simple nest, a gall in an oak, should create such a refined material—black ink. And with a little iron sulfate added, and gum Arabic thickening, the ink would bind to paper.

The thrum of boils and escaping steam filled Bianca's laboratory down the corridor. Bianca held her quill above the linen, poised, for so long that the ink on its tip dried. Setting it back down, she leaned over the desk, running a finger across the smooth surface of the vellum where she'd write the final draft of her discoveries. But first she had to know how to start, how to explain her ideas in a way that men would listen. Men, who would already expect a woman's work to be imprecise, who might not accept, for example, that the variation in doses and strengths of her distillations and extracts had been deliberate. She hoped to find a dependable cure once she'd tracked the full cycle of the disease. But that would come later; she couldn't document what she hadn't yet done.

Dipping her quill in the ink, slowly Bianca traced the first words across her parchment. *I soon will have the means to cure my husband, or to kill him, and the rest of Florence. My cures can rescue citizens from the malaria that crushes our city.* Malaria. *It's not bad air or bad people that cause this disease—if it was, all of Florence would be affected at once—but some danger inside the body. The sick will be all of us eventually, and we need to protect ourselves with a medicine that heals.* Scratching out *heals*, she wrote *cures*, then, *giving us back our health.*

But what would people understand of the paper? Would they see her evidence for a general idea after delivering the details? Details she had in plenty, gleaned from the sickroom in Pratolino, about the balance she had to strike between a body's weakness and the strength of cure that the body needed. Would they believe these discoveries to be hers, a woman's? And did she really need their critiques before putting her ideas to their final test on Francesco?

Bianca wrote for another week. She barely slept and she didn't taste the food Francesco made her eat. Roll after roll of parchment unspooled over her desk, filled with recipes-turned-procedures, as steps of the cure spun from her pen. Sheets began stacking up, each precise description rendered neatly and set aside to present to the most learned men in Florence.

After days of writing, Bianca wondered how she could have ever doubted her work. No doubt some people lived today because she'd given her cures to them, and her formulations of the cure described the conditions she'd accounted for. Others trying to follow what she'd done wouldn't have to test again different ways to harvest herbs, or how to set the temperatures of the distillations, or which solvents to use. The next time Francesco became ill, she'd treat him with carefully timed doses, a mix of distillate and infusions, spaced so she could learn how high a dose a body could handle. And once she did, she could lay out detailed guidelines to apply to different stages of the sickness, including at the end when death seemed almost a given. Then, Florence's great fear of malaria would be gone.

Had she successfully carried out her mother's mission? If Pellegrina had had a son instead of a daughter, the pages stacked in front of Bianca would already be printed and circulating, even though she hadn't yet fitted the final pieces into place. Bianca had had to fight each step along the way for the right to do what she'd done. Now she was ready to fight again, for the chance to present the progress of her work at Francesco's Crusca, and to make the Academy accept what she, a woman, was creating. Their emblem, a shovel sweeping away the chaff, the *crusca*, of the Florentine language, applied to the reasoning and rhetoric of scholarly findings, too. Bianca would be chaff to them unless she proved herself otherwise. And what would that take, to break into a world of self-absorbed scholars with their own agendas, alliances, and patronage? Far easier for them to reject her outright than for her to convince them to listen. And far harder for Bianca to ever persuade anyone to take her seriously if the Academy judged her thoughts wanting.

As evening fell Bianca sat at her desk, staring unseeing at the page in front of her. She had done it: the ink was drying on her final words. The writing would be enough, or it wouldn't be, for Crusca, but it was everything she had.

Stretching her stiff muscles, she got up from the chair. She found Francesco in one of his galleries, arms folded, staring at a new painting.

"What do you think?" he asked her. "Too bright? I told the artist I didn't like that red. I'm going back to Florence to tell him."

"Francesco?"

"Yes, love?" He turned to her, opening his arms.

"I'm finished," she told him. "I'm ready for the men at Crusca."

Francesco laughed. He stopped when he saw her face. "Bianca, you can't. I told you already; I thought you understood." He shook his head. "Perhaps I can bring your work to show them, but they don't welcome new faces. Only insiders can keep up with them. And no woman has ever been an insider." Francesco took her hand. "Bianca, please."

"Francesco, listen. Perhaps I'll be the first. Once I've convinced them, I will have won Florence. They have sway over everyone, including—"

"Including my brother." Leaning against a wall, Francesco ran his fingers through his hair.

"I hope he listens to them. His own ideas, I'm sure, wouldn't stand up to their scrutiny. Mine will." Bianca stilled Francesco's hand. "If I was a man, you wouldn't be trying to talk me out of this. They've heard papers on the Medici alchemy before, yes?"

"Porcelains, metals. Not an alchemy that cures."

"Not a scientific alchemy, you mean. Francesco, my work is the language of experiments, argument, rhetoric. It's an alchemy they can understand."

Francesco moved away from the wall and started pacing. "You're right, they wouldn't object to the substance of your ideas. It's not what, though, but who." He paused to face her. "I tell you, I'll take your cure regardless. You don't have to do this."

"I'm going to your Academy. Will you help me or not?"

Francesco started pacing again. "You don't give me much choice, do you? All right. I'll send a letter, but first go listen. Don't say anything before you've seen who's there, and what their arguments are like. After that, if you still want to present—"

"Which I will. And when I do, they'll have questions, but they'll hear me first." They would, she was all but certain. "I'll go listen, and then I'll thank you for sending your letter of introduction. Although you should thank yourself. This will help me make a cure for you." She touched his cheek. "For now, rest. Forget your painting."

"I'm fine, Bianca." But as he followed her from the gallery, he wiped a sheen of sweat from his forehead before taking her arm. "You'll be leaving for Florence in a week, I suppose. It's unfortunate timing. I'll be off to Poggio by then, to hunt. My brother suggested it. Unlike him, isn't it? I think he's finally starting to realize he's been too hard on me, on both of us. I'd hoped you'd want to join me."

"Nothing about him interests me. I'd come if you were sick." She laced her fingers in his. "But you promise me you're not, yes?" She peered into his eyes.

"I'm not sick."

"If you were, this would count as day one of your disease—should I get my notebook?" As Francesco shook his head, her frown turned into a smile. "Then on to Crusca," she said, tilting her head. Soon she'd be among the most learned in Florence—where she belonged.

28
Crusca

Tucking a satchel of notes and papers under her arm, Bianca stepped out of her carriage along the near side of the building. Midmorning in October, and the Academy of the Crusca was in shadow. She would have missed the entry if Francesco hadn't told her where to find it.

"You'll see," Francesco had said back in Pratolino. They'd both been packing, she to return to Florence, he for his hunting trip in Poggio. Bianca would join him after Florence, hoping that by then Francesco's brother would have come and gone. Had the cardinal ever been in the countryside for a week of sport? Would he trade his red robes for something less formal? Or perhaps he'd change his mind, and not come at all.

"Crusca is the biggest headache you're likely to get all month," Francesco had told her, cramming his riding boots into a bag. "Once they start talking, they don't stop." At least he hadn't joked about the men's screams of horror at finding a woman among them, or tried to talk her out of going. Not that he could have.

Now, Crusca's grim stone façade rose up in front of her. Stopping, she closed her eyes, splaying her fingers against the stone wall. It was warm from the mid-autumn heat stored during the day and released at night, leaving the auditorium cool for the learned men inside. What else did these walls hold? How much knowledge? Today she'd find out, or at least begin to. Still, she couldn't shake the feeling that she should be somewhere else. Prepping her assistant. Sitting in the palace court. But no. This was Bianca's time to talk to men about research. And best let them see her from the first as she was: a woman, independent, working on her own. Not as someone's wife with household secrets to give, but as someone with scientific alchemy to share.

Bianca opened her eyes. There it was, still before her. She made her way to the entrance, its opening flanked by two stained wooden doors, roughened with small divots. Bianca peered through the foyer. One man stood on a dais at the front of the room, shouting and gesturing to those seated before him, many of whom shouted and waved back. The sound of someone pounding on a bench drowned out any words Bianca might have understood. One of the nearest men glanced her way. He could have recognized her from the palace, but unless he'd been in Pratolino, he wouldn't know her as a healer. Still, she had enough of a reputation that people knew her when they saw a woman in a place no woman should be, if not enough of a reputation—yet—to convince them that she belonged there. Bianca let her shoulders slump, her hood shadowing her face. She wanted to pounce, not cower, but blending in would be impossible then, and she'd learn more if she observed without being recognized.

As men scurried for the last seats in the auditorium, the opening lecture ended. The chairs with deeply curved arms and wide leather seats had been taken, leaving only spots on polished wooden benches or folding chairs. As Bianca stepped farther into the hall, the din echoed, scavengers feeding on conversations, turning in on themselves to whisper or outward to laugh out loud, but never, just as Francesco had predicted, silent. Some held papers, loosely bound. Others had books. All talked among themselves, with few listening to the men at the front who seemed to be trying to instill some order in the hall. Most whose eyes fell on Bianca simply moved their conversations away from her, turning their backs or sliding a space or two down their benches. One man, stooped and wrinkled, paused to ask her, "Have you lost your husband?"

"No." Bianca gave him a cold smile. "I'm looking for a seat."

A tall man with a gray beard shot her a sharp look, then moved away. Next to him, a younger man with hazel-green eyes approached Bianca, nearly dropping the stack of papers tucked under his arm. "Madam, there may be a seat in the front?" He scrambled to straighten the pages.

Where everyone would look at her? She pulled her hood forward. "I'm here to observe."

"So long as you're comfortable. Let me introduce you to—"

"No," Bianca said, perhaps too sharply. The man clearly knew her. Was he from Pratolino? His courtesy was more welcome than the other men's rudeness, but she wasn't ready to have her presence known yet. "I'll sit in the back," Bianca told him. She took the farthest of three unoccupied seats, her nearest companions two men so deep in conversation that they didn't even glance at her as she smoothed her skirt and sat down.

Just as a white-haired man ascended the platform in the front of the room, though, someone paused in the aisle. "Is anyone sitting here?" A young man slid into the chair next to her. "The seats are filling."

Bianca nodded, scooting her chair sideways along the floor tiles.

As the speaker in the front of the room cleared his throat to begin his presentation, the young man asked, "Are you a writer?"

It was an easy answer. "I write, yes." Bianca set the satchel down and folded her hands in her lap.

"Like Ammannati's wife?"

Bianca's eyebrows lifted. "You mean the mistress Battiferri? Laura Battiferri. She has a name, you know. Do you think one of the greatest poets of Florence signed her poems 'Ammannati's wife?'"

The man shifted in his chair, cheeks flushing. "And so you're a poet, too?"

"No. I'm not a poet. But I know Battiferri's writing. She's spoken here?"

"Once." He looked up at her. "She speaks as if each word is sweetened with honey. You feel it here." He thumped a fist to his chest. "But she also makes you think."

"I agree." A man behind her spoke up, leaning toward them. "And the gentleman speaking now." He tilted his head toward the dais. "Today he's presenting scholarship, something from manuscripts. He sweetens his words, and also uses humor, but don't let him fool you. Pay particular attention to how he offers, then refutes, points, but still, he needs to be careful with his evidence."

How long had it been since she'd heard anyone talk this seriously about important ideas? Bianca shook her head, smiling. The more she listened, the more she understood. Like learning to grasp the Florentine accent when she'd first left Venice, once she had heard it enough, she knew she'd cease hearing it at all. And the man behind her was right. The scholar at the front of the room spoke eloquently for almost an hour about old manuscripts he'd been translating for years. Twice someone stood up and disputed his claims. The second time, Bianca found herself clutching the edge of her seat, waiting for one or the other of the men to strike a wounding blow. The only violence was verbal, but by the time the man presenting sat down, he looked shaken, clutching his manuscript to his chest as though to shield the ideas he'd presented from being further trampled into the ground. "Good showing," Bianca's neighbor commented. "But he should have been ready for that argument. Present anything incomplete and you might well not survive to complete it."

This seemed to be true. No one challenged the next man's study of the philosophy behind architectural styles, but the man who followed him was shouted from the podium before he'd even finished explaining his thoughts. Over the next hour, Bianca became more comfortable, picking apart sentences, many with complicated structure quite unlike the simple banter of the Court in the ducal palace. Even Francesco grew bored when she tried to discuss concepts with him at this level. No, this was something different altogether. Her style of writing would fit in here, better than she'd dared hope. But what about her arguments? She'd envisioned her presentation as a sharing among scholars who might offer new ideas to add to hers. Those who came with work unfinished, though, left with work ripped to shreds. Was she going to have to tell Francesco he'd been right, that bringing her paper here would be a mistake? Bianca frowned and kept listening.

One man finished and another took his place, lecturing on the history of astrology and chemistry in Florence, though with no reference to the Medici cosmos or the alchemist's studio of darkly boiling substances. Another's analysis of Michelangelo's art had Bianca nearly holding her breath. All through his speech, she wondered what this man would say if she stood up now and told him she'd been performing science for years among forgotten shards in the artist's garden.

Others shifted impatiently in their seats, but Bianca didn't stir. In the early afternoon, when the last speaker set down his notes, Bianca sat motionless in her chair even after the men around her began to stand. She wouldn't linger with them to debate over what she'd heard, though only because no man would take her seriously. But as she'd seen today, it took a great deal of careful evidence to make members of the Academy listen, much less change their minds.

These men didn't just borrow ideas; they countered them. They grounded them in other thoughts, other philosophies, creating new knowledge. But Bianca had been doing that for years, challenging every assumption or weakness in her own arguments with different ideas. Her detailed notes, much of it could stand up to any counterpoint she could imagine these men making. She could explain how artemisia functioned, its different effects, and how the process of distillation had allowed her to create a cure. How to use that cure, though—that was the question she still couldn't answer. And it was bound to be the first these men would ask. She was asking it herself.

Still, she had doubted herself for years, when the only thing she should have doubted was her belief in men who knew no more than she did. She understood more about healing than any of them; had even one of these men ever caught a sick child's vomit in a pot or cooled a fever with a poultice they'd made themselves? None of them, learned as they were, could be harsher critics than she herself had been. And if she wasn't harsh with herself now, then they'd squash all her work for its weakness. She would present here, but she couldn't yet, not until she'd answered her final questions. Not until she'd seen the disease unfold, connecting doses to severity of sickness.

The room had almost emptied. Bianca needed to go before someone noticed her sitting. As she began to rise, grabbing her satchel, somebody gave her an arm.

She looked up into a warm, inviting face. The man who'd sat next to her. "Well, mistress, will you be presenting someday?"

"I may." She stood, her hand on his elbow. "Did someone ask if I would be?"

"The first speaker on the dais. He's here regularly. But then, so am I. I could put in a word for you." He bowed. "I could tell from how intently you watched and listened today that you're interested in what we discuss."

"Perhaps." Would she even need Francesco's introduction?

Bianca nodded at her escort, then walked back through the entrance. Winding her way around the corner, blinking in the bright sunlight, her face broadened into a wide smile. The Academy had released some of its mysteries, and she'd kept hers, close to her heart, where they'd stay until she had the last piece of the puzzle.

Malaria would kill more people by then, but not her, and hopefully not Francesco.

Bianca turned toward her waiting carriage. Before she reached it, though, a servant, breathless, stopped in front of her, his hands by his side, panting in time with the horse he'd just dismounted. "Mistress. I come from Poggio, where your husband—"

"—is hunting, yes, I know." With his loathsome brother, if the cardinal had actually left Rome. Bianca looked into his eyes. "What's wrong?"

"The cardinal hasn't come yet. But the grand duke is ill." The servant lowered his voice. "The heat disease."

At first the words meant nothing. Then, gradually, they sank in. He was sick and she was here. He was alone, and only she could cure him. "Ride ahead and prepare the fastest carriage you can. Meet me at the side entrance of the palace," she said. "I'll be right behind you." Her notes and papers were with her now; the rest of what she needed was already in Pitti Palace. Bundles of herbs, flasks of steeping artemisia, an alembic, at least several doses of distillates. "Go," she told the servant, who was still staring at her, wide-eyed. "He won't die; I have medicine. I know how to cure him."

29
Illness at Villa Poggio a Caiano

Wet flakes of festering slime reflected the blaze of sun in Francesco's ear. Just for an instant he stirred, lines of blood snaking from his ruptured eardrum, converging down his neck. Bianca wrung out a wet cloth and dabbed at the rusty trickle. Such a small gesture, but all she allowed herself to do. She could have given him the stronger artemisia three days ago when his fever again spiked and every day since. Sometimes she still couldn't believe she hadn't.

Within an hour of her arrival she had converted a corner of her room into a miniature laboratory, setting up the alembic she'd brought with her from Florence, organizing her vials, lighting a small fire in the hearth so she could boil water without creating too much heat, giving Francesco some steeped artemisia whenever he needed more liquid. In that first hour, though, Francesco had woken twice. "Not yet," he'd insisted both times. "I don't need your cure—not yet." He'd said as much again this morning when, for a few minutes, his eyes had flickered open.

How had Francesco moved so far—from scorning her experiments in the garden, spurning her infusions, being suspicious of her testing—to this? Perhaps he knew that this kind of proof, from testing her doses to curing those dying, was the only way for her to find a place there? Or was it?

How had presenting her work at Crusca come to mean so much to her? The perfect argument with the perfect cure—and what exactly was that worth now? The idea of observing the progress of the disease from the beginning, noting it, recording it for what she'd discuss there, and in front of those men? Her husband lay dying before her. Had she really thought the only work that remained was to monitor the progression of the disease? And why? It was easy to blame her failures on the doses, on the timing, on not knowing enough about the disease itself. But perhaps all the others had died of complications from malaria over which she had no control. In which case, why not give the strongest dose now? Bianca steadied her shaking hand; only then was she able to wipe the sweat from her own face. What had her mother said? She'd warned her about pressing her own knowledge; at the same time, she'd wanted Bianca to find it. But not at the cost of another's life.

Poor Francesco. Had he thought that her triumph over malaria would be easy and the risks—seizures, even death—small, a half-truth he'd convinced himself of? A question had hung unspoken between them: if he died, where would that leave her? Florence wouldn't care that she'd tried to save him. But if he lived?

If he lived, she'd be known for having saved Florence's grand duke. Her adopted city would see her in the end for the scientist she was. A healer, a defender—if he lived. Science the way Bianca practiced it was exact. Precise amounts of artemisia leaf and flowers in infusions and extractions to give a strong dose for malaria at its peak, free of any impurities—that's what he needed. Too potent and he'd vomit all the remedy. Its simple alchemy told her she could do this.

Picking up a clean cloth, Bianca wiped his dripping forehead. The villa's ceramic floor tiles had captured the sweltering heat of the unusually warm October day. Even with the open windows, the thick, smothering air felt sticky, harsh smells rising from the bowls of filth that the servants whisked away, only to promptly replace them with more basins. The one blessing she could count right now was that the cardinal was decidedly absent. She'd always halfway thought he'd back out; a week in the countryside was the last thing she could picture Francesco's brother enjoying.

Bianca kneeled to take Francesco's hand and laid her head close to his heart, listening to the frantic wheezing of his chest pushing out air, then sucking it in again. Feverish as he was, and with the color draining from his face, court doctors would have bled him, killing him. But was she doing any better? She had to act, despite his protests. True, he could get sicker. If the patient she needed had to be close to the brink of death, she had one in front of her now.

"Francesco, it's time." Bianca spoke softly.

Eyelids flickering, he shifted in bed. Could he hear her? What if she'd waited too long, and he'd fallen into a sleep impossible to recover from?

"I never should have agreed to let you do this," Bianca said under her breath. "If I'd dosed you when I first got here, you'd be out hunting now." When he'd given the same instructions at Pratolino—*wait*—there had been signs of the disease then, but he hadn't been drowning as he was now in a pool of phlegm drenching his lungs. He hadn't had this burning fever. Last night, she'd nursed him through convulsions, forgetting to breathe herself until his stiff body relaxed and he gasped air in and out at last.

Francesco's eyes rolled back. Had she lost him? Was another seizure coming? Then in a faint voice, he muttered. "Is it time? Do you know what you need to . . ."

Did she? She'd watched the progress of the illness, and had written down notes of how Francesco's body responded to every brew. Every few days, another round of chills, fever, sweating, as the disease set in again. She'd measured his pulse in each phase, tracked his fever's rise and fall, jotted down how symptoms developed and in what sequence they worsened. She'd known a seizure meant the illness had advanced and when a patient was too dehydrated or too malnourished to accept treatment. But now she knew, too, at what stage fluid in the lungs would make it impossible to swallow, making certain treatments unsafe. In the past two days she'd come to the conclusion that in a patient like Francesco, who had no other complications, it wasn't the strength of the medicine that was so important as the timing of its delivery. Wasn't that right? Bianca ran over in her mind each of her cases at Pratolino, each man or woman whose body had been so weak she'd been afraid to give them pure distillate—or was it that she was afraid to waste it on those almost dead. After watching the rhythms of Francesco's disease, she wondered if waiting for any next stage of it was pointless, and that she should just give the cure now. All this she'd devised from observing Francesco, the man who lay before her, in pain. All this she'd learned so that, ultimately, she could save him.

"Yes." Bianca blinked back a tear. "I know enough." His eyes had closed again; she didn't think he heard her. That didn't matter. Sick as he was, she had no time to waste, and further words would only slow her down.

Bianca reached for a vial on the side table and poured it all into a cup of lukewarm brew. One dose now, the rest over the next two days. Clasping his head in one arm and lifting his chin, she tipped the contents of the cup to Francesco's lips, wiping stray streams of the medicine into his mouth. She closed her eyes, and for a minute saw her mother sipping what Bianca had prepared, and the girl at Sant'Elisabetta, and then all the women in the brothels, and the patients in Pratolino. So much artemisia, so many gardens. Some of the experiments had gone badly. Not enough distillate, or perhaps too much. The time for such errors was over. At least, she hoped so. Soon she would know.

Tucking another pillow behind Francesco's head, she told him, "Sleep."

Francesco settled into the bed and sighed.

In the hours that passed he seemed more restful, but nothing could ease her doubt about the risk she'd taken. And Francesco? Had he really understood what he'd agreed to? He liked big gestures, but he often failed to think about the consequences. When he'd promised to let her test on him, had he actually pictured this? He could have changed his mind at any point, and he hadn't. But he likely didn't realize just how sick he was.

Of course Bianca had put herself in danger too, waiting this long to cure him. A saved life would mean her success, leaving no room for any to doubt her science, but his death would mean her downfall. Already, few loved their grand duchess, and no wives had ever fared well once their Medici husbands were dead. Add to that the cardinal, next in line after Antonio for the dukedom, and Bianca's future could only be seen as grim. Had Francesco really risked any more than she had? Both of them depended on her cure bringing real recovery and change. Both would live or die by her skill. Which meant that both, she knew from all her years of work, would live. They had to.

All at once, Francesco half-rose in the bed, gagging. A great gob of acid liquid ran down his chin onto his nightshirt, soaking it with sour fluid. Bianca's stomach turned at the smell of bile. Malaria hadn't left any of her patients, even the mildest cases, without a fight. Pulling off his shirt, Bianca then lowered him back to the bed, covering him with a fresh linen sheet. Water and cool compresses would ease his discomfort a little, but she could do nothing more until he stopped retching.

After he was settled again, she took her notebook and sat by his bedside. She'd recorded everything: what she put into Francesco's cure and when, how much of the pure distillation, the changes she'd seen as he drew back from malaria's grip. Choosing words to describe the changes in his color and the sweat beading on his face, less pungent now and stinking more of a man's clammy body than of death, she watched Francesco shift under his thin sheet, his eyelids flickering. Once they opened, but he seemed to stare through Bianca without seeing her. She scrawled another note, not wanting to look away from him for the time it would take to write clearly. *Late morning, three hours after first dose. Seems near waking.* The next time his gaze met hers, would he know her name?

The following morning, a servant tapped at the door.

"Can't it wait?" Bianca asked, crossing the room to speak with the man so they wouldn't have to raise their voices. Francesco's sleep finally looked more restful, and his fever was beginning to ebb. It might rise again in the evening, though. She needed him undisturbed until then.

But the servant shook his head. "It's a message from the cardinal, Mistress. I was told to give it to you right away."

"The cardinal? Of course. Thank you." She held out her hand. The scroll the servant gave her was small, but its scarlet wax bore the cardinal's unmistakable seal. Bianca tore it open without waiting to watch the servant leave. Suddenly she was sweating, her palms clammy. A quick glance at the letter was all it took. The cardinal was en route, and not because he'd decided he wanted to go hunting after all.

He'd given no salutation, no acknowledgment of the woman he must have known would read his letter. *I have been informed of the progression of my brother's illness. I'll soon be arriving at his bedside. Francesco de' Medici must not pass on without Rome's blessing.*

Rome's curse, more like. Bianca let the parchment drop to the floor. If she'd had doubts this morning about whether now was the time to bring Francesco back from the brink to which his illness had taken him, those doubts were gone. The cardinal would revel in Francesco's death. Bianca wouldn't be surprised if the man was coming just to make sure it happened, and to preside at the funeral of the brother whose wedding he'd refused to bless. Well, he wouldn't get the chance. Bianca kicked the scroll under the bed and turned to a corner table. Time for another dose, a strong one. Francesco was going to live.

She'd have to add something to fight the nausea so Francesco could keep it all down. She hadn't brought any peppermint with her, but they'd surely have some oil in the kitchen. Bianca sighed.

Since she'd arrived, sharp herbal smells had filled the room, mixed with alcohols and acrid smoke. Bianca had felt the servants' sidelong glances, their whispers growing more intense each time they passed in and out, bringing hot water and clean cloths when she asked for them, but always muttering when her back was turned about the mistress's witchcraft. *It's science, not witchcraft, and it's going to save his life*, she'd wanted to say, but who would listen? She wasn't about to leave his side, not even for a quick trip to the kitchen. So, reluctantly, she rang the bell to call a servant.

The woman who stood at her door looked familiar, though she hadn't answered the bell before. Grease spatters stained her apron. "Mistress," she said, meeting Bianca's eyes more willingly than the other servants had. "I'm the head cook. How can I help?"

"Oil of peppermint?" Where had she seen this woman before?

"Certainly; I'll get it for you."

Bianca waited, but the woman didn't leave. Was she waiting to be dismissed? Bianca said, "Thank you, truly."

"Thank *you*." To Bianca's amazement, the woman stepped into the room and knelt down before her. "You saved my daughter's life. I brought her to you in Pratolino. We were there cooking for the duke when she became ill with the heat disease."

Bianca nodded. "Of course. She's doing well, then?" The girl had been one of her early successes, albeit a mild case. And yes, she'd most likely survived because this woman, her mother, had brought the child to Bianca in time. Bianca couldn't remember the girl's name, but each symptom was still fresh in her mind. "Your daughter fought her sickness well." Bianca touched the woman's hand. "She's strong."

The cook beamed. "I'll get your peppermint, Mistress. And anything else, anything at all, that you need." She lifted her hands as if holding something round. "You look exhausted. Perhaps you'd like to wash in a basin?"

Bianca shook her head. It had been days since she'd paid attention to what she needed for herself. What else did Bianca want that the woman could provide? Nothing, but the woman's warmth was a nice change. Bianca returned to her table, preparing a sweet infusion to which she would add the peppermint. And whether because of all the studying, all the work she'd put into her writing, or because of the cook's grateful confidence, Bianca poured the second vial down Francesco's throat without her hand even shaking.

Once he'd swallowed, Bianca bent over him. "You may feel worse before you feel better, love." Could he hear her? The room spun as she moved from his bedside. She must have stood up too fast. Bianca braced her hand on a wall. When had she last slept? Though lack of sleep hadn't made her dizzy before.

Pressing her fingers to her temples, Bianca closed her aching eyes. Once or twice Francesco had teased her, admiring her clear skin and asking if she was quite certain that she wasn't a witch, that she hadn't made some deal with the devil to keep from getting sick herself. Bianca had brushed off his questions. She had no time to get sick, and besides, she dealt so much with artemisia it probably ran in her blood, and if Francesco wanted to see a devil he should go find his brother. The truth was, though, she'd spent no more time with artemisia than her mother had, and it hadn't protected Pellegrina. Bianca simply never had been sick and never would be. That's how it was.

For just a moment, she allowed herself to sink into the bedside chair. Yes, she was tired, but her work was almost done. She'd given two doses already to Francesco. He'd need one more before the cardinal arrived. She had finished that distillation this morning, exactly the right amount of cure to save Francesco. Francesco, but not herself.

Bianca hadn't meant to fall asleep, but the next time her eyes opened, the room was growing brighter with glints of morning sun. It felt cold, too, though Francesco had thrown off all his blankets. Shivering, she stood, catching her balance on the back of the chair as, once again, the room swayed.

Francesco had blinked himself awake. "Bianca?" He lifted a shaking hand to the cloth at his head. "What?"

Even as his gut gurgled, warning of another purge, Bianca couldn't keep the smile from her face. He knew her, and his eyes weren't feverish. Already the cure was having an effect. She filled a cup with water, then knelt at his side. "Please drink?" She touched his forehead. Cool, his face and neck dry.

He drank it in two swallows, lying back against the pillows when he finished. Soon, all she heard was light snoring, so different from days before, when his cries had shaken the whole villa. A rosy color, pink, not yellow, had returned to his face. She laid her head on his chest, listening for a heartbeat. Steady, a pulse stronger than hers. And that was it. His fever lowered, his flushed face calmed, tense limbs loosened. The heat, the illness, was fading. He'd need more medicine to drive the last of the sickness from his body and prevent a relapse. But he'd get it. Francesco lived, and Bianca had won.

She had everything she needed now to add to her waxy sheets of fine vellum—a paper documenting the entirety of her cure. After that, she'd manufacture her medicines, and Florence would finally recognize her for the healer she had always been. The most expensive botanicals would be at her fingertips in her own pharmacy. And she'd have any seeds she desired to grow in her gardens. She'd dispense cures. And the cardinal? Once he saw how she'd revived Francesco, he'd have to accept the outcome, saving his holy oils for those actually dying. She'd sleep now, resting a little longer in this dismal country house. All her weakness would be gone, surely, before the cardinal arrived.

She closed her eyes.

30
The Price of a Cure

Sinking in a deep, inky pool, Bianca trembled as the water seeped into her clothes. But she needed to wake. Her eyes flickered open. *It's just tiredness*, she told herself, and she sat up, her movements slower than the urgent messages in her head. She was on Francesco's bed, the front of her dress damp from his sweat. Francesco lay next to her, flat against his yellowed pillows. The mottled flush had faded in his face, his breath only slightly uneven now. Bianca's heart was racing, but it shouldn't be. She'd healed him. What Francesco had wondered about all his life, Bianca had found.

Couldn't she sleep a little longer?

Bianca shook her head. Light poured through the window—perhaps she'd been too tired to close the shutters. At one point she'd been resting in the chair. She'd woken, hadn't she? And helped Francesco take some broth down his throat. Then she'd sat down beside him. Or had she lain down? She'd meant to give him another dose last night before they'd both fallen asleep. But it wouldn't matter if that dose was a little late, as long as he got it. She'd healed him.

Bianca lifted herself onto a nearby stool. When the doorway darkened, she thought at first that her eyes had just fallen closed again. Then Francesco let out a cry. It sounded like his brother's name.

The cardinal. Eyes still bleary, she blinked. There he stood. Bianca lurched to her feet.

The man couldn't enter a room without filling it. As he pushed his way in, his robes a dark crimson one shade brighter than the crusted blood on Francesco's face, Bianca searched for a fitting greeting. With a bob of his head, he took a place standing opposite her on the other side of the bed, stiff in the armor of his cardinal's garb. Bianca gave him a slight nod. "Cardinal."

"Well?" The cardinal barely glanced at Bianca as he snatched the cloth from Francesco's head and held the back of his hand to his brother's brow. "I was told you were dying. But you have no fever. The servants said you couldn't speak a few days ago."

"Ferdinando . . ." Francesco muttered in a tired voice, pulling himself onto the pillows.

The cardinal faced Bianca as he paced along the side of the bed. "What have you been doing to him?" He shook his head. "I can smell the sickness. Foul linens, rank vomit, the malaria. And sulfur, which means someone has been playing with chemistry. For good or ill, I wonder? For God, or for the devil?"

"Ferdinando, sit, so I can see you fully." Francesco pointed to the chair that had been Bianca's these past days, eyeing his brother as he sat. Bianca lowered herself onto the edge of the bed. "There, we're all sitting." Francesco's voice rasped. "Brother, it's a new medicine."

Bianca glanced at Francesco, then set her eyes on the cardinal. The man's lips tightened.

"That's not possible. I was told you were delirious." The cardinal leaned toward Francesco. "Was this your metals after all? How did you concoct something while on your deathbed?"

"Not my work."

Looking down, Bianca found her fingers twisting and knotting one of Francesco's sheets. She forced her hands still.

"What do you mean, Francesco?" The cardinal's face stiffened.

Bianca would have stood if she thought she could have without shaking. Instead she lifted her head. She'd have to do this again and again: tell a man who hated her that she'd accomplished what he never could. She steadied herself, meeting his gaze. "It's my medicine, Cardinal."

One eyebrow flicked as he looked her up and down. "Are you still playing that game?" He lifted one of the empty cups to his nose. "Yes, this does stink of weeds. One of your brews from sneaking around smutty brothels?"

Bianca held the cardinal's stare. She wasn't ten again, creeping through the aunties' palace with her herbal brews, trying to explain to old women how she knew more than they did. She'd been right back then, but so had they; her cures had been strong, but not strong enough. Now she knew to distill what before she'd only been able to boil and steep. She had power, and the man in the bed was her proof. Any miscalculation would have killed him. In her hands, he lived. She swallowed. "My brews, yes—medicine for your family."

A hoarse voice added, "For all of Florence."

The cardinal let out a harsh bark of laughter. "This is nonsense." He pointed to the bed. "Do I need to grab these linens and wring the wet from them? Bring them to your face, my duke, to smell the acid vomit? Or show you all the other poisons in this room?"

Francesco lifted his head. "Listen to me. Bianca's cure for the heat disease works."

The cardinal again leaned over the bed, putting his hand on Francesco's shoulder. "Listen, brother." The cardinal's face reddened. "Some get sick and some don't. Some recover, some die; that's how it's always been with our family—and in all of Florence. There's no cure, Francesco. God is the cure. What does she want to do next, raise the dead?"

Bianca glanced at Francesco, then the cardinal. "Cardinal—"

The cardinal spoke over her. "Francesco, it's clear that this is all God's doing, not some woman's."

"Francesco, rest," Bianca said softly. How satisfying for the cardinal if Francesco relapsed now. If he died today, no one would dare suggest that it was because his brother infuriated him when he most needed quiet. No, they'd probably thank God that the cardinal was at his bedside when it happened.

Bianca took Francesco's hand. "You won't change his mind. He can't even see what's in front of him, or he'd see it's his god that has given me a special gift, the gift of curing."

"Have you never thought your cures might be curses? We're meant to die with dignity when we're called; isn't that right?" The cardinal stood, towering over both of them. "Tell me about this medicine you have so much faith in. A medicine made by a woman?"

Bianca raised her voice. "I'm in the room, Cardinal; you don't need to talk as if I'm not."

Nostrils flaring, the cardinal raised his hand, letting it slap down on a table by Francesco's bedside. A spoon clanked to the ground. "This is blasphemy."

"This is my medicine, Cardinal. It's my work."

"Your work?" He raised one eyebrow. "You have work, other than seducing my brother?"

Using his elbows, Francesco propped himself against the bed's backboard. "Listen to me carefully, Ferdinando. Bianca's been practicing her medicine in her own laboratory. Once I'm well, I intend to make it known that her skill as a healer carries weight, and any others who wish to treat the sick should look first to her."

"Brother, you go too far. You'll not soil the Medici name that way, allowing a whore to run your affairs, not as long as I draw breath." The cardinal fixed his gaze on Bianca. "I think it's time I learned a little more about this cure of yours, don't you? I see you've made yourself a little laboratory here."

In two steps he stood in the corner Bianca had set aside for preparing her cure. Her extracts and distillate, and on a desk, a pile of notebooks. Everything she needed to cure Francesco. Embers glowed in the hearth at the center of the room, ready to heat the brew for Francesco's treatment, which had already been steeping in a thick clay pot.

"All these weeds and books you think you need." The cardinal picked up the notebook on top of the stack, thumbing through it. "Sketches, numbers, scribbles." Bianca imagined the feel of the pages under his fingers. She'd want to wash anything he touched. The room swaying, she braced her feet against the ceramic floor to stand, to go and take it from him, but she couldn't steady herself. Francesco had fallen back on the pillows.

"I'm cold," the cardinal announced, and tossed her notebook onto the hearth's red embers.

By the time she'd stumbled over to the cardinal, the room spinning, nothing was left of the pages but flames. As she reached for his arm he moved aside, grabbing a bundle of dried artemisia and adding that to the crackling fire. A second bundle followed, and another notebook. In the bed, Francesco started coughing, the smoke from the burning herbs too much for his already raw throat. Bianca felt her own lungs protesting. The cardinal, however, merely looked amused. "Francesco, it's sweltering hot in here. What were you thinking, allowing your woman to have a fire going in this hearth? I'll put it out for you." Bianca lunged for his arm again, only to feel his fist in her face. She fell, half-catching herself on the bed, as a splash and a hiss filled the room, the sound of liquids being poured over flames. Then the dull thud of a sturdy clay vessel, the one with the distillate, hitting the floor and breaking.

Bianca pulled herself up until she was sitting on the bed next to Francesco, her head pounding from the cardinal's blow. Francesco reached for her hand. His fingers shook as he grasped hers. "Bianca—?"

Bianca shook her head. "It doesn't matter," she said, loud enough for the cardinal to hear. "Francesco's had enough doses. The next was just for good measure. And I have copies of all of those notes in a place far from here." Some notes at Pratolino, yes, and some in Florence. Her latest notes, those documenting Francesco's illness, were nowhere else but in her head, but they wouldn't be difficult to reconstruct from memory. Every moment of fear and success from these last few days was surely cemented in her mind. Bianca looked up at the cardinal. "We'll have to hope you don't catch malaria yourself, Cardinal, as without my herbs I wouldn't be able to cure you."

"Cure me? As if I'd let you touch me. The only one who cares about what you're doing is this dying man here." His fist rose again, the heavy rings on his fingers glinting in the window's light. "Bianca, you're worthless."

Gritting her teeth, Bianca let seconds pass. "If your opinion mattered, I'd care. My work on artemisia will be read." Francesco squeezed her hand. "My work, explained in just one paper—at Crusca."

"Nonsense." The cardinal let his hand fall so the sleeves of his robe covered his fist, but his voice had lost none of its anger. "Know this, Bianca. Florence is a Medici Florence, protecting the Church and its teachings. There's no room for a woman's mind. You think you'll present at Crusca, among the most educated of men? I suppose next you'll be giving them directives, imagining they'll all do your bidding just as my fool brother does. But women aren't capable of such thinking. The sooner you learn that, the easier things will go for you."

"It's my alchemy that's cured him, Cardinal. A woman scientist saved your brother. A woman gave him the medicine he needed." Bianca paused. "Science to you is the business of a few men in palace rooms, dead ones buried in your churches," she said. "Science to me is men and women, together, observing, learning, working."

"A woman who fits your description doesn't sound like a scientist to me." Clasping his hands together, the cardinal drew back. "She sounds like a witch."

Taking in the cardinal's face, his robes, the gleam of gold around his neck, Bianca rose, saying, "You expect the whole world to be like your church, run by a few wealthy families, Medici in a seamless lineage, one corrupt cleric following another. You think science is the same?"

"I think you know nothing of the Church or science."

"Remember, Francesco was dying. He now lives. He's given me the buildings I need, and his Crusca will open its doors to me as soon as they learn what I've done." She lifted her chin. "When they learn I've saved his life."

The cardinal raised an eyebrow but didn't speak.

Bianca let the room fill with silence, breaking it with, "Your brother recognizes my work. And that I've done more than any man has managed. One day you can read about it. You could have done so today if you hadn't burned my papers."

The cardinal's eyes narrowed to slits. His face was so like his brother's, but with a smile colder than any Bianca had ever seen on Francesco's lips. "This game has gone on long enough, Bianca. My brother promises you science? I promise you exile, and for that you should count yourself lucky. You called Francesco back when God was ready to call him home." He faced Francesco. "Isn't that true?"

Francesco tried to sit up. The effort was too much. He fell back against his pillows. "Little brother, you are the uninvited guest here." His voice was sharp.

"Is that right, Francesco? Now let me explain a few things to you about *my* uninvited guest." The cardinal pointed to Bianca. "I can ban your wife from the Church—and from the city." He nodded at the both of them. "And I will."

"You'll have to kill me first." Francesco's jaw clenched.

"Don't think that can't be arranged, brother. We're Medici." The cardinal paused. "And if she's still in Florence at midday tomorrow, by tomorrow night I'll name her witch and have her hauled away."

Bianca opened her mouth, but no words would come. So that was it? She'd been exiled, and they'd just given him the grounds to do it? Her eyes darted to Francesco. She shook her head, signaling him not to speak, not to play the cardinal's game. The man wanted Francesco to bargain and plead. They had to find another way.

Banishment would mean an end to everything Bianca had built. There was nowhere for her to go where she wouldn't be recognized, a highborn woman with alchemic knowledge, and shamed, declared by the Church to be unholy. Bianca could never be safe, let alone practice her science. Not as long as the cardinal lived.

As long as the cardinal lived.

No one knew better than Bianca how thin that line was, between life and death. How easy it was to cross. She'd spent her whole life keeping as many people as she could on this side of it. Would all that work, and all the future lives she might have saved, be lost? Because one man continued to live?

The cardinal, from what she could see, was only a mass of flesh—bleak, soulless. Bianca let her eyes lose their focus, trying to see him as he really was, no robes of taffeta and velvet, no beating heart, just a skeleton. The man was already dead. Bone on bone, nothing living. Bianca's gaze met Francesco's. What had the cardinal just said? Francesco's death could be arranged; they were Medici, after all. If one brother killed the other it wouldn't be a first, not in this family. Only, the death needed here wasn't Francesco's.

Francesco gave a nod so slight that no one who wasn't looking could have seen it.

Bianca turned to the cardinal, a smile fixed on her face. "If you're banishing me, I trust you won't expect my hospitality. You'll leave Francesco and me alone on our last night."

As she'd imagined, the cardinal shook his head. "No, now that you mention it, I would like a meal in your house. Perhaps if you prepare it well I won't make your banishment a lifelong sentence." He took a step closer to Francesco. "Yes, much as I'm sure you'd enjoy one final night with your whore, Francesco, I'll be expecting supper with you tonight. I don't imagine your woman can cook. But hopefully your servants can."

"I can cook, actually. I make a fine . . ." What would the cardinal be most likely to eat? "I make the best tarts in Florence." All the Medici loved sweets, she knew that. "Cooking is just another kind of chemistry, you know."

The cardinal snorted. "Oh, I'm sure that's why my brother snuck away to your bed for years. Perhaps during your decades of exile you'll learn it's the only science that should concern you." Turning to Francesco, he said, "If you're as cured as she says you are, I trust you'll join me tonight? Your wife, I'm afraid, is not invited, but I'd like to dine with you."

Bianca took Francesco's hand. Let him be seen, dining with his brother, one last time. Had Francesco thought the same thing? His eyes said yes, though from the lines around his lips Bianca knew what the effort of this meal would cost him.

"Why, yes, Ferdinando; I'm feeling better." Francesco didn't look at her and Bianca didn't dare nod, but she squeezed his hand. A beat passed, and then he squeezed back, his grip firm and sure. "Yes," he told his brother. "We'll eat together tonight. On one condition. Banish Bianca if you must, but apologize to her now. She's not a whore and never has been, and her cure will save lives, as it did mine."

Bianca bit her lip. Didn't Francesco understand her plan? Dining with his brother would give her the opportunity to prepare a tart for the cardinal, a very special tart indeed. From his nod and his look, she'd been sure Francesco's mind had moved in step with hers. Was he going to risk it all for this? She didn't care what the cardinal called her. What she cared about was seeing him dead.

The cardinal gazed at Francesco. He could storm out of the room now, back to Rome, and her banishment would be set. "Francesco," the cardinal said. "Do you know the meaning of the word whore? Hasn't it ever occurred to you she married you for more than your charm? But never mind. If I've offended you, Bianca," he turned to her. "Forgive me. Perhaps I could have spoken the truth with more tact."

Francesco sat up. "You'd better go. Now."

"Ah, but we're still planning here. Let's see, apples and plums fill your storerooms, do they not? Bake them well, and your husband and I shall enjoy them while you pack your bags for your travel. I'll pray for your departure as a penitent." And in a rustle of red, he swept from the room.

"You pray, Cardinal," Bianca said beneath her breath.

She waited until the door had clicked shut and the thud of the cardinal's boots had faded. Only then did she look at Francesco.

Tonight she'd extinguish a candle, suffocating it, the light flickering as if in pain, gasping for the last pockets of air. She was more Medici than he knew.

"I don't think I've ever heard you say that word." Francesco's soft laugh turned into a cough, but a smile still played in his eyes. "Has my brother finally converted you?"

"He's converted me to ridding Florence of a wicked man determined to deprive people of cures, determined to stop scientific minds from creating them."

"He's made you a baker tonight, but be careful, Bianca. You're used to a laboratory, not a kitchen. It'd be too bad, wouldn't it, if you mixed up some ingredients?"

Bianca touched the tip of her finger to his smiling lips. "Ah, well, you Medici men. Unable to resist a bit of sweet. Apple's your favorite fruit, isn't it?"

"It's my brother's too. Give him the apple, red like his robes. I'll take the plum. I don't think I'll be hungry anyway. Now, Bianca, let me look at you. You're bruising already from where he hit you. Is that why your face is so flushed?"

"I'm fine." Bianca swayed, digging into her heels for balance. The room couldn't be spinning; she was just tired. "You know, you didn't have to make him apologize to me."

"Of course I did—he touched you. Besides, I'd hardly call that an apology. Now, I'd better get ready for this meal. And so had you. You'll want to stop by my study. There's a little tin . . ."

Bianca's lips formed a thin line. "Of white powder. Though why you keep it here I don't know." She shook her head. "Wait, I'll help you up."

Every cure had its price. This cure had taken Francesco's strength, even though it had saved him. Opening her arms toward Francesco, she said, "Shift your weight, love, toward me." Francesco slid out of the bed and stood, his legs shaking.

He kissed her cheek, his face cool. "Bianca, so warm?"

Sweat pooled on her face. Surely it meant nothing.

Bianca held Francesco's waist as he bent over a washbowl, water splashing along the sides, scrubbing his own face for the first time in days. He seemed steady enough on his feet, almost more so than Bianca herself. The next dose of her infusions and distillate, now dampening the ashes of Bianca's herbs and notes, would have meant that the heat disease was broken for good. Even without that dose, though, as long as nothing new arose in his body to have to struggle against, he'd recover, she was certain. Tonight it was the cardinal, not Francesco, who'd be fighting for his life.

31
When Alchemy Kills

Steadying herself in the kitchen passageway, Bianca glanced behind her at the stairs she'd just clambered down—hardly like the stealthy feline she'd once considered herself. How did the servers make this journey back and forth carrying their dishes? The dining room, like the bedrooms, was on the floors above. The kitchen, outside. Francesco and the cardinal might, even now, be drinking wine right above the place where Bianca stood. Down here in the storerooms, though, all was chaos. Making her way through them, she passed piles of dishes and pots on countertops. She'd have to work carefully. The tin in her pocket bounced against her hip as she moved. Mistakes could be unforgiving, even fatal.

In the kitchen, flour covered the nearest table, and a young woman kneading dough by the windows didn't look ready to welcome another baker. The next counter space overflowed with partially chopped vegetables. Bianca pushed past a boy holding tongs and a muscular woman with a partially plucked chicken in her arms while a pot behind her boiled loudly. Smoke fumes twisted toward the ceiling. Her lungs burned. She was used to the steam of steeping herbs in the air, not scalding fats. At a corner table one woman sat, stacking pastry cloths. Bianca approached, speaking only to burst into a fit of coughing. At least it made the woman look up. Clearing her throat, Bianca tilted her head toward the table. "I need this workspace, ma'am."

"This is my kitchen," the woman scolded. "The bakers report to me. You—"

"I think you'll find it's *my* kitchen." Bianca drew herself up. True, she'd never set foot in here before, but shouldn't this woman recognize her? "I'm Bianca, the grand duke's wife. Now, please may I have this table?"

The baker blinked, then turned and fled.

Bianca reached into her pocket and pulled out the small metal tin she'd taken from Francesco's study. A staple of every Medici household, if not in the kitchen, then in the master's bag. Today she'd use it as some extra sweetening—it certainly looked the part. Yet no one knew the properties of arsenic better than the Medici. Bianca laughed to herself. Her husband's family and their poison. If anything, it was effective. Combined with strychnine, it killed rats. Certainly, on its own, it could kill a mere mouse of a cardinal.

As Bianca wiped down the surface of her small table, she went over the plan in her head. Apple tarts for the cardinal. That must be the one thing he shared with his brother, a love of that sweet autumn fruit. Apples red as the cardinal's robes, and a plum tart for Francesco, who would barely touch it, sick as he'd been. "I'll eat it, though," he'd promised as they ironed out their plan. "My brother will get suspicious otherwise. Besides, it's not every day you bake for me."

She pressed her hand to her temple. She was sweating, but she felt cold, not hot. Leaning on the table, she braced herself. Had she still not recovered from the long nights at Francesco's bedside? Healers didn't have time to get sick. Bianca shook her head and kept going.

She'd need flour. There was plenty of that in this kitchen. And lard was already on the table. Bianca motioned to a passing servant boy. "Sugar, salt, and about a half dozen eggs, and whisk them for me, please." The boy nodded. "Apples and plums—and soft cheese,"

Bianca added before he darted away. Red apples for the cardinal, like his robes.

By the time the boy returned, Bianca had rolled up her sleeves. She'd assembled the rest of what she needed, mixing bowls, cups, and water. He laid out the ingredients she'd asked for, setting down the fruit last. Bianca nodded her thanks to the boy and began pouring flour and sugar, adding salt and spices, and then working in the lard. She whipped the soft cheese into the egg mix. Stirring, she combined all the ingredients and divided the batter into two copper pans. There; now she could begin the fruit topping. Bianca started cutting plums, harvested from the Medici orchards. They leaked dark juice into the bowl, warm and red as blood against Bianca's hands.

"Mistress?"

Bianca jumped.

"Was the peppermint oil all right?" It was the cook, the one whose daughter Bianca had treated. As Bianca blinked at her, trying to focus her eyes, the woman stepped closer. "Mistress, are you well?"

"Of course." But, suddenly, she didn't want to look at the deep-colored juice pooling at the edge of the table.

"Only, your face looks a little rosy." The cook glanced at Bianca, then looked down. "No offense meant. You're beautiful as always; you just look tired. I've never seen you in the kitchens before, Mistress. I understand, though, baking must be a comfort after the scare you had with the duke's illness. Tell me if you need anything, anything at all. I'll be over—oh, that's my soup boiling. I'd better go." She hurried away.

Head spinning, Bianca supported herself with one hand on the table. Her mother had loved baking when she could, and Bianca had watched those dough-covered hands with strong fingers that worked only to feed and heal. She'd never found joy in the task herself, though. The peace of her garden in Florence or her laboratory in

Pratolino, that was what she wanted. But both would be lost to her if she failed in her task today. She reached for the basket of apples.

And frowned.

Francesco had always loved autumn's first apples. So why was something telling her these were for the cardinal, and the plums were for Francesco? The cardinal would never touch Eden's forbidden fruit, much less let a real-life Eve give it to him. And Francesco had always, always loved apples. And there, that was all of them cut. Bianca set the apples aside.

Now, how much of Francesco's special powder to measure? She looked through the spoons in a cupboard drawer, she needed something big, one for pudding . . . more than a pinch for the cardinal today. Her hand trembled as she opened the tin and scooped the arsenic into the spoon, then into the plum filling. It was done.

The nearest oven had room for both tarts on its top rack. Bianca slid them in, then staggered back. Sweat poured down the side of her face. The oven's heat, that had to be it. She just needed to rest. There was a chair, pushed up into a corner within sight of the ovens. Her knees giving way, Bianca slumped into it.

Trembling, she grabbed the sides of the chair, even as its uneven wooden legs rattled on the floor. In Florence, if Francesco had come to her like this she'd have forced him into bed right away, then run to her beloved garden shed, the laboratory she'd built for herself, to make him the strongest medicine she could. But, for herself? "Please, Francesco, another dose," she heard herself say. Then, darkness. She dreamed of the cardinal. His twisted face stared at her, a look of hatred and glee, Bianca trying to wash the red plum juice from her fingers. The man had invited himself to his own funeral.

Bianca jolted awake. A pitchy smell filled the room. Glass? Something burning. Tarry smoke rose from the glass candleholder beside her, the candle wasting away to the end of the wick. How long had she been here?

Taking bunches of her sticky hair, she pushed it all into a cap she'd pulled from a side pocket. The cook stood before her with two perfect bubbling tarts. Bianca glanced down at her fingers, then folded her hands, hiding the plum's purple stains.

"I thought I'd take these out before they baked too long." The cook smiled, but her eyes were full of worry. "You looked so tired, I wanted to let you nap. Are you sure you're all right? I'll help you back to your bedroom if you like. My stew meat's simmering, midday meal tomorrow," she said. "But I have a little time."

Bed was a luxury she couldn't afford. But she also wasn't sure if she could stand. She had to, though—someone had to serve the tarts. As long as she didn't move, the room didn't spin, but her legs were weak, and everything from the past several hours felt like a dream. The air in her lungs felt almost too heavy to breathe.

"Not bed—I'll be fine in a minute. Just . . . would you mind serving the tarts?" She'd meant to do it herself, but she couldn't let the cardinal see her like this.

"Of course. The apple's for the grand duke, I'm guessing? I know he loves them."

Bianca opened her mouth to answer, then shut it again. He did love apples. But so did the cardinal. "Give him the apple." That was what Francesco had said. "The apple's for the cardinal," Bianca told the cook. "Francesco knows," she added. Yes, that was a relief. Even if Bianca forgot, Francesco would know which was his.

"Apple for the cardinal, plum for your duke." The cook nodded. "You just rest here while I serve them. Don't worry about a thing." And she was gone. Closing her eyes, Bianca leaned back against the wall and let the darkness come.

"Mistress? Mistress?" The words sliced through the air.

Bianca sat up, blinking. The cook was back, hands now empty. How much time had passed? "What's wrong?" Bianca asked. The worry in the woman's voice had been unmistakable. Had she dropped the tarts?

"I served them." The woman glanced at the floor, then Bianca. "The duke reached straight for the plum. But he . . . he . . ."

Bianca's chest tightened. "He what?"

"Please, Mistress, it's late, but if you can walk," the cook said, "I think you'd better come see."

Her mouth formed an O, but she couldn't scream. Taking the cook's hand, Bianca rose to her feet, almost pulling the woman off balance. Once she'd taken a few steps, though, Bianca pushed away the woman's offered arm. "Stay here." Whatever waited in the dining hall, this woman would be safer away from it.

But the cook shook her head. "Please Mistress, you'll need my help. I think the grand duke is ill. Here, take my arm, quickly now, across the way."

"No, he can't be." She'd only just saved him from malaria. Bianca's heartbeat thundered in her ears. Pushing the cook away with a strength Bianca hadn't had a moment ago, she stumbled outside, setting her sights on the door to the storerooms and stairs. One foot in front of the other, each step like lead sinking in clay. Halfway there, she turned. The cook, hands clenched, fingers entwined, was watching her. Bianca nodded reassurance to the woman and kept going.

Once inside, others' eyes followed her too, but the bakers, servers, and washwomen trundling up and down the nearby stairs might as well have been shadows. Climbing up those same stairs, Bianca reeled forward, bracing herself on a table at the top. Was that the cardinal's voice she heard coming from beyond the door ahead of her, or just someone bellowing at a serving boy? Bianca staggered through the door.

At the polished table in the center of the room sat the cardinal, tall and upright, his red robes spilling over the chair and reaching around like sticky tendrils. A half-eaten tart sat on a plate before him.

And across from him, another form slumped, motionless, his dark hair matted back. Francesco. Another tart, hardly eaten, lay before him.

Bianca sank against the doorpost. She must have gasped or cried out, though she didn't hear her own voice. The cardinal turned. "Why, Bianca. You've decided to join us. Sadly," the cardinal added, "I think your cooking doesn't agree with him." He nodded toward Francesco's plate. Filling spilled from the tart, dark and gelatinous, like clotted blood.

Time blurred. She'd seen the plum juice, oozing like blood next to those rosy apples, and she'd been thinking about killing the cardinal. Thinking about having his blood on her hands. Those plums. She'd mixed the arsenic into the bloody filling.

Give the apple to the cardinal. I don't think I'm going to be hungry. That's right, he'd planned to eat the plum so his brother wouldn't be suspicious, so they could see their plan through.

She'd poisoned her husband.

A drum beat in her head. Bianca cleared her throat several times before she forced out a word. "Francesco?"

But it was the cardinal who answered, his lips curled. "Your poison succeeded, Bianca." He stood up, opening an arm as if to welcome her to the table. "But on whom, eh?" In three strides he crossed the room, his robes billowing behind him. He grabbed her arm, bringing Bianca close to his face. "You don't look so well yourself. Trouble standing? Perhaps it's done its job on you, too."

His words pounded in her head. Was he right? Had she eaten arsenic, and forgotten? No, Bianca knew ailments better than that. Francesco, if he was still conscious, must be wracked with stomach cramps. Bianca simply felt feverish and weak. She had cured Francesco, only to catch the sickness herself. She had cured Francesco, only to poison him.

The cardinal's fingers tightened on her arm. "Look at me, you reckless whore. I know you tried to kill me." He laughed. "A fine mess you've managed." With his free hand he pointed toward the slumped figure. "Too bad your husband likes sweets too. And look how well he trusted you. I imagine the two of you cooked up this plan together. We both love apple, but he insisted on taking the plum. Well, what went wrong?"

Bianca stumbled forward. Without the wall at her back, would her feet hold her? The cardinal's fingers seared like burning spikes, and her tugging at them just made the cardinal grasp harder. She shut her eyes, letting her knees give way, finally jerking free of the cardinal's grip. Forcing herself to crawl, she moved one arm's length forward across the floor. Then another. The cardinal must see her as no threat at all—he could stop her if he wanted. Well, maybe he was right. But she was almost to Francesco's chair. Bianca stretched out her hand and touched its wood. She whispered his name.

All at once, two boots filled her vision. Bianca looked up. The cardinal loomed above her, his hands on his hips. "Not going to admit it, are you? But it doesn't matter. It's clear what you planned."

The voice that answered sounded like hers, but it was too small, too far away. "Admit what?"

"Whore." His fingers again dug into her arm. "You thought you could kill me, leaving you free to ruin Florence right alongside your husband." He hissed the words in her face, his breath hot. "Poison, was it? I always told Francesco he'd run into trouble with that stuff someday. Playing with alchemy, ignoring God's will . . ."

The room was spinning. And dark. Had someone snuffed all the candles? She'd have to tell Francesco they'd need to be lit. Wait, no, Francesco was . . . Francesco . . .

A harsh, ringing voice, sharp as a blade, cut through the haze in her head. "Witch." The cardinal's hand lifted her chin, forcing her to look at him. "You want to be with your husband? Do you think he can protect you?"

Bianca twisted her head back, pulling away.

"You killed him, you witch."

A thousand minutes, and no minutes, passed. She was on her knees, her arm burning from the squeeze of his fingers. Bianca lifted herself up, clasping the chair like rungs of a ladder, until she had Francesco by the shoulders, shaking him. "Francesco, please, please . . ." If he could just gag or cough, he'd vomit the poison. He wouldn't choke; she'd be there to save him. But . . .

"Just let him die, Bianca, as God wants." The cardinal shoved his brother's chair, kicking it hard.

Francesco moaned, falling to the floor. His lips moved, a single word. "Bianca."

She heard it in her ears and in her bones. "Francesco?" She willed him to answer. But he lay still, limbs splayed unnaturally against the floor. He was . . . unconscious. He couldn't be dead. Bianca pressed in close, her hand shaking as she placed it on his chest. She wouldn't let him die. But she couldn't even stand. With one push of the cardinal's heavy hand on her shoulder, she was sprawled on the floor again.

The cardinal spoke above her. "This might be where you atone for your sins, Bianca."

"Atone?" Her voice sounded thin and scratchy. "I've never murdered a brother."

"And I still haven't," the cardinal said. "Someone saved me the trouble. But you'd have killed me, wouldn't you?"

"Nor frightened a young boy, nor hid under red robes."

"Hmm. What are you trying to say, Bianca?"

Bianca rolled to her side, inching away from the cardinal, just as he thrust his boot into her back. She cried out, "Nor whored myself to a church."

The cardinal loomed over her. "Whore? The only whore I see is the one who poisons her own husband by mistake, and catches the same disease she thinks she's curing. Yes, I can see now you're not poisoned.

You're a lunatic, is what you are." The cardinal shook his head. "Shall we summon someone to take away my brother's pathetic body?"

"He's not dead." Bianca's voice cracked.

"Isn't he? You're the healer, you'd know. Go ahead, see if he's breathing." The cardinal stood back, arms folded. "I won't stop you."

Bianca turned toward Francesco, crawling over to him. She bent over his body. Surely if she was still enough she'd hear his heart. So many times she'd lain beside him, his pulse steady, his chest easily rising. And now . . . she felt for his pulse, but there was none.

"Hmm. Satisfied?" the cardinal asked. "As for you." He stood in front of Bianca, aiming his boot at her chest. This time, the impact knocked her backward, dizziness sending black clouds through her vision. His voice echoed. "I was going to banish you. Now I'll bury you."

Her head hit the ground. Blood trickled along her jaw, seeping into the crevices between the floor tiles. Had she bitten her lip? She curled into a ball, pressing a hand to her head, a throbbing pain closing in. How much time did she have to think before she entirely lost track of where she was?

Malaria. She knew the disease, every part of it. This was how people died.

The cardinal motioned to the servants in the doorway. "She'll be dead soon. Take her anywhere. Bury her wherever you want. She's not a Medici." Turning to Bianca, he spat on the ground. "No one cares where they dig your grave."

Bianca's head rang. And her cure? Some of the notes he'd burned she had copies of elsewhere, safe as long as he didn't discover her workrooms at Pratolino. But even if he did, there was still her garden shed. She hadn't had her time at Crusca yet, her chance to make her cure known to all and secure a place for herself as Florence's healer. She had to live. *Please*, Bianca thought. Please, God, if there was a God. Let her live another day.

Red pulsated behind her eyes. Opening them, she looked around the room, her head splitting. Wasn't there another person to find? Her lips shaped his name. Antonio. Francesco would take care of him, wouldn't he? Save their little boy? No . . . no . . . wait. Francesco was dead. The last word he'd ever speak had been her own name.

Her stomach heaved and she gasped for air. "Antonio?"

"You mean the royal *heir*?" The cardinal towered over her. "You can forget your son, Bianca."

Tears filled her eyes. As she looked at the cardinal's angry red face and hands, his robes seemed to crackle, fall apart, disintegrate.

"He's going away." He leaned close to her face, his breath hot. "To a place of prayer where no one will find him. Locked in forever under my directives—of purpose in the light of God and discipline in civil work. Yes, I'll take care of Antonio."

Antonio. The clever one, standing in her garden, playing in her laboratory. He'd be the one to escape malaria. To escape the cardinal. Wouldn't he? She gagged, then spit in the cardinal's face.

His hand struck the side of her head.

Bianca rolled into a ball, gasping. Black dots rose and fell in her vision. Antonio . . . Antonio. The cardinal wouldn't protect him; he'd destroy him. But no. Antonio could save himself. He was young. He had her blood. Like her, he would do anything to survive. She'd been his age when her mother had died, when she'd first learned to be strong. *Be like a woman, Antonio. Fight where you must. Serve if you have to. But stay alive.* She could have shown him so much more in the laboratory. If she just had another day.

The room pulsed, then faded into black.

Strong hands reached in the dark to grip Bianca's shoulders. Pain surged in Bianca's chest, her legs convulsing into one tight ball of flame. Someone was moving her. Where? Into a fiery kiln? The kiln for Francesco's porcelain that he'd make no more. Bianca forced her eyes open. The dark ceiling, the underside of a table. The strong hands that pulled her into the light. A woman's face bent over her. A stranger? No, the woman with the sick daughter—the cook.

"Francesco?" Bianca asked.

"Hush. The cardinal's taken him away. But we're not safe." The woman grunted as she lifted Bianca's shoulders and began dragging her, her spine grating against ceramic tiles, pain crushing her chest. She cried out. "I'm sorry, Mistress. There's no other way. I got one of the stable workers to find us a carriage; no one else wants to risk angering the cardinal. You must stay with us. Just a little longer." Bianca lost the thread of the woman's voice. Welcome darkness descended again.

When she next came to, her head rolled to one side, the smell of fermented grasses filling her nose. The whole back of her body throbbed with pain. A horse whinnied low. Another answered. She fought to keep her eyelids open.

"We're taking you away," the cook said in a small voice.

"I'm . . . I'm sick?"

"Yes. Do you know where you are? Do you understand what's happening, Mistress? You're in the stables. Can you move?"

Black filled her vision. If she couldn't force her eyes to stay open she'd sink into the darkness.

"Help me lift her into the wagon." The words flew somewhere over Bianca's head.

"We're digging our own grave." A man's voice. "You're not going to get her farther than the church here." The man's rough hands grabbed Bianca's body. "I'm taking a horse and running once you two are on the road. Better that than face the cardinal."

"Better that than let him get away with killing her. She saved my daughter's life." The cook positioned her arms underneath Bianca's legs. "Take her head. I have her feet." Then she spoke to Bianca. "No fear, Mistress."

Bianca writhed. "No, Francesco, I can't leave him. Please."

"Hush." The cook tapped softly on Bianca's leg. "He's gone to God."

"Then, Antonio—"

"Shhh . . . wherever the cardinal sends him he'll have that tutor at his side, that young man from Pisa, and from what I'm told, he's no friend of the cardinal." She lowered her voice. "But His Eminence doesn't know that. Now rest and let us lift you."

"Tutor?" She remembered Francesco saying something about the tutor. Antonio might be safe, then. "But . . . where are you taking me?"

"To a Sick House. You're ill, Mistress."

"I have malaria. I know I do. But . . . not a Sick House, please." If she spoke louder, could the cook understand her words through the rasp? "Please, you must take me to my garden in Florence."

"Mistress, Florence? Is there no help here?"

Help? No one could cure Bianca's malaria but her. Francesco might be dead. But Antonio was alive, and so was she. Still alive, in this moment, and she'd hold on to the next, and the one after that.

"Please," she whispered, then shut her eyes.

Clip-clop. Clip-clop.

Bianca could hear, but her eyes couldn't see. How many times had she opened and shut them in a single day without thinking about it? What her brain wanted, her body wouldn't do. She'd been in the stable, and now she was moving, lurching, clip-clop. Each jolt of the cart sent a wave of nausea through her, followed by pain. Pain was good, though; pain meant she wasn't dead, didn't it? Clip-clop, clip-clop. This cart had boulders, not stones, under its wheels, each bump in the road a shattering blow. But if she hurt, she must be alive.

Woods—a smell that was crisp and fresh, and with pine all around. Bay laurel, maybe a bough overhead? How nice the sweetness. Did she think it or did she see it, above her, so many shades of green? A pale lime, the color of her gown at that first ball with Francesco, or like the limes on the ceiling outside Francesco's mother's chapel.

A hunter green, too, blending dark colors of the forest. Juniper and cypress and pine and pretty green moss. Light sage: she'd wanted that color for the big wedding, but no. Too melancholy, Francesco had said. The green reminded her, though, of home, of seafoam and seaweed. And what about the bright green of that tiny emerald Francesco had given her? One gem hidden among artichoke leaves, and with a bite of pickle. She'd laughed, and joked that he was trying to poison her.

Now it was night, no? The greens she was seeing were just shadows. What she wanted to see was Antonio.

Yes. There he was. Antonio, all grown up, with a man about ten years older. Antonio had become handsome, like his father. Smiling, he walked around her old garden laboratory, talking about something . . . experiments? And the friend talking back. The friend knew something about science, too. Bianca tried to call her son's name, to catch his eye. But he didn't turn. That was all she was, a pair of eyes. She didn't have a body or a voice. She could only watch.

"I wish you'd known my mother," Antonio, now in the garden, called out to the other man. "She wouldn't work in our casino when it was my father's, but I think she'd love it now with me there. If you could have studied here with her . . ."

Antonio, a scientist.

A jolt, then pain, the whole world was pain. A hot trickle down her face, why couldn't she wipe away the blood? The healer with malaria, who couldn't cure herself. Was that how she'd be remembered? But she would be in her garden soon. Would Antonio be there to greet her? But no. Antonio was too young still, too young to see his mother so ill. And his father . . .

Tears filled her eyes, forcing the lids apart, letting in the faintest light. A little dam, broken. And why? She'd lost something, someone. "Francesco . . . Francesco." Someone had killed him.

"He's not here, Mistress." A voice, so far away. Her throat hurt. She needed more words. The voice continued. “He’d want you not to give up. You’re going to make it. We’ll be there soon enough.”

Where? The smell of the air was no longer fresh and pure but layered with odors of town roads. Bells tolled near her garden, such a sorrowful sound. Hadn’t she just been here, in her garden with Antonio? Or, maybe the bells were from a church farther away?

“Take me to my garden.”

“Yes, mistress, soon.”

Bianca’s lids flickered. Pink sky, fiery clouds. The dawn of another day.

Author's Note

As with any history, we only know part of the story. The Medici were renowned for their internal family drama and uneven skill in ruling, as well as alchemic practices, particularly Cosimo I and his son, Francesco I de' Medici. I've filled in as best I could, embellishing some details and in a few instances extending time (for example, Francesco's diplomatic travels away from Florence in 1565) or shortening it (Bianca and Piero's affair in 1563 is reduced to several months) and omitting some events for the sake of narrative cohesion. I've also taken liberties with the design of buildings and grounds (the San Marco Casino and nearby gardens) and their artwork (in particular, in the Hall of the Five Hundred in Palazzo Vecchio). The Crusca Academy serves multiple purposes in my rendering. Dates and places in the book usually follow the generally-agreed-upon version of history, but still, opinions vary. Malaria, a word of Italian origin, is used interchangeably with terms such as "the heat disease," although more common at the time was "tertiary fever," suggesting something about the disease's recurrent pattern every several days. Terms that may seem modern, such as "science," "chemistry," "laboratory," "experiment," "patient," even "sample" and "subject," actually are relatively old; even the idea of a clinical trial is centuries old, some say dating from the time of the Bible. Interestingly, the Nobel

Prize in Physiology or Medicine was awarded in 2015 to the Chinese woman scientist Tu Youyou, who, without a doctorate or medical degree, with her team discovered the anti-malaria drug artemisinin, derived from artemisia—what she called in the title to her Nobel Lecture "A gift from traditional Chinese medicine to the world."

The Sant'Elisabetta convent is a composite of multiple convents, hospitals, orphanages, and apothecaries at the time including Sant'Apollonia, Sant'Orsola, Sant'Agata, Santa Caterina da Siena, Santa Maria Nuova, San Matteo, and Ospedale degli Innocenti. Many orders of nuns served in these institutions, including Benedictines and the Oblate Hospitaller Augustinian and Franciscan nuns.

Most of the characters in this book are historical figures; minor characters have been excluded from the narrative (for example, there's little mention of a stepmother of Bianca's, siblings of Piero). I rarely name secondary characters, and I have avoided similarly named characters. Thus, Bianca's daughter is named Virginia instead of Pellegrina—Pellegrina was the child's grandmother's name. Ferdinando, to avoid any confusion with the older brother, Francesco, is mostly referred to as "the cardinal" throughout the book.

Numerous sources say Francesco and Bianca died in close time and space proximity to each other in the villa of Poggio a Caiano. Francesco's remains rest in the Chapel of the Princes, the Medici tombs. Some records indicate that both Francesco's and Bianca's viscera are entombed in a church near Poggio. Stories abound, but Bianca's body has never been found, nor when she died confirmed.

Acknowledgments

A number of friends, colleagues, editors, and family have sustained me in researching and writing this book. At She Writes Press, I am indebted to publisher Brooke Warner for her unwavering support of this project, and also to senior editorial project manager Shannon Green. I am grateful to all my editors, including the inimitable Susan S. Brown, who coached me into writing a voice-driven story. I thank the many others who have given feedback and editorial advice along the way, including Ruth Lydia Richter, Carolyn Brantigan, and Kristin Van Bodegraven. Thanks also to colleagues at Western Washington University who supported me in this project. A good friend, Annamaria, planted the idea for this book and introduced me to the historical Bianca; one day as we were walking across Piazza della Santissima Annunziata, she recounted that some Florentines say the bronze statue of the once-Cardinal Ferdinando, atop a horse, is looking at an ever-open window high on a wall, where the spirit of a woman dwells. Many thanks, too, to Stefano Corazzini, a scholar in Florence, with whom I've held numerous conversations about Bianca and Francesco, who are subjects of his work as well. I am particularly grateful to Raffaello Bocciolini, also in Florence, whose knowledge of Florence history is unparallelled, as are his fact-checking skills. My family helped with this book in many ways. Jim, my partner in life and in writing, showed up when I needed editing assistance; our son, Ian, built the stunning writing cabin in our woods whose refuge contributed to my appreciation of the wonder and enigma of the Renaissance mysteries I dove into; and our daughter, Emily, inspired by exemplifying a young, dedicated female scientist. Lastly, I thank Rose Engelfried, a strong and tireless reading and editing presence throughout this project. Every writer needs a meticulous, creative editor like Rose. My gratitude goes out to all mentioned here, but any errors in this text remain mine alone.

About the Author

photo credit: AJ Barse

Gigi Berardi hails from Hollywood, California, and is an academic and a freelance writer of books, numerous articles, and several hundred reviews and features. A former Fulbright Scholar in Italy, her graduate degrees are in science and performing arts.